# TAKING HER
## TO
# *Mykonos*

Writing With A View Books

# TAKING HER
## TO
# *Mykonos*

JULIE SNEED WOMACK

*For Mom and Dad*
*I love you both dearly. Thank you for everything.*

# Chapter 1

*Anna's ashes are locked in the car. Of all the freaking moments to lock the keys in the car. But, it's okay. I'm handling it.*

Katherine has decided that her purpose today is to be positively useful. She has been the head of the fund-raising committee at her twins' school for the last three years. In that time, she has put together three flawless galas whose live auctions each raised over seventy-five thousand dollars for Coleman Hall Academy.

Planning a funeral has its similarities. It's all about the delegating. She doesn't want Anna's parents or Kevin to have to worry about any of this. They were relieved when she stepped in. They were able to focus on grieving, and this is her way of showing her love and condolences to them.

While Katherine waits next to the inaccessible car on the sidewalk in front of the Good Shepherd Catholic Church, she skims through her mental checklist. *Anna's brothers are passing out the pamphlets. Her niece and nephew have been practicing their readings for days, and Ashley has done a beautiful job with the flowers. The organist had just begun playing "Ave Maria" when I was alerted to this mess. So here we are.*

Anna's husband Kevin was panicking, of course, and Katherine sent him inside the church to greet loved ones, assuring him that she would handle it.

Katherine Collins is African-American, with dark brown hair and caramel-colored skin, which makes her contrasting light blue-green eyes so shocking that it can make your eyes water when you look at them. In a good way. Her hair is now in a sleek ponytail with hair wrapped around the elastic band to dress it up, one of her signature do's. She wears a black BCBG sheath dress, a blazer, and black heels. At work as an attorney, she is always wearing some variation of a power suit. When she is casual, she still looks polished in Ann Taylor and Banana Republic. She lives in an English Tudor in San Marino.

Katherine is the one you always want on your team, the one classmates wanted to partner up with on group projects in school. She's always prepared, proactive, articulate, and diplomatic. If there's a problem with a neighbor, she'll get it resolved with no bridges burned. She's the one the neighbors enlist to speak at the city council meeting to get speed bumps installed in the neighborhood to prevent speeding where their children play in their front yards. She's a yes person, and she uses practically every second in the day (and some in the night) to accomplish it all.

She is married to James, and together, they have been a power couple since they met at the end of their first year of law school. They have eleven-year-old twin boys, Beckham and Brice. Katherine and James were thrilled when they learned from the ultrasound that they were having twin boys. James couldn't wait to have sons to play baseball with, and Katherine was pleased with the convenient plan of scheduling one C-section, having her tubes tied when her O.B. was in there, and being back at work in six weeks, her family complete.

The AAA guy jimmies the lock with a slim jim. The lock pops.

Katherine smiles. It's not a joyful smile, obviously, but an appreciative smile that says, *Thank you kindly for being skillful at breaking into cars so we can proceed with my friend's funeral on time.*

The AAA guy swings the door open for Katherine and hands her a clipboard on which she signs her electronic signature.

"You're a lifesaver. Thank you so very much."

"You're welcome, ma'am. My condolences."

Katherine furrows her eyebrows. *Does he have tears in his eyes?* She exhales, almost impatient. *The Triple A guy is more feeling than I am. What the hell is wrong with me?*

"I appreciate it."

She excuses him with a polite nod, ducks into the front passenger side of the car, unbelts the white urn that is secured in the front seat, and leans over to pick it up. Upon doing this, she spots the car keys on the back seat.

She can picture how it all went down. Kevin was assisting Camila and Alexa out of their seat belts. Perhaps one of them was having a meltdown, understandably, or a crisis buckling her patent leather shoe. Kevin finally got the girls out, and, distracted and bereaved, closed the door to the already locked car, stranding the car keys—and his beloved's ashes—inside.

Katherine kneels on the front seat, reaches and grabs the keys from the back seat, then most carefully picks up the urn, hugs the precious cargo to her chest, pushes the car door closed with her hip, and takes off toward the church.

*Let's do this.*

Katherine enters through the front doors of the church. Several people linger in the narthex. Kevin stands with Anna's parents, Irma and Jose, and they receive friends and family, accepting hugs and words of condolence.

Camila, seven, and Alexa, five, quietly cling to Irma's waist. They have dark brown hair and heart-shaped faces, just like their mommy. Camila's eyes are hazel like Kevin's, and Alexa's are brown just like Anna's. They wear petal-pink dresses, pink tights, black patent leather Mary Janes, and pink frilly bows in their hair. Anna specifically requested that they not wear black. She didn't want them to look like they were in mourning, she wanted them to look like princesses.

Kevin spots Katherine as she approaches him. She gives him a thumbs-up. *The package is secure.* Kevin nods, relieved, but still broken. She silently hands him his car keys and keeps moving.

Katherine reminds herself to look sad. Her default demeanor when she's in productive mode is swift and efficient. She's not meaning to be insensitive. She's just trying to make things happen.

Katherine places the urn on a table across from the closed doors of the center aisle where the priest and altar servers wait. Stephanie, the church lady meant to assist with the funeral, also lingers here. In reality, it is Stephanie's job to handle the funeral arrangements, but Katherine relieved her of most of her duties, keeping her on for assistance the day of.

"Okay, everything is all set," Katherine says for everyone in the narthex to hear. "Stephanie, will you please inform the organist that we are ready to begin?"

"Of course," Stephanie confirms and heads upstairs to the choir loft.

Through the open doors of the bride room, Katherine spots a woman sitting in a chair, muscular legs crossed, wearing nude Christian Louboutin heels. She approaches and finds Rishika sitting with Craig standing behind her, one hand on her shoulder. They exist in painful silence, in the dark.

Katherine smiles gently. "We're about to begin."

Katherine strides down the side aisle towards the front of the church and peruses the congregation as she does so. *Wow. There are a lot of people here. Two hundred? Two-fifty? Anna was very loved. …Are all of these people coming to the house afterwards? Yikes. Will they all fit? Will there be enough food? Should I drive through KFC and pick up a few buckets of chicken on the way? That's kind of tacky.* Katherine shrugs. *But let's be real, everyone loves fried chicken. It will go well with the catered food. Yep. Some chicken and some biscuits.*

Katherine steps into the fourth row and sits next to James. She leans over and whispers in his ear. "Let's drive through KFC after this."

James furrows his eyebrows, smiles a tight, concerned smile and takes his wife's hand in his. "Okay, honey."

# Chapter 2

Ashley Fitzpatrick stands by the altar, which is flanked by a few enormous matching flower arrangements, and drops a few aspirin into each tall vase. To her horror, the flowers are looking a little droopy, and they are her responsibility. There are also sprays of carnations and daisies and smaller vases of roses sent by other friends and family.

She sniffles as the organist plays background music that somewhat covers up the creak of the wooden pews, nervous coughs, low voices, and sobs.

*"Ave Maria,"* such a beautiful song.

Before that, it was "Amazing Grace." The music is heart wrenching, mostly because Anna knew she was going to die so she picked out all of the music herself, hymns that she loved from growing up in the Catholic Church.

Ashley has blonde hair and blue heavy-lidded eyes. In college, she was an absolute knockout. She looked like she could be a Playboy bunny with her petite and buxom figure, crystal-blue bedroom eyes and demure sweetness. At some point over the years, her sweetness began to translate to homeliness and her curvy figure became maybe a little bit frumpy.

She used to be a well-paid accountant, but when she had her first of three children, she became a stay-at-home mom. She is mother to ten-year-old Elizabeth, six-year-old Teddy, and three-year-old Ryan. Ashley is still very beautiful, but she has forgotten this fact, presumably because her husband stopped telling her ages ago. Most of the time she wears yoga pants and a workout top, regardless of whether or not a workout will take place. When she volunteers at her kids' school, she wears nice jeans and a sweater set from TJ Maxx. She now wears a black sweater set, slacks and ballet flats. Of the five friends, she strayed the farthest from Los Angeles, where they met in college, moving up to San Francisco where she lives in a light gray Edwardian house with white trim. However, she may have to move soon.

Ashley's face contorts into an ugly cry. She's been hysterical since she woke up this morning all alone in a depressing hotel room. Every time she hugs someone at the church she dissolves into tears.

*God, I'm such a mess.*

She shakes her hands and takes a deep breath to rein in the tears. *Focus on the flowers.*

Ashley stands back and assesses them. She insisted upon taking on the flower arrangements even though there is a lady at the church who normally arranges them. But Ashley wanted to take care of the flowers out of love for Anna, and so Katherine relieved some lady named Stephanie of this task.

Ashley flew down from San Francisco a few days before the funeral, went to a florist and bought several bunches of stargazer lilies, Anna's favorite, along with some greenery. Alone with her pathetic thoughts, she arranged them in large vases in the church's parish hall.

Stargazer lilies. Dark fuchsia petals with white tips and burnt orange stamens. They remind Ashley of her senior prom. She was on the prom committee, so with five other classmates, she spent the entire day before arranging twenty giant flower arrangements. The perk of being on the prom committee was being allowed to skip class for stuff like that. When she thinks about it, that's when her love of flower arranging began (and party planning, for that matter). The creative act of working with something from nature is so therapeutic-making something that is already beautiful even more beautiful.

*Yes, this helps.* Ashley nods, caressing the petals, attempting strength. Her nose involuntarily scrunches. *I'm not fond of how stargazers smell, however. They're so overpowering. Like an entire bottle of perfume has spilled. It takes me back to prom completely.*

Each table had a giant towering vase full of stargazer lilies in the middle of it. You couldn't even see the four people on the other side of the table, that was how big the arrangement was. There were four silver goldfish swimming around the water in each vase. That was really cool. Ashley's idea. Something to make it over the top and special. Ashley loved planning all of the details for her first big party. The theme song was "How Do You Talk to an Angel", sung by the guy who had been Donna's bad boyfriend on *Beverly Hills 90210*, and so they went with that theme and made the decor look heavenly. It was so romantic. She wore a long white sequin gown with a halter top and a high slit up one leg, and she had a pile of blonde curls pinned to the top of her head. Her goal was to look like a sexy angel.

*I lost my virginity to Jason Novitsky that night.* Ashley squints her eyes, recalling the evening. *What was I thinking? Well, I was thinking that I was in love with him. He was totally hot… and a total player. I'd had a crush on him through my entire high school career, and then he finally asked me out a few months before prom. It was an obsession, really. That was when my bad judgment in men began. The sex was… not good. Pow, pow, pow, pow, pow. And then he dumped me.*

Ashley's eyes widen and she claps her hands over her mouth. *Oh, my gosh! Don't think about sex right now. That's totally inappropriate.*

"Ave Maria" ends and segues into "On Eagle's Wings." Ashley

leaves the area below the altar and rushes to her seat, mortified with herself.

She slides into the fourth row pew next to Katherine and James, Lorelei and Adam.

Rishika and Craig walk quickly down the aisle. Rishika makes eye contact with no one. They sit down in the second row behind Anna's family.

*Poor Rishika,* Ashley thinks. *I mean, poor all of us, but poor Rishika.*

# Chapter 3

After a few moments of a silent and still congregation, the altar servers process down the aisle past Lorelei carrying a cross, followed by a priest wearing white vestments. Anna's four brothers carry a plank on which the urn rests. Behind them, Anna's parents follow, and then Kevin with Camila and Alexa on either side of them, their little hands in his. To Kevin, no one else is around. Tears stream down his face. His eyes are up. Begging to God? Begging to Anna? Each family member carries a long-stemmed stargazer lily.

The pallbearers carefully place the urn on a table below the altar, right next to a poster-size photo of Anna Camila Finch. Her heart-shaped face is framed by shoulder-length dark brown hair. She has big, deep brown eyes and a warm smile. Each family member places a lily next to the urn. This was Lorelei's idea, and it is a lovely gesture.

Lorelei leans against her husband, Adam, for strength, and he puts his arm around her. She dabs at her eyes with a tissue and shakes her head in sorrow as she watches Camila and Alexa file into the first row with their daddy and grandparents.

Lorelei Leibovitch has big, curly auburn hair and bright, green eyes. She has freckles that used to look kind of dorky when she was a kid, but now they are really lovely and add a youthful essence to her fair skin. She's very au naturel, mostly because, as a mother of six, she's too frantically busy to care about putting on makeup. Phoebe, Aislinn, Hadley, Atticus, Celeste, and Gideon range from age twenty to age five. Her house, in a subdivision in Rancho Cucamonga, always looks like a bomb went off inside, but is always full of love and noise. And chaos.

Lorelei is a high school art teacher. She's the quintessential creative and unorganized person. Her classroom is always kind of cluttered, but her students love her and fight to get into her class. Her class is an experience. She has a way of unlocking their inhibitions, presumably because her eccentric, open and nurturing personality and unconventional teaching methods encourage a safe space where her students can be whoever they are.

After college, where she double-majored in studio arts and art history, she planned on living the artist life, temping during the day, staying up super late when her creative juices started flowing, painting and sculpting. Things didn't quite work out that way. Given the opportunity, Lorelei could probably create brilliant art. But, with a full-time job and a big family, she's always in survival mode.

She has a style all her own, a little gypsy-esque. Large dangly earrings always peek out from under her huge cinnamon curls. She loves a good flowy kimono top to cover up her tummy that has been stretched out so many times in pregnancy. She carries twenty-four extra pounds, four for each child. She sometimes grabs a new kimono top when she's at Target buying toilet paper and vitamins for the family. She wears a black one now, over a black silky tank top, with a long, flowy, black and pastel floral skirt and cushioned Mary Janes that are practical for teaching on her feet all day.

As the priest says the opening blessing, Lorelei stares at the backs of Camila's and Alexa's little heads. *Those poor precious girls. They're wearing the bows I bought for them on the day of the home tour in La Canada. Obviously, Irma has curled their hair. It looks beautiful. But*

11

*eventually, Irma will have to go home. I've got to teach Kevin how to do little-girl hair. I don't want Camila and Alexa to go to school looking like orphans.* Lorelei's eyes widen at her own thoughts. *Oh, that's a bad thing to say. I didn't mean that. It's an expression. Or at least it used to be. You shouldn't infer that orphans are not well-groomed. I guess that expression was used more in the eighties when we were all watching Miss Hannigan drinking excessively and yelling at little orphans to clean the orphanage to shine like the top of the Chrysler Building. Regardless, I'll make sure Kevin has lots of hair bands and bows to put in the girls' hair. And bottles of No More Tangles.*

*That was a beautiful home tour. Katherine had tickets for herself and Anna, and then she couldn't get away from work so she gave me her ticket. Anna and I had a wonderful time together admiring all of the over-the-top homes. It was really more Katherine's scene. Anna and I were like tourists. We took photos, even though we weren't supposed to, so we would be able to incorporate some of the decorating ideas into our own homes. At the last home, there was a boutique and food trucks. Anna and I ate falafels at an outdoor table and talked about which houses we liked the best. What a lovely memory. Then I saw those adorable pink grosgrain bows at one of the vendors' tables and I bought one each for Alexa, Camila and my Celeste. Great. Now when Celeste wears her bow, I'm going to think about Anna's funeral and how Alexa and Camila don't have a mother anymore. Those precious, precious girls. They're going to need all the love they can get.*

Tears stream down Lorelei's face, and she wipes her face with a worn and wet tissue. She turns and rummages through her huge purse looking for a new one, but damn it, all she sees are receipts, granola bars, handwipes. *I really need to clean out my purse. I really need to organize my life!*

Katherine dutifully offers her a small package of tissues.

"Thank you," Lorelei whispers.

Katherine nods and smiles compassionately. It's kind of a rehearsed compassion, but compassion nonetheless.

Lorelei pulls out a fresh tissue and blows her nose loudly.

# Chapter 4

From the second row, Rishika's head turns and her gaze lands on Lorelei. Rishika does a double take, and her eyes widen when she notices that Lorelei's face is streaked and smeared with mascara. *Holy shit.* Agog, she takes a beat before returning her attention to the priest.

Rishika is Indian, with long glossy black hair and dark brown almond-shaped eyes. She's in tip-top shape because she gets up at four-thirty a.m. five days a week to make it to her five o'clock CrossFit class before work. In fact, her body is a rare female one in that it's stronger and more toned than it was in college.

She is a creative executive at a major film studio, finding and developing incredible scripts to pass onto production. She is always in control, yet also relaxed, possibly due to the full-body massage she gets once a week at the studio.

Rishika is always fashionable and well-groomed, in a way that is cool. She knows what's cool. Even her dog is cool. Rishika's black labradoodle, Penelope, is her baby. Penelope has her own Instagram account and has three thousand followers.

Rishika shops at boutiques and obscure clothing stores so she's always wearing clothes that no one else is wearing. She would never buy clothes at, say, Target, because she thinks it deplorable to see someone wearing the same clothes you have in your own closet. Her nails are always manicured- short, squared, and painted with a nude polish. She now wears a simple sleeveless black above-the-knee shift dress with an exposed zipper in the back, nude Christian Louboutin heels, and her hair in a fat bun at the crown of her head. The look is simple and classy, allowing her to look stylish even though her world has been turned upside down. She lives in an impressive Mediterranean house in the Hollywood Hills.

Rishika sits between her husband, Craig, and her parents. Her mom and dad sit tall and strong, wearing white traditional Indian clothing, communicating their respect to Anna and her family. Anna was like a daughter to them, but they offer strength to those around them by remaining stoic.

Rishika digs the fingernails of her left hand painfully into her right hand. *Let's get this over with!* -she screams in her head. *No more crying. Do not cry. Why did I make that photo of Anna so big? It's such a gorgeous picture of her, but she's staring at me, and I just can't handle it. We don't need a photo. We know who's up there in that urn. And looking at her sweet face is torture.*

Rishika feels her eyes welling up with tears so she digs her nails in harder. She glances down, red half-moons dented into the flesh at the base of her thumb. She takes a cleansing breath. Focusing on something as mundane as her hands momentarily distracts her from her devastation. She narrows her eyes as she studies her skin. *My hands look old. These are not my hands.* She flexes both hands, fingers fanned out wide. *Where did all of these spots come from? I need to start wearing sunscreen on my hands. I've heard that you should do that because your hands get sun exposure when they're propped up on the steering wheel. My commute to the studio is forty-five minutes in the morning and an hour and fifteen minutes in the evening. That's two hours of my unprotected hands aging five days a week. I should have them zapped. I'll make an appointment with Dr. Baker this week. And put a tube of sunscreen in my car.* Rishika straightens out her light brown fingers and watches them tremble, bringing her back to the present. A few tears escape from her eyes and she quickly dabs at them with a tissue. *Don't cry. This fucking thing isn't even halfway over. Oh. Don't say "fucking" right now. You're in a fucking church! Shit. Sorry. I'm so sorry.*

"And now," the priest says, "Rishika Badami Cooper, Anna's best friend, would like to say a few words."

*Oh, God.*

Rishika looks up. She takes a cleansing breath as Craig grabs her hand and squeezes it. She rises and scoots past her parents, who offer encouraging nods.

As she steps onto the marble floor below the altar, she hears the click-clack of her heels echoing through the church and the sound of her quickening heartbeat pounding in her ears.

She walks in front of Anna's beautiful giant photo and climbs the steps up to the podium.

*Exhale…*

"Anna was the best person I've ever known." Rishika's voice shakes as it echoes out through the church. She takes another deep breath. *Just pay tribute to her. You can do it.*

"Our moms met when they were pregnant with us, so I've been blessed to know her all my life. How do I keep this brief? I could tell you a hundred stories about every phase of her life. As far as friends go, she was best—encouraging and loyal. She always had a comforting hug to give."

Rishika sees people nodding in agreement.

"You felt good about yourself when you were in Anna's presence. She had great positive energy. She was so much fun, and she had a contagious laugh, surprisingly loud for someone so little. "

Rishika smiles in spite of herself. *Yes. You can do it.*

"Anna had a particularly happy childhood growing up in Altadena, California, which is why I think she was obsessed with all things eighties- *The Goonies*, *The NeverEnding Story*, *The Princess Bride*, reruns of *The Golden Girls*. Our first concerts were to see New Kids on the Block and Milli Vanilli."

People laugh, pleased. They want to remember Anna happily.

"Anna loved musicals, and she would randomly break into song if a situation evoked a relevant musical lyric. *Les Miserables* and *Rent* were a few of her favorites, but she used to sing the most obnoxious songs from *Annie* and *The Music Man*. And *Cats*."

Rishika shakes her head in feigned disgust and there are some chuckles from the pews.

"Anna played soundtracks from Broadway musicals while she drove, but peppered in some nineties hip-hop, specifically Dr. Dre, if the girls weren't in the car.

Her favorite food was her mama's cooking, particularly potato tacos with homemade salsa. I could never believe how she ate such spicy food, even as a kid."

Irma smiles and wipes her eyes with a tissue. Jose leans his head against his wife's.

"She also had an incredible sweet tooth. She adored chocolate. She used to joke that she had Aztec ancestors and that explained why she loved chocolate so much. When we were kids, we used to say we were going to the park and instead we would walk down the street to See's Candies and pool our money together for a few chocolates. I don't know if you knew that, Irma and Jose, but that's what we did."

Irma and Jose both smile and shrug that they didn't.

"Anna was so intelligent. She was a great student starting in kindergarten. Again, I would know. I was there. She worked so hard through Westridge High School, Loyola Marymount University, and Loyola Law School, trying to be the best she could be. But, really, she was like that in every aspect of life.

"She was a social butterfly. She had many circles of friends. Friends she grew up with, friends from every school she attended, friends from her neighborhood, her Zumba class at the YMCA. She organized get-togethers, reunions, and girls' nights. She called old friends out of the blue and kept in touch with them. It takes a lot of effort to keep in touch with that many friends, but Anna prioritized friendship. She was the best friend I've ever had. She was my *sister*."

Rishika's voice trembles at that, and a tear streams down her face. She wipes it away quickly and pushes on, determined.

"Anna was a loving, fun and patient mother. She was one of those moms who played with her children. She would put Camila and Alexa on her lap and ride down the slides at the park. She would climb on the jungle gyms with them while the other moms sat on picnic blankets and talked. Camila and Alexa loved to play with her old Barbie dolls, and she would sit on the floor for hours helping them change in and out of the plethora of little clothes when their little hands couldn't navigate the tiny arm and leg holes. Anna loved her daughters fiercely. She worked really hard to get them, and she always said that they were her greatest treasures."

She looks at Kevin. It was Kevin who told her all of this when she asked him what she should say about the girls. He nods at her through his tears.

"And Kevin. God, she loved Kevin so much."

The tears really begin to flow down Rishika's cheeks now. It isn't like Rishika to show anyone her feelings. Her emotions are never public, but fuck it, this is for Anna, and she is going to lay it all out there.

"I was there when Anna met Kevin, and once he was in her life, she had a new look in her eye that was just for him. She laughed at all of his jokes. Even the ones that weren't funny. But she was amused *because* they weren't funny. And she loved being a mom and dad with him. He was the absolute love of her life."

*Oh, God, it's not fair that they were so happy and now she's gone.* Rishika shakes her head, trying to ignore her thoughts.

"Anna came from a really great family, and she loved her mom and dad so much, and her brothers, too. Her brothers were always her protectors. Anna was a shining example of how to be a devoted daughter and sister, a loving partner, and a committed friend. I learned so much from her. I learned *so much* from her," Rishika repeats, her heart wrenching. "In every aspect of life. Most amazing to me was how somehow she made every person she loved feel like they were the most important to her. How did she do that? Or maybe it's that she had so much love in her heart that she was capable of loving us all endlessly. Anna, I will love you forever, and I will never forget you."

Now that Rishika has made it to the end of her eulogy, a sob bursts out of her mouth. Her hands fly to her mouth to cover it, but she can't stop, and the sobs tumble out of her. The congregation is also distressed, yet quiet and surprised.

Rishika has finished her best friend's eulogy, but now what? Where does she go from here? She is stranded up here on this podium, vulnerable, lost and emotionally demolished. This is the worst moment of her life.

Suddenly, Rishika feels a hand on her back. She looks behind her and Irma is there, her face wet with tears, her eyes sad and compassionate. Irma opens her arms, and Rishika turns to lean down and hug her. Rishika lets loose and just cries. The dam has broken. Little Irma rubs Rishika's back, like she has done so many times through the years, as Rishika towers over her sobbing.

"That was beautiful, mi hija. Just beautiful."

# Chapter 5

The street of Anna's mid-century modern house in the San Diego neighborhood of Scripps Ranch is packed with cars. She would have been pleased that so many people are in her home together toasting to her life. She and Kevin loved entertaining, filling their home with fun and laughter, creating memories. They often invited families over from the girls' preschool and elementary school. They would grill hot dogs and steaks, and the kids would run around while the parents sat around the fire pit drinking wine.

This is where Anna always hosted the annual Christmas brunch for Rishika, Lorelei, Katherine and Ashley. The five of them were sorority sisters at Loyola Marymount University. Anna was a bridge builder, someone who brought people together. She was the one who kept a strong relationship with each of them, even though their annual Christmas brunch was the one time every year all five of them usually got together.

People mingle around Anna and Kevin's kitchen, dining room and living room, speaking quietly as they sip beverages and hold plates of food. Katherine bustles around, refilling glasses and picking up used paper plates and napkins.

Rishika stands at the wet bar area in the living room making herself a vodka soda. Everyone else is drinking coffee or white wine, and it is only eleven in the morning, but she just barely got through her best friend's funeral, so who's going to judge? And who cares if they do?

Since the service ended, she's been bombarded with people telling her what a wonderful job she did, delicately avoiding the topic of her inconsolable breakdown. The people who didn't approach her regarded her with looks of pity and sadness. Lorelei, Katherine, and Ashley hugged and complimented her beautiful eulogy while assessing her incredulously. It's quite possible that in all their years of friendship, they have never seen her cry before.

Craig appears behind her. "Hey, honey," he says gently. "How are you doing?"

She takes a deep breath. "I'm okay."

"Can I get you something? Have you eaten?"

She hasn't eaten. She is avoiding the kitchen where both her and Anna's parents are sitting at the table, as well as the dining room where Anna's brothers are filling their plates, eating and talking. She loves them all, but it's so hurtful to be with Anna's family right now. Rishika's heart breaks for them. They will never be the same. And Rishika is just too exhausted to comfort them or chat with them about their lives.

"I'm good, babe. Just… I'm trying to have a quiet moment. Here." She grabs a bottle of beer out of the wine fridge below and hands it to him. "The guys are out back."

He smiles at her, recognizing the not-so-subtle hint, gives her a kiss on the cheek and goes.

As Rishika hears overwhelming layers of conversation all around her, she can pick up on key words such as "cancer", "brain tumor", "poor girls", "too young". For a single moment she is able to drown it all out and focus on the clear crystal sound the club soda makes as she pours it over cubes of ice into the glass. And then the fizzy effervescence swells and blooms into every crevice around the ice. She inhales a deep breath, and then she lets it out.

If Anna was here she'd be a ball of fun energy. She'd be like "Yeah! Par-dee!" And Rishika would be making two vodka sodas.

She squeezes a wedge of lime into her drink, then takes a sip and closes her eyes.

A few times before Anna passed, she tried to tell Rishika something. "When I die," she would start. But each time, Rishika stopped her. "Don't talk that way. That's not going to happen. You've got to keep fighting." She never wanted Anna to lose hope, even when it was clear that death was inevitable.

*I should have listened to her. What did she want to tell me?*

\*\*\*

In the backyard, Camila and Alexa play on the play structure with their cousins. Lorelei holds a plate of sandwiches, fruit and cookies and beckons for them to take a break and eat. Craig, James and Adam sit on patio furniture, drinking beer and catching up, though their moods are solemn.

James rises from an Adirondack chair and enters the living room from a sliding glass door. He joins Ashley and Kevin, who are standing in the center of the living room.

"I'm so sorry Pierce couldn't make it down," Ashley tells Kevin. "He sends his condolences."

"No problem. I understand," Kevin answers in a monotone voice.

Ashley looks at Kevin sympathetically. She really wants to be there for him. Even though she's known him for decades, she can't think of anything to say that doesn't sound trivial or cliche.

"Hey, man." James puts his hand on Kevin's back. "One day at a time."

"I'm just trying to get through today."

"And, you're doing an amazing job. Hang in there."

*That was good, James. It was cliche, but at least it was supportive,* Ashley thinks. She should have looked up funeral conversation etiquette.

"We're here for you," James continues. "Don't hesitate to call for anything."

"Yes," Ashley agrees. She walks away and blows her nose as the tears begin to fall again.

"We're outside if you want some air," James says to Kevin and heads back outside.

Rishika walks up to Kevin and hands him a Bud Light in a bottle. "Who are all of these people, and when can we make them leave?"

"Thank God there is one person I can count on to keep it real." He sighs. "This is so weird. I can't even explain how numb I feel right now. My mind is numb, my body is numb. I feel like I'm sleepwalking. And even though this house is full of people right now, it feels so empty."

Rishika nods. What can she possibly say?

"Hey, can I talk to you?" Kevin asks. "I want to tell you something in private."

Rishika looks concerned. "Of course."

Kevin leads the way and Rishika follows him into the kitchen, which is full of people, including Anna's and Rishika's parents, so he keeps going and steps into the laundry room.

"This is probably not the right time to say anything, but you're here, and I'm just trying to think about what Anna wanted and to cross things off of my very strange and morbid to-do list."

Rishika furrows her eyebrows. "Okay…"

"If anything ever happens to me, Anna and I would like you and Craig to take care of Camila and Alexa."

Rishika's face contorts into surprise and skepticism. For a

moment, she doesn't say anything. "Wow. I don't know what to say. First of all, that's not going to happen."

"I know, but it was really important to Anna to prepare for every scenario while she was here. She felt like she had to tie everything up and make sure everyone she loved would be okay without her."

Rishika's mind races. "Is she *sure*? Are you both *sure*? I'm not the most maternal person. Anna, of all people, knew that. What about her parents? And her brothers and sisters-in-law?" Anna did, after all, have five brothers. "What about your family?"

"We are sure." Kevin smiles an exhausted smile.

Rishika's eyebrows remain furrowed. What was Anna thinking? Rishika is pretty much the least qualified person for this very important job, definitely the least fit out of her group of Supermom friends. She notices the look on Kevin's worn-out face. Her expression of doubt relaxes.

"I'll do anything you guys want. I would never say no to any of Anna's wishes."

# Chapter 6

Lorelei stands outside the laundry room holding a plate of food that she has prepared for Kevin, determined that he will eat and keep his strength up. Her face is utterly white and her mouth hangs open.

*What was Anna thinking?*

Rishika is the last person anyone would leave their precious children to. Rishika is many wonderful things, as confident and as fierce as they come, successful at all that she ventures to tackle in life, yet she has made it very clear for years that motherhood will not be one of those ventures.

Lorelei rushes away from the laundry room back into the living room where two couches face each other with a coffee table in between. Katherine and Ashley sit there eating fried chicken and drinking chardonnay. Lorelei silently sets Kevin's plate of food on the coffee table next to a bottle of chardonnay and sits down across from them, her eyes darting back and forth as she thinks.

"Are you okay?" Katherine asks. Lorelei doesn't look up. "Lorelei," Katherine repeats.

"Uh…" She shakes her head as if to wake herself up. "I just heard the most unexpected conversation. That's one way to put it," she mumbles to herself. "Another way to put it would be *insane*."

Katherine and Ashley look at each other.

"Lorelei. What was it?" Ashley asks.

"Kevin and Rishika were having a private conversation in the laundry room"—Katherine and Ashley exchange glances again—"and Kevin asked on behalf of him and Anna, if something ever happened to him, that Rishika and Craig take custody of Camila and Alexa."

"What?" Katherine asks, baffled. "What?" she asks again.

"I know. It's almost laughable, right?" Lorelei says with a weird, delirious laugh.

"Why her?" Ashley asks. "I mean, not that it's a competition, but every one of us is more suitable for that role than Rishika is."

"That's what I was thinking," Lorelei agrees. "And besides us, what about Anna's parents and siblings? And Kevin's? It's so strange."

"Well, Kevin's parents and his sister's family live in Florida. Maybe they wouldn't want the girls to be uprooted out of California," Ashley reasons.

"Okay. There's that logic. But…" Lorelei searches.

"I mean," Katherine chimes in, finding her words, "would Rishika even *want* to do that?"

"Right?" Lorelei gesticulates at Katherine with both hands, indicating that Katherine has just made her point. "Rishika hardly even spent time with them. Anna told me they would always leave the girls with Kevin or a babysitter and go to a spa or out to dinner when Rishika came down to visit."

"Wow," Ashley says. "I mean, I get wanting adult time, but all Rishika has is adult time. It wouldn't have killed her to get to know…"

"Oh. Incoming," Katherine says and picks up her glass of wine and takes a sip so as to act natural.

Rishika appears holding a plate of food and an almost-empty cocktail glass and sits on the couch next to Lorelei, who smiles gently.

Rishika looks at the plate on her lap and sighs. "I'm not even hungry. Going through the buffet line was just something to do." She sets her plate down on the coffee table.

"I know what you mean," Ashley says.

They sit in silence for a moment.

"I can't believe we're here," Lorelei says. "Even though we knew it was coming, I can't believe we're here."

"I feel so removed from the situation right now," Katherine says. "I think I might actually be in shock. Do you know that I haven't cried yet?"

"Really?" Lorelei replies, surprised.

"Nope. Not once. Isn't that strange? When you called me with the news," she says, directed at Rishika, "I left work, drove down here, went grocery shopping, let myself in here with the hidden key and stocked their fridge and freezer. When Kevin and the girls came home from the funeral home, they found me here vacuuming." Lorelei, Ashley and Rishika exchange weirded-out expressions. "I've kept myself busy ever since."

"Huh," Rishika says.

"I can't *stop* crying," Ashley says. "I just can't stop crying." Her face contorts as she begins to cry again. "I just miss her so much."

"See?" Katherine says as she puts her arm around Ashley. "That's what I should be doing. I'm a heartless animal."

"You're not," Ashley says through her tears, her blue eyes red and puffy. She reaches up to her shoulder and pats Katherine's hand. "People deal with tragedy differently."

"We should be reminiscing about her," Lorelei says constructively. "The only way we're going to get through this is by remembering all the good times."

"Okay," Katherine agrees. She looks away for a moment in thought. "When I think of Anna, I think of adventure. It's how she viewed life.

When you think about it, she squeezed a lot into forty-two years, studying abroad sophomore year in Japan and then backpacking through Thailand the following summer. She loved to travel."

"I'm so thankful that she got to do all of those things," Lorelei says.

"She should have more time to do more," Rishika says gloomily, not in the mood for optimism. Anna's life was cruelly cut way too short.

Lorelei pats her hand. "I know, but she did more than many people do in eighty years. She lived a full life. That's what we need to focus on."

Rishika shrugs, dismissive.

Katherine laughs. "Okay, maybe not so appropriate that I just envisioned this, but I just had the funniest thought about how when we were in the French Riviera, Anna insisted that we sunbathe topless. 'When in the French Riviera,' she said. Remember, she said that everywhere we went?"

Ashley smiles and nods.

"'When in Amsterdam. When in Rome.'" Katherine continues. "And she thought it was hilarious to say that when we were actually in Rome. Anyway, we did sunbathe topless and our boobs got so sunburned that we kept the aloe vera gel in the hotel mini fridge just to get some chilling relief. And then, of course, we screamed when we applied the freezing cold gel, and it was quite a production."

"Oh, my!" Lorelei exclaims and giggles. "I could never sunbathe topless."

"Well, we were twenty-two."

Ashley and Katherine smile, fondly remembering the memory.

"She did often instigate ridiculous scenarios," Rishika admits.

"Gosh. Has it really been twenty years since our backpacking trip?" Katherine inquires.

"Well, yeah," Rishika answers. "Our LMU twentieth reunion is in the fall."

"It can't be," Katherine says. "Because I have not been out of college for twenty years," she jokes.

Ashley sighs. "I feel like it's been a million years."

Lorelei shakes her head regretfully. "I can't believe I missed that trip. It was the trip of a lifetime and I missed it."

"Life is what happens when you make plans," Ashley says. "And life literally happened in the form of Phoebe."

"Timing was not ideal, but yes, it was a worthy trade-off," Lorelei says and smiles.

"I think about that trip a lot," Katherine says thoughtfully. "It was life-changing."

"Europe is life-changing," Rishika interjects.

"We should do it again someday," Ashley says wistfully.

Lorelei claps her hands together. "Oh, my gosh! Can we? Can I actually come this time?"

"Of course," Katherine says.

"You have to go," Kevin says.

The ladies turn to the side and Kevin is there. Their eyes shoot to each other. They're mortified, as though they've been caught doing something wrong.

"Kevin," Lorelei says.

"We're so sorry," Rishika says.

"About what?" he asks.

"We shouldn't be happy right now," Rishika answers.

"We were reminiscing," Katherine explains.

Kevin nods. "Anna wants you to be happy. She would love that the four of you are here laughing in our home. She would want me to refill your wine, which is what I came over to do." He sets a vodka soda on the coffee table in front of Rishika, as well as a fresh wine glass for Lorelei which he fills with chardonnay. He proceeds to refill Ashley's and Katherine's glasses. "Anna would love for you all to be talking about that trip. Trust me, I heard about it repeatedly. I know stories about that trip that I probably shouldn't."

The ladies break into smirks.

"Could you maybe keep those stories to yourself?" Katherine asks.

"I've stayed quiet this long."

They laugh.

"But really. You should go back to Europe. If anything, I think we all realize how short life can be. Don't just say you should go back. Do it." Kevin's demeanor abruptly changes. "Um. Actually… would you guys mind following me?"

# Chapter 7

They have all been in this room many times before and especially in the last month when Anna was in hospice and it was evident that it was time to come and say goodbye. The hospital bed, IV stand and various medical paraphernalia have been since been removed. What remains in Kevin and Anna's bedroom is the beige and white Bohemian bedspread that Anna once picked out and the dresser covered with framed photos of Anna and Kevin's wedding, Camila and Alexa as babies, and more recently Camila and Alexa wearing leotards and tutus.

Ashley looks down at the floor. Even though she is a very close friend, it feels like an invasion of privacy to be in here. This is Anna and Kevin's bedroom. This is where they slept together every night. This is where Anna took her last breath. Her absence is palpable.

On the wall is a large vibrant framed painting of the Old Port of Mykonos, a beige sandy beach with a short pier jutting out into the turquoise water. Fishing boats of different hues float in the harbor. On land, the buildings are whitewashed a simple and bright white, but the window frames are painted in splashy primary colors. White awnings canopy cafe tables.

"You've all seen this painting before," Kevin says.

They all nod.

"Mykonos. It was Anna's favorite destination from our trip," Rishika says.

"Yes. It was," Kevin says. "We always said we would go back someday."

Rishika, Lorelei and Ashley look at each other.

Katherine stares at the painting. She was with Anna when she bought it. Once a year, she and Anna used to meet in Orange County and go to the Costa Mesa Swap Meet. They would eat hot dogs as they walked up and down the countless aisles of vendors who filled the giant fairgrounds parking lot. They'd try on clothes, look at bargain-priced jewelry, buy little trinkets for their kids, and watch in awe as the man with jinsu knives demonstrated chopping through entire melons. One year they both bought a set. About six years ago, they were walking by a stand that displayed paintings and Anna exclaimed, "Look! It's Mykonos!" She rushed into the pop-up tent and gushed to the artist about how beautiful it was. She bought it, and they lugged the cumbersome painting down crowded aisles back to Anna's minivan where they had to fold down the seats in order to lay the painting on top.

"There's something I've been grappling with, and you've just given me an idea," Kevin says.

The ladies exchange glances.

"Anna recently pointed at that painting and said, 'I want to go there.' I said, 'I know you did, honey.' And she replied, 'No. I still want to go. I want my ashes spread on the warm sand and sprinkled in the clear water.'"

Ashley puts her hand on her heart.

"That's perfect," Rishika says quietly.

"So perfect," Katherine repeats.

"Would you ladies be willing to do that?"

Lorelei's jaw drops and her hand flies to her mouth. Katherine and Rishika look at each other with wide eyes.

Ashley bursts into tears. "I'm sorry."

"Isn't it too soon to talk about that?" Rishika wipes her face.

"No." Kevin smiles sadly. "It's not."

"But don't you think it's something you, Alexa and Camila should do together?" Lorelei asks.

"Trust me, I've been asking myself that. But it would be too hard on us." He gestures at the painting. "Look at that place. Mykonos represents Anna's happy memories, the places she still wanted to go, the things she still wanted to do. It breaks my heart. It pains me to look at this painting, but I can't bring myself to take it down either." Kevin shakes his head. "We said goodbye today."

Lorelei grabs Katherine's hand. Ashley wipes at her tear-streaked face.

"Of course we'll do it," Rishika says firmly. "We'll take her to Mykonos."

# Chapter 8

Lorelei, Rishika, Katherine and Ashley embrace excitedly when they meet at gate 154 in the Tom Bradley International Terminal at LAX.

Yes, the primary purpose of this trip is to disperse Anna's ashes on a beach in Mykonos, but they are on their way to backpack through Europe together, and it's impossible to not be excited about that.

Lorelei furrows her brow when she gets a good look at Rishika. She must've lost almost ten pounds since the funeral, and it's not like she had weight she needed to lose. By the quick glance exchanged by Ashley and Katherine, they, too, have noticed. Rishika looks tired and defeated. And defeat is something that Rishika has never shown. She has always been confident to the point of cockiness.

"Okay, ladies. I have a gift for each of you." Lorelei beams as she pulls out a stack of pink t-shirts and passes them out.

Katherine holds one up to herself and reads the bold black text. "'Cool Chicks Backpacking Europe'. Hmmm." She looks to Ashley for help.

"Cute," Ashley says politely.

"Nope," Rishika shoots down. "I'm not wearing that."

"Rishika," Lorelei whines. "This is my first time in Europe. I'm excited. And we're all together. It's a big deal."

"I know it's a big deal. But, you're not a cool chick if you have to put it on a shirt."

"Please…"

"I'll wear it," Ashley acquiesces.

"I will, too," Katherine says with a hesitant expression.

Donning various combinations of casual shirts and Ann Taylor jeans, black leggings and navy blue sweatpants, Katherine, Ashley, and Lorelei pull their new t-shirts over their heads, giggling as they check each other out.

Rishika tisks and shakes her head. "Give it to me."

"Yay!" Lorelei cheers as Rishika puts the t-shirt on.

Rishika points her finger at each of them in a scolding fashion. "No social media while we're wearing these."

"Alright, but can we get one picture just for us?" Lorelei asks, working her big doe eyes.

"You're pushing it."

***

One by one, Rishika, Katherine, Lorelei and Ashley hand their tickets to the airline employee to be scanned and walk down the jetway to get on the plane that will take them to Germany.

Rishika is pretty conflicted. On the one hand, she gets to go back to this beloved continent with her friends. But, doing it without Anna will be agony. Places all over Europe will be painful reminders of her. It feels disloyal to go on an amazing vacation and attempt to have fun amidst this tragedy. It's too soon. Rishika does, however, feel an obligation to scatter Anna's ashes in one of her favorite places in the world, and she will do what Kevin can't. Anna deserves to be put to rest in such a beautiful and special place. It's a sense of duty that overpowers all of it. It's this sense of duty that had Rishika take off an insane amount of time from the studio without batting an eye, that has her leaving Craig and Penelope, and that has her wearing this dumb t-shirt that could ruin her carefully built image.

Navigating large purses and tote bags in front of them, they make their way down the aisle of the airplane. Lorelei leads the way.

"This is so exciting," she exclaims. "I feel like we're about to have so many trips in one. I can't believe all of the amazing places we're going to go to. Paris!" She claps her hands. "Mostly, I can't wait for Paris."

"Lorelei, is this your first time traveling internationally?" Katherine asks.

"I've been to Mexico, but this is my first time crossing an ocean."

"Wow," Rishika comments, surprised Lorelei hasn't traveled abroad before. "You're going to love it," she says, attempting to be a team player. *We're traitors. We shouldn't be going backpacking through freaking Europe after our best friend died. We shouldn't be making new memories without her.* She shakes her head as if to shake the thoughts out of it. Her subconscious has been bombarding her with jabs of guilt, loss and pain for the last month. They remind her to mourn. They remind her to not feel joy.

"I think my last big trip was my honeymoon," Ashley says. "For years, wherever we've taken the kids, we've been at the kiddie pool. So it just always made more sense to drive somewhere less than a few hours away. Why take an expensive and miserable airplane ride to somewhere exotic if we're destined to be at the kiddie pool?"

Rishika inwardly makes a face. She can't at all relate to hanging out at a kiddie pool. It sounds like hell. When she and Craig go to a resort, they always lounge on the opposite side of the kiddie pool. Or the adults-only pool, if that's an option. But she's really trying to be agreeable so she attempts to relate. "It's so hard for us to go very far for very long when we can't bring Penelope with us. We have a good doggy hotel near us, but we just hate to leave her there too long."

Katherine glances at Ashley and rolls her eyes. Ashley widens her eyes in a nonverbal, *Are we really comparing my kids to a labradoodle?* Katherine stifles a laugh.

"As a result, we just don't travel internationally very often because, you know, you kind of want to stay for a while if you're going to go so far."

Ashley's expression remains neutral. She hates when Rishika makes her life feel small. "Right."

"Our trips usually involve camping or Palm Springs," Lorelei responds. "It's so close to us. Why go anywhere else?" Her ginger hair is pulled back into a big, slightly messy bun on the top of her head. Leaving for the airport this morning was a mad dash. She kissed each of her kids goodbye in their beds before the Uber picked her up for the hour-and-a-half ride to LAX. She mentally vows to actually do her hair for the rest of this trip. "Buying plane tickets for the eight of us is nearly impossible, but when we sprang for it and went to Disney World a few years ago, I was in the seventh circle of hell. I was making sure everyone's needs were met, everyone was entertained, everyone had gum so their ears would pop when we were climbing in altitude and then decreasing in altitude. Making sure everyone had snacks so their sugar levels and moods didn't crash." Lorelei exhales and smiles. "I can't believe I'm about to be on a plane for ten hours and I don't have to take care of anyone." She laughs indulgently. "I'm going to sleep. Possibly the entire time."

"A few cocktails might be nice," Rishika suggests.

"Definitely. And I have Nina Blake's new book!"

Nina Blake was one of their sorority sisters at Loyola Marymount University. She's now a *New York Times* bestselling author who lives in Oklahoma and writes romance novels from her lakeside home. Nina sent a beautiful spray of pink roses for the funeral with a small pink and green banner that said "Love in DKZ." Pink and green are the signature colors of the Delta Zeta sorority. It was comforting and sweet to see that reminder up at the altar that their sisterly love had transcended two decades since college.

"Oh, yay!" Ashley cheers. "Can I borrow it when you're done?"

"Of course."

"That's us right there," Katherine says, pointing to the seat numbers just ahead of Lorelei.

They stop and lift their carry-ons in the overhead compartments.

"This is going to be utter bliss. I'm so burned out. The high school spring art show was last week and was great and is, thankfully, over." Lorelei audibly exhales from mental exhaustion. "You know what else I'm excited to do on this trip?"

Rishika brightens, anxious to hear her fun idea.

"Shave my legs. I never shave my legs anymore."

Rishika physically reacts. "*Why?*"

"I have no time."

"You need to go to a different country to have time to shave your legs?" Rishika asks, appalled.

Lorelei sidesteps into the row of seats and sits down. "I have six children and a full-time job." She shrugs. "I wear pants. Every day. I'm in dire need of alone time. And sweet relaxation." She sighs contentedly and turns to her left to find that the woman in the seat next to her has a boa constrictor wrapped around her neck.

Lorelei yelps in fear. Rishika leans around Lorelei.

"Hi," the snake lady replies.

"What the hell is that?" Rishika asks.

"This is Gerald, and I'm Sue. Say hello, Gerald."

"No, that's okay. Why is Gerald with us?" Lorelei asks weakly.

"He's my comfort pet. I get really anxious on planes."

Lorelei looks thoroughly aghast. "You don't say."

Rishika chimes in. "Ever try vodka? Xanax? Trains? Ships? Stay at home with your snake?"

Lorelei reaches behind her and pinches Rishika's thigh.

"Ow!"

Lorelei whispers out one side of her mouth to Rishika, "Don't anger the snake lady." She turns back to Sue. "He's lovely."

Gerald's tongue slides in and out, tasting the air. Lorelei jumps out of her seat, into Rishika's lap.

"Will you switch seats with me?"

Rishika makes a squeamish face. "Sorry."

A flight attendant walks by. "Ma'am, I'm going to need you to take your seat in a minute."

"Oh, hi! Excuse me, are there four available seats somewhere else? Or one seat? Just one seat would work." She mouths *sorry* to her friends as she attempts to abandon them.

"I'm sorry, we are full, and we're about to close the door. So please sit in your own seat." The flight attendant continues down the aisle closing overhead bins.

Lorelei's polite expression contorts, and she whispers to her friends, "Really? No one else thinks this is crazy? Didn't anyone see *Snakes on a Plane*? It didn't go well."

Katherine and Ashley cast freaked-out, sympathetic expressions her way.

Lorelei returns to her seat and inches as far to her right towards Rishika as she can. "Will you be my comfort pet?"

Rishika places a few items from her purse onto her lap as she gets settled. "Of course."

Lorelei strokes Rishika's arm. "Oh, no. I took a sleeping pill before we boarded. I can't sleep! If I fall asleep, Gerald is going to unlatch his jaw and swallow me!"

"Don't worry," Sue says. "He ate a mouse this morning. He's completely satisfied, and he's a total sweetheart."

Lorelei nods and smiles sweetly at Sue. She reaches over onto

Rishika's lap where she has a pen and a notebook. Lorelei grabs the pen, clicks the ballpoint out, and holds it tight. "Just in case I need to cut my way out."

# Chapter 9

Katherine's tray table is down and she is typing away on her laptop. A few files are stacked on her lap.

"You brought work?" Ashley asks.

"Of course. How else do you think I'll be able to stay away for so long? I have a colleague consulting on my cases, but I'll be e-mailing and conference-calling constantly."

Ashley wrinkles her nose. "Oh."

"We can't all be stay-at-home moms." After a moment, Katherine's fingers stop moving around the keyboard. "That was bitchy. I'm sorry. My tone is me being stressed and anxious about leaving work."

"It's okay."

"I'm so worried about my cases falling apart while I'm gone. One of them has been totally consuming me. And now I'm leaving Brice and Beckham for two weeks, and with baseball season in full swing, it's just a lot to manage. But I know I can count on Shu to keep things shipshape." Shu is the Collins family's Chinese au pair. On top of being super-organized and caring, she has been speaking to the boys in Mandarin since they were babies.

"Nonetheless, Brice and Beckham are angry at me for leaving them." *Actually, Brice and Beckham don't really care that I'm leaving for two weeks. They're used to me not being around. And that's worse. And, God, Italy. After all this time, I'm going back to Italy.* Katherine rubs the back of her neck to defuse some stress.

"I get it," Ashley sympathizes. "It's not a good time to leave my kiddos either. I hope Pierce can handle it all. And actually, I'm probably going to go back to work soon."

"Really? I didn't know you wanted to."

Ashley hesitates. It seems like she wants to explain further, but she just shrugs. "I guess it's time." She furrows her brows.

"Oh." Katherine turns back to her work. She glances back at Ashley, who just sits and stares at the seat in front of her. "Are you going to read or something?"

"I'm just going to think for a little while."

"Okay," Katherine says quizzically. "Are you good?"

"Yep," Ashley answers a little too quickly. She continues to stare at the back of the seat in front of her.

"Okay," Katherine says, unsure, and she returns to her work.

Ashley flew down from San Francisco last night and spent the night at Katherine's house so she could be on their flight. Katherine was pretty preoccupied getting everything buttoned up at home before the trip, but now that she thinks about it, Ashley was somewhat distant. She seemed her usual cheerful self when Katherine or James engaged her in conversation, and when they sat down to dinner she asked Brice and Beckham all sorts of questions about school and baseball, but there were moments when she seemed lost in thought. To be honest, she doesn't look great. Her brow has a permanent furrow, and she just looks… dull. Perhaps Anna's death is taking its toll on her.

*** 

The call button above Katherine's seat is lit. She has tucked away her laptop and files for the time being.

The flight attendant appears with plastic cups and mini-bottles of Prosecco for each of them. Katherine went to the galley and complained to the flight attendants about Lorelei being seated next to a comfort snake. She demanded excellent service and bottomless complimentary alcohol to discourage her and her friends from taking further action and reporting emotional trauma to the airline.

"Thank you," Katherine says, pleased, and she passes the cups and accompanying bottles down to each of the ladies.

After the ladies fill their cups, Katherine lifts hers. "So begins our journey."

"I can't believe we're actually doing this," Ashley says, enthusiastically.

"I can't believe we're doing this," Rishika repeats, a little morbidly.

Lorelei eyes Gerald. "Cheers." She knocks her Prosecco back in one sip. Rishika refills her cup.

"We should toast to Anna," Rishika says. "We're doing this for you, Anna." She holds her cup up.

The other three lift their cups of bubbly to meet hers and toast in unison.

"To Anna."

A baby begins to fuss a few rows back.

"She should breastfeed that baby or give him a bottle," Lorelei tells Rishika. "Helps the baby's ears to pop as we rise in altitude." Rishika nods, neutrally.

Out of her oversized tote, Katherine pulls out a thick, weathered paperback guidebook called Let's Go to Europe 1996. "Remember this?"

Rishika's eyes widen. "You still have that?"

"I wondered where that went!" Ashley says.

Katherine turns the pages. "All of our places are highlighted. There are notes in the margins about the spots we loved. Bar napkins, train tickets…"

"There's Anna's handwriting," Lorelei says with wonder.

Katherine smiles and nods.

The baby a few rows back starts screaming. The mother is already frazzled by the stress of quieting her baby in such tight quarters jam-packed with strangers. Lorelei pushes the flight attendant button. "That girl's gonna need a drink." She stands up and calls across the rows to the young mom. "Give me just a minute, honey, and I'll hold your baby. You poor thing, you're going to need a break. Prosecco is on the way."

"Thank you," the lady says gratefully, her initial skepticism about a complete stranger holding her precious first-born overruled by the anticipation of a timeout and alcohol to soothe her frayed nerves.

*Yes. Please hold that baby and shut him up,* Rishika thinks to herself.

"That's kind of you," Ashley says.

"It will give me a reason to leave my seat," Lorelei explains.

"Okay, let's talk about our travel plans," Katherine begins.

The day after the funeral, she called Rishika, Ashley and Lorelei one by one to confirm that they could and would go to Europe and sent a group text to throw out possible travel dates. Two days later, after they all arranged time off for work, she retrieved their credit card numbers and bought plane tickets for all of them to leave at the end of the first week in May, one month after the funeral. The other three ladies put their trust in her, and so Katherine mapped out a general course of travel. However, they haven't really discussed the details of their route.

"We don't have as much time as we did before," Katherine points out. "Two weeks instead of six. Obviously we can't hit all of the cities we visited before, and we'll only be in each city for a few days, so we're going to give Lorelei the highlights tour." Lorelei smiles and scrunches her shoulders to her ears in excitement. "We'll enjoy a few days in Munich, Interlaken, Bruges, Paris, Nice, Rome, Athens and then Mykonos where we will perform Operation Ashes."

Rishika looks appalled. "Can we not call it that?"

"Sorry. Giving it an impersonal title makes it easier for me to process." Rishika looks around Katherine at Ashley, who furrows her eyebrows. Katherine continues explaining logistics. "I've looked into lodging in each city. Most of our hostels are still around."

"Hostels?" Lorelei cries. "Oh, my gosh! What an adventure."

Ashley winks at Lorelei. "I'm excited for you."

"For the cities we are traveling to," Rishika says, "let's stick to the original details as much as possible. It will be like a memorial for Anna." By going through the motions of their original trip, they can think of her and pay homage to the wonderful moments they shared. It will be hard, but it will be an act of love.

"We can do that," Katherine concedes.

"Great! I want to do everything you guys did anyway," Lorelei says.

"I like that idea," Ashley agrees. "Everything the same."

"We'll take Anna on one last trip," Rishika says.

# Chapter 10

Lorelei yawns and smiles as she opens her eyes. Gerald's head and several inches of his body are on her lap. Lorelei's eyes contort into horror. She opens her mouth wide and screams silently.

Sue smiles. "He likes you."

"Is that good?" Lorelei asks.

"Yes." Sue's smile fades. Lorelei gulps.

Next to her, Rishika is in a deep sleep. She dreams she's in the backyard of Anna's childhood home. She's a kid again, scooping wet mud into plastic dishes. Anna is inside the playhouse setting the little table with plastic cups and plates. Rishika can hear Anna happily singing "I Dreamed a Dream" from *Les Miserables.* It's eerie to hear a little girl sing such a sad, heavy song with such a sweet voice. Rishika hums along as she squishes the lovely cold mud in between her fingers.

"Come here, Rish," Anna calls. "There's something I need to tell you."

"Be right there," Rishika answers.

The kitchen window is open and Irma is making potato tacos for lunch. It smells so good. Irma's potato tacos are the best.

Rishika looks to her right and Camila and Alexa are there playing in the mud next to her. Alexa looks Rishika in the eye.

"Why are you here?" she asks in a bratty voice.

Rishika makes a face at her and takes a mud pie into the playhouse, but it's empty. There's no more little furniture, no more plastic play food, no little dishes. No Anna. Nothing. Panic rushes through her. Where is Anna? She looks out the little door and through the kitchen window of Anna's actual house to where Irma is happily humming the song that Anna was just singing.

"Anna is gone!" Rishika screams.

"It's okay. The tacos are ready," Irma says calmly.

Why won't Irma listen to her? "Anna is gone!" Rishika screams. "Anna is gone!"

Rishika sits up abruptly in her seat. She's drenched in a cold sweat, and she pants, attempting to catch her breath.

To her right, Katherine is asleep with her laptop open in front of her. On the other side of Katherine, Ashley sleeps, snuggled up to her cardigan that is rolled into a ball.

Rishika glances to her left at Lorelei who starts to doze off and catches herself, sitting up straight and alert, raising the ball-point pen in protection. The poor thing looks exhausted. Lorelei swivels around and her horrified, bloodshot eyes look straight into Rishika's.

"We've got to get off this plane."

# Chapter 11

The ladies exit the plane and enter the Munich International Airport.

"We made it!" Lorelei dramatically drops her large tapestry carry-on bag and collapses down on the airport floor, spread eagle.

"Gross, Lorelei," Ashley says. "Get up. Who knows when our first shower will be."

"I've been in fight-or-flight mode for the last ten hours. I'm exhausted," Lorelei pouts.

Unfazed by her friend lying on the floor, Rishika pulls an aerosol can of Evian out of her Louis Vuitton tote and mists her own face to freshen up.

Katherine looks at her, deadpan. "A little help?"

"Oh. Sure." Rishika sweeps a circle of cool vapor around Lorelei's face.

"Aww, sweetie. You poor thing. Now, get up." Ashley offers Lorelei a hand and helps her up off the floor.

"Lorelei," Katherine says, smiling brightly, "you're in Germany. Welcome to Europe!"

\*\*\*

Rishika heaves her backpack off the conveyor belt. She squats down, slips her arms through the thick straps and lifts the heavy load with her legs with ease.

Lorelei, Ashley and Katherine study the revolving conveyor belt, waiting for theirs.

Rishika glances out through the sliding glass doors to the curbside. She sees Anna out there. Rishika does a double take, but Anna is still there wearing jeans, a white v-neck t-shirt and a large backpack.

"What the…" Rishika squints her eyes, trying to look closer. Anna sweeps her dark hair off her neck and pulls it into a ponytail. "Anna," Rishika says under her breath. Anna begins to walk along the curb as if to catch a ride. Rishika drops her giant backpack onto the floor.

"Watch my bag!" she shouts to Ashley and runs off.

"Where are you going?" Ashley calls.

Katherine rolls her eyes at Ashley. "Oh, no. She's going rogue on us already."

Rishika's heart pounds in her chest as she races through the crowded baggage claim toward the exit, her eyes glued on Anna.

Rishika dodges travelers with suitcases. A man with a luggage dolly meanders right in front of her.

"Excuse me. Move!"

She darts around him, leaps over a group of suitcases. She gets to the curb. A truck passes by, revealing that Anna is gone. Rishika looks around frantically, but of course, Anna is nowhere to be seen. She doubles over, puts her hands on her knees and gasps for air, totally confused.

# Chapter 12

Ashley, Lorelei, and Katherine carry their heavy backpacks out to the curbside of the airport. Ashley and Katherine drag Rishika's backpack, each holding a strap.

"Where the heck is Rishika?" Lorelei asks.

"She just took off," Ashley answers.

"Are we walking from here?" Lorelei asks.

Ashley shakes her head. "It's probably a twenty-minute drive to the city center."

"Should we get in the taxi line?" Lorelei asks. "Grab an Uber?"

"Well, it's best not to take taxis. They totally jack up the prices for tourists and will take us on a lengthy scenic route. I don't know… is there a public shuttle? When I'm with my kids, I have every detail planned out. I've forgotten what it's like to be spontaneous." Ashley chuckles.

"We're not going anywhere until we find Rishika," Katherine says.

"Girls." Rishika appears in front of them. "I found us a ride."

Katherine feels annoyed, but relieved. "Where were you?"

"I thought I saw… someone I knew."

Katherine searches Rishika's face. She appears erratic and ruffled.

"Come on," Rishika insists.

Moments later, the girls are throwing their backpacks into the back of a cargo truck.

"What is this? Who are these guys?" Katherine asks. She can partially see the face of a man in the small side mirror on the driver's side door. His head nods slightly in greeting.

"I don't know. They're just delivering cargo," Rishika answers.

"What cargo? To who?" Katherine asks.

"I didn't ask for their business plan," Rishika quips. "I said 'Munich' and they gave me a thumbs-up."

"Do they speak English?" Ashley asks, warily.

"Munich. That's all we need to communicate."

Ashley and Katherine climb into the very back of the truck behind Rishika.

Lorelei hesitates. "Are we really doing this?"

"Yes." Rishika waves her in impatiently. "Come on. This is backpacking."

Lorelei shrugs, incredulous, and climbs in.

A second man appears at the back and waves to the ladies.

"Oh, hi." Katherine waves back to him. "Danke schoen," she says, unconfidently.

"Great," Lorelei complains. "Our entire German vocabulary is from a Wayne Newton song."

The man pulls down the sliding door and it slams shut. The ladies all jump.

"We can't even see where we're going?" Lorelei shrieks.

"They're going to drop us off near the city center," Rishika explains. "Lorelei, you have to trust us. We've done this before."

"Twenty years ago," Katherine pipes in. "I stopped doing a lot of things I did twenty years ago."

Rishika furrows her eyebrows at Katherine's negativity. "What the heck? I thought we were duplicating this trip."

"There are a few things we will not be duplicating."

"Well, obviously," Rishika says, annoyed.

They settle down in the empty areas between unmarked boxes.

"I mean, really. This is dangerous," Lorelei persists. "We have children to go home to," she says without thinking.

Rishika glares at Lorelei and then lays back with her head on her backpack. She crosses her arms and closes her eyes. *Great*, she thinks. *Am I going to have to hear about children non-stop for this entire trip?* Rishika has never really had a thing for kids. It's not like she had a particular negative experience with children. She's just never had a natural affinity for them or opportunities to bond with them as she was growing up. She's an only child. She was never into baby dolls or playing mom. She never babysat neighbor kids or had young cousins to help out with. She just doesn't have much experience with kids, and, as a result, doesn't relate to them. Also, they're loud and time-consuming.

The four ladies bounce along in the back of the truck in silence. Ashley leans against a stack of boxes. Katherine lies down with her head in Ashley's lap. Lorelei sits upright and tense, crisscross applesauce.

Ashley texts on her phone. Pierce is asking her where Teddy's baseball gear is and directions to get to practice. Ashley blows out a breath of annoyance. She spent a week preparing a detailed eleven-page typed-up itinerary so he would know what to do without her there and the kids would have everything that they needed. So that she wouldn't have to be doing this, communicating with him practically the moment they landed. What an incapable buffoon. She texts back, agitated, *Just ask your ten-year-old daughter. She knows everything that you don't.* Surely Pierce hastily texted Ashley, interrupting her before he bothered problem-solving on his own. Her poor children. How could she leave them with him?

Katherine digs through her backpack and fishes out a protein bar. "Anyone want one?" Ashley and Lorelei shake their heads no. Katherine peels back the wrapper and takes a bite. She leans back against Ashley. She reads the negative energy and raises her eyebrows to no one but herself.

Lorelei raps her fingers nervously on the metal floor of the truck. Obviously, she is excited about this trip. But, she didn't anticipate that they were going to be reckless like girls in their twenties. She was already on high alert for the entire flight making sure a boa constrictor didn't eat her. Her nerves are completely shot. Her tapping fingers make a rhythmic echo in the hollow of the truck. Ashley glances at her, annoyed, as she continues to text Pierce.

"Mark my words," Lorelei says, "we're going to wake up in bathtubs full of ice with a note that says, 'Call an ambulance. Your internal organs have been harvested.' This is exactly the kind of stuff I warn my kids about, and now I'm in this situation. I actually watched the movie *Taken* last week, just to remind myself to be vigilant so we don't get kidnapped and sold into human trafficking. You know, none of our husbands are anything like Liam Neeson, so we're scr—"

"Lorelei!" Ashley shouts. "Shut up!"

Lorelei looks shocked and offended. Frankly, Katherine and Rishika are a little surprised at Ashley's outburst, as well. It's not like her.

They ride along in awkward silence for a little while. Lorelei eyes Ashley.

"I'm sorry," Ashley says, still a little agitated. "I'm dealing with something right now." She turns back to her phone.

Lorelei shrugs. "It's okay." But it's not. She already feels like she's a third wheel. Yes, Katherine, Rishika, and Ashley have done this before. They've hitchhiked before, they've seen the world, and they've done all these crazy and daring things and she hasn't. But they don't need to rub it in her face.

"For the record," Rishika mumbles, "Craig has some Liam Neeson-like qualities."

This makes Katherine inwardly smile. Craig is an absolute sweetheart. He's extremely smart and laid back, but he doesn't have any killer Liam Neeson qualities. She glances at Ashley and Lorelei to see if they're thinking the same thing, to share a humorous moment and defuse the tension, but they are both currently in their own heads.

Craig and Rishika are an unlikely pair, but a great one. He is not who the ladies would have picked out for her, or who they would have expected Rishika to choose in a husband. But he is so good for her.

Rishika was always a party animal— the instigator of the party, the life of the party, and the person that wanted to keep partying long into the night after the party ended. When they had all started calming down in their mid- to late twenties, spending more time staying in with their men on the couch or with a small dinner party of other couples, sitting in a backyard drinking wine, Rishika was drinking martinis at Bar Marmont or taking shots at Miyagi's on Sunset with her single friends or with the hot and emotionally unavailable guy of the moment. She'd end up at parties at houses in the Hollywood Hills owned by people she didn't know with backyards full of people who weren't her friends, and doing the occasional recreational drug.

At that time, Rishika was an assistant to a creative executive at the studio. She was an absolute go-getter during the day. She would read the Hollywood Reporter first thing every morning and keep up on the industry news. She was an efficient, likeable assistant and had a great rapport with her colleagues. When she got home from work, she would go for a run, read a script, take a short nap and then go out at night and drink way too much. Somehow she'd managed to pull it off day after day. She enjoyed it, but eventually the party scene started to get repetitive and tedious.

One night she was at a dinner party hosted by Shirley, the executive she assisted. They started out in the living room drinking chardonnay and eating canapes. She glanced at her phone to check the time. She had plans to go out afterwards with some guy named Dean who she'd been on a few dates with. He was also an executive assistant at a different studio and she'd met him at a party at a stranger's house in Silverlake. She noticed that she had a message from him, standing her up for the second weekend in a row. As a result, she was sliding into a shitty mood.

When the guests all went into the dining room for dinner, she was the last one in because she'd stepped outside and called Dean and told him to lose her number. When she walked into the dining room, there was one seat left next to a guy who smiled at her. He stood up when she approached her seat and he pulled out her chair. *Oh, here we go*, she thought, unexcited about feigning polite conversation all evening with a boring guy, but she knew to be on her best behavior since this was a work thing. He pushed her chair in and introduced himself as Craig. He asked her questions about herself to which she replied, a little bit curt and uninterested. And then, as she was explaining how she knew Shirley, per his question, she realized that he was looking right into her eyes, really listening to her. And right then, as the salmon and risotto were being placed in front of her, she thought, *Huh. What would it be like to date a sweet guy with substance?*

The following week they met for coffee after work, and the following weekend he took her to his favorite Mexican restaurant. None of it was trendy or flashy, but they had a lot to talk about. Rishika discovered that Craig had grown up in Indiana and had two brothers and two sisters. He'd grown up spending a few weeks every summer at Lake Michigan renting a big lake house with lots of cousins and aunts and uncles. He used to go camping and fishing with his dad, just the two of them. He'd been the only one of his brothers who wanted to go and it had inspired him to become an Eagle Scout.

Craig was calm and laid-back, a gentle giant. She enjoyed discussing things that mattered to them, their individual passions, what they both wanted out of life. Rishika found herself thinking about him when she was at work and falling in love with him more every time she saw him. Even though she was a strong woman, Craig made her feel safe and at ease. Little by little, she let him chip away her hard shell and she revealed more of her truths, the ones she was proud of and the ones she felt were less desirable.

So, even though Craig is nothing like Liam Neesom, and even though he is too sweet and gentle to have any killer instinct, he's a superhero. He has tamed Rishika.

\*\*\*

The ladies continue to ride along in silence. Ashley continues to text angrily. Lorelei finally settles down and falls into a deep sleep on her backpack. Katherine checks her e-mail on her phone.

Rishika's eyes remain closed, though she is not asleep. Her anger about the "having kids to go home to" comment has dissipated. It's fine. By now, she is used to the "no kids" comments. It pisses her off, but is not super hurtful. What now consumes her mind is the incident at the airport. *What the hell was that?* she wonders. *I swear I saw Anna. It was the craziest thing. It could have been someone that really looked like her. But, no, it was totally her. I know her like I know my own reflection. Maybe I was hallucinating. Maybe I'm having like a delayed shock thing. Losing Anna has been really traumatic.*

Suddenly the truck brakes. Lorelei wakes from the abrupt stop. The ladies all look at each other, startled and unsure.

Lorelei jumps up and heaves up her backpack, poised to throw it. "It's happening! Get ready to throw something at them!"

The door slides up. The man who closed the door earlier stands there and yells at them, "Out! Out! Out!"

The ladies all grab their backpacks and carry-ons and scamper out. They stand on the side of the road in shock.

"Okay, thank you!" Ashley calls to the truck as it pulls away from them. "That was abrupt."

"They're not supposed to pick up hitchhikers," Rishika explains.

"Fuck!" Katherine yells suddenly.

"What's wrong?" Ashley asks.

"My tote bag. I left it on the truck!" She covers her mouth with her hands, her eyes huge.

"Oh, shoot," Ashley replies.

Rishika pats her back. "It's okay. We can go shopping. We'll buy you whatever you need."

"Anna's ashes are in that bag!"

# Chapter 13

"Fuck!" Ashley exclaims.

They all look at each other, panicked.

Without a word, Rishika takes off in a sprint after the truck. The ladies yell at her in encouragement. She pumps her arms, and her strong legs stride out as far as they'll go. But the truck is too far ahead. Rishika may be in great shape, but she can't outrun a truck.

She slows to a jog and looks around. A pick-up truck is approaching. She waits for it, begins running again like she's waiting for a baton hand-off, and as it passes she jumps on the back and climbs into the bed of the truck.

The driver sees Rishika and waves her off. He rolls down his window and shouts something in German.

She points at the cargo truck. "Catch that truck!"

The driver nods with a determined look. The pick-up truck accelerates and catches up with the cargo truck.

Rishika waves frantically at the driver of the cargo truck. The man in the passenger seat rolls down his window.

"Stop! Please! My bag is in your truck!" Rishika shouts.

The cargo truck slows to a stop. Rishika doubles over in the bed of the pick-up truck to catch her breath.

"Oh, my God." She climbs out of the back of the truck.

The man in the passenger seat jumps out of the cargo truck, jogs to the back and pulls up the sliding door. He hops in, grabs Katherine's tote bag and tosses it to Rishika. He gives her a thumbs-up, gets back in the cargo truck and it drives away.

The driver of the pickup truck gets out. "Vow. You're fast," he says with a German accent.

Rishika lunges at him and hugs him tight. She gives him a kiss on his cheek.

"Thank you," she pants as she pulls away, relieved and out of breath. He looks at her like she's crazy. "You have no idea what you have done for me. Thank you."

"You're velcome," he says with a big smile.

Rishika walks back towards the girls. She holds the tote bag triumphantly over her head. "I got it!" she shouts. "I got it."

Ashley, Katherine and Lorelei cheer, jumping up and down. They run up to Rishika and hug her.

"Rishika!" Ashley squeals. "That was amazing!"

"You did it!" Katherine says and embraces Rishika. "Thank you. I never would have forgiven myself."

Lorelei pats Rishika on the back. "You are such a badass. I can't even believe you."

"Thank God I just ran a 10K," Rishika says.

"Oh, my God," Katherine says with her hands placed on her cheeks. "What would we have told Kevin?"

"That Anna decided to go road-tripping with new friends?" Ashley proposes.

Katherine swoons at the thought.

Lorelei elbows Ashley. "That's not remotely funny."

Rishika peeks in the tote bag. "You know your passport and wallet are in here, too."

"That would have been very inconvenient. But replaceable.

Rishika, you're my hero."

Rishika returns a victorious wide smile.

The four of them walk down the street arm in arm.

# Chapter 14

The streets of Munich are gray cobblestone, and the sidewalks are lined with old-fashioned black lamp posts. The buildings are of Bavarian architecture, constructed out of plaster and stone, spotted with lots of multi-paned windows and topped with steep roofs. The restaurants and shops look like cozy and charming chalets. It's so quaint and pretty, and the city has such an old, historic feel to it.

This moment is Lorelei's first taste of European culture, and she is overcome with the excitement of *being* in Europe. As she walks along the cobblestone street, she takes constant pictures on her phone of the buildings. "Just look at this architecture! I feel like I'm in Fantasyland at Disneyland. It doesn't even look real!"

"I can tell your students are going to benefit from all of this inspiration," Ashley says and squeezes her arm.

"I hope so. I set up a separate Instagram page solely so I could share with them what we see and do."

"That was brilliant," Rishika compliments.

"Thanks. Gosh, I can already feel a special intangible energy in the atmosphere. I'm so excited to become an artist again on this trip."

"What are you talking about? You're an artist every day," Katherine refutes.

Lorelei scrunches her face in rebuttal. Yes, she is an art teacher, but she herself hasn't created original, inspiring art in years. She doesn't have stories to tell. She hasn't really *lived*. But here in Europe she will have adventures. So many escapades to keep her inspired for years to come.

"How much further?" Rishika asks as they walk down the street. "My feet hurt."

Ashley laughs. "You sound like Ryan."

"I did sprint after a moving vehicle."

Katherine looks at her phone. "We're close. Should be up on our left in a little bit."

"I kind of feel like we're cheating by using a phone," Ashley remarks. "Backpacking was much more hard core twenty years ago. We didn't have GPS or internet. We had our trusty <u>Let's Go To Europe 1996</u> guidebook. We had to overcome language barriers and communicate with locals in order to figure out directions."

Rishika nods in agreement. "We didn't even *have* cell phones. We called our parents once a week from a pay phone just to tell them we were alive."

"It was much more of an expedition back then," Ashley adds. "A blind journey."

Lorelei nods.

Katherine's breath catches. "There it is! We're here!"

"Oh, my gosh, a real-life hostel! This is so exciting!" Lorelei exclaims.

"I feel like I'm twenty-two again," Ashley says, beaming.

The women jump up and down in celebration.

***

The ladies enter the hostel excitedly. They look around as they walk through the lobby into the main room, where an eclectic mix of young twenty-somethings of various ethnicities socialize. The room buzzes with chatter in various languages and accents. Some lounge on the couches. Some play board games at small tables. On the far side of the room is a table with a few computers. A young woman with dreadlocks plays a guitar while a guy sings an alternative tune with emotion. It's a very laid-back, cool vibe.

Lorelei, Katherine, Rishika and Ashley look at each other and nod, anxious to mix in with these groovy young people. For a moment, Lorelei imagines them lounging on the couches later, singing along with the guitar player and their new carefree friends.

Almost all at once, all conversation halts to an awkward silence.

"Oh, my gosh," a female voice says, "why are there *moms* here?"

Rishika's jaw drops. Lorelei's and Ashley's eyes widen in shock.

Katherine's eyes follow the voice and she sees a petite young woman with a blonde pixie cut wearing cut-off jean shorts, a tank top and no bra. She dresses like she doesn't care, but she looks like a supermodel.

"Woohoo!" a male voice shouts. "Cool Chicks Backpacking Europe!" The room erupts in laughter. Lorelei, Katherine, Rishika and Ashley stand there, stunned, humiliated, and deflated.

Rishika clenches her jaw. "We are burning these shirts."

# Chapter 15

It's evening. A long room with wood floors houses two rows of wooden bunk beds.

It's like a scene out of the children's book <u>Madeline</u>, only instead of sweet little orphans in matching blue dresses, the characters are young women of various ethnicities and styles. This particular corner of the room is inhabited by a group of solemn American women in their early forties. They lounge on their bunk beds, Lorelei and Rishika on top bunks and Ashley and Katherine underneath them.

"I've never felt so old," Katherine pouts.

"We're not old," Rishika refutes. "We're forty-two and we're kicking ass."

Katherine tilts her head towards some scantily clad young ladies who are primping, presumably preparing for an unforgettable night out in Munich. "Well, compared to them, we're old." Her eyes widen. "And flabby."

Rishika agrees by nodding, begrudgingly. Except for the flabby part.

Ashley sighs. "It didn't even occur to me that we were old. You guys are going to laugh at me, but I felt like this was our second chance. I actually felt like we were just doing this trip a second time around, and we were still in our twenties. That's so dumb. What did

I think? That the plane was a time machine?"

Katherine nods in agreement. "No, I was thinking that, too."

"Fooorties," Ashley says dramatically and shudders. "That sounds ancient. When my parents were in their forties they were boring and so uncool."

Lorelei looks up, thinking about her own parents, and nods in agreement.

"When my parents were in their forties," Rishika says, "they were already successful doctors." She considers this. "But they were also really strict. And boring and uncool."

"I'm so embarrassed," Ashley says and hides her face in her pillow.

"Well, you know what?" Lorelei says, breaking her silence. "This is my first chance. And I don't want to lie around and pout on my first night in Europe." She climbs down the ladder of her bunk. "We may be in our forties, but I, for one, am prepared to act like I'm in my twenties."

Katherine grins. "Attagirl! I love that idea. Thank you for some perspective."

Ashley claps her hands together. "You are totally right. What are we doing? We're in Europe!"

Rishika looks over at the bunk bed next to her. Anna lies there on her stomach with her feet in the air. She writes in her journal as her feet sway front and back. Rishika does a double take. Her eyes widen in shock. She shakes her head to snap out of it, but Anna is there, writing in her journal just like she would have done twenty years ago. Anna was always writing in her journal.

"Anna?" Rishika whispers. Rishika frantically looks at Katherine, Lorelei and Ashley, but they are oblivious to Anna's presence.

"I'm going to shower and put on something fabulous," Lorelei says. "I bought new outfits for this trip."

"A shower definitely needs to happen," Ashley agrees as she rises from her bed. "I need to wash that plane ride off me."

The ladies' conversation blurs into the background as Rishika looks back to Anna, who rests her chin on her hand, propped up on her elbow. Anna looks right into Rishika's eyes and smiles. "You should get ready, too. Have fun, okay?"

Rishika's jaw drops. "Anna!" She reaches across the way to the other top bunk for her beloved friend, loses her balance and falls the long way to the wood floor with a painful thud.

"Oh, my God!" Katherine shouts.

"Rishika!" Lorelei cries.

Lorelei and Ashley are at Rishika's side instantly. Katherine jumps off her bed and rushes to Rishika who lies on the ground in shock.

"Are you okay?" Ashley asks.

Rishika groans. "Ugh. I don't know. Shit." She rubs her hip. They all help her up and guide her to sit on Katherine's bottom bunk. "I swear, I just saw Anna. She was writing in her journal."

Katherine, Lorelei and Ashley look at each other, caught off guard. After a moment, Ashley sits down next to Rishika.

"That is probably what she would be doing if she was here," Ashley says gently, as she rubs circles on Rishika's back.

Katherine looks down at Rishika with new eyes. She's been friends with this woman since they were eighteen years old. Rishika has always been the tough one, the one with unbreakable confidence who knew she would get whatever she wanted—and *has* gotten everything that she's wanted. Rishika is the one that has your back and is ready to fight for you. Rishika has always inspired Katherine to be confident and believe in herself. It's now, in this moment, that she sees through Rishika's tough exterior. She has dark circles under her eyes. She looks… fragile.

"Hey," Katherine says to Rishika as she sits down on the other side of her. "How *are* you?" Rishika shrugs. "Have you been sleeping at all?"

Rishika exhales, painfully. "I can't sleep without dreaming about her. I can't do anything without thinking about her," she says and sniffles.

"You've been through a lot," Katherine says as she slips her hand into Rishika's. "You will get through this. We'll get through it together."

Lorelei kneels down in front of Rishika. "Sweetie, I think you need to eat something. Let's go get some dinner." Rishika nods and exhales a breath that is laden with heartache. Lorelei rubs her knee and smiles at her. "Let's go have some fun."

As Rishika slowly makes her way to the shower, Katherine stops Ashley and Lorelei. "I've never seen Rishika this vulnerable. We need to keep an eye on her."

# Chapter 16

After a hot shower, a teeth-brushing, and fresh clothes, the ladies have a new lease on life. On their way to dinner, they walk through Marienplatz, the main square of Munich, named after Mary, the Mother of Jesus. They mill around the crowded square for a while, admiring the incredible Neo-Gothic architecture of the Old Town Hall and the New Town Hall, which look more like grand cathedrals than government buildings with their steeples and pointy spires. In the middle of the square stands the Mariensaule, a column topped with a golden statue of Mary that pays homage to Mary as the protector of Bavaria.

The ladies are just in time for one of the performances of the day by the little statues in the Glockenspiel, the legendary clock located in the tower of the New City Hall.

Lorelei is in awe of this famous clock in this square where hundreds of people from all over the world gather each day to watch this moving piece of art and culture that was crafted hundreds of years ago.

The bells chime melodically, and Lorelei steadies her phone, filming as the scene begins to unfold. It is a reenactment of the 1586 wedding celebrations of Wilhelm V and Renata of Lothringen. The Bavarian duke and duchess watch a procession of jesters, musicians and other processors carrying flags. And then the armored knights on horseback enter, traveling towards each other, lances raised. As the characters circulate, the scene begins again. This time the golden knight spears the silver knight, who falls back, defeated. Below them, dancers in matching costumes spin and celebrate. It's like a giant music box.

Lorelei smiles widely, her heart full that she is here witnessing this in person, and it's only the first day of a two-week European adventure. It's just so incredibly exciting! She stops filming and glances at her friends to see how they feel about this moment. Her smile fades.

Rishika is dazed, presumably missing Anna. Lorelei doesn't fault her for that, but come on! They are in Munich, Germany. Enjoy it! Katherine has walked off and looks focused on whoever she's speaking to on her phone, probably a colleague. Ashley looks pissed and texts furiously with her head down. To Pierce? Who knows? What does Ashley have going on in her life right now that has her so grumpy? I mean, I guess they've all seen the Glockenspiel before, but still.

For a moment, Lorelei is thoroughly annoyed with all three of them for taking this moment for granted. *This is going to be an interesting trip*, she thinks. It's day one and they have already lost patience and snapped at each other.

It's strange. There is actually so much that she doesn't know about these ladies. She's known them for about twenty-four years. She, of course, knows their families, what they do for a living and a little bit about what their kids are into, but other than that, what does she really know about them anymore? She knows them on a superficial level, only getting her annual update at the Christmas brunch. They are, naturally, always excited to see each other, but other than the occasional comment on a family vacation photo on social media, they don't really communicate with each other between one Christmas brunch and the next.

Anna had strong relationships with each one of them individually. She saw and spoke to each of them multiple times a year. God bless her. She was the glue that held them together. With her gone, will they continue to do their Christmas brunch? Who will host it? Or, will they all retreat even more into their own lives, their friendships eventually fading completely? Other than Anna keeping them connected, what do they all have in common? They all have very different personalities, different interests, different political views. Even with Rishika in Hollywood, Katherine in San Marino, and Lorelei in Rancho Cucamonga, all within fifty miles of each other, they pretty much only get together once a year.

They love each other because they loved each other years ago during the formative years of adulthood. What they have in common is that they share wonderful memories of great times. That is what bonds them. Is that enough to sustain a friendship?

# Chapter 17

"Welcome to the legendary Hofbrauhaus, one of Munich's oldest beer halls," Katherine says to Lorelei with her arms outstretched as they walk into the bustling tavern. In addition to planning the trip, Katherine has decided to play tour guide as well. She's going to give Lorelei the deluxe experience.

They walk through the crowded restaurant under cross-vaulted ceilings that are painted with colorful frescoes in the baroque style. Wall sconces and pendant lights emit a cozy glow. Black walnut wainscotting halfway up the walls and framed pictures combine to create an inviting atmosphere.

There are long picnic-style tables full of people, drinking beer and talking happily. The delectable aromas of sausages and potatoes permeate the room.

"This level is called the Schwemme," Katherine continues, "and, believe it or not, it is where the beer was once brewed." Lorelei nods, glad that Katherine is back in the moment to enjoy this experience and have fun with her.

A five-piece band plays traditional Bavarian folk music in the center of the room. The musicians bob to the tune as they play the guitar, large bass, harp-like zither, trombone, and accordion. The music is infectious, and Lorelei bops along as she and the ladies find a picnic table with room for them. They sit on either side facing each other.

"Willkommen," greets a waitress wearing traditional female lederhosen.

"Hallo!" they return.

"Girls, shall we just share a bunch of food?" Katherine asks. They all nod. Katherine turns her attention to the server. "We would like some pretzels and beer cheese, sausages—both weisswurst and bratwurst— with sauerkraut and mustard, potato salad, cabbage salad, and spaetzle. She glances at Lorelei to explain. "Noodles and cheese."

"Sounds amazing," Lorelei gushes. "I will eat whatever you order."

Rishika takes note that she can eat the sausages, sauerkraut and mustard, likely the only things on the menu that fall under the paleo umbrella.

"Wow," Ashley compliments. "You remembered."

"I have rehearsed this moment." Katherine quickly turns her attention back to the waitress. "Oh, and at the end, apple strudel! With the vanilla sauce and whipped cream. Danke schoen."

"Of course," the waitress says. "And to drink?"

"Weissbier for all of us, please!" Ashley says.

"Oh, yeah," Rishika says, excitedly. "Keep the weissbier coming!" Rishika is in dire need of a nice big weissbier. Not paleo, but you can't come to Germany and not drink the beer. She's still shaken by the previous events, but a hot shower has soothed her, and she's prepared to be a good sport. She hurt her wrist and her hip when she fell off the top bunk, and Lorelei went down to the reception desk and got a bag of ice and an ACE bandage from the first-aid kit. She has to admit, it's exciting to be here at the Hofbrauhaus. The fun atmosphere and cheerful music are contagious, and her mood is lifting.

Lorelei puts her hand up in a little wave to the waitress. "I'll have a chardonnay, please."

Rishika shakes her head at the waitress. "No, she won't."

The waitress nods and leaves.

Lorelei scrunches up her nose. "You know I've never been a beer person."

Rishika winks at Lorelei. "You've never had weissbier. It doesn't taste like a frat party, I promise. It's liquid gold."

Ashley can see that Rishika is making an effort to have fun. The poor thing has circles under her eyes, but she's attempting to be pleasant. Ashley grabs Rishika's hand on the table and smiles. "This is going to be a great trip."

Rishika smiles and nods. She glances at Ashley's hand on hers. "Where's your wedding ring?"

"Oh, I didn't want to travel with it."

Rishika nods. "That was probably smart. Shoot, now I wish I'd left mine at home."

Katherine looks around. "There are so many young people here. They're kids! And they have that sanguine look in their eyes. You know?" The other ladies nod. "Do you remember that feeling, that you had all the time in the world to accomplish your goals? That you were going to change the world?"

"Absolutely," Lorelei says, wistful.

"Totally," Rishika agrees. "But, actually, we've each accomplished a lot of our goals. We should be really proud of that."

"True, true," Katherine agrees. "But I'm so busy all the time, moving onto the next task, that I don't celebrate the victories. They don't realize that this is the best part right now, the part *before* everything happens. The anticipation."

"Do you really believe that?" Rishika questions. "You seem to love your work."

"I do, I do. I'm just so busy. I need a gap year in my life." She laughs it off.

"You get a gap two weeks," Ashley offers.

"I'll take it."

"My problem is complacency," Lorelei chimes in. "My plate is so full, and even though I still have that dream of being an artist someday, I'm too uninspired to actually make it happen."

"Really? You're so creative and dynamic," Ashley says.

"Well, thank you, but it's like I use all of that up on everyone else. If I find myself with a little time just for me, I choose Netflix over painting."

"Mmm," Katherine nods. "Complacency can be a dangerous thing. It's what causes years to pass without you even noticing. I kind of want to go up to some of these guys and ask them, 'What's your plan? Tell me how you're going to take the world by storm.' And maybe some of their rose-colored optimism will rub off on me."

"Katherine, you don't strike me as complacent at all," Rishika counters. "You're an absolute go-getter."

Katherine ponders this. "Not complacent. I'm just… losing steam. I have so much to do"—she exhales—"and not enough time. I could use a jolt of inspiration to remind me why the rat race is so important. It's just not always as fun as it used to be."

"Hmm," Rishika muses. "The race is what keeps me going. I love scrambling to the top."

"What do you when you get there?" Katherine asks.

Rishika smiles. "Revel in it."

"What gets me about these young adults is that they have their entire lives ahead of them," Ashley says. "They haven't made mistakes yet that will impact their lives long-term."

Rishika and Katherine look at each other and raise their eyebrows.

"I just mean they don't understand that the choices they're about

to make are going to determine what their life is like in twenty years."
*So choose wisely,* she thinks.

"Damn," Katherine says. "Are you regretting quitting accounting all those years ago?"

"No, it's not that."

"I think I know what you're trying to say," Lorelei chimes in. "We've made our choices. Our paths are pretty much set. My path to motherhood started when I was twenty-two. It led me to make more and more choices that took me away from the path that I had planned on taking. I don't regret it, of course, and I wouldn't trade it for anything, but I do sometimes wonder what an alternate path would've looked like."

"Hmm," Katherine ponders. They each contemplate the conversation in silence for a moment.

"I wonder how many of these guys have absolutely no idea what they're going to do with their lives. I did so much searching before I went back to school to get my accounting degree." Ashley had gotten her bachelor's in liberal arts, but had struggled with finding a career path she was passionate about after college. "I felt so lost. Good Lord, the random jobs I took. Phone sales, temping, and then all the first dates that went nowhere." Ashley shakes her head and chuckles.

"I loved all that!" Rishika exclaims.

"Oh, my gosh, I didn't," Ashley disagrees. "It seemed like more of a chore than a luxury at the time. I just wanted to get on with it already. I wanted to figure myself out. And then I met Pierce and he became the mission." She nods. Rishika, Katherine and Lorelei wait for more. Ashley deflects to Rishika. "What searching did you do? You were always firmly set on the film industry path."

"Yeah… but I started at the bottom. First as an intern, then as a production assistant, then as an executive assistant. I enjoyed the climb. Besides, I did searching in other ways. To me, searching indicated that the possibilities were endless. I had fun with all the trial and error."

"Trial and error," Katherine jokes. "Is that what we're calling it?"

"Ha ha. Yes, I was wild. We get it. I actually think it's kind of nice that we've gotten through our formative years," Rishika says. "I like feeling secure. We know where our lives are headed."

"That we do," Lorelei agrees. "We are committed. We've chosen our husbands, our careers, we've had our kids. But sometimes I wonder what's left. Is there anything else to search for?"

"Now we need to search for something to search for," Katherine jokes.

"Ugh. You guys are morbid," Rishika says with a disgusted expression. "I disagree with all of this. I love my life. I love my job. I'm happy with the choices I've made to get where I am. It took me a while to grow up, but I'm thankful that I got all of that out of my system and don't have any regrets." Lorelei nods and purses her lips, introspective. Rishika exhales, pained. "What I'm afraid of is losing people I love. I feel like the rug has been pulled out from under me. Losing Anna has shown me that I'm not in control. And I like to be in control. No matter how prepared I am, no matter how diligent I am or how hard I work, in the grand scheme of things I'm not in control, and it's terrifying."

This leaves the group very quiet.

The waitress breezes by carrying four clear glass mugs of cloudy, golden ale and slams them down on the table.

"Good timing," Katherine says and passes out the beer.

Lorelei takes a tentative sip and her eyes widen in delight. "Oh, my gosh."

"Right?" Katherine takes a huge gulp and closes her eyes.

"I didn't expect it to be sweet." Lorelei takes another sip. "It takes like banana and bubblegum. I love it!"

"Oh, it's so good to taste this again!" Ashley exclaims. They all take a moment to savor the cold, yeasty weissbier.

"Rishika, you're totally right," Lorelei says, returning to the topic. "There are a lot of things we don't have control over. But some things we do. I think what I've learned from losing Anna is that life is short. If there's something we still want to do in life, we'd better do it. There are no guarantees of years and years to come."

Rishika nods.

"So true," Katherine agrees. "I think the only advantage these young adults have over us is their outlook. They're all in the head-space that they can conquer the world. And the crazy thing is, like you said, Rishika, we've all accomplished a lot of great stuff, yet we're nostalgic about the day when our outlook was more rosy, when we believed that anything was possible. You guys, we're in Europe! Europe is magical! Anything *is* possible!"

"Yes!" Lorelei exclaims. "I've been waiting for this my whole life. Promise that this is our mantra from this moment on. Anything is possible." She looks at each of them, asking them to join her on her journey to jumpstart their attitudes about life. She raises her mug of weissbier and Katherine follows, matching her excitement.

Ashley smiles. She used to be an optimist. Is it really true? Could things take a turn for her? Could she still have everything she wants in life? The realist in her doubts it, but the weissbier and Katherine and Lorelei's contagious sentiments are swaying her to feel hopeful. She raises her beer mug as well.

They all look at Rishika, who looks hesitant, likely because she is too cool to get swept up in emotion. But, Lorelei's big hopeful doe eyes are irresistible, and Rishika raises her glass to join theirs.

"Yay!" Lorelei cheers.

They exclaim in unison as they clink their glasses together. "Anything is possible!"

# Chapter 18

The middle of the table is filled with a smorgasbord of sausages, potatoes, pretzels, sides and accompaniments. They reach across each other tasting everything with enthusiasm and delight. The waitress slams down another round of overflowing beer mugs onto the table.

Lorelei's eyes shine mischievously. "Do you remember the drinking game 'I've Never?'"

"Oh, my gosh, yes!" Ashley shouts as she dips a chunk of pretzel in mustard.

Katherine claps her hands together. "Let's play."

"Okay! Remember, someone makes a statement about something they haven't done and if you've done it, you drink," Lorelei says.

"Right," Ashley says and chuckles. "Although all of my juicy secrets are from twenty years ago, and you know all of them."

"I'll start, then," Lorelei says, her eyes flashing. "I've never been to Jamaica."

Katherine audibly scoffs. "Lame. I'll start. I've never had anal sex!" she shouts.

"Let's just jump right in, shall we?" Rishika says dryly.

"Oh, my God," Ashley mumbles.

People look weirdly at Katherine. Some people laugh. Lorelei covers her face. "I'm so embarrassed."

"I'm sorry. I've always been simultaneously terrified and intrigued about this topic," Katherine explains. She leans in, mischievously interested. "So… who drank?"

Ashley shakes her head. "As if." She looks next to her at Rishika.

"Oh, hell, no," Rishika replies, appalled. "Because… ouch."

Ashley snickers.

Rishika looks at Katherine. "So, is that a no for you?"

Katherine shakes her head thoughtfully. "It's a no. I have logistical questions."

Rishika chuckles. "Such as…"

"Such as, does the receiver actually experience pleasure? And secondly"—Katherine naturally raises her voice—"how the hell does he get it in there?"

People from surrounding tables look over at them and snicker.

"For God's sake, Katherine," Ashley says, eyes wide. "Would you please stop shouting outrageous things to the general public?"

Katherine puts up both hands in apology. "Sorry, sorry. I got caught up in the moment. But surely I'm not the only one who wonders these things."

"You've been awfully quiet, Lorelei," Rishika says. Lorelei looks at her. "You're the only one who hasn't answered."

"Oh," Lorelei says. She coyly takes a sip of her beer. The girls scream.

Ashley hits Lorelei in the arm. "What?"

"This is going to be a more interesting game than I thought," Rishika says as she picks up her beer mug with both hands.

Katherine leans toward Lorelei. "Do tell."

Lorelei shrugs. "Adam and I have conceived six children together. We've tried pretty much everything."

"I had no idea you were so kinky," Katherine says, truly surprised. "I'm fascinated. Like I said, so many questions."

Lorelei laughs. "Okay, I'll answer them. But I'm going to need some more liquid gold first."

\*\*\*

After another round weissbier, satisfying Katherine's deep curiosity, and a few more "I've Never" questions, the ladies stuff themselves with apple strudel until they cannot eat another bite.

They begin to mingle with other patrons. There is a lot of clinking of beer mugs with strangers who quickly feel like friends while others dance to the cheerful folk music. It's so cool to be in a room of people from all over the world. They infuse each other with their dreams and energy.

Katherine and Ashley meet Marcus and Tom, who are honeymooning from London, as well as Hank and Rosanne from Michigan, who are celebrating their fortieth wedding anniversary.

Meanwhile, Lorelei is obsessed with approaching all of the youngish people. She meets twenty-four-year-old twin sisters from New Zealand who are on the quest for love, and thirty-year-old Emma, who quit her job as a receptionist at a doctor's office and is backpacking Europe by herself in a soul-searching quest to uncover what to do next with her life. Twenty-two-year-old Christopher is here in Germany to learn about his dad's side of the family and meet a few distant cousins he found through an ancestry website. Christopher tells her about a disco a few streets over, and she files this information away for later. Lorelei admires all of their missions of self-discovery and she basks in their excitement for the unknown.

After a few more conversations, Katherine finds what she's been looking for. She meets Melinda and Renee, two friends who met when they were pre-med. They decided to take this trip before they begin medical school in the fall. They can't wait to save lives, to really make a difference. They are impressed that Katherine went to law school and is an attorney at a prestigious law firm. They compliment her and validate her and ask her what her career goals are. She tells them that she has always wanted to become a partner in her law firm and that she's close. She just needs to keep pushing. They tell her that she can do it. She tells them to go get it. She's an inspiration to them, and they to her. She feels that fire within her starting to smolder again.

Rishika meets Diana, a recent screenwriting graduate from Australia who is using this trip as fodder for movie ideas. Diana's goal is to think of each city she visits as a possible setting. She anticipates that after her eight planned destinations, she'll have eight possible movie ideas. Meeting this go-getter rubs Rishika the wrong way. She was like that in her early twenties. Hell, she was like that a few months ago. But how could she possibly think of possibilities when she barely wants to continue?

# Chapter 19

When the ladies are ready to say goodbye to the Hofbrauhaus, Lorelei convinces them to try out the disco that Christopher suggested. They enter the crowded club, the bass pounding through the speakers and pulsing through their bodies. A DJ spins tunes in a corner of the dance floor. Bright lights and colors bounce off every surface, making everything appear disjointed. Rishika, Katherine, Lorelei and Ashley look around.

Lorelei claps her hands together. "This is amazing!"

Ashley nods. "I haven't danced in ages!"

"Let's go get some cocktails," Katherine says as she starts to lead the way.

A girl in her early twenties saunters up to the ladies. Katherine recognizes her as one of the people who so rudely commented on their arrival at the hostel. She's petite and waifish with a blonde pixie cut and delicate features, and she's followed by her posse of three beautiful twenty-somethings. One has full lips that seem to be in a permanent pout, one wears low-rise jeans exposing a butterfly tattoo on her hip bone, and the last wears a halter top and her tanned shoulders are dusted with body glitter.

"Well, well, well. If it isn't the moms from our hostel," Pixie Girl says with sass.

Katherine raises her eyebrows.

"Is that supposed to be an insult? Being a mother has been my most satisfying life experience," Lorelei says proudly. "And I have a daughter around your age, and I hope she would never speak to a stranger that way."

Pixie Girl looks baffled.

"What's your problem?" Katherine asks.

"Just that we're here to explore the world and find ourselves without parents looking over our shoulders, and suddenly you're everywhere we look."

"Trust me, we don't care what you're doing," Rishika says.

"We want you to find yourselves," Lorelei says. "I'm still finding myself."

"Shit," Pouty Lips says. "It's going to take that long?"

"Are we offending you somehow?" Katherine asks.

"Yeah," Butterfly Tattoo says defiantly. "I'm offended by your friend's mom jeans." Her eyes trail down Lorelei's body.

Lorelei's jaw drops.

"Oh, no, she didn't," Katherine says.

"I got these at Forever 21," Lorelei says defensively.

"Well, you should not be shopping there because you are not forever twenty-one," Butterfly Tattoo says.

"Is there a store called Pushing Fifty?" Body Glitter jokes. They all crack up and high-five each other.

"Fifty?" Lorelei blurts out. "We're forty-two!"

"Oh, my gosh," Ashley mutters and hides her face with her hand.

"For the record, I'm not a mom," Rishika states and puts her hands in the air innocently.

"Really?" Katherine turns towards her. "That's what you're offended about?" Rishika shrugs. Katherine turns back to the twenty-something gang. "We settle this now."

Pouty Lips gets in her face. "Oh, yeah? How?"

Katherine grits her teeth. "Dance-off."

"You're on," Pixie Girl says dangerously.

"It's the four of us against you and your little prepubescent friends."

"What the heck are you doing?" Lorelei whispers behind Katherine.

"Ugh," Ashley complains. "I just want a Moscow mule and to dance a little."

Rishika nods. She just wants to find the VIP section and find out if this place has bottle service.

"We've got this," Katherine says over her shoulder. She gets in the ringleader's face. "I get to pick the song."

"Deal," Pixie Girl says, "but don't pick anything by New Kids on the Block." She retreats back to her trio and they cackle obnoxiously.

A switch flips deep inside Rishika and her head snaps toward Pixie Girl. Anna's favorite band as a preteen was New Kids on the Block. She had a pillow case with Jordan Knight's face on it. She used to practice kissing on that pillow.

"Bitch!" Rishika yells. "NKOTB were awesome!"

Ashley's head whips towards Rishika. "Whoa. Where did that come from?"

"She just made it very personal," Rishika seethes.

"Okay," Ashley soothes and rubs Rishika's back.

"Aww," Lorelei sighs. "My first love was Joey McIntyre."

"For me, it was a tie between Ricky Schroder, Michael J. Fox, and Kirk Cameron," Ashley says with a chuckle.

"Girls. You are not helping the cause," Katherine says over her shoulder.

"What exactly is the cause again?" Ashley asks, observing the absurdity of the situation.

"The 'we're not pushing fifty' cause!" Katherine retorts.

"What are we about to do here?" Rishika asks.

"I'm getting tired," Lorelei says. "What time is it?"

"I have a plan," Katherine says, ignoring Lorelei. "Senior year, Greek Week, lip-sync competition. The routine."

Rishika nods. "It's risky, but it just might work."

Lorelei's jaw drops. "I can't dance like that after all these years!"

"For Gods sake, maybe you *are* pushing fifty!" Katherine barks. Lorelei looks wounded.

"I don't think I remember it," Ashley remarks. "I'm *buzzed.*"

"Your body will remember it," Rishika says. "You can do it. That routine was epic."

"It *was* epic," Lorelei says. "Okay. I'm in."

With her new attitude, Lorelei steps up to the group of twenty-somethings who are huddled up discussing their plan. "You are going to regret the day you were born!"

"A little harsh," Ashley says, trying to impart a little perspective on the situation. "Remember, we're just cool chicks backpacking Europe, having fun at the club."

"Let's do this." Katherine struts up to the DJ and whispers in her ear.

"Please clear the dance floor," the DJ says through the microphone in a confused voice. "I guess we're having a dance-off."

People hesitantly vacate the dance floor while the two opposing teams take to the dance floor. They face each other and stare each other down.

"I guess it's the old people versus the young people," the DJ says into the microphone.

Katherine deadpans.

Moments later, the first few well-known roboticized notes of 2Pac's "California Love" featuring Dr. Dre and Roger Troutman echo through the bar.

The two groups start to bop their heads a little, a slow start to a brutal dance-off in the name of fighting ageism.

The melody brings Katherine, Lorelei, Ashley and Rishika back to a moment in time, circa 1996, when the only pressures of life included studying for exams, who to take to the next formal, and winning a lip-sync competition for the honor of their sorority. And just like that, 2Pac, Dr. Dre and Roger Troutman trigger the muscle memory in their bodies from another era, and they dance in spectacular unison. Their mouths move, knowing every lyric.

Surprised by the powerful start, the twenty-somethings are thrown off and look at each other with concerned eyes. They also hadn't planned on lip-syncing and they don't know all the words, although their parents probably do. They dance a little awkwardly, not quite knowing what to do.

"Get it together!" barks Pixie Girl.

They snap out of it and each begins to dance back with modern moves.

The crowd cheers.

Both groups of ladies take turns with solo dances.

Rishika does the Running Man. Pixie Girl does a move from Fortnite. Katherine does the Roger Rabbit. Pouty Lips does a move from Fortnite. (Sadly, the crowd really responds to these Fortnite moves.) Ashley and Lorelei couple up and do the Kid n' Play.

Body Glitter and Butterfly Tattoo start to grind on each other. The crowd cheers.

"They're getting sexy!" Katherine cries out. "We're losing the crowd!"

This was the moment in the routine when Anna did the MC Hammer shuffle in her parachute pants back and forth. Out of respect for Anna's solo moment, the ladies freeze. They don't know what to do.

Katherine has a sudden idea and goes for it. She dives to the floor and transitions into the glorious rhythmic movement of the Worm. The crowd goes berserk. Ashley, Rishika and Lorelei, as well as all four twenty-somethings, stop dancing out of shock and awe. They stand there watching Katherine with their mouths hanging open.

"Final pose!" Ashley shouts.

Ashley offers Katherine her hand and pulls her up, while Rishika and Lorelei get on all fours. Katherine climbs onto their backs and settles with an arm and leg on each one of their bodies. Ashley climbs onto Katherine's back and straddles her like she's riding a horse, throws her arm up and rotates her wrist around like she's roping a steer. The twenty-somethings watch out of sheer curiosity.

The music stops and the crowd erupts into roaring applause and shouts. It's obvious who the winners are tonight. The twenty-somethings realize they've been beaten.

Ashley and Katherine climb down and help Lorelei and Rishika up off the floor. They scream and jump up and down, going absolutely ballistic, because no matter what age you are, nothing feels as good as the validation of a crowd after throwing your body, mind, and soul into a lip-sync battle set to 90's rap.

Lorelei and Rishika struggle to lift Katherine on their shoulders and then parade her around the dance club in victory. Club-goers high-five her and pat her on the back.

Pixie Girl approaches Katherine. "No fair!" she whines. "You guys totally practiced that."

Ashley smiles victoriously. "Honey, we've been practicing that since you were in utero."

"Pre-choreographed dancing was not prohibited in any previously discussed conditions of the competition," Katherine spouts off as she ungracefully hops down from Lorelei's and Rishika's shoulders.

Rishika tilts her head towards Katherine. "Our lawyer. She passed the bar while you were watching Sesame Street."

"How does bitter defeat taste in your mouth?" Katherine asks smugly.

Pixie Girl returns a squinty glare. She breaks. "Alright, that was *savage.*"

After a beat, "Oh, is that good?"

Pixie Girl smiles. "Totally."

Katherine softens. "Thanks! Your dancing was pretty savage, too."

"I'm Vanessa." Pixie Girl offers her hand.

"Katherine," she reciprocates.

"I hope I'm exactly like you when I'm middle-aged."

Katherine looks at Vanessa, deadpan. She ponders the sentiment and shrugs. "I'll take it."

"I want to buy you a drink." Vanessa throws her arm around Katherine's shoulder and they walk towards the bar. "So, where'd you learn that dance anyway?"

"Well, we were seniors in college. It was Greek Week and our sorority had been undefeated in the lip-sync competition for five years until the previous year. *That* was the routine that won back our title."

The bartender slams shots down on the bar for the ladies. "The dancing mamas! These are on the house," he says.

"Still not a mama," Rishika retorts.

"Oh, drink the damn drink," Katherine says.

They throw the shots back. The twenty-somethings gather around them. When another round of shots appears on the bar, the two groups of ladies throw those back, too.

Lorelei holds a shot up into the air in a circle of her friends and the twenty-somethings who challenged them. "Now, for future reference, we women need to support each other. No more cattiness. Let's start a movement of love and support. No matter what our differences are, we are women, beautiful and strong!"

The mixed group of ladies cheer and knock back their shots.

Pouty Lips turns to Lorelei. "You are so right. I just love you."

"I love *you*!" Lorelei returns and puts her arm around her.

"Okay, so teach us the dance," Body Glitter says.

They all move onto the dance floor together. The DJ plays "California Love" again and the ladies begin their routine. Other club-goers join in.

The rest of the night becomes a staccato series of events.

A round of Cosmopolitans.

Dancing.

Shots of Jaeger.

More dancing.

Group selfies.

Group pyramids on the dance floor.

Shots of Jose Cuervo.

Shots of…

# Chapter 20

A stream of bright sunshine bakes Ashley's face. With her eyes closed, one of her hands rises to wave it away. Her eyes slowly blink open. She has cotton-mouth and she is so, so thirsty. Parched. But, when she makes the slightest movement, she realizes how badly her head hurts. *The pressure. Oh, the pressure!* She can't possibly get up to get water. A small moan escapes her shriveled lips.

"Help. I want to die," she squeaks.

The ladies are draped in various positions on their bunk beds in the hostel. Lorelei and Rishika begin to stir.

"Never again," Lorelei croaks.

"What were we thinking?" Rishika moans.

"We can't do shots anymore," Lorelei says. "We're too old for shots."

"Please stop talking about it," Ashley says weakly.

"Do not say we're old," Rishika mutters. She shifts her weight with her wrist and winces in pain. In fact, her entire body is sore from falling off the bed the day before. "We were epic." She raises her arm in victory, eyes still closed.

"Shh," a voice shushes from somewhere in the room. All of the other beds are full with sleeping and presumably hungover women.

"I didn't say we're old," Lorelei whispers. "We're not old. But we are too old for shots."

"We acted like we were at our first frat party," Rishika remarks. "We know better than to mix beer and hard alcohol. Amateurs."

"I'll give you one thousand dollars to stop talking about it," Ashley begs. She gags, scrambles out of bed and runs off.

Rishika and Lorelei hear puking.

"Oh, sweetie," Lorelei says. She reaches her arm out in the direction of the sound of Ashley vomiting in a trash can in the hallway. At the moment, she can only hold Ashley's hair in spirit.

Katherine stirs, her eyes covered with a silk sleep mask. "My neck. Ugh, my neck hurts. This mattress is shit."

Rishika slowly sits up and swivels around to put her feet on the floor. "Whoa. I've got to get a hot dog or something. A weinerschnitzel."

"Shut up!" a voice shouts, a few beds away.

"Sorry," Lorelei whispers.

Katherine tries to sit up and grabs her neck. "Oh, my God! I really can't move my neck!"

***

Lorelei, Rishika and Ashley sit in the stark waiting area of a Munich hospital with all of their backpacks. They wear sunglasses and clutch cardboard cups of coffee to their chests. Rishika eats a bag of salted almonds from a vending machine. Lorelei scratches her left arm furiously. Ashley takes focused breaths in an attempt to soothe her nausea and pounding head.

"I just can't get over it. We drank so heavily before and it never slowed us down. Never."

"Do I really need to spell it out to you?" Lorelei asks, annoyed.

Katherine approaches them wearing a neck brace. She faces straight ahead and can only turn with her entire body.

"It's nothing serious. I just strained my neck and need to take it easy."

"Take it easy?" Lorelei says, concerned. She leans down and pulls the pant leg of her jeans up to scratch her leg. "We're going to Interlaken today. How do you expect to take it easy?"

Katherine shrugs and winces. "Ow."

Lorelei sits up. She reaches back and sticks her arm down the back of her shirt and scratches furiously. Rishika watches her.

"What is happening?" Rishika asks.

"I am so itchy right now. Is there anything wrong with my back?"

"Come here." Rishika pulls up the back of Lorelei's t-shirt to reveal her red and bumpy back. "Oh, my God. You're covered in bites."

Katherine takes a peek and inhales. "Whoa. I think you got bed bugs or something."

Lorelei's face contorts into a pout. "Really? I'm on vacation and I have to deal with this? I just assumed that since I wasn't bringing my kids that I wouldn't have to deal with communicable diseases." She sighs in frustration. "Okay. We're going to have to handle this."

"How?" Rishika asks, aghast.

"Well, I have to decontaminate myself. And I have to wash all of my clothes since I put last night's pajamas in my backpack with everything else I brought. Lice has gone through our house so many times. I know the drill."

Rishika looks thoroughly disgusted.

"I'm on it," Katherine says. She holds her cell phone far out in front of her, since she can't bend her head down, and taps at the screen. "Okay, there is a waschsalon a few streets away."

Rishika and Lorelei rise and throw their backpacks over their shoulders. Ashley sighs heavily and follows suit. Katherine gazes at her giant backpack in despair.

"You're lucky I love you," Rishika says as she attempts to pick up Katherine's backpack with her own on her back. "Oh, dear God."

"I'll help you," Lorelei says. She grabs the other strap.

Rishika cringes. "Just make sure your little friends don't jump on to me."

Katherine smiles. "Thanks, guys."

Moving slowly and painfully, they leave the hospital, lugging their heavy backpacks. Ashley concentrates on her measured deep breaths. They are a pitiful bunch.

"Ashley, are you okay?" Katherine asks.

Ashley shakes her head. "Talking… makes me want to puke."

Katherine makes a sympathetic face. "Okay."

"I think you messed your neck up when you were doing the Worm," Rishika says.

"Oh, my gosh, the Worm!" Lorelei exclaims, excitedly. "That was badass. You're my idol!"

"Nope. Not the worm," Katherine disagrees. "I'm positive it was that bunk bed. I should've brought my special pillow."

Ashley dumps her backpack and runs to the side of the road and throws up.

# Chapter 21

The ladies divide and conquer. Rishika begrudgingly washes all of Lorelei's clothes and her backpack at the laundromat and Katherine finds a drug store to pick up some hydrocortisone cream. Lorelei and Ashley go back to the hostel, where Lorelei takes a shower and washes her hair three times while Ashley pukes twice more in the bathroom. An hour and a half later they all reconvene and finally make it onto a train headed southwest.

Sadly, the time spent at the hospital and dealing with bedbugs makes defunct the plan to visit the Munich Residenz, the lavish four-hundred-year-old palace that belonged to the royal Wittelsbach family. There isn't very much wiggle room in their travel plans from country to country. They have a lot of ground to cover in a short period of time.

In a private train cabin, Katherine and Rishika sit across from Lorelei and Ashley, all clutching their cups of the third round of coffee. Ashley still wears sunglasses. After an hour of agreed-upon quiet time for resting and nursing their hangovers, Katherine breaks the silence.

"Happy Mother's Day, ladies."

"Oh, my gosh! I forgot!" Lorelei says.

"We'll have to call our kids later," Ashley says. She taps the screen on her phone to check the time. "They're probably not awake quite yet."

Rishika smiles. "Happy Mother's Day, girls."

"Thank you," Lorelei returns with a smile.

"Today is going to be a hard day for Kevin, Camila and Alexa," Katherine observes.

"And Anna's parents," Rishika adds.

"Those poor little girls," Ashley says.

Sad silence fills the train car.

"Honestly," Katherine starts, "how are they all going to make it without Anna?"

They all look at each other shaking their heads, finding no way to answer that question.

"How is Kevin doing, Rishika?" Lorelei asks.

"He's in survival mode. Irma and Jose are still staying with them, but last I spoke with Kevin, he felt like they needed to try things on their own."

"That's a step in the right direction," Lorelei offers.

"It's hard. Irma and Jose are helping with the cooking, housework, and the girls, and they're family, but it's such a long time for Kevin to have house guests. He feels like he and Camila and Alexa need some time just the three of them."

"I feel so horrible for him," Ashley says as she nibbles the last of the one cracker she has managed to get down. "How is he going to raise Camila and Alexa on his own?"

"He just is," Lorelei answers matter-of-factly. "And we're going to need to swoop in and help him out. We've really got to be there for him and those girls."

"I remember when Anna and Kevin met," Rishika remembers. "It was the disco fever-themed SigEp mixer sophomore year. He was wearing those gigantic bell bottoms and had fake curly chest hair glued to his chest with his shirt unbuttoned. He looked ridiculous, but he owned it. Anna loved how he was kind of dorky, yet confident."

They smile at the memory.

"They were meant for each other," Ashley says.

"You know how people say, 'After fifty years, my grandparents are still head over heels in love with each other?'" Katherine asks.

"I hate that," Ashley interjects. "It sounds like such a crock because how can you still be truly *in love* for that long?"

"I love Adam very much. But 'head over heels' is pushing it," Lorelei admits. "We all know that marriages go through stages. The beginning, of course, is the lust stage, then there's the in-love stage, in both of which you are feeding off of the addictive spark." Her wistful tone turns matter-of-fact. "When you have kids, you enter the teammate stage, which, by the way, Adam and I have been in for half of our lives. And then, of course, there's the roommate stage when you're not connecting at all and you just live together."

"I think there's probably a companion stage," Ashley adds. "You know, where you're just satisfied being together. When you are content to sit on a porch swing and really talk and go on cruises together."

Rishika makes a face. "So the old people stage."

Ashley shrugs. "I don't know. It sounds nice to me."

"James and I continue to be in the co-worker stage. When you see each other at work all day and then you see each other at home, and you're like, '*Oh, hello again.*' We have no time to miss each other. He is so fierce in the courtroom, though. I wouldn't go into battle with anyone else. However, I will admit that the spark is more like a dim lightbulb."

"You and James are a fantastic couple," Ashley interjects. "James and Katherine. Katherine and James. You're inseparable."

Katherine tilts her head from side to side, only moderately accepting the statement.

"Craig and I are still in love," Rishika interjects.

"That's because you don't have kids," Ashley says. Rishika's face contorts into an argumentative look. "No, really. Kids complicate things. Don't get me wrong, I love and adore my children, but there's more to fight about—more stress, not seeing eye to eye on parenting, less sleep, less money, less sex. *Your* life is easy."

"My life isn't *easy*," Rishika says defensively.

"You and Craig can focus on your careers and each other. Your evenings and weekends are carefree. Every night is date night. You probably get home from work and make cocktails every evening." They all look to Rishika to protest, but her silence confirms that when she and Craig get home from work, they make cocktails. Ashley continues. "You don't have soccer games and children's birthday parties to monopolize your weekends. You don't have to help with homework or wipe butts or wake up at two a.m. when someone is puking and have to change the sheets."

Lorelei scrunches up her nose. "That is an accurate depiction of family life."

"But Craig and I made that choice and it makes me angry that I have to defend it. Our life together has other stuff going on. Just because we don't have kids doesn't make it a walk in the park," Rishika says. Ashley shrugs. "I resent that, Ashley," Rishika says, irritated.

"Let's not fight, guys," Lorelei interrupts.

Rishika looks out the window with her arms crossed. Ashley looks down at the floor.

"Well," Katherine jumps back in, "My point *was*, it always sounds like a crock of shit when people say they're still in love after all that time, but Anna and Kevin would have been that couple. She was always laughing so hard at him, and you could tell that he still felt like she was out of his league. She was this lovable, beautiful and smart woman, and he always wondered how he got her. And they stuck together through thick and thin. Obviously."

"It's true," Lorelei says. "They had a very special relationship."

They sit in solemn silence for a moment.

Ashley blows out a pained exhale. "Pierce left me," she says in a small voice. She leans back against the wall and crosses her arms.

The girls all look at each other.

"What?" Lorelei says as if she truly didn't hear her.

"Ashley," Rishika says. "What do you mean?"

Ashley shakes her head. Her sunglasses hide her expression, but a tear runs down her cheek.

"Ashley," Lorelei says sympathetically.

"Take your glasses off," Katherine says.

Ashley removes her sunglasses to reveal teary eyes full of hurt. She sniffs and lets out a whimper.

"Honey. What happened?" Lorelei asks.

"He's been having an affair," Ashley blurts out. "For eight months. We're filing for divorce."

Lorelei covers her mouth in shock.

"What?" Rishika says, bewildered.

"How could he?" Lorelei asks.

"Easily," Ashley says. "They're in love."

"Wait a second," Katherine interjects. "James and I had dinner with you guys in February. You two seemed fine."

"Yep. He was having a full-blown affair then. I just didn't know it yet. I found out a few weeks later."

"Why didn't you say anything to us sooner?" Rishika asks.

"I didn't want to tell anyone at first. I was humiliated. And I couldn't believe it was happening. And then, you know, we needed to focus on Anna. Of course the funeral wasn't the right time. And I didn't want to put a damper on our trip."

"I hate that you've been enduring this on your own," Lorelei soothes.

"My parents know."

"Oh, Robert and Jane must be pissed," Rishika says.

"They are."

"I knew something was up on the plane," Katherine says. "You stared at the seat in front of you for hours. Oh, this is why you have to go back to work."

Ashley nods.

"What about the house?" Rishika asks. "Do you and the kids get to stay in it?"

"I'm going to have to find something smaller."

Katherine blows air out of her mouth, concerned.

"Did you sense that anything was off?" Lorelei asks.

"Well, to refer back to our previous conversation, I guess I just thought we were in a roommate phase." Ashley shrugs. "And things with Pierce have never been *easy*. But I assumed we were going to be married forever. I thought we had all the time in the world to get through it. I figured this is just what marriage is like. Sometimes it sucks. "

"I'm going to kick his prissy little ass," Rishika says.

"Can I ask," Katherine says, "who's the woman?"

"He met her at jury duty. They sat next to each other in the jury assembly room for hours and went to lunch together on their break."

"The whore," Rishika spits out.

"They were in love by the time they were dismissed at four o'clock. They decided it was their civic duty to do each other in the parking structure."

"Whoa," Katherine says.

"I can't believe it," Lorelei says, shaking her head.

"Is it wrong that *I* feel betrayed?" Katherine asks. "Pierce and I always got along so well. We had so much in common. You know, we always geeked out about wine. We discussed *Downton Abbey* and *Game of Thrones*. He was my buddy. But he was lying right to my face the last time I saw him. And now I can't be friends with him anymore. The prick."

"He was lying to a lot of people. He's a big fat liar."

Katherine, Rishika and Lorelei exchange concerned glances.

"Okay, forgive me for asking *this*," Lorelei starts, "but are you willing to work on things?"

"After that?" Rishika retorts. "Who could get past the infidelity? I couldn't."

Lorelei pats Rishika's hand. "Let's hear Ashley out."

"I wanted to. But Pierce says it's no use. He said he isn't in love with me anymore. He wants to be with *Maggie,*" Ashley spits out.

"Ugh, *Maggie*," Katherine commiserates.

"I'm sorry," Lorelei says. She grabs Ashley's hand and squeezes it tightly.

"If I'm honest, I don't think he was ever really in love with me. Maybe it was bound to happen. I was the one who always pressured him to get married."

"You can't honestly blame yourself," Katherine says.

Ashley takes a deep breath and lets it out, looking down at her lap. "It really doesn't matter who's at fault, the outcome is the same."

"Of course it matters," Rishika says. "It's Pierce's fault, and I hate him with a vengeance."

"That's right," Katherine says. "I *hate* him."

"I loathe him," Lorelei agrees.

They gather around Ashley in a seated group hug.

"Never in my life did I think I would ever get a divorce. I feel like

I've failed. I've failed as a wife, and I've failed my kids."

"You did not fail," Rishika says firmly.

Ashley bursts into another fit of sobs.

"Sweetie," Lorelei soothes. Ashley lays her head on Lorelei's shoulder.

"Do you need a lawyer?" Katherine asks.

"Yes," Ashley says, resigned.

Katherine squeezes her shoulder. "I know someone."

# Chapter 22

The ladies solemnly get off the train at the Interlaken Ost train station, carrying their humongous backpacks. They look tired, hungover and depressed. They are now helping Ashley carry the dissolution of her marriage.

Katherine also feels a pang of panic. *Italy. Every time we get off a train, we are closer to being in Italy.*

Outside the train station, they board a bus. They ride along quietly, looking out the windows. The beauty of the Swiss countryside begins to pull out some smiles. The grass and foliage are a vivid green, as are the grandiose mountains, capped with snow. Deep blue gentians, white tulips, sunny daffodils, and of course Switzerland's official flower, edelweiss, are just some of the alpine wildflowers that blanket the earth. The water of Lake Brienzersee is a brilliant combination of icy white and turquoise.

"The colors are so vibrant," Lorelei exclaims. "I've never seen anything like it. Paint colors are screaming out to me."

Ashley smiles. "I forgot how beautiful it is here."

The grandeur of the scenery brightens their moods, and by the time they step off the bus in front of the Interlaken Adventure Company, they are bubbling with excitement.

After they check in at the activities desk, they suit up in wet suits, life jackets and helmets, and complete a short instructional and safety training.

Katherine has told the employees that she simply woke up with a stiff neck and that she's a little sore, no big deal. She isn't missing this for anything. During their original trip, they planned on river-rafting—it was something Anna really wanted to do. But, unfortunately, a thunder and lightning storm thwarted their plan, and they headed off to the next city without checking this adventure off their list.

Now they stand on the side of the Lutschine River, water gushing by, waiting for instructions to climb into their raft, which is being held steady by several Interlaken Adventure Company employees.

"You guys," Lorelei says, suddenly anxious, "this is really dangerous. Maybe this is a bad idea."

Rishika puts both hands on Lorelei's shoulders and looks into her eyes. "No regrets, girlfriend. We're doing this."

"I'm scared," Lorelei squeaks. "I realize that I want to be daring and have all of these crazy experiences that I've never had, but in actuality, I'm a total wimp. I always tell my students to be brave and daring, but I'm not. I'm a fraud!"

"Come on," Ashley says as she links her arm through Lorelei's. "It's a first for all of us. We'll get through it together." Ashley recognizes the blessing of this trip taking her away from her problems at home. These adventurous moments are the first things that have evoked sincere rushes of excitement inside her in months.

The anticipation of this excursion sneaks up on Rishika, and she begins to jump up and down. She catches herself. She momentarily forgot that she gets a second chance to do this, but Anna doesn't. Is it right to do this in Anna's honor or is it unfair to do it without her? A female guide in her late twenties with blonde dreadlocks comes up from behind them and interrupts Rishika's thoughts.

"Welcome, ladies," she says with a Swiss accent. "I'm Mila. Are you ready to have some fun?"

Katherine and Ashley cheer as Mila climbs into the raft. Lorelei watches with apprehension, and Rishika looks like she's at Anna's funeral all over again.

Mila eyes Katherine's neck brace and then points at it. "Is *that* going to be okay?"

"Oh, yeah," Katherine answers. "Fine, fine. It's just a precaution."

"Okay, then. Come on in."

One by one, they take the guide's hand and step into the raft. Once the ladies are in position with Lorelei and Ashley sitting in the front of the raft, Rishika in the middle row, and Katherine and Mila in the back row, the employees give the raft a push, sending it down the river.

"Here we go!" Ashley cries.

In the back of the raft, Katherine touches her neck brace. "Soft and gentle, soft and gentle," she chants, willing the rapids to take it easy on her. Mila glances at her like she's crazy.

Lorelei takes nervous deep breaths. "Oh, man. We have absolutely no control."

"You're okay," Ashley says. "Just enjoy it."

Lorelei shakes her head.

"Hold the shaft with one hand and the T-grip with the other like you practiced during the lesson. Paddles in the water," Mila instructs. "Begin to stroke."

The ladies put their paddles in and stroke, a little awkwardly at first, and then more uniformly. On either side of the river, tall spruce trees reach into a brilliant blue sky dotted with cumulus clouds.

"Wow, this is gorgeous!" Ashley exclaims.

Rishika digs her paddle into the water with determination. *Germany, check. Switzerland, check.* She will be checking off her way through Europe, check, check, check, until she gets to Greece. She just needs to get through all of this, and then… and then *what*? Move on with her life? Once Anna's final wish has been carried out, what exactly is Rishika supposed to do next?

Rishika looks over and sees Anna sitting next to her on the raft, paddling with fierce pulls through the water. Rishika stops paddling, entranced. Anna looks Rishika in the eyes and smiles, then she throws her arms up in the air and lets out a whoop. Here she is rafting down the Lutschine River, like she wanted to so many years ago. She looks fearless, euphoric.

Anna always lived with such vivacity and complete abandon. Her enthusiasm often rubbed off on Rishika, who was always the more serious one, even as a child. Will Rishika ever feel true happiness again? With no limits? Or will she always think, *This is great, but it would be so much better if Anna was here?*

Meanwhile, Katherine sits in the back of the raft trying not to move, being careful of her neck. "Pretty cool," she says, unsure, but she's trying to be a good sport. She strokes only with her arms, not her entire body, with pathetic strokes that don't even penetrate the water.

The raft floats over a few small rapids, evoking cheers from the group.

"Ooh. That's kind of fun," Lorelei says, warming up a bit.

"Bump!" Mila says. The ladies bring their paddles in the boat until they pass over the bump. "Very good. Okay, ladies, we need to steer this raft together." The ladies paddle. "The rapids are going to get bigger down here. Let's paddle harder."

The ladies pull their paddles through the water with muscle as they go over a series of bigger rapids. The bumpy water causes Katherine to fall off her seat into the raft, and a quick succession of rapids tosses her around.

Her neck *snaps* audibly.

Lorelei's, Rishika's, Ashley's, and Mila's heads swivel to look at Katherine.

"Oh, my God!" Ashley cries.

"Are you alright?" Mila asks.

Katherine's eyes are wide with terror and then the look of concern disappears. "It's okay! I think that fixed it!" She moves her head from side to side to confirm it. "Yep. I'm good!"

The other ladies nod, relieved. Ashley gives her a thumbs-up, and Katherine climbs back onto her seat.

"Focus, ladies!" Mila says. "All hands. Here comes a big one."

The ladies turn their attention back to the rapids and take deep breaths in preparation. As they bump over a large rapid, the raft dips and rises rapidly, the inertia catapulting Lorelei out of the raft and into rushing whitewater.

Ashley screams.

"Lorelei!" Rishika shouts.

Lorelei flails around in the water. She grabs the nearby paddle before it is swept away and pulls it into her chest, hugging it with both arms.

"Oh, my God! Oh, my God!" Ashley exclaims.

"Remain calm," Mila instructs, yet her voice is laced with concern.

"I'm trying!" Ashley shouts. Mila casts Ashley an annoyed look and refocuses her attention on Lorelei.

"Extend your paddle toward the raft," Mila commands over the loud rush of the river.

"Extend your paddle toward the raft!" Katherine repeats, attempting to take charge.

Lorelei reaches her paddle toward the raft. "It won't reach!" she panics.

"Assume the white-water swimming position," Mila instructs.

"Assume the white-water swimming position!" Katherine mimics.

Mila grits her teeth, having had it with this group.

Lorelei lies back with her feet pointed down the river, per the ten minute instructional session. The guide looks at the water ahead. "Bend your knees slightly and brace yourself for the upcoming rapid." Lorelei bends her knees.

Ashley looks down-river and panics. "Oh, my god. It's coming! Brace yourself!"

Lorelei's eyes fill with terror. "Ahhhh! You guys! Tell my kids I love them!"

"Be strong, Lorelei!" Rishika beckons.

"This is not the end!" Katherine yells to Lorelei. "But we love you!" she adds, just in case.

"Jesus, take the wheel!" Lorelei pleads, in position.

The raft and Lorelei sail over the rapid. "You're doing great!" Mila calls out. "The rapids will slow soon." They go over a few smaller rapids. "Extend your paddle." Lorelei extends her paddle and Mila leans out, grabs Lorelei's paddle, and pulls her towards the raft. Lorelei grabs onto the outside safety line on the perimeter of the raft. "Hang on."

Katherine takes Lorelei's oar and tosses it into the boat while Lorelei hugs the raft for dear life. Rishika clutches Lorelei's hand and they lock eyes as the raft bobs over a few last small rapids.

Ashley and Katherine watch, speechless and relieved, catching their breaths from the intensity of the situation.

The raft slows down and employees of the adventure company pull the raft out of the water. Two employees help Lorelei out of the river. She collapses onto the riverbank. The employees squat down next to her, talking to her and assessing her condition.

Rishika, Ashley, Katherine, and the guide jump out of the raft and rush to Lorelei.

"Lorelei!" Katherine cries out as she envelops Lorelei into her arms.

"Are you alright?" Rishika asks.

Lorelei looks all around, a little crazed, and her teeth chatter.

"She's in shock," Mila says. "What's your name?" she asks, per her first aid training.

"Lorelei Olive Leibovitch," she replies with a far-off look in her eye.

"Your initials are L.O.L.?" an American Interlaken Adventure Company employee questions with a stoner surfer-dude voice. "That's fantastic."

Mila casts a scolding glance his way and continues her emergency protocol. "What year is it?"

"Oh. My. God," Lorelei says. "I almost *died*." The ladies look at each other, concerned. "It was exhilarating!" she exclaims, suddenly animated. "I've never felt so alive in my life! What a rush!"

Katherine and Rishika look at each other and begin to laugh, Lorelei's excitement contagious.

"Honey, I'm so happy for you," Katherine says.

Overwhelmed, Ashley pulls Lorelei into a bear hug and begins to whimper. "That was intense. Thank God you're okay." Tears run down Ashley's cheeks. Lorelei hugs her back, smiling with her eyes closed.

Rishika pats Lorelei on the back. "See? When push comes to shove, you are daring."

# Chapter 23

A bus stops and the ladies exit, talking effusively and walking buoyantly, despite the weight of their backpacks. They are on absolute highs from their adrenaline-spiked voyage down the Lutschine River.

As the bus drives away, the four of them stand on a sidewalk in Downtown Interlaken staring at their next hostel.

Katherine touches her neck. "I can't do it. Don't make me."

Lorelei instinctively starts to scratch her arm and then her back.

Ashley bites her lip in thought. "I have an idea." She sets off walking towards the entrance of the hostel.

"I can't go in there!" Katherine rips the neck brace off her backpack strap and velcroes it onto her neck.

"Just trust me!" Ashley calls behind her.

The other three follow her into the hostel. Ashley walks through the lobby into a common area where a melange of young men and women are hanging out.

She pulls the <u>Let's Go To Europe 1996</u> guidebook and a pen out of her backpack, sets it down on a table and starts writing on the inside cover. She looks off in thought for a moment before she continues to write. The other ladies appear at her side.

"What are you doing?" Katherine asks.

Ashley finishes writing and puts the cap back on the pen. "With all due respect, I think it's time we retire this thing."

Rishika's mouth drops. "That *thing* is priceless. It's like a scrapbook. We have souvenirs in there. Anna's handwriting is in there."

"I agree with Rishika," Katherine says, concerned.

Ashley points to her head. "We have it all up here. Don't you think?"

"But I thought we were going to do everything the same," Rishika protests with furrowed brows.

"Well, we could try," Ashley answers. "But it's not going to be the same. Anna isn't here."

The ladies look at each other sadly.

"It's true," Katherine says. "We were kidding ourselves. It's... not the same without her."

"Of course it isn't," Ashley says. They hang their heads for a moment. "It's okay, though. Let's not be discouraged. This is a new experience. I think Anna would want that for us. We have Lorelei here with us this time." Ashley grabs Lorelei's hand and she smiles. "And we're in a different phase of life. I feel like there are some new and different adventures in store for us this time."

Katherine nods in agreement. "River-rafting was incredible and that was a first for all of us."

"Exactly," Ashley agrees.

"Yes, but it was supposed to happen on our first trip," Rishika counters.

"Should we just throw out the whole plan and be completely spontaneous?" Lorelei asks.

"Hold on, daredevil," Katherine says. "We need somewhat of a plan to keep us on schedule."

"Agreed," Ashley says.

"Okay," Rishika says, "but can we go to the same cities, for old times' sake?"

"Of course," Ashley says. "I'm just saying, we can be a little more flexible than we previously planned to be. If new fun opportunities pop up, let's go for it. Starting with not staying at this hostel."

"Thank the Lord," Katherine says. "I'm on board with that plan."

"Okay," Rishika says more to herself. "Okay."

"You know, there might actually be some perks to us backpacking at this stage in our lives," Ashley suggests.

They look at her for more.

"We have money now."

They break into grins.

"We sure as hell do," Katherine says.

"We love you, <u>Let's Go To Europe 1996</u>," Ashley says. She kisses her fingertips and touches them to the book.

"You never steered us wrong," Katherine says and follows suit.

"You led us to destinations that we'll never forget," Rishika says and follows.

Lorelei kisses her fingertips and touches the book. Ashley slides the book onto a shelf with books and board games, and they walk out of a youth hostel for the last time.

# Chapter 24

The first destination on the new and improved semi-spontaneous agenda is Interlaken's best clothing boutiques. A plethora of apparel is tried on. Four credit cards are swiped repeatedly. The ladies ditch their gigantic backpacks and replace them with suitcases. They emerge from the final store, not in their jeans, t-shirts, and tennies, but in linen pants, silky tops, gauzy scarves, flowy sundresses, and sandals. They look like Cool Chicks—no, Grownup Chicks with Money Backpacking Europe.

***

They enter a spacious lobby with marble floors that are so shiny they can practically see their reflections. Maroon silk drapes with gold tassels frame grand windows, and a massive chandelier is the centerpiece of the space, branches of hand-polished crystals throwing a myriad of tiny rainbows onto the far wall. The ladies look around, impressed and excited, as they head to the concierge to check in.

Moments later, their luggage is whisked away to their room, and they are seated at a table in an upscale restaurant rated with three Michelin stars and nineteen Gault & Millau points. The space is luxurious, with white linens, crystal chandeliers, contemporary chairs, fine white plates, crystal stemware, and highly polished cutlery. After a knowledgeable sommelier recommends a brut champagne, they sip bubbly and laugh like they don't have a care in the world. Ashley takes a few sips to participate in the high life and then switches to Perrier as she nurses the tail end of her hangover.

Two waiters appear, one with a silver fondue pot and the other with a silver platter. They set both on the table and simultaneously lift the silver lids with flair. The ladies clap. A savory aroma of gruyere, garlic and white wine wafts from the fondue pot. The platter is adorned with cubes of bread, boiled potatoes, cocktail gherkins, onions and pickled fruit. A plate holds rosti—golden, crisp potato pancakes fried in butter. Another platter is filled with alplermagronen, which is a traditional Swiss gratin made of potatoes, cheese, macaroni, cream, and onions. Stewed apples are served on the side.

They try to act well-mannered and civilized in this very fancy setting, but they are starving. Their post-river-rafting sandwiches wore off hours ago, and the delicious aromas and tantalizing visuals of this feast are irresistible. They waste no time passing platters and adorning their plates with scrumptious bites.

Rishika surveys the carbohydrate laden spread before her. Is she actually going to dip pickles in cheese and call it a day? Damn it, it's the bread, potatoes and freaking macaroni that she really wants.

"Oh, screw it." The ladies look at her. "I will succumb to the carbs. When in Europe."

"Yay!" Lorelei cheers.

Ashley holds a portion of alplermagronen over Rishika's plate in offering, and Rishika nods as the steaming cheesy potatoes and noodles are lowered onto her plate. She takes a bite before she can change her mind and her eyes roll back into her head.

"Oh, my God! This is like mac and cheese on crack!" she says with her mouth full.

Lorelei, Katherine and Ashley look at each other and laugh silently as they witness the unlikely moment.

"Welcome to the party, girlfriend," Katherine says.

Lorelei picks up a cube of bread with a long fondue fork and swirls it around in the melty cheese, which warms over an open flame. She gently blows on it before tasting it. She closes her eyes.

"Do you think we should order some meat or a salad?" Ashley asks.

"I'm good with bread, cheese and potatoes," Rishika responds. She laughs and they all begin to giggle along, mouths full.

"Europe is magical. Anything is possible," Lorelei jokes, so happy to see Rishika eating with such gusto.

Katherine stabs a gherkin with a long fork and plunges it into the cheese. In the midst of the motion, she feels like she's falling and her fingers submerge into the fondue.

"Whoa. I think I actually just fell asleep for a second." Katherine wipes her hand with a cloth napkin. "Sorry."

"Yes," Ashley agrees. "A clean, comfortable bed sounds amazing."

# Chapter 25

Their Swiss hotel room totally kicks their Munich hostel's ass when it comes to plush accommodations. It's not huge, but it's lovely. There are two sumptuous full-sized beds lavished in poofy white comforters and numerous soft pillows.

Dressed in their pajamas, Lorelei and Rishika lounge in the beds as *I Love Lucy* dubbed in German makes background noise.

"I'm so happy right now," Katherine says, cozy under the covers with her baby blue silk sleep mask secured over her eyes. Her ibuprofen has already kicked in, staving off any remaining neck pain. "This mattress is so good. Pillow good." She's practically slurring as she nods off.

"Maybe we needed that horrible hostel experience to truly appreciate all that will follow," Lorelei muses.

"Mmm." Rishika makes a doubtful expression. "Well, I'm so comfy and full of cheese and bread, I'll ride with you on your silver lining."

Ashley enters the bedroom from the direction of the bathroom swaddled in a bathrobe, hair wrapped in a towel. She's just had herself a good cry in the shower. The steamy solitude was the perfect situation for some emotional release. She's had the most extraordinary day, seeing the exquisite scenery of the Alps and the Lutschine River, the rush of adrenaline after their river-rafting adventure, and then the amazing dinner they had in the elegant hotel restaurant. She wants to tell Pierce all about it. Well, maybe not Pierce, but someone. She feels the loss of not having *her person* to share things with. She feels alone. She has her children, and most of the time, they fill her up and keep her busy. But she desires companionship, someone to go through life with. There has been quite a bit of loneliness in her marriage, but at least she had the illusion of a partner with Pierce. Now that illusion has vanished. She is alone.

She settles into an armchair in the corner of the room and smiles. She's gotten pretty good at turning off her private moments of sadness and transitioning back to being present with whoever she is with.

"I've got to tell you guys something," Rishika says suddenly in a serious tone. It isn't like her to confide her feelings to others, but she just has to get this off her chest.

Ashley and Lorelei look at her, concerned.

"What is it?" Lorelei asks.

"Hey, Katherine, are you awake?" Rishika asks.

"Yeah, yeah," Katherine mumbles.

"This is going to sound… strange." Rishika takes a deep breath. "Okay, I'm just going to say it. Since we arrived in Europe, I've been *seeing* Anna. Like she's physically here or, well, her spirit is here."

"Seeing Anna," Katherine mumbles.

"What do you mean?" Lorelei asks.

Ashley sits forward in the arm chair, eyes wide.

"Wait, what?" Katherine asks, sitting up and removing her sleep mask.

"I know it sounds totally crazy, but there have been a few situations where I've looked over, and I've literally seen her. She was *there*. I saw her hitchhiking outside the airport. That's why I took off and ran outside the baggage claim. I saw her writing in her journal in the bed next to me at the hostel, which is why I reached for her and fell off the bunk. And she was rowing right beside me when we were river-rafting." Ashley, Katherine and Lorelei look at each other, stunned, and back to Rishika, who continues. "At first I thought maybe I was having some sort of flashback of her from our first trip, but it's Anna as we knew her now, forty-two-year-old Anna. At the hostel she looked me right in the eye and spoke to me."

"What did she say?" Katherine asks, cautiously.

"She said to have fun."

Ashley, Katherine and Lorelei glance at each other again.

"We've all felt really big emotions since Anna's death," Ashley offers. "Do you think you're still in shock from losing her? Could you be hallucinating?"

Rishika shrugs. "I don't know. I wondered that myself at first. Maybe."

"Maybe it's your way of coping with all of this," Ashley suggests. "Perhaps your subconscious is projecting your desire for Anna to be here with us."

"I think that explains it," Katherine agrees. "And I think it goes even deeper than that. Rishika, I think you want Anna to give you permission to have fun, and you know in your heart that Anna wants you to be happy."

Rishika nods just to be agreeable. These are all reasonable theories, but in her heart she believes that her interactions with Anna are real.

"Well, I believe you," Lorelei says. "I believe that Anna is here and that you see her. Is she here now?"

"No."

Lorelei looks a little disappointed. "Hmm. If I'm honest, I'm a bit jealous. I want her to connect with me, give me a sign. Why is it just you?"

Rishika shrugs again.

*It's just her because Rishika thinks everything is all about her,* Katherine thinks. *Even her subconscious believes that she's the only one with a special enough friendship with Anna that Anna would come back from beyond for.*

"Well, it makes me happy that she's on this trip with us," Lorelei says. "She should be. I feel like she is."

"Where are her ashes anyway?" Ashley asks. "They shouldn't be stuffed in a bag."

"In my suitcase," Rishika replies. She took them over after the cargo truck debacle.

"May I?" Ashley asks. Rishika shrugs.

Ashley goes to Rishika's suitcase that is propped up and opened on a suitcase rack. Rishika feels a dull burn in her chest as Ashley pokes around her suitcase looking for Anna's ashes.

Ashley pulls out the tupperware and closes the top flap of the suitcase. "You'd love this room, Anna. Humongous bathtub. Swiss chocolates on the pillows." Ashley carries the tupperware over to the window that showcases a view of Switzerland's famous three peaks—the Eiger, Monch, and Jungfrau. "Just look at this view," she breathes.

Katherine and Lorelei smile sadly at each other.

"Please put that away," Rishika says in a low voice. "I'm not going to talk to her ashes."

Ashley's smile fades. "Okay."

"Why do you get to decide what is and isn't appropriate when it comes to Anna's ashes?" Katherine asks.

"It just feels ridiculous parading the tupperware around the room and giving her a tour. It's demeaning."

*Yet you're talking to her invisible spirit, and that's okay,* Katherine thinks, but keeps to herself. She doesn't feel like fighting with

Rishika. She just wants to table this conversation and sleep off the jetlag.

"We could do a seance," Lorelei offers brightly. She used to be into all that tarot card, palm reading, horoscope kind of stuff. But then she found Jesus while building houses in Mexico with an on-campus service organization her junior year and retired all of that.

"No," Ashley, Katherine and Rishika chime in simultaneously.

"Yeah, you're probably right on that. Well, I still want to talk to her spirit," Lorelei says. "I couldn't bear not doing that."

"I think we should all do what's in *our own hearts*," Katherine says with a little attitude.

Ashley nods. She walks to the window and looks at the snow-capped mountains. "You'd love this view, Anna. It's just beautiful." But her voice is forced and lacking the joy it had a moment ago. The moment is gone.

# Chapter 26

Lorelei rolls over uncomfortably. She sits up and attempts to reach the middle of her back to scratch her rash. She glances at her phone. It's just after two in the morning. She looks around. Katherine snores softly next to her, and Rishika is dead to the world in the next bed. But, next to Rishika, the bed is empty with the covers pulled back.

Lorelei sleepily climbs out of bed and looks around. She sees a dark silhouette move on the balcony. She grabs the tube of hydrocortisone cream off the nightstand, unscrews the cap, and blots a few dabs on her arm as she goes to the door and opens it.

Ashley sits in the dark on a slightly reclined chaise lounge with her legs extended, hugging a mug to her chest.

"What are you doing out here?" Lorelei whispers.

"I'm wide awake. My internal clock is all messed up."

Lorelei nods, though she suspects it's more than that. "Would you mind rubbing some of this on my back? These bites are driving me crazy."

"Of course." Ashley sets the mug on the floor, sits up, and holds her hand out to take the tube as Lorelei sits down in front of her on the chaise.

"So… how have you been dealing with everything on your own? First Pierce and then Anna?"

Ashley squirts a blob of ointment onto her fingers and lifts the back of Lorelei's shirt. "It's been a rough few months. I think what has saved me has been having to keep it together for the kids."

"How are they?"

Ashley rubs Lorelei's back in small circles. "Elizabeth is really pissed off at Pierce. She kind of gets it. I've tried not to talk badly about Pierce in front of the kids, so it was really confusing and vague at first, but now she knows, since he has moved in with *Maggie*. She's really grossed out and confused and angry. Teddy and Ryan don't really understand what's happening." Ashley pulls Lorelei's shirt back down and pats her back.

"Thanks." Lorelei rises and moves to another chair. "Have they met her yet?"

Ashley wipes her hand on her pajama pants. "No. I feel like it's too soon. I haven't even met her. I'm too disgusted by the thought of her."

"So, where are they staying while you're here?"

"Pierce is staying at the house with them, you know, to try and keep things *normal.*"

Lorelei nods. "I'm going to say something, and I don't know how you're going to receive it."

Ashley tilts her head, surprised. "Okay."

"I feel like you changed over the years as a result of being with Pierce."

"How do you mean?"

"Like you were afraid to be yourself. Like everything you did was to please him. You did all these wonderful things, like hosting amazing dinner parties and keeping an immaculate home. I'm sorry to say, it seemed to me like you did it all for him and he never seemed to notice. He took you for granted. It always bothered me, but I never wanted to say anything about it."

Ashley doesn't say anything. Lorelei is absolutely right, but it's embarrassing to hear. It makes Ashley look desperate. Like she was always trying to impress her very own husband, but she never succeeded despite all of her elaborate efforts. She's humiliated that she wasn't enough. She feels her chest grow warm and blotchy.

"What I'm trying to say is, maybe this is a blessing in disguise. He wasn't good for you."

Ashley picks up her mug and takes a sip of her tea. She purses her lips and nods. Finally, she speaks.

"This is not a blessing. I have had to accept the fact that the life that I have so carefully planned is not mine anymore. It's a disappointment to my parents. My kids are now from a broken home. They will have to move out of their childhood house. I have to know that while Pierce has a brand-new shiny relationship with a woman who hasn't earned it, I will be alone raising my three children. I've had to mourn the death of a close friend without a partner to lean on. And my future has absolutely no certainty. Trust me. This is not a blessing." Ashley downs the last gulp of her tea and rises from the lounge chair.

"Ashley, that's not what I meant."

"And I know he's an asshole and a cheater, but you know what? I *loved* him." Her voice wrenches with emotion.

"Of course you did."

The sliding glass door closes hard as Ashley disappears into the room.

Lorelei is left to sit by herself with a pit in her stomach. "Damn it."

# Chapter 27

Rishika tightens the laces of her running shoes in front of the hotel. She had awoken with a start from a disturbing dream—about Anna, of course.

She leans her head from side to side, stretching her neck, and then takes off in a jog. Workouts are her only release these days. She needs to relieve the tightness she feels in her shoulders, neck and jaw. She had a restless sleep and had to get out of that hotel room. She's accustomed to being in her office at the studio for long periods of time, mostly only interacting with her assistant and phone conversations that end concisely with the click of a button. This traveling with her friends is a lot of never-ending social time. It's a lot for her.

Also, she hasn't eaten bread for two years. She dove headfirst into that amazing meal last night and then all that beer at the Hofbrauhaus. All the carbs and cheese has her constipated just two days in. She can't just let herself go to hell while she's here. She has barely been able to bring herself to eat since Anna died. Craig harassed her every day, making her smoothies in the morning, putting protein bars in her work bag, asking her in the evening if she had taken her vitamins that day. He's been treating her like a child. She does appreciate it, even if it drives her crazy. She has just not been hungry. At all. But now, oddly enough, her appetite is coming back and she's eating like an animal, so she'll have to sneak in workouts whenever she can.

She jogs through Interlaken. Striding out her long legs feels fantastic. *It's good to be here*, she thinks. Of course, it is. She is not so spoiled and unappreciative to not relish being in Europe again. It is special to be jogging in Switzerland right now. But she has so much going on in her head.

The whole Camila and Alexa thing. Should she tell the ladies about it? Maybe they could give her a little perspective about it, make her feel better. But she can imagine the looks of shock on their faces. In what universe would Anna choose Rishika to care for her precious children? She must've been high on pain meds when she made that call. Rishika knows they would judge her. They've already made digs about her not having children in the two days that they've been on this trip. No. She won't put herself in that situation.

***

The aroma from the little coffee pot in the kitchenette permeates the hotel room and awakens Lorelei and Ashley. Katherine is on the balcony with her laptop open. She's been at it since seven. She's exhausted, but she had to prepare for a conference call that she'll jump on when they're on the train later. She's gazing out at the mountains in her own little world when she senses movement inside the room, turns and waves at the ladies.

They waste no time in calling in an order to room service, and when Rishika returns from her jog through Interlaken, as well as lunges, squats, and burpees in a nearby park, the small table in the room is covered with silver platters. There are omelettes, fresh fruit, whole wheat toast and various jams—a healthy selection to offset the indulgent choices from the previous day and the likely indulgences to come.

"Did you eat anything yet?" Lorelei asks Rishika.

"I don't work out on a full stomach."

"Come here, I'm making you a plate," Lorelei says as she dishes up a generous serving of everything.

"I think I'll shower first." "Here you go," Lorelei says pleasantly as she shoves the plate toward Rishika.

"Okay, okay," Rishika concedes. "Thank you."

For the time being, Ashley and Lorelei have swept the discomfort of their early-morning conversation under the rug. Likewise, they have all avoided their awkward moment of not seeing eye to eye on the topic of whether to talk to ashes or to not talk to ashes. There have been so many things to sweep under the rug over the years.

Sweep. Sweep. Sweep.

# Chapter 28

Bruges is a medieval city covered in cobblestone, with canals and old romantic bridges interspersed throughout. It's dotted with pubs, churches, parks, museums and squares. When the ladies arrive that evening after traveling northwest by train for the better half of their day, the city is lit up and magical.

Having eaten sandwiches on the train, as well as having slept off their jetlag for the majority of the ride, they are ready to jump right into one of Bruges' main industries—chocolate.

When they walk into the first chocolate shop of many, their senses are overpowered. The aroma hits them first. To simply say that it smells like chocolate would be understated. It smells clean and sweet, like pure quality ingredients, but also complex, laced with so many subtle essences. The conglomeration of aromas results in a round and sumptuous fragrance that will likely remind every customer of a different moment in their lives—when their mother was baking a chocolate cake, getting a box of Valentine's chocolates from their first sweetheart, or making mugs of hot chocolate with whipped cream for their children on a rainy day. The shop is cozy, with wooden shelves covered with many varieties of elegant gift boxes tied up with ribbons.

The ladies split up, dispersing to various glass cases displaying exquisite little edible works of art, each following what beckons to them. It's like each of them is a character in *Charlie and the Chocolate Factory* and Willy Wonka has just removed his cane from their path, giving them permission to explore his entire scrumdiddlyumptious wonderland.

There is something for everyone's imagination. There are cases that hold chocolates in various shades from pure white to milk chocolate to the darkest and most intense. Some chocolates gleam in their simple glossy forms. They are molded from different shapes—round, square, hearts, shells, leaves. The chocolate is so high-quality, the pure flavor stands alone. Others tempt with chopped pistachios, flaked coconut, impressive gold flakes, a single coffee bean.

Other cases hold colorful creations, each color foreshadowing what flavor waits inside. There are floral and fruity flavors such as rose, violet, elderflower, cherry blossom, kaffir lime. There are more exotic essences such as Earl Grey tea, curry, saffron and matcha. Some have almondy marzipan tucked inside, some crunchy pralines, some caramel, some an airy meringue. There are round truffles dusted with cocoa and nuts, and vibrant macarons in a kaleidoscope of hues. On the one hand, everything looks so exquisite you hate to eat it, but you would be a fool not to.

As Rishika studies the beautiful chocolates, Anna appears next to her beaming, taking in the selection.

Rishika looks at her with confusion and longing. *What is happening? Is this escapism? Am I so traumatized by Anna's death that I am escaping my pain and reality by imagining that Anna is here with me? Should I be worried that I'm going crazy?*

Anna looks at her. "Pick that one. It has rum in it." She waggles her eyebrows.

Rishika smiles. That's just like Anna. Historically, Rishika would be stressing about something, and Anna would defuse the situation for her and put things in perspective. She's been doing that for

Rishika since they were kids. Rishika was a high-strung child, always pushing herself, feeling the stress of the world and pressure from her parents to accomplish high marks. Anna was always like a warm cup of tea that comforted her. She was the yin to Rishika's yang.

Rishika waves the shopkeeper over to select the chocolate with rum in it. Whatever *is* happening, Rishika decides, she is thankful that it is. Given the option, she would surely choose to be a little delusional to keep Anna around in any form.

***

From a different case of chocolates, Lorelei notices Rishika's gaze. It holds both confusion and joy. She knows, without a doubt, that Rishika is being blessed with a visit from Anna. Lorelei is a very spiritual person. She believes in things like this. She can see the happiness that it's bringing Rishika. Lorelei misses Anna so much, and God, she wishes she could have just another moment with Anna for herself.

# Chapter 29

The ladies visit three different chocolate shops. They pick out assortment boxes to enjoy, and they have some shipped home to their family and friends.

They find a place to sit along the picturesque canal as swans swim by in the moonlight. With boxes open, they display their wares, sharing and tasting.

Ashley bites into a glossy dark square and flavor bursts into her mouth. "Oh, my goodness, this one has orange caramel inside with a hazelnut praline. Taste it." She shoves her hand in front of Rishika's face.

Rishika laughs. "Okay, let me finish the one I'm eating first. Lavender marzipan. Don't rush me." She slowly chews with her eyes closed. Then she swallows and accepts the bite that Ashley feeds her. "Oh, yeah. That's heaven."

"This one is champagne and strawberries in milk chocolate," Lorelei says with her eyes closed as she savors the delicate flavor.

"I've got white chocolate with mango lime. Oh, wait, there's a little chili pepper at the end," Katherine says, in awe. "Yes," she says in a sexy, baritone voice. "Oh, that's good."

Rishika laughs. "Girl, you've always loved your chocolate."

"When we get home, I'm going to learn how to make chocolates,"

Ashley says. "It won't taste like this, of course, but it would be so fun to come up with interesting flavor combinations." She looks at the inside of her chocolate, studying it and scheming about how to recreate it.

"I'm sure you could do it," Katherine says. "I will gladly be your taster." Everything Ashley makes tastes amazing. She often enjoys something at a restaurant and somehow recreates it at home with great success. A few years ago, Katherine, James and the boys were in San Francisco when Brice chose to write a report on Alcatraz. Ashley and Pierce invited them over for dinner, and Ashley made coq au vin and a caramel apple cheesecake, both of which they'd recently eaten at a locally acclaimed restaurant. She'd attempted to recreate them and had been very successful. James still reminded Katherine of that meal from time to time.

Ashley loves it here. Bruges was her favorite city in Europe on their previous trip. She smiles as she savors the taste in her mouth. "How is anything we eat after this going to be impressive?" Ashley asks. They all shrug. "We've been broken. Broken in Bruges."

"Is that like *Sleepless in Seattle*?" Rishika asks.

"Yes, just with more eating," Ashley jokes.

Rishika laughs. She loves a good movie reference.

"This is the most fun I've ever had," Lorelei says. "This day ranks right behind the days my children were born."

Katherine laughs. "Belgian chocolate can do that."

Lorelei smiles, then her expression morphs to thoughtful. "Um, do you guys feel a little guilty about this?"

"About what?" Ashley asks.

Lorelei looks at them more seriously. "I'm having the adventure of my life, and Anna's not here. Yet she's why I'm here. I feel"—she searches for the word—"remorse. I feel remorse that I'm having such a ball at Anna's expense."

"It's not at her expense," Ashley says. "I think she would be disappointed if we were moping around, especially here, together."

"It's just like how Rishika envisioned Anna telling her to have fun," Katherine says. "Deep down, her subconscious knows that Anna would want that."

There's something about how Katherine explains it that rubs Rishika the wrong way. Like Katherine knows the logical explanation of what's happening with Rishika. Clearly Katherine doesn't believe that Rishika is really being visited by Anna. It makes Rishika sorry that she shared it. From now on, she will keep it to herself. But she understands exactly how Lorelei is feeling. Rishika knows that she will always put limits on her joy. She may have fun, but not too much fun.

"I feel it, too, Lorelei. Without a doubt." Lorelei nods and shares a sad smile with Rishika.

"I actually felt like she would've hated her funeral," Ashley says. "Well, not the ceremony, the ceremony was lovely. But the reception. It was so glum. Exactly what she didn't want."

"Everyone did the best they could," Lorelei says.

"We should've put on "Mo Money, Mo Problems" and started a dance party in the living room," Ashley says with a smile.

"In theory, Anna would've loved that, but that would've felt wrong at the time. I wasn't capable," Rishika says.

"True. But I do agree with you, Ashley. Anna would be upset if we were here and didn't embrace it. Now, we *are* able to enjoy ourselves. We can't squander all of this," Katherine says with open arms.

Even though there is truth to what Katherine is saying, Rishika thinks it's insane that Katherine still hasn't cried over Anna's death. It seems heartless and disloyal. It's like Katherine doesn't care *that* much.

"It's an opportunity to reminisce about her," Ashley suggests.

"Okay," Lorelei concedes. "Then tell me about your first trip. Which countries did you go to then that we won't make it to this time?"

"Aaah." Ashley smiles and thinks. "Austria. We went to Salzburg and took *The Sound of Music* tour. You know Anna and her musicals."

"Oh, that's perfect!" Lorelei interjects.

Katherine continues. "We saw the house that was used in the movie from across the lake and the trees where the children were swinging in their newly made outfits that Maria made from the drapes. It was so surreal. It was like we were in the movie. And then we listened to Mozart music performed at the Hohensalzburg Castle."

"Wow," Lorelei gushes.

Rishika cracks up. "There was this old man sitting in the row behind us, and he had this thick, phlegmy cough."

"Gross!" Lorelei comments.

"He was sitting right behind Anna, and every time he coughed, Anna looked so repulsed. She'd scrunch up her face like this." Rishika makes a face. "You know how expressive Anna's facial expressions were."

"Right," Lorelei says, nodding, into the story. Katherine and Ashley smirk, remembering.

"And so," Rishika continues, "Ashley got the giggles. Every time the man coughed and Anna made a face or arched her back because she felt like she was getting contaminated, Ashley lost it a little bit more." Ashley nods and begins to giggle. "She was wiping tears from her eyes, her shoulders were bouncing up and down, she was doing the Ashley snort..."

"Oh, my gosh," Lorelei interjects, "I forgot how you used to snort!" Ashley covers her mouth, amused and embarrassed at the memory.

"Meanwhile, Katherine was scolding Ashley, trying to shush her so we wouldn't get kicked out. Finally, Anna had had enough of the coughing, so she turned around and glared at the old man, and he looked at her, completely innocent, and said, 'What?' We all exploded into laughter, as people all around us stared, and we gathered our things and got out of there as fast as we could."

They crack up at the memory.

"That's hilarious," Lorelei says through a chuckle.

"Oh, my gosh," Ashley says, catching her breath. "I had forgotten about that."

"Where else did you go?"

"We loved the Netherlands," Katherine chimes in. "In Amsterdam, we went to Anne Frank's house. That was crazy to see. Really moving."

Rishika nods in agreement. "Incredibly moving."

"Remember how we spent like six hours on a train looking for 'cute Holland?'" Ashley chimes in.

"What's 'cute Holland?'" Lorelei asks curiously.

"Anna was dead-set on having her picture taken in a field of colorful tulips in front of a windmill," Ashley explains. "She called it 'cute Holland.'" Goodness, we spent an entire day riding the train. We finally found it, and she was right to be so adamant that we find it. It was amazing."

"I can totally picture that," Lorelei comments. "It's like a photo on a calendar. That must've been gorgeous." Ashley nods.

"We went to the Heineken Factory and the Van Gogh Museum," Rishika remembers.

"I love Van Gogh!" Lorelei says. "Ugh. I'm really bummed I missed that."

"We'll take you to the Louvre when we're in Paris," Katherine promises. "You are going to see a ton of art on this trip."

"Thanks."

"Then we spent a few days in London, seeing, you know, the touristy stuff— Big Ben, the Tower of London, Westminster Abbey." Rishika shakes her head wistfully. "I loved London."

"Wow. I know this isn't a very insightful statement, but it's incredible how much there is to see in this world, in Europe alone," Lorelei says. "We're barely going to scratch the surface. I'm forty-two years old, and I'm on a different continent for the first time. I feel like I'm behind."

"You're not behind," Katherine reasons. "This is the trip of a lifetime. Some people may never do something like this. We're really lucky." Lorelei nods.

Ashley bites into another chocolate and chews it thoughtfully. She loves reminiscing about their first time in Europe. But, oddly enough, there's something about it that gives her a weird sensation in the pit of her stomach. Is it regret? Is it simply nostalgia? She can't quite put her finger on it. She noticed it when Rishika was recounting the Salzburg Mozart performance. Does she feel this way because she knows that Lorelei was right about what she said on the balcony last night? Pierce did inhibit her. He did change her. Or rather, she allowed herself to change in his presence. She used to be so happy. At some point, she started censoring herself and behaving properly. She evolved into someone else entirely.

\*\*\*

As twenty-two-year-old women, an intense immersion in Belgian beer and chocolate-tasting was the extent of Anna's, Rishika's, Ashley's and Katherine's cultural research of Bruges. As it turns out, and to Lorelei's surprise and delight, there is a ton of art in this city.

With one more day here, and, surprisingly, without extensive planning by Katherine, the events of the day are up for grabs. Lorelei decides to cram as many art museums into her itinerary as possible. Ashley expresses an interest in going to the Kantcentrum to see how Belgium lace is made and learn about the history of the Bruges lace industry, and has somehow managed to convince Katherine to go with her, Rishika preferring to go with Lorelei.

The Expo Picasso contains art by Picasso, Rodin, Renoir, Degas, Claude Monet, and other Impressionist artists. The exhibit contains one hundred original works by Pablo Picasso. Another section of the museum showcases art from the twentieth century, including original works by Matisse and Chagall.

Lorelei is beside herself. Witnessing her pleasure and awe in seeing these great artists' works in real life is really warming Rishika's heart. It's crazy how they used to spend so much time together. She hasn't done anything one-on-one with Lorelei in ages. It's nice.

Rishika and Lorelei were freshman roommates. She and Anna decided that since they were starting college, they should be open to new experiences and friends. So they should room with other people, instead of each other. Actually, this was Anna's urging, and Rishika just went along with it. Anna was placed with Katherine, who, like her, was a political science major.

The housing gods had paired up Rishika and Lorelei, and at first, Rishika thought Lorelei was kind of strange. Okay, she thought she was completely weird. Lorelei was and is quirky. She was an art major, a quirky creative. She listened to Tears for Fears, Brit-pop, and 3T (Michael Jackson's three nephews. Rishika hadn't even known there was a band containing Michael Jackson's nephews... whose names all began with the letter T.). She was one of those people who went to the Renaissance Fair every year... in costume. Lorelei had her own style. It was like she tried to follow trends, but she got them wrong somehow, but either she didn't know it or didn't care. She had huge untameable hair and hung tie-dyed scarves over her lamp on her desk.

At first, Rishika and Lorelei did their own thing. They didn't have any classes together. They came and went from their dorm room without a ton of communication. Little by little, Rishika realized that Lorelei was hilarious and undeniably herself, which Rishika appreciated. In addition, Lorelei was incredibly sweet and had huge innocent green eyes that somehow chipped away at Rishika's tough exterior. For all of these reasons and more, Rishika began to find Lorelei endearing. Rishika started putting Lorelei in her student films. On an artistic level, they connected. One night, she invited Lorelei to join her, Anna, and Katherine at a frat party, and they all had a blast together. The four of them started to become a cohesive group. Then in the spring they all went through sorority rush and each decided on Delta Zeta. Ashley ended up being in their rush class.

Lorelei and Rishika were one of those classic cases of opposites attract. Until they were so opposite that they stopped really communicating at all.

# Chapter 30

An evening train heads southbound through bountiful fields of lavender, endless rows of purple and sage under a changing sky. Travel time is often when the ladies catch up with their families at home.

Katherine talked to Brice and he told her all about his baseball game and how he struck out six kids. Sadly, Beckham himself struck out so Katherine had to give him a quick pep talk. James has been swamped with work so he is going to have his mom take the boys for a few days.

Lorelei's call home was a marathon one, beginning with Adam, who sounded happy to hear from her, but a bit frazzled. Celeste gave her a play-by-play of the Girl Scout spring camping weekend. Hadley was conflicted about two rival birthday sleepovers and which one to go to. Atticus has been spending a lot of time in the garage practicing his drums, and Gideon was building a Lego Ninjago set. Lorelei didn't get to talk to Phoebe and Aislinn, her older ones. They were off doing their own thing.

Craig updated Rishika about a spontaneous DIY fire pit he's been working on in the backyard. It will be a perfect place to drink after-work cocktails. Penelope is fine, but she whines at night for Rishika.

Pierce didn't answer the phone when Ashley called, so sadly, she missed talking to any of her kids.

Now, Katherine works on her laptop. Rishika reads a script on her iPad. Ashley began searching for accounting jobs on her phone, but her heart just wasn't in it. She now peruses recipes on Pinterest.

Lorelei studies the Louvre website, obsessed with the thought that she will be in the quintessential city of artists in a few short hours. "Gosh, I can't wait to see the Mona Lisa. The artists of the Renaissance! Donatello, Michelangelo, da Vinci! I'm already thinking how I can plan lessons around this. A self-portrait in the style of the Mona Lisa. Painting contemporary subjects using the styles of the Renaissance. It will be so interesting to see how my students interpret that," she says. "I'm already so inspired by what I learned at the Expo Picasso. My students are really reacting positively to what I've posted on my Instagram."

Ashley puts her phone down. "Lorelei, you amaze me."

Lorelei makes a surprised face. "What do you mean?"

"You have six children, three more than me, and you still manage to hold a full-time job, inspiring angsty teenagers to create art and encouraging them to have a creative outlet, a place to put their thoughts and emotions."

"Thank you," Lorelei says sincerely. "Well, I love it. It's *my* creative outlet. It's almost like a hobby. A hobby that keeps me extremely busy," she adds.

"Why does it keep you so busy?" Rishika asks. "Isn't school out at like three?"

"Yes, but I'm constantly revolving student work in the display cases in the hallway by my classroom. I have two student exhibitions each year and that takes some after-school preparation during the weeks leading up to them. I also incorporate a lot of art history into my classes so I have lectures and corresponding quizzes to plan."

"You're an amazing teacher," Katherine praises.

"Well, I don't know about that. When I go home, I don't even think about it. And, when I'm at work, I don't think about home. I only have enough room in my brain to think about where I am at the time. So I always feel like I'm behind. I get to work and realize I'm not quite prepared, and I get home and realize I have no groceries for dinner. I always feel frazzled and disorganized. I feel like I don't give anything in my life a hundred percent."

"It sounds to me like you give it *all* one hundred percent," Ashley says. Lorelei scrunches up her nose and shakes her head in disagreement.

"You're present, though," Katherine points out. "Wherever you are, you're present. I admire that. I give work five hundred percent and everything else twenty percent."

"That's interesting math," Rishika teases.

"I think about work when I'm at work, when I'm driving, when I'm tucking my kids into bed, when I'm brushing my teeth, when I'm having sex, when I'm in Europe." She fans her hands out to indicate her open laptop and the lovely scenery outside the window. "I have no balance in my life."

"When you're having sex?" Rishika exclaims.

Katherine blushes. Should she not have admitted that out loud? "Maybe a little," she says, guiltily. Lorelei, Ashley and Rishika stare at her. "Okay, I'm embarrassed."

"Having balance is something everyone struggles with," Lorelei says. "I think."

"Well, I'm great at it," Ashley says. "But only because I don't have a job."

Katherine scoffs. Ashley is practically the equivalent of Martha Stewart. When her children were babies, she made all of their organic baby food from scratch. She has a vegetable garden. She hosts forty people at Thanksgiving every year and makes all of the food. She sews her kids' Halloween costumes. She is the room mom for all three of her children's classrooms. Katherine admires her for having different mom strengths than her. She's also a little envious of those qualities and the time to practice them.

"Are you kidding me?" Katherine says. "I've never seen anyone do 'Mom' better than you. You actually make me feel bad about myself."

"No!" Ashley says. "That's silly."

Rishika looks thoughtful as the idea wheels turn in her head. "You know, Ashley," she says, "you could totally be an influencer."

Ashley makes a face. "What do you mean?"

"Everything you do is huge right now. Everyone wants to make adorable DIY decor for their homes, prepare beautiful food, craft interesting cocktails, throw amazing themed parties. You could have a zillion followers on Instagram or write a lifestyle blog. You could be the next Joanna Gaines. Women would want to be you, and I think you could have fun with it."

"Really?" Ashley asks, surprised.

"Totally," Rishika confirms.

"Huh." Ashley never thought she was doing anything exceptional. She's just a stay-at-home mom. She was a successful accountant and willingly gave that up to give her children the wholesome family life that she had in Minnesota. However, she does often feel like an underachiever when her go-getter friends speak about their demanding jobs. All three of them are overachievers in every way. The truth is, Ashley started doing her domestic duties a little over the top to impress Pierce, to be the best wife she could be for him. To make him happy. To make him proud. But, really, it didn't seem to faze him. He came to expect it. She suddenly realizes that, despite it all being lost on him, artfully turning their home into a haven is something that she really enjoys. She actually takes great pride in all that she does.

"I could help you set up a blog and an Instagram page if you'd like," Rishika offers.

"Thanks. That's sweet of you. I'll think about it." A warm and rosy joy blooms inside of her.

# Chapter 31

The air in Paris is a pleasant seventy-four degrees and the ladies meander along gray cobblestone sidewalks adorned with planters of bushes and trees. They gaze in shop windows and rush into the ones that look interesting.

Rishika has just bought two Louis Vuitton purses, one for her mom and one for Anna's mom. Rishika has been very blessed in the mom department. Her own mom is driven and successful and has given her the tough love and inspiration to become successful doing what she loves. Irma is the soft mother figure in her life, the one she went to for hugs when something upset her in elementary school. The one whose smiling face put her at ease when she stood nervously, on stage at the podium, at the fifth-grade spelling bee. Rishika has received different kinds of support from both moms throughout her life, and she knows that Irma is going to need *her* support for many years to come.

Shortly after Ashley leaves yet another message on Pierce's voicemail, her phone rings.

"Finally," she says when she sees his name on the called ID. "Hello?" she answers, annoyed. "Oh, hi, sweetie! It's Teddy," she explains to the ladies. Lorelei gives her a thumbs-up and points at a wine shop as she, Katherine and Rishika slip inside.

Ashley can see them through the window walking up and down the aisles of bottles as she listens to Teddy as he tells her about his weekend.

"Oh, that's fun, sweetie. Which beach are you at, China Beach?" Her face scrunches up, confused. "Wait, Santa Barbara? Why are you guys all the way down there?" She purses her lips, but she keeps her tone calm and pleasant for her son's sake. "Oh, really? Can I talk to Daddy for a minute, please? Okay, I love you so much. Have fun."

Ashley paces back and forth a few lengths as Pierce gets on the phone. She can feel her face instantly grow hot. "Pierce, I told you, I didn't want them staying with her yet. I haven't even met the woman. I'm not having my children stay with some stranger." She shakes her head angrily. "Well, even though you are very acquainted with her vagina, she is still a complete stranger to me." She shrugs. "Well, what the hell can I do about it? I'm thousands of miles away and you're not following the rules. How are we going to be successful at co-parenting if you're not going to listen to me at all? Yes, of course, I want to talk to them. Put Elizabeth on, please." Ashley exhales and attempts to calm her breathing and adjust her mood. "Hi, sweetheart! I miss you so much. Tell me everything!"

\*\*\*

The Rue Cler Market is a most impressive sight. A melange of tables out in the open air boast colorful produce, cheeses, and fresh-baked baguettes and pastries. There are buckets of peonies, seafood laid out on ice and rock salt, sausages hanging from hooks, light brown eggs stacked on cardboard crates. It's a visual overload to register all of the tables of goods. As per a plan they devised over a lazy breakfast of coffee, croissants and raspberry jam in their plush hotel robes, they rented bicycles, which they have just parked, and they will now each choose a few items for a collaborative picnic lunch.

Locals stroll from table to table, presumably purchasing a few items for their dinner—a vegetable to saute, a loaf of bread, a wedge of cheese. Here, they do not tend to overflow their grocery carts at the supermarket once a week. Instead, they buy a few fresh ingredients almost daily.

Rishika, Katherine and Lorelei take in the big picture, wondering where they should begin. Ashley glides past them and heads over to the fruit several tables away. Her negative energy is palpable.

Katherine gestures towards Ashley with her head. "What's with her?"

"She had a fight with Pierce," Lorelei says. "He and the kids are staying with the girlfriend. Against Ashley's wishes."

Katherine frowns. "Jeez. Let's give her some space."

They find themselves attracted to a table holding tiers of what look like colorful candies in the shape of fruits and vegetables.

"What are these?" Lorelei asks.

"Marzipan," answers the fragile-looking old man that runs the booth.

They ooh and aah at the selection of marzipan creations—little vividly red strawberries, light green artichokes, dark green peas in a pod, bright yellow bananas, and deep purple eggplants made entirely out of sweet almond paste.

They purchase a few of the small candied bites for later, then Katherine and Lorelei meander to the salamis and cured meats while Rishika floats to the next table, which is laden with the most beautiful variety of cheeses.

"We're going to have to be careful with all this cheese," Rishika remarks. "Remember what happened last time?"

Lorelei looks up from the salami, curious. "What happened?"

"We ate so much Brie and goat cheese that none of us could poop for like three days," Rishika answers.

"Oh, my gosh," Lorelei says with a giggle.

"That was uncomfortable," Katherine says, remembering.

"We bought an over-the-counter laxative," Rishika continues, "but the instructions on the box were in French, so we guessed on the dosage." She makes a face. "It caused a bit of a situation."

"An epic chain of events, more like it," Katherine remarks.

Lorelei laughs. "Oh, no! Gross."

"I don't know, girls," Rishika says. "This selection is amazing. It just might be worth it." The three of them chuckle and continue to peruse the wares.

Rishika picks up a very soft and creamy Camembert. "Oh, yes," she says quietly to herself.

Anna appears next to her. "Cheese, glorious cheese!" she sings theatrically, in the tune of "Food, Glorious Food" from the musical *Oliver*.

Rishika looks up and smiles at her, pleasantly surprised, but not shocked that Anna is standing there before her. She glances at her friends. They are oblivious to Anna's presence.

Anna observes as Lorelei presents a jar of honey to Katherine. "I just love that Lorelei is here this time. It's a joy to witness her experiencing all of this."

"Mmm," Rishika agrees.

Over at the fruit table, Ashley rummages through clementines. She looks really stressed out.

Anna purses her lips, concerned. "Poor Ashley. Pierce is such a jerk. Give her some love for me, will you?" Rishika frowns and nods.

Anna picks up a wedge of Roquefort cheese and smells it. Her eyes widen and she crinkles her nose. "Whoa, this is a ripe one. It smells like a yeast infection."

A boisterous belly laugh escapes Rishika's mouth.

Lorelei jumps in surprise and furrows her brows. "What was that?"

Rishika clears her throat, embarrassed. "Oh. Nothing. I just thought of the most random thing."

"What?" Lorelei asks.

"Um. Nothing."

"You scared me to death," Lorelei says, as she moves onto a table abundant with baguettes and loaves. She squeezes through the paper sleeve. "Wow, that's soft."

Anna continues to sniff the cheese. "Gracious, that's potent. Oh, my God."

Rishika stifles a smirk. "Then stop smelling it."

"I can't," Anna says. Sniff, sniff, sniff. "It's oddly addicting." Sniff, sniff.

"Did you say something?" Katherine asks from the table behind her.

"Just that cheese sure is smelly. Especially these blues," Rishika answers, pretending to be very attentive to a wedge of Gorgonzola.

Anna puts the Roquefort cheese down. She smells her hands. "That's an understatement. I smell like I need a prescription cream. Rish, you've got to smell this." Rishika clenches her lips together and closes her eyes, trying not to laugh. She shakes her head in refusal. "You've got to," Anna continues. "C'mon. Don't you wanna smell my fingers?" She fans her fingers at Rishika, who snickers.

"Gross," she utters.

Anna lunges at Rishika with her stinky hands. Rishika screams in laughter and jumps away.

A couple at the marzipan table turns to look. Her friends stare at her in surprise.

Embarrassed, Rishika covers her mouth with her hands, her eyes wide.

"She's here, isn't she?" Lorelei asks, mystified. She looks around, trying to see where Anna might be. "Anna, I miss you. You can visit me, too. I'm open to it." She waits for a minute like something might happen, then throws her hands up. "What am I, chopped liver?" She walks off, pouting.

Onlookers look confused, and the atmosphere feels awkward.

Unsure of what to say, Rishika shrugs at Katherine and Ashley.

"Rishika…" Katherine starts, concerned.

"I actually don't want to talk about it," Rishika replies curtly. She hands some money to the vendor for a few wedges of cheese and strides off toward the bikes.

# Chapter 32

It feels wasteful to be in a bad mood in Paris. The ladies pedal along under a canopy of trees. The baskets on their bicycles are stuffed with their wares from the market.

Anna's ashes are nestled in the basket of Ashley's bicycle. It has become an unsaid thing that they bring Anna's ashes with them on all of the big excursions. It feels like the right thing to do, since this trip is Anna's last hurrah. Her ashes will be with them at all of these beautiful and legendary landmarks until the ladies scatter them on a beach in Mykonos, laying Anna to rest.

They ride quietly. Lorelei feels hurt from the previous incident in the market. She has now twice witnessed Anna connecting with Rishika. She sees that it can happen. It's possible! She longs for more time with Anna or a sign that proves that Anna will always be here on this earth in some form. So why is Rishika the only chosen one? Of course she is. Rishika was Anna's best friend from birth. No matter what, no matter how great your connection was with Anna, the history and bond that she and Rishika had together can not be topped.

Katherine doesn't know what's going on with Rishika. Katherine believes in heaven, but she's too reasonable to believe that Anna is making appearances while they're river-rafting, at the Rue Cler

Market, and such. How likely is it that Rishika is experiencing a miracle? Rishika isn't even consistent about her religious beliefs. She follows the trends. When Madonna got into Kabbalah, so did Rishika. Katherine has decided that when they get back to the States, she's going to have to have the unpleasant conversation with Rishika that she needs therapy. She'll have to put her feelers out and have some names ready.

As Rishika rides along the tree-lined street, she feels very embarrassed. She made a scene at the market and exposed herself. She's been trying to keep the Anna visits on the down-low. If Anna wanted to communicate with the others, she would visit them, too.

Ashley is still edgy from her conversation with Pierce. She's furious that he went against her wishes. How are they going to provide a stable environment for the kids if he just does the opposite of what she wants all the time? He's so fucking inconsiderate. They agreed that they would break the kids in slowly with their exposure to Maggie. Ashley wanted to meet her first to make sure she wasn't a psychopath. Obviously Ashley isn't excited to meet the home-wrecker at all, so she may have been putting that off a bit. She has absolutely no control in this situation. Pierce is calling all of the shots. The kids are pretty much her department and now Pierce and Maggie are moving in on her territory. What if Elizabeth, Teddy and Ryan begin to like Maggie? Ryan is such an affectionate little guy. What if he wants to snuggle with Maggie? Ashley couldn't bear that.

They ride down cobblestone streets lined with horse chestnut trees, passing patisseries, sidewalk cafes, and street vendors. As they ride along, in the therapeutic ambience of Paris, their moods begin to lift. The optimism and possibility of this city is contagious.

They turn a corner and the Eiffel Tower comes into view.

Lorelei's face transforms into amazement. "Oh, my God! I can't believe it!"

They pedal into a park that is manicured with perfect lawns and enter a bike path. Gray, wrinkled and smiling, an elderly couple rides toward them on a bicycle built for two. Ashley watches them ride past and witnesses their companionship. They are a pair sharing a reliable bond, pedaling in unison through life. Ashley's thoughts wander to the symbolism of what this sweet old couple has that she does not. The physical reminder is too much. Her handlebars swivel, and she loses control of her bike.

"Ashley!" Katherine cries.

Ashley crashes onto the asphalt and the Tupperware flies out of her basket, bounces on the ground, and breaks open, spilling all over the ground, Anna's ashes everywhere. Katherine, Lorelei, and Rishika pull over, hop off their bikes and rush to her. She lies on her side, surrounded by ashes.

"Oh, no," Rishika whispers, horrified.

"Are you alright?" Lorelei asks as she grabs Ashley's hands and helps her up.

Ashley looks around as she surveys the gray ashes that cover the bike path. "Oh, my God!" She bursts into tears. "Look what I've done!"

"It's okay," Katherine says soothingly, even though she, too, realizes this is quite a predicament. "We'll just scoop her up."

They all get down on their hands and knees and scoop up handfuls of ashes and dump them back into the Tupperware. There are thin layers of ash on the ground they can't scoop into their hands.

"We can't get it all. I'm so sorry! I'm so, so sorry!" Ashley remains kneeling on the ground, completely disheveled. She covers her face with her hands and cries. Her face is streaked with tears and wet gray ash.

"Meh, just leave a little here," Lorelei attempts flippantly. "Anna loved Paris." Rishika and Katherine look at Lorelei, deadpan. "She'll be mostly in Mykonos and partly in Paris." She exhales as the ladies continue to stare at her. "Silver lining moment."

"But it's not Kevin's plan. This is the purpose of the entire trip and I've just totally fucked it up! My whole life is fucked up!" Ashley covers her face again and totally lets loose, her entire body shaking with every sob.

Katherine and Lorelei look at each other with concern and compassion in their eyes.

Katherine kneels down next to Ashley and grabs her hands. "If anyone would support deviating from a plan, it would be Anna. Don't you think?"

Ashley doesn't answer. She just looks into Katherine's strong and calm blue-green eyes. Katherine helps her up and dusts off Ashley's knees with her hands. Lorelei takes a wet wipe out of her purse and cleans Ashley's streaked face.

Meanwhile, still on her knees, Rishika has not stopped pushing small bits of ash into the palm of her hand, desperately trying to get every last particle. She stops for a moment and watches her friends take care of Ashley. They know how to comfort her, how to mother her. Ashley is an absolute mess right now and Rishika can't bother herself to get up and attempt to help her. She sucks at making people feel better, at being compassionate. How the hell would she be a worthy guardian to two young girls? But she does know this—from now on, she's carrying Anna's ashes.

# Chapter 33

A baguette, a wedge of Camembert, a log of goat cheese, peppered salami, some radishes, a few clementines, a small collection of little marzipan fruits and vegetables, and a perfect bottle of Bordeaux are arranged like an edible art gallery on a blue blanket with the ladies sitting in a circle around it. The magnificent Eiffel Tower looms above them. After finding a bathroom and washing up, they now break pieces off the baguette and pass around the cheeses and salami on a paper plate. Katherine uncorks the wine and pours it into waxy paper cups.

"You guys, I saw that sweet old couple ride by on their bicycle built for two, in perfect companionship, with the stability of knowing they having someone to love and count on forever," Ashley explains. "I realized that I'm not going to have that." Rishika passes a cup of wine to her and she takes a swig.

"Don't say that," Lorelei says.

"It's true," Ashley says. "It's ironic, actually. Today is our wedding anniversary."

"Oh," Rishika says with a disturbed expression.

"I didn't realize that," Lorelei says.

"It wasn't noteworthy enough to mention until my spill."

Rishika cringes. *It was, literally, a spill,* she thinks, *but I'm not going to point that out.*

"As we speak, my husband and children are at *Maggie's* beach house in Santa Barbara, playing house. Pierce and I have been married for eleven years. You know, we used to talk about what we would do when he retired. We thought about cashing out of L.A. and settling down in my sleepy hometown in Minnesota where we could experience the four seasons. Where I would garden and he would fish. We'd have some land and a huge house so that one day, when we had grandchildren, they would stay with us for weeks at a time. We'd buy a four-wheeler and take the kids off-roading and we'd have a fire pit for roasting marshmallows."

"That sounds nice," Lorelei comments.

"That surprises me, actually," Rishika says. "It doesn't sound like Pierce at all."

Ashley nods. "He had his moments. Months ago, when I was desperately trying to save our marriage, I begged him to move us to Minnesota. I thought, if I could just take Pierce away from all of the stress, away from the rat race and keeping up appearances, away from Maggie, maybe we could fix us. But, really, we would have just been taking a bad marriage somewhere new. I see that now." Ashley shrugs. "Well, it doesn't matter now. It's not going to happen. That bitch is going to get my house in the country."

"Get your own damn house in the country," Rishika barks.

Ashley smiles at her. "You're right. But it's not just the house. It's everything. It's companionship. When I married Pierce, I was investing in a future with him, the person I was going to grow old with."

"It may not happen with Pierce," Katherine says, "but it could totally happen with someone else."

Ashley scoffs. "Yeah, like I'm going to start dating again."

"Of course you will," Lorelei says. "When you're ready, you will."

"You have your whole life ahead of you," Katherine retorts. "Love is not done with you."

Ashley crinkles her face and shakes her head. "That's the beauty of getting married. You don't have to date anymore. And, oh, my gosh, to be intimate with someone again! I would be mortified."

"Really?" Rishika asks, surprised.

"Oh, I can't imagine," Ashley continues. "My body has been through three vaginal deliveries, and have you seen my kids' heads?" Rishika looks like a deer in the headlights and attempts to shrug neutrally. "They're not small. I've looked down there with a hand mirror and it is not pretty."

"Oh, don't look," Katherine says, aghast. "Never look."

Lorelei shrugs. "You should see mine," she says, attempting to be constructive.

Rishika looks mortified. Inside, she's thanking her lucky stars that her cervix is still in-tact.

"Who else is going to want to go down there?" Ashley continues.

"Tons of men will *love* going down there," Katherine says supportively.

"Girls, I don't want to start over. I wouldn't even know how. I was eleven years in! *Eighteen*, if you count the years that Pierce and I dated."

Ashley dated Pierce for six and a half years before he finally proposed to her. Her friends always kind of hated him for it. It felt like he settled for her.

"I invested all that time and so much energy and emotion on him. I've given Pierce practically half of my life! All of that is lost now. Do you know how daunting that is?"

Rishika and Lorelei look at her sympathetically.

"I'm so sorry, Ashley," Katherine says. "That really sucks."

"Katherine," Lorelei scolds.

"It does," Katherine says, defensively.

"We need to be positive," Lorelei says. She's already tried being brutally honest with Ashley about how she feels about Pierce, and it didn't go over well at all. Clearly, Ashley is still mourning the loss of Pierce and isn't ready to entertain the thought that moving on could be a very good thing. When Lorelei went back to bed that night in Switzerland, she made a decision. She will just be a good listener for Ashley, a shoulder to lean on, someone to lift her up.

"But as much as we need to tell Ashley that it's going to be okay," Katherine counters—

"Which it is," Lorelei interjects—

"Yes, but I think we also need to commiserate with her."

"He's a fucker," Rishika jumps in aggressively. "And he's not even that cute."

"Rishika!" Lorelei scolds.

"What?" Rishika questions. "Ashley can do better. I've always thought so."

Lorelei glances at Ashley, worried about her reaction.

Ashley chuckles. "You know what? This is helping. Tell me more."

Lorelei looks confused.

"My turn," Katherine says. "He's a total dork. In eighteen years, I don't think I've ever seen the man without khakis on. I mean, who wears khakis to a Guns N' Roses concert?"

Ashley laughs. "It's true. It's so true."

"Remember at your fortieth," Rishika starts, "when Craig handed you a really nice bottle of champagne, and Pierce said, 'Actually, this is sparkling wine. It's only truly champagne..'"

Katherine and Ashley chime in with nasally, stuck-up voices, "'...if it's from the region of Champagne!'"

"That crossed my mind in the restaurant in Switzerland when we were truly drinking champagne. Most likely better champagne than Pierce has ever had," Ashley says smugly. Her gaze locks on to Lorelei's skeptical face, and she understands her hesitation. "It's okay." She nods encouragingly. "I do want you to be honest. Say your worst."

"Okay," Lorelei says tentatively. "All Pierce cares about is Pierce."

"Mmmm," the other ladies agree. However, this doesn't evoke laughter as Rishika's and Katherine's comments did.

Lorelei knows she can do better. "Okay, I got one. Remember when we got really drunk at Rishika's wedding reception and afterwards we all went skinny-dipping in the hotel pool?"

Ashley nods, interested, and takes a huge swig of wine from her cup.

"I saw Pierce's penis, and it was really small!"

Silence.

Katherine and Rishika swing their heads towards Ashley, open-mouthed and mortified. Ashley covers her mouth with her hands. Their eyes all dart around to each other.

"Shit," Lorelei squeaks. "Did I say too much?"

Red wine sprays out of Ashley's mouth.

They erupt into laughter. Ashley wipes her dripping chin with a napkin. Their guffaws escalate higher and higher until they are all wiping tears from their eyes.

"I'm crying!" Katherine exclaims. "Oh, my God, I'm crying!"

Ashley emits an enormous snort.

"Oh!" Rishika claps her hands. "The snort is back. Yay, the Ashley snort is *back*!"

Ashley continues to giggle and snort uncontrollably, covering her nose, embarrassed and shocked.

"Oh, my gosh," Katherine says, clutching her stomach, "my abs hurt."

Lorelei sighs. "I've kept that to myself for thirteen years."

This sets them off again. Lorelei falls over with her head in Rishika's lap.

"I'm impressed," Rishika snickers. "You're like a steel vault."

"Okay, okay, okay," Katherine says, attempting to pull herself together. Lorelei, Rishika and Ashley contain themselves. "A toast." They hold their paper cups of wine into the air in the middle of their circle. "To Lorelei, who can keep a juicy secret for more than a decade."

They laugh. "To Lorelei!"

"And to Ashley. You are an absolute gem, and true love is going to find you. You will meet an amazing person who makes you happy. Someone who encourages you to be yourself. Someone who truly deserves you."

"To Ashley! Cheers!"

Ashley wipes a tear from her eye as she catches her breath from laughing. "Oh, thank you," she breathes, smiling as she imagines the possibility.

# Chapter 34

There are six hundred seventy-five steps to the top of the Eiffel Tower. The ladies start off strong, fueled by the adrenaline of climbing this legendary monument.

Lorelei holds her phone out in front of herself on selfie mode and records. "I'm climbing up the stairs of the Eiffel Tower! This is an epic, bucket list moment!"

Rishika trudges ahead of them, taking the steps two at a time, pumping her arms, enjoying the opportunity to exercise her glutes. It's been weeks since she's had a chance to do her weekly stair workout at the 4th Street stairs in Santa Monica. But this is obviously way better. She's climbing into the sky. In Paris!

Down a bit, Lorelei glances up towards Rishika, and her mind goes to Rishika on all fours on the bike path, frantic and grief-stricken, trying to scoop up every last grain of Anna's ashes. Perhaps Anna was visiting Rishika, and Rishika alone, because she was the one who needed it. Lorelei's expression softens and she slides her phone into her back pocket. "Hey, Rishika!" Rishika looks down to her. "Wait up!"

Rishika slows to a stop until Lorelei reaches her. Lorelei breathes deeply, catching her breath, and smiles. They begin to ascend the stairs together.

"I want to say something to you," Lorelei begins. Rishika cocks her head to the side and waits. "I'm sorry about how I acted at the market. It was childish and selfish. I'm happy for you that you get to see Anna."

"Oh… I shouldn't have told you girls about that. I'm sure you all think I'm crazy."

"I don't," Lorelei says quickly. "I believe you. This is something extraordinary. Don't you worry about what anyone else thinks about it. I think you should not question it. Just go with it, and enjoy it completely."

Rishika stops walking. She looks into Lorelei's kind green eyes. "Thank you."

Back aways, Katherine follows lethargically, putting one foot in front of the other. "We should've drunk the wine after we did this. I need a nap."

Ashley nods. "Me too. I feel sluggish. So sluggish."

"Push, girls!" Lorelei cheers ahead of them.

Katherine and Ashley look up and see Lorelei and Rishika twenty steps above them.

"Come on, girls. We're waiting for you!" Rishika calls.

"Ugh," Katherine groans.

From above, Rishika watches as Anna strides past Katherine and Ashley below. "Sayonara, slowpokes!"

Rishika laughs and jumps up and down. "Hurry!"

"Ever hear of leisurely sightseeing?" Katherine shouts in return. She remarks to Ashley, "I don't know where that girl gets her energy."

"Last one to the top buys dinner!" Rishika calls.

Ashley sighs, tired. "That could be expensive." She breaks into a labored jog.

"Just add it to my tab," Katherine resigns.

Ashley laughs. "No, come on." She waits a few steps up and grabs Katherine's hand.

Anna wrinkles her nose cutely at Rishika as she approaches her. Rishika takes in the glory of the moment as Anna breezes past her.

Rishika and Lorelei wait until Ashley and Katherine finally catch up.

Fifteen minutes later, they arrive at the second level. They board the lift and head to the top level of the Eiffel Tower.

When the elevator door opens, Rishika sees Anna at the rail. Rishika rushes to the rail to join her, her friends at her heels.

Lorelei sucks in her breath, astonished.

"It's magnificent, isn't it?" Ashley smiles.

Lorelei is speechless. She wipes a tear from her eye.

"Oh," Ashley says, touched at Lorelei's emotion.

"Here we are again, Anna," Katherine says. "After twenty years, we made it back to the top of the Eiffel Tower."

Unbeknownst to Katherine, Anna stands just a few feet away from her on the other side of Rishika. She looks out over all of Paris, sadly. Rishika sees her expression.

"I always thought I would bring my girls to Paris," Anna says. "We'd go shopping, I'd introduce them to the wonders of French baked goods, and then I would bring them up here." Her tone becomes wistful. "We would look at this incredible view and I would tell them, 'The world is your oyster. See and do as much as you possibly can.'"

Rishika looks down and blows out a pained breath. "Anna wanted to bring Camila and Alexa here."

Ashley, Katherine and Lorelei look at her. They frown and nod.

"I'll do it," Katherine announces to Anna, wherever she may be. "I promise I'll bring them." She smiles and nods.

"Thank you," Anna says with a contented smile. Rishika looks troubled, disappointed in herself for not thinking of it.

They all stand silently for a little while, leaning against the rail, with so much of Paris to study.

"Wow," Lorelei breathes. "Look, there's the Louvre! And there's Notre Dame. The Arc de Triomphe. It's spectacular."

"The world is our oyster," Rishika says softly, looking at Anna.

"What?" Katherine asks.

Rishika extends her arms out and yells, "The world is our oyster!"

Lorelei, Katherine and Ashley laugh at her uncharacteristic enthusiasm.

Anna smiles at her. "You're damn right it is. And please don't forget it again."

"I actually feel that way right now!" Ashley says like a lightbulb is igniting in her head. "Like we can do anything."

"Why not?" Katherine remarks.

"I just had the craziest epiphany," Ashley says. Her friends look at her. "The youth don't have a monopoly on dreaming. And I think I need to dream again."

Rishika clicks her tongue. "There's our next t-shirt."

Lorelei brightens and opens her mouth. Rishika raises her hand to stop her. "Not literally."

The four of them put their arms around each other as they look out over Paris... the five of them, that is, including Anna.

# Chapter 35

To wake up in Paris, is to wake with a feeling of possibility and delight. The ladies begin with pain au chocolat and cafe au lait and power through a full morning of sight-seeing. The Arc de Triomphe, the Champs-Elysees, Notre Dame.

Lunch is, in and of itself, an event. Ashley insists that they eat at Benoit, one of the Barefoot Contessa's favorite restaurants in Paris. They feast on duck confit and fish in a savory saffron broth, and they finish with coffee and decadent Armagnac Savarin, a cake soaked in brandy and topped with whipped cream.

Being at the Louvre is a dream come true for Lorelei. Rishika, Katherine and Ashley have to attempt to keep up with Lorelei as they approach the iconic pyramid. The Louvre is overwhelmingly big and Lorelei feels anticipation, yet a hint of anxiety at only having an afternoon to see it. There is just so much to explore  the Italian Renaissance, Egyptian antiquities, Italian sculptures, Greek vases, Islamic art, to name only a handful of subjects.

As they move from room to room, section to section, Lorelei is emotional in the presence of all this historic art. She sees pieces that she once studied as an art history major. The Mona Lisa! The Wedding Feast at Cana! Psyche Revived by Cupid's Kiss! The Young Martyr! She's beyond moved. But there's also something else there, a sadness or regret that she hasn't put her finger on.

When the ladies are exhausted, they end at the gift shop where Lorelei buys postcards of some of her favorite works that she viewed today, a book about the history of the Louvre and its collections, a sketchbook and pastels. Why did she not think to bring art supplies with her in the first place? On the other hand, her Louvre sketchbook and pastels will be special and inspiring for her.

When the others are ready to go back to the hotel, Lorelei excuses herself to go down to the Seine to sketch like the true artists of Paris. Here, at this epicenter of creative energy, she finds many artists with easels and paints, likely with the same goal as her. This is such a creative place, a creative moment. After twenty years of missing her first opportunity, Lorelei is finally here. She finds a bench and sits, opens her sketchbook, gets out a sharpened pencil and takes a deep breath. She looks at the Seine and waits expectantly.

She takes it all in—the calm green water, the occasional barge, the sandy walking path, the trees that line the streets above. Wispy cirrus clouds stretch across the cornflower-blue sky like pulled cotton balls. Does she hear a street musician in the distance? It's *perfect*.

She always tells her students to figure out what they want to say. Let their mood come out in their brushstrokes. She sits with her pencil poised, a smile on her face, waiting for her pencil to move. But it doesn't. God, she's been waiting for a moment like this for decades. She doesn't have a child wanting a snack or help with their homework or a ride to practice. She doesn't have a child here on this entire continent. This is her opportunity to create. So what is the problem? Maybe after all this time, she has nothing to say. Or maybe she has so much to say, but she doesn't know where to start.

*That's okay*, she thinks. *Just draw something and it may become something special.* Another one of her teaching slogans. She thinks about her first time at the Eiffel Tower yesterday—how she felt up there, the immensity, the magical, limitless feeling of being so high above this legendary city. She begins to sketch its strong vertical lines in the center of her page. Okay, good. Yes, she just needed to get started. She draws the different levels of the Eiffel Tower and then opens her pastels and rubs in some trees and grass below it. She adds details of a Parisian cityscape behind it. She smiles. It certainly is pretty.

She glances around. Of the two canvases of fellow dreamers that she can see, one is of the Eiffel Tower and one is of the Seine. Like hers, they are very pretty. But they are unoriginal, and let's face it, basic. As is hers.

A lump forms in her throat as a thought suddenly hits her. *Those who can't do, teach.* Lorelei knows she's a good teacher. She loves to teach and feels the satisfaction of inspiring and encouraging young people and sharing her love of art with them. Yes, she's a good enough artist to sketch out and paint examples for her students, to teach technique. But perhaps she's not a groundbreaking artist in her own right with any original perspective that would set her work apart from anyone else's. She's a teacher, but not actually an artist. This epiphany is heartbreaking.

Lorelei sees a young woman setting up her easel. She sits down on a stool and looks around at her setting. She is glowing. She knows that this is an incredible time in her life, that anything is possible. Lorelei and her girlfriends have been talking about this concept a lot on this trip. Isn't it amazing what a powerful concept it is? But when real life at home takes off in the form of children, a job, and keeping a house clean, we forget that anything is possible. We are too busy making dinner.

But the problem for Lorelei is that she never had the opportunity to apply the 'anything is possible' concept. One moment she was a promising art student, thinking her whole life was ahead of her, and the next moment she was getting a crash course in motherhood. This young woman could have been her. And even if this young woman finds out that she is not destined to be an amazing artist, after all, at least she will have given it a shot and will move onto another dream or something more practical instead of pining over it for decades.

Lorelei hasn't exactly pined over it, has she? Perhaps her subconscious has. She just always thought someday she would have time to realize her artistic dreams. *Someday, someday, someday.* It's a dangerous word that allows years to pass. She didn't even give much thought to how much she missed out on until this trip. She just ground it out every day. She loves her family and her job, but being away from it, seeing the possibility in this world, the possibility that young people see, has caused her to mourn for the young girl in her who had to skip that small but invaluable phase in her life.

*** 

When Lorelei goes down to the Seine and Ashley and Rishika head back to the hotel, Katherine decides to stay out a little longer. She says she wants to try a hot chocolate place that she's heard about, which is true, but she really just needs a moment alone.

She sits at a lovely little outdoor table by herself sipping the decadent dark chocolate, relishing that she is here in Paris… because there isn't anything looming over her in Paris.

She is days away from going to the country that, after she swept everything under the huge proverbial rug, she assumed she would never go back to. Even though Italy is an amazing country and she loved it so much there, it would just be too hard. She has never needed to deal with this. She has never *wanted* to deal with this. Even on this trip, she's been able to focus on staying caught up on her work, has been so consumed by having so much fun on all of these European adventures that she's been able to mostly avoid these thoughts and feelings. But now she is only two train rides away.

A church bell clangs somewhere. Katherine's dark brown hair attracts the warm sun and makes the top of her head feel hot. Additional church bells layer and compound more clanging, and the result is overwhelming. The sweet, rich chocolate is starting to make her feel nauseous.

# Chapter 36

The train rattles south down the tracks towards Nice, France. Lorelei, Katherine, Rishika and Ashley sing the Greek alphabet that they learned when they were rushing Delta Zeta. "Alpha, Beta, Gamma, Delta, Epsilon, Zeta, Theta, Eta, Iota, Kappa, Lamba, Mu, Nu, Xi, Omicron, Pi, Rho, Sigma, Tau, Upsilon, Phi, Chi, Psi, Omega, that's all." They crack up and throw their arms around each other.

"It's amazing that I could still sing that song in my sleep, yet I can barely remember my mother-in-law's birthday." Katherine laughs.

"That's selective memory," Ashley says.

Lorelei's cell phone rings. She glances at it. "Oh, it's Phoebe." She presses the FaceTime button. Phoebe's angelic face surrounded by light auburn curls appears. She's the spitting image of her mother with Adam's bright blue eyes. "Hi, sweetie!"

"Hi, Mom."

"Hi, Phoebe!" Katherine calls.

"Hi, Phoebe!" Rishika and Ashley chime in.

"Hi, everyone," Phoebe says, forcing a smile.

"I'm on a train to the French Riviera, can you believe it?" Lorelei says.

"That's so great, Mom." She sighs. "Look, Mom, I have something I need to tell you, something I just found out. Will you take me off FaceTime, please?"

"Sure, sweetie," Lorelei shrugs at her friends and pushes a button to disengage FaceTime. She puts the phone to her ear. "Okay, just me. What is it?" She listens. "Uh-huh. Uh-huh." Lorelei's face does a double take. "Pregnant? You?"

Ashley, Katherine and Rishika look at each other with wide eyes.

"What?" Katherine exclaims.

"Put her back on FaceTime," Ashley says.

Lorelei activates FaceTime again. "No, you didn't just say that."

"I'm pregnant," Phoebe repeats.

"I heard you!" Lorelei yells. "No. Okay, let's just relax for a moment. I'm sure you're about to get your period. We've all had a scare like that."

"Oh, yeah. Yeah. More than once," Rishika, Katherine and Ashley confirm respectively in the background.

"This is just a little scare," Lorelei begins calmly in her mom voice, "because I know you and Brad wouldn't be that careless and stupid!" she shouts. "Especially since you've worked your ass off your entire high school career and these first two years of college, and you're about to go to Yale!"

"Mom. I took two pregnancy tests. Besides, I can't keep anything down. I'm puking nonstop. This is for real. It's happening."

"No," Lorelei says, shaking her head in refusal of the facts.

"I guess I should tell Yale that I'm not coming. I can continue at Chaffey for another quarter or two, and then finish my degree in a few years."

"No! Don't you dare do that!" Lorelei shouts. "Brad can transfer to a school near Yale."

"Mom, he's playing football at UCLA. He's living his dream."

"*His* dream? What about *your* dream, Phoebe? What about *your* dream?"

"I don't know, Mom. Maybe I can go to Yale later."

"*Later?*" Lorelei asks. "*Later* doesn't exist. *Later* is a synonym for *never.*"

Rishika, Katherine and Ashley glance at each other, concerned about both Lorelei and Phoebe.

"I'm so sorry, Mom. Oh." Phoebe's voice becomes uncomfortable. "Uh-oh." Her face disappears from the screen and all that is heard is the horrible sound of her vomiting.

"Oh, God," Lorelei says.

Rishika, Katherine and Ashley look sympathetic and grossed out as they listen to Phoebe puking her guts out.

"My baby," Lorelei says, so concerned.

Phoebe appears again, with a pale and haggard face, her hair disheveled. "Mom, I've got to go. I love you. I'm really sorry." Phoebe ends the call.

Lorelei bends over completely, hanging her head between her knees. Katherine, Ashley and Rishika look at each other with wide eyes, unsure of what to say.

Ashley rubs Lorelei's back tentatively. "It's going to be okay."

"Nope." Lorelei shakes her head. "Not happening."

Ashley keeps rubbing her back. "It's going to be okay." She can't think of anything else to say.

Lorelei finally looks up. "What are the chances?" She looks right into all of their eyes. Rishika, Katherine, and Ashley shake their heads. "I mean, what are the fucking chances of this happening again to my own daughter? The same daughter I had as a result of the same situation! I mean, does a trip to Europe mean that someone's plans for the future have to get screwed?"

"It is a horrible coincidence," Rishika says. Ashley widens her eyes at Rishika. Rishika shrugs, as in *What else am I supposed to say?*

"Right? It's just so ironic." Lorelei continues to get amped up. "If this trip has emphasized anything to me, it's how much I missed twenty years ago. I missed my youth, my opportunity for self-discovery, the livelihood that I truly yearned for and have fantasized about for twenty years. Because of an early, unwanted pregnancy."

Ashley jumps a little at this last statement. Lorelei is the most nurturing and maternal person she knows. She has six children! It's uncomfortable hearing her talk so regretfully about her pregnancy with Phoebe, reducing her to an *unwanted* pregnancy. Ashley can't imagine speaking that way about one of her own kids. But she does make a mental note to talk to Elizabeth in great detail about abstinence, birth control, and consequences in the coming years.

"At least I graduated from college. Phoebe has worked towards this goal for years. AP classes in high school," Lorelei continues. "Captain of the cross-country team, chess club, volunteering for the charity league. Then getting all of her general ed requirements done at community college. It was a carefully laid out plan. She's been so patient and methodical. For what?" She rises from her seat and paces around the small space of the train room. "I wanted more for her. I wanted the world for her. But I know how this turns out. She won't go to Yale. She won't go backpacking with her friends after college. She won't get her dream job."

"She can still do all of those things. Other people do," Katherine says.

"Totally," Rishika agrees. "She can finish her degree online. She can start that right away."

Ashley nods. "She can have help with the baby and eventually she can still build up to a successful career."

"Maybe," Lorelei says as she takes a deep breath. "But it will be really hard. I should know. Oh, my God, I'm going to become a grandma. A grandma! And I've barely experienced anything!" she shouts. She glances at her friends, who are sitting stunned. "I'm sorry.

I'm totally going off the deep end here. I should probably go home."

Katherine's eyebrows furrow. "No! You are not leaving. This is finally *your* turn. You are always putting everyone else before yourself."

"Besides, what can you do to help the situation? The baby is barely a grain of sand," Ashley reasons.

"Phoebe needs me. You heard her. She can't keep anything down." Lorelei fans herself and takes deep breaths.

Rishika nods. "Sounds like she deserves it, the little slut."

Lorelei whips around to face Rishika. Ashley's eyes bug out of her head and Katherine's mouth hangs open. Lorelei's wide eyes search Rishika's. Rishika sits tall, her expression serious and unchanging, almost like a challenge.

Lorelei bursts into laughter.

Katherine and Ashley look at each other, confused, as Lorelei releases bellows of guffaws. Lorelei bends over with her hands on her knees as she continues to let it out, sound pouring out of her. Is it laughing? Is it crying? Is it a combination of both?

She straightens up and punches Rishika in the arm. "Thank you," she says, as she continues to laugh, wiping her tear-streaked face.

Rishika exhales. "Phew. That was risky, but I went for it."

Katherine shakes her head. "You're crazy," she says to Rishika.

"I was prepared to let her punch me in the face if that was what she needed to do," Rishika explains.

Ashley begins to giggle and Rishika and Katherine join in.

"'Haven't experienced anything,'" Rishika continues. "Who else can say they've had a near-death experience in the Lutschine River, you ungrateful bitch?"

Lorelei wails with laughter and puts her arm around Rishika. "Oh, my gosh!" Tears stream down her face. "Oh, Rishika." She attempts to catch her breath. "I don't always understand you, but I really do appreciate you."

# Chapter 37

The water of the Mediterranean Sea sparkles as Lorelei, Katherine, Ashley and Rishika recline on lounge chairs under blue and white striped umbrellas sipping foofy cocktails. Soft sand glitters around them like a mixture of graham cracker crumbs and sanding sugar. The Phoebe pregnancy situation has been the topic of conversation for most of the day, and though Rishika was able to defuse the initial shock of the situation, it has certainly put a damper on Lorelei's first time in this legendary seaside playground of the elite.

Ashley, of course, feels badly about the sudden change in Phoebe's life plans, but she is more troubled about Lorelei's reaction to the news. Of all these girlfriends, Lorelei has always been the one Ashley related to the most in recent years. Lorelei was their crusader into motherhood. She has been a role model for Ashley. Where Ashley is super organized and structured, Lorelei is carefree and go-with-the-flow in her parenting philosophy and practice. Lorelei's family life may appear chaotic to some, but to Ashley, it has always resonated warmth, boisterous fun and love. Lorelei was an example to embrace the process, not the product. Where Ashley used to freak out about painting or making slime in the kitchen because of the impending mess, she has learned to embrace the creative self-expression of the child that happens during the process, all due to Lorelei's example.

Now, Ashley is completely perplexed by the implication that Lorelei regrets getting pregnant with Phoebe. She has to get it off her chest.

"Lorelei," she starts. "I'd like to talk to you about something." Lorelei looks up as she plucks a maraschino cherry from her frozen drink and pops it into her mouth. "What you said on the train. You basically implied that all of your hopes and dreams were crushed because of Phoebe." Katherine and Rishika look up from their magazines. Ashley has tears in her eyes. "You called Phoebe an unwanted pregnancy." Lorelei looks a little surprised. Katherine and Rishika pretend to turn their attention back to their magazines.

"I said that? I thought I said 'unplanned'."

Ashley shakes her head slightly.

"Oh," Lorelei says, remembering her rant. A wave of embarrassment and shame washes over her. "Wow. I was upset. I certainly wasn't carefully choosing my words while I reacted in front of my girlfriends."

"I'm not judging you. I just…"

"Well, actually, it feels a lot like you're judging me." Lorelei gets up from her lounge chair. "I need a walk."

She takes off, trudging through the hot sand, down to the water's edge, and walks along the shoreline until she seems to disappear.

\*\*\*

Forty-five minutes later, Lorelei returns. Ashley, Katherine, and Rishika have since taken a dip in the water and returned to their seats. They look up from their various reading material when she approaches, and they wait for her to speak. Ashley looks remorseful.

Lorelei sits at the foot of Ashley's lounge chair. "I'm sorry I snapped at you. This is… a lot."

"I'm sure it is," Ashley says, sympathetic.

"Of course I didn't mean what I said. I love Phoebe with all my heart. I mean, at the time, when I was twenty-two years old, getting pregnant was a total shock that turned my world upside down. It was certainly unplanned, but it was also such a blessing. I loved Phoebe as soon as I heard her heartbeat for the first time, and I can't imagine my life without her."

"I know that," Ashley says. "But do you really feel regretful about your life turning out differently than you planned?"

"Not regretful. Just… I wish I could have had that time."

"You know, I got pregnant with Elizabeth ten years after you got pregnant with Phoebe. I had all sorts of time and look at me now. It's not like things worked out better for me. And yet I wouldn't change it. I love my three kids to death. And if my failed marriage to Pierce is the price I had to pay to get them, then so be it."

Lorelei nods. "That's really good perspective. You know, the funny thing is, I realized that I reacted exactly how my parents reacted twenty years ago. My mom *flipped out*. Oh shit. I'm going to have to tell my mother the news. She's going to make this my fault. She's going to say, 'Now you know how it feels.'"

Ashley makes a sympathetic face.

"It's okay," Lorelei thinks out loud. "That's not important. This is not about me. What's important is being supportive of my daughter."

"Good for you," Ashley says. "You've got this."

"Thank you. The crazy thing is, it's almost like God has prepared me for this situation, firsthand. After clearing my head, I realized that Phoebe's got some challenging times ahead and I know that I need to be there for her. I need to be steadfast and strong. So I called her."

"Well done," Katherine praises, looking up from her magazine and deciding that it's now safe to join the conversation.

"How did that go?" Rishika asks.

"Really well. She sounded… really relieved to have me in her corner."

"Of course she is," Ashley says. Lorelei pats Ashley's feet and rises from Ashley's chair and returns to her own. "I feel much better. But I could use another frozen bellini."

"You got it," Rishika says.

"Let's get Anna one, too" Katherine suggests. "We'll drink it for her, obviously, but it'll be symbolic."

Rishika signals a waiter. "Monsieur? Encore cinq, s'il vous plait." She holds up five fingers and points to her drink. Her year of high school French has really paid off.

The waiter nods and walks away.

The ladies stretch out on their chaises in delicious relaxation. Today, they have no plans. They will play it by ear and simply enjoy this gorgeous setting.

Anna appears on an empty lounge chair next to Rishika. "My own bellini. Thanks! Will you get buzzed for me, too?"

Rishika smiles at Anna and nods, discreetly. She takes a long sip of her almost-empty cocktail through the straw with a smirk.

"I'm glad you're having fun, Rish." Anna sighs, content. "This is spectacularly gorgeous. I'm glad I can see it clearly. It totally sucked when I lost vision in my right eye." Sadness appears in Rishika's eyes. "It was like I kept losing pieces of myself and I had no control of it. I had to be strong, though, for Kevin and the girls. Now that it's a done deal, I can admit how shitty it was." At Rishika's changed body language, she says, "No, no. I'm not here to be a buzzkill. What's done is done. It's your job to have an amazing time for me. That's partly why I'm here, you know. To live vicariously through you."

Rishika turns to Anna, confused. "What's the other part?" she whispers.

Anna ignores the question. "Are you hearing me? Live for me."

Rishika searches Anna's lovely face and nods. She turns her gaze to the water. The shimmering lapis lazuli sea expands farther than she can see. The day is lovely, warm and sunny, and here she is in freaking Nice, France. Anna is here in spirit, but only in spirit. Rishika owes it to Anna to enjoy this world for the both of them. If that's what Anna wants, she'll do it.

"Whew," Anna says. "It's hot out here. Time for a dip." Anna stands up, stretches, unties her bikini top, swings it around over her head dramatically, and lets it drop to the ground. She runs into the ocean with her arms outstretched, letting out a few whoops.

Rishika revels in the sight of her very best friend being crazy in the French Riviera. As usual, Anna is reminding her to be brazen and live in the moment. So that's it, then? Anna wants to live vicariously through Rishika? Well, then Rishika better show her a damn good time.

Rishika stands up. "Ladies?" They look over at her. "When in the French Riviera!" She unfastens the back of her navy blue athletic-style bikini top, pulls it off and drops it like a mic. It lands on the sand in front of her shocked friends.

Ashley, Lorelei and Katherine sit up in their chaises with their mouths hanging open.

Casually pumping her arms, Rishika runs down to the water, leaps through small waves and dives under with the grace and ease of a triathlete.

Anna whoops for Rishika, and they giggle together in the water.

"Really?" Lorelei says, dryly. "That's easy for her to do. She hasn't breastfed any children."

"Oh, yeah. I'm in!" Ashley stands up and wriggles out of her yellow tankini top. "Woo!" She giggles as she trots into the water, cupping her breasts with her hands.

Katherine and Lorelei gawk at each other.

Katherine shrugs. "Oh, what the hell." She stands, ditches her coral halter tankini top and takes another approach. "Confidence is key." She throws her shoulders back and walks with her head held high down to the water.

"Yeah, girl!" Rishika shouts as Katherine struts her stuff.

Lorelei scoffs, sitting on the lounge chair, self-conscious, feeling like a fuddy-duddy.

"Do it! Do it!" chant Rishika, Ashley, Katherine, and Anna splashing around the water obnoxiously. Sunbathers watch the spectacle.

"Oh, God," Lorelei mutters under her breath.

"I thought you were throwing caution to the wind!" Rishika shouts.

Lorelei groans. "Yeah, with my clothes on," she mutters.

"Lorelei! Lorelei!"

"Do it, girl!" Anna cheers from the water, though only Rishika can hear her.

"Ah, heck." Lorelei stands reluctantly, and the ladies cheer. She struggles with her bathing suit top. "These control-top suits are hell to get off," she explains to an old lady who is sitting nearby. She finally rolls the tankini top over her head. "I can't be scandalous when I'm a grandma," she announces. She cups her breasts and runs down to the water in her bathing suit skirt, shrieking.

Anna, Rishika, Ashley and Katherine laugh and scream as Lorelei ungracefully plunges into the water.

They splash and clap and celebrate, all the while laughing hysterically.

"I can't believe I did that!" Lorelei exclaims, her hands clapped to her blushing cheeks.

"That was amazing! What an adrenaline rush!" Katherine boasts.

As their laughter and cheering dissipates, they float blissfully in the calm waves with their naked upper bodies glistening under the water.

"So… how do we get back to our chairs?" Ashley asks.

"Yeah. I didn't really think that part through," Rishika says. "I was in the moment."

# Chapter 38

Laughter erupts within the sultry vapor of the steam room in the hotel spa. The ladies lounge, swaddled in white towels, their faces and shoulders glistening with dew.

"They were engaged in wholesome fun on their family vacation, happily building a sandcastle together," Lorelei recounts, "and then the sweet little boys see an army of boobs coming towards them."

"'Look away, sir,'" Katherine chimes in, channeling Rishika. "'Look away!'"

"Well, why was the dad staring at us?" Rishika shrieks. "He was examining our breasts."

"How could he not?" Katherine replies, snickering. "We emerged from the water like a *Baywatch* episode. His wife was trying to cover both sons' eyes and he was just sitting there entranced."

"Paralyzed!" Lorelei adds. "She was so pissed."

"And we all skulked back to our chairs," Ashley says.

"Yes!" Lorelei agrees. "We totally skulked."

They sit in contented silence for a moment while the moist air penetrates their sinuses and opens up their pores. They blot their faces with ice-cold washcloths that have been infused with peppermint oil.

" I propose that we continue this pampering in our suite with fluffy robes and room service," Katherine says.

"Oh, that sounds good," Lorelei agrees.

It's quiet and the girls lean their heads back and relax.

Ashley opens her eyes, her brows furrowed. "I have kind of a confession to make."

The girls open their eyes and wait. Ashley sits up. "Um," she begins hesitantly. "A few days before my wedding, Anna told me that she didn't think I should go through with it." The girls sit up and adjust their towels. "She said that she didn't see Pierce having my back and she had a really bad feeling that it wasn't going to work out." The girls listen, quietly. "You know, Pierce was kind of showy and made everything elaborate. It didn't bother me then. I kind of liked it, actually. I thought we were going places, together. In hindsight, I think he thought I was just along for the ride."

"How did you react when Anna said that?" Lorelei asks.

"Well, I was furious. You girls were all married by then. It took Pierce so freaking long to propose to me. I said that it was finally my turn to be happy and that she was trying to sabotage that. I accused her of being jealous because Pierce was more successful than Kevin was."

The girls look at each other and cringe.

"Ouch," Rishika says.

"I know. I was a total bitch."

"What happened?" Katherine asked.

"I told Anna that if she didn't support the marriage, she shouldn't show up to the wedding." The girls all look at Ashley, wide-eyed. "Obviously, she was one of my bridesmaids and she was standing right up there next to you all. We just swept it under the rug. But, unfortunately, it was kind of always lurking in our friendship." The girls nod. "I always felt like I had to overcompensate and pretend my relationship with Pierce was amazing, like I had to prove we were

going to make it. She was just trying to help, and"—Ashley scoffs—
"it turns out that she was absolutely right."

"But she didn't want to be right," Katherine reasons.

"I know that." Ashley's voice cracks. "Over the years when things
weren't great with Pierce, I was kind of angry with Anna for being
right. I, uh, actually called her and told her about Pierce's affair when
I found out. I had to confide in someone. Of course she didn't say 'I
told you so.' She was sweet and told me that she was so sorry how
things had turned out with him. I told her that I was sorry that I held
anger for her over the years when she was only trying to protect me."

"You resolved it then," Katherine says. "Good for you."

"Yes, thank goodness. I regret having that negative energy about
it for so long."

"We all make mistakes," Katherine says.

"She saw it clear as day way back then. That Pierce and I weren't
right for each other. And as hard as it was to do so, she approached
me about it."

Katherine looks away. The truth was, they all had their doubts about
Pierce. Anna was the only one brave enough to say anything about it.
Katherine loathed him at first, with his high-and-mighty attitude. But, she
chose to try to bond with him in order to be supportive of their
relationship. In the end, she *had* found things she had in common with
Pierce. He was a good guy in many ways. But he was not good for Ashley.

"Well, we've already covered this," Lorelei says. "You got the best
part of Pierce in the form of Elizabeth, Teddy and Ryan."

"Plus," Rishika jumps in, "some of these things we just have to
find out on our own."

Ashley nods. "That's very true."

"Sometimes," Rishika continues, "even if we know something's
not good for us, we do it anyway, because we want to." The ladies
nod in agreement.

A startling hiss commences and white vapor fills the room.

"Okay, I'm hot. Let's get out," Katherine shouts.

They rise and feel their way through the cloud to the door and escape the overwhelming heat. Ashley closes the door and the hissing muffles instantly.

Rishika pours a cup of ice-cold fruity and herby spa water for each of them and they take it gratefully. Katherine grabs an apple out of a shallow gold bowl of apples, oranges and bananas before joining Ashley and Lorelei on the chaise lounges.

Rishika takes her water and walks down the steps into the pool. She crosses her arms on the side of the pool in front of her, facing her friends.

"So. I was thinking. As nice as the robe and room service plan sounds, we're a hop, skip and a jump away from Monte Carlo, for God's sake."

"What are you suggesting?" Lorelei asks.

***

After cappuccinos and a trip to the hotel boutique and beauty salon, the ladies step off the elevator and into the hotel lobby. They are dressed to kill in glamorous, sexy ball gowns.

Ashley looks like a Greek goddess in a moss green flowy gown with one asymmetrical strap. Her blonde hair is loosely French braided back and pinned up.

Katherine looks like a classic film star from old Hollywood in a strapless red gown with a large flat bow at the base of her back. Her dark hair lies in long defined waves.

Rishika wears a sleek form-fitting yellow dress with spaghetti straps that show off her muscular CrossFit shoulders and arms. Her glossy black hair is pulled back in a chignon at the nape of her neck.

Lorelei wears a floral dress with cap sleeves and a full skirt in bold jewel tones. Her hair is swept up loosely with curly tendrils escaping from the updo.

Heads turn as the four of them strut through the lobby like it's a catwalk.

# Chapter 39

On a hilltop above the Mediterranean Sea, a taxi pulls up to the entrance of the palatial Casino de Monte Carlo. A grand fountain anchors the middle of the turnaround where valets in uniform open doors for guests and park Lamborghinis, Porches, Bentleys, and the like. The doors of the taxi open, and Lorelei, Ashley, Katherine and Rishika attempt to climb out gracefully. As each one emerges, they take in the opulence of the setting, their facial expressions reflecting their awe.

The famed Casino de Monte Carlo is a magnificent structure of beige and cream, in the grand Belle Epoque style of architecture. Two domed towers with verdigris bronze statues welcome its guests. There are splendid balconies, and ivory canopies tent the top of the windows. Palm trees are scattered around the grounds, adding to the essence of paradise for the rich and the visiting. Ornate wrought-iron pendant lights dangle like earrings from the wrought-iron Art Nouveau overhang that shelters the stairs leading up to the wooden and glass front doors. A clock is perched high above the entrance, hinting that the guests of the Casino de Monte Carlo may all turn into pumpkins once their fairy tale night has come to an end.

When the ladies enter the main hall, the scenery gets even more impressive. High ceilings in stained glass. Red velvet draperies.

Marble columns. Soft golden lighting emanates from wall sconces and chandeliers. There is a buzz of energy and money.

"Wow," Ashley says in awe. "This is like a James Bond movie!"

"Where do we even start?" Lorelei asks.

"The bar," Rishika replies.

Moments later, the ladies hold up their martinis, shaken, not stirred. If there ever was a place to people-watch, this is it. With women in gorgeous gowns and sexy cocktail dresses and men in smart suits and tuxedos, it is like being on the red carpet at the Oscars.

\*\*\*

After a few rounds of martinis, Katherine takes a deep breath. "I need to find a Ritz cracker or something. All I've eaten is olives." She looks down at her empty martini glass. "Several olives."

"Let's go find something to eat," Lorelei suggests. "There's got to be a buffet in this place."

"What do you think this is, the Excalibur?" Rishika asks.

"We'll find something," Ashley says.

They walk through the casino. Rishika carries Anna's ashes in her Louis Vuitton tote, as she just feels better having them with her.

As they pass by the roulette tables, Lorelei hesitates.

"I've always wanted to play roulette." She grins. She opens her purse, pulls out a hundred-dollar bill and puts it on the table. Ashley's eyes widen in surprise. The dealer exchanges the cash for a chip. "Black, please," Lorelei says sheepishly.

The dealer places her chip on the black area of the felt and waves his hand over the table to indicate that there will be no more bets. The ladies all giggle as the dealer spins the small white ball around the roulette wheel.

"Oh, my gosh, oh, my gosh," Lorelei chants nervously.

They watch as the ball goes round and round, whizzing over red, black and occasional green numbers, and finally slows down. It lands on red.

"Oh." Ashley frowns. "Sorry, hon."

"Bummer," Lorelei says, disappointed. Ashley, Katherine and Rishika begin to walk away from the table.

"Hmm." Lorelei thinks for a moment. She leafs through more hundred-dollar bills and places a stack on the felt. Ashley happens to glance back at Lorelei.

"Whoa," Ashley says. "Where'd you get all that?" Rishika and Katherine turn back.

"I went to the ATM back at the hotel," Lorelei says. She turns her attention to the dealer. "A thousand dollars on black."

"Are you crazy?" Rishika asks.

"I've recently realized that I need to take more risks in my life."

Katherine, Rishika and Ashley look at each other with wide eyes.

"Yes, madam." The dealer spins the ball, and it blurs around the wheel of numbers. The ladies watch, hopeful. It lands on red.

"Oh, shit," Katherine says.

"Ouch," Ashley says. "Let's go."

Rishika puts her arm around Lorelei. "One day, Adam will think this is funny. In like ten years."

They all turn and begin to walk away. "Well, that sucked," Lorelei says, disgruntled. She stops. "You know what? No. Go big or go home, ladies." She turns and walks back towards the roulette table.

"No," Katherine calls to her. "Quit while you're ahead."

"That ship has already sailed," Rishika mumbles.

"Lorelei," Ashley implores.

They follow her back to the table where Lorelei fishes out another stack of cash and puts it on the felt. "A thousand dollars on black."

"How much more of that do you have?" Ashley asks.

"Not much," Lorelei says.

Katherine, Ashley and Rishika look at each other, worried. Lorelei looks both terrified and hopeful. For a high school art teacher with six kids, she really doesn't want over two thousand dollars to go down the drain. "I'll probably never be here again. So…" She shrugs.

The dealer spins the ball. Lorelei takes deep breathes while she watches. Ashley holds onto Rishika's arm. Katherine covers her mouth with her hands folded as in prayer.

Ashley closes her eyes and leans her head against Rishika's shoulder. "I can't look."

# Chapter 40

The ball whizzes around the wheel. It begins to slow down. It passes a red number, a black number, a red number, a black number, and it comes to an almost stop on a green zero. The ball rolls onto black twenty-eight.

Lorelei, Katherine and Rishika erupt into boisterous screaming. They jump up and down.

Ashley uncovers her eyes and sees the ball on black. She sucks in her breath and joins her friends jumping up and down.

Lorelei looks like she's going to pass out. "Thank you, Jesus."

"That was incredible!" Katherine says, grabbing Lorelei by both arms and shaking her.

"You almost gave me a heart attack," Rishika says.

The dealer pushes a stack of chips toward Lorelei.

"Wow," Katherine muses. "That's a lot of cheddar."

"They ain't dollar chips," Rishika quips.

"Shh," Lorelei says. "Act natural. Act like we belong here."

Katherine scoffs. "We don't belong here."

"Okay, I'm playing," Ashley says.

"Me, too," Rishika chimes in.

"But with much smaller bets," Ashley adds.

They all pull out money and put it on the table. The dealer gives them chips. They start reaching across the table, putting chips down on various numbers.

Katherine places a chip on the table and asks Ashley, "Will you please put this on number fourteen?"

"Sure." She does so.

"Anna's birthday," Katherine explains to the ladies.

Ashley nods and puts one of her own chips on number fourteen as well.

"Oh, put me down on that," Rishika says.

"Great idea," Lorelei says and leans over to place her own chip on number fourteen.

The dealer spins the wheel, and yet again the little white ball that decides the fate of so many victories and disappointments takes its circular journey around the numbers.

Red number fourteen hits. The ladies go crazy.

*** 

A party forms around the roulette table as the ladies continue to win. A cocktail waitress weaves in between players and spectators delivering libations.

A man on the other side of the roulette table notices Ashley. He's in his mid-forties with piercing blue eyes, sandy blonde hair in a longish crew cut, and the rugged beginnings of a five o'clock shadow. He observes as Ashley bites the olive off the toothpick in her martini and it falls into her cleavage. She looks around to see if anyone has seen, rounds her back in order to reach in and fish the olive out of her cleavage, and pops it into her mouth. The man laughs.

He catches Ashley's eye and nods and smiles at her. She instantly notices his movie-star good looks and how his buff body fills out his tuxedo. She finishes chewing her olive and looks behind her to see who he's smiling at. Ashley points at herself and mouths, *Me?* The man laughs and nods. She flushes.

Suddenly Ashley has a hankering to read a cheap paperback novel about a big brawny Viking with lush blonde hair and bulging muscles seducing a fair maiden who looks a lot like her, wearing a dress with a very low-cut bodice and full skirt. There would be pillaging and plundering, and a whole lot of rollicking around below deck on rough burlap sacks of sugar and potatoes.

Katherine notices the exchange between Ashley and the handsome stranger. "Ashley, I think your luck in men is about to take a turn."

"Is that well-dressed Viking real?" Ashley says. "Or am I hallucinating?"

Katherine laughs. "He's real, and he is checking you out!" She pats Ashley on the back and steps away as the man approaches.

"Hello," he says.

"Hi," Ashley says, a bit shy.

He extends his hand. "My name is Andrick."

Ashley offers her hand. "Ashley." Andrick lifts her hand and kisses it.

"I've never heard the name Andrick before. What is its origin?"

"It is Swedish for 'manly and brave.'"

Ashley's eyes widen and she knocks back the rest of her martini.

"Are you married?" Andrick asks as they step back from the roulette table.

Ashley blows air out of her mouth in a not-so-lady-like way. "That's a complicated question."

"It's a yes-or-no question," he returns with a smile.

A happy warmth washes over her entire body. She smiles back.

"I do not have a husband who is mine." She narrows her eyes, waiting to see if the answer takes.

Andrick chuckles. "I'm glad to hear that. May I buy you dinner?"

"What, now?"

"There's a wonderful restaurant upstairs."

She smiles. "I could really use some dinner."

"Great."

"Give me one second." She steps forward and whispers into Katherine's ear. "I'm going to have dinner with the Viking."

A huge smile spreads across Katherine's face. "Go get him, girl. We'll find you later. Be careful."

Ashley smiles at her with excitement in her eyes and then walks away.

"Yes!" Katherine does a celebratory dance and fist-pumps the air.

Andrick takes Ashley's hand and leads her across the casino. She makes eye contact with a woman she doesn't know and silently screams. The woman takes in the sight of Andrick, mouths *Wow, good job*, and gives Ashley a thumbs-up.

*** 

After the momentum slows at the roulette table, Lorelei, Katherine and Rishika move to a blackjack table. They each have cocktails and hold a hand of cards.

Lorelei shows her hand to Rishika. She has a jack and an ace. "Oh! Is this good?"

Rishika looks at her like she's crazy. "Yes!"

# Chapter 41

At an intimate table for two in Le Train Blue, Ashley and Andrick are seated across from each other on red velvet chairs, sipping champagne. The carpet is red jaquard, the dishes are rimmed in gold and small gold lamps on each table emit a warm, intimate glow. The ambiance is cozy, luxe and outrageously romantic.

"You're a very long way from California," Andrick says as he cuts into his rare steak.

"My girlfriends and I are heading south tomorrow." She takes a bite of her langoustine and rolls her eyes at its buttery, melt-in-your-mouth flavor. Andrick grins, enjoying her appreciation of the meal. "Rome, and then Athens and then... Mykonos at the end of this week." Andrick stops cutting a piece of steak, wondering at the cause of change in her tone. "We're, uh, going to scatter our friend's ashes there. That's really the purpose of this whole trip."

Andrick's face falls. "I'm very sorry. That must be incredibly hard."

"It really is." Her eyes fill with tears without warning. She shakes her head in an attempt to shake off the sadness, surprised to show such emotion in front of this handsome stranger, right out of the gate. "It's been an amazing trip, but it's daunting that that moment is inching closer. It's going to be really difficult for us. We've been reminiscing about Anna a lot, but now that I think about it, we've been avoiding the topic of what we are actually going to do in Mykonos. Look at me. I can barely say it myself."

He takes her hand and squeezes it. "Perhaps the closure will be good."

Ashley thinks about it. "I'm not sure I want closure yet. I don't want to move on." She chokes up and fans herself with her hand.

"Go ahead. There is nothing wrong with crying. You are showing your love for her."

"I don't want to cry right now. I have cried plenty. But thank you." She takes her hand back and dabs the corners of her eyes with her linen napkin.

"Anna clearly had strong friends for you to come so far to do this for her."

"We were all very close with her. Oddly enough, each of us was close with her, but we weren't necessarily still super close with each other in recent years."

"Yet here you all are together."

"Yeah. This trip has really bonded us." Ashley looks thoughtful. "How about that."

"That's wonderful."

"Oh, my gosh! We just met and that's the conversation I led with. You must think I'm crazy."

"I think you're honest. And lovely."

Ashley blushes. "Thank you. Can we change the subject?"

"Of course."

She searches for a safe topic. "What do you do?" she asks and takes a bite of artichoke. "Oh, my gosh," she whispers.

"I create international schools all over the world. My mother was a teacher, so I've always admired and respected educators, understood how hard they work and the support that they need. She instilled the value of education in my brothers and me since we were young. Also, school was not easy for me. I am dyslexic and I was kind of a trouble maker as a child, as a result. But some special teachers didn't give up on me. So, when I sold my first business and needed to think about where to invest that money, I was pleased to put it into schools."

"That sounds very noble."

He shrugs. "Thank you. What is your passion?"

Ashley laughs. "Okay." And then she thinks about his question and looks simultaneously confused and amused. "I'm not sure anyone has ever asked me that. I used to be an accountant, but now I'm a stay-at-home mom. However, I think I'll be going back to work very soon."

"If that's what you want, good for you."

Ashley nods and forces a smile.

"So, which one is your passion?"

She butters a roll, thoughtfully, and takes a bite. Ashley's instinct is to be humble, buttoned-up and polite, but her head reminds her that eighteen years of that got her absolutely nowhere with Pierce. It stifled her. As Pierce's wife, she never allowed herself to shine. She did things in an impeccable way in an effort to shine for Pierce, but when it fell on blind eyes, she didn't shine at all. She dimmed over time. She realizes that Pierce is only half to blame for that. She holds the other half of that blame. She allowed herself to go on that way for so long. In this moment, she decides that she will never again compromise herself for anyone. She will be her true self, unapologetically.

"I'm pretty good at accounting. Numbers have always made sense to me. But I wouldn't call it a passion. I love being a stay-at-home mom." She brightens. "It's so nice to be able to pick my kids up from school at the drop of a hat if they're sick or to drop off their lunch if they forgot it. I enjoy helping the teachers with math centers and class parties. I love picking the kids up from school and bringing their friends home with them and hearing stories about their day as I lay snacks out for them. Sounds indulgent, but I just love catering to their every whim. You know, now, while they're little."

"You sound like a very dedicated mother."

"Thank you. I am."

"How old are they?"

"Elizabeth is ten, Teddy is six, and Ryan is three. I know it sounds provincial, but I'm a kick-ass homemaker." Andrick smiles, intrigued. Ashley has never been one to sing her own praises, but Andrick has opened up Pandora's box, and she's on a roll. "I never really thought about what that term means. Making a home. It's actually pretty special. *That's* my passion. I'm a great cook. Like, really good. I love to make things from scratch and cook all kinds of cuisines. I love to arrange flowers, and boy, can I put on a party. I just find it all really fun." Ashley glows from within. Andrick's eyes shine. She can see that he is impressed with her. She suddenly feels a bit self-conscious and blushes. "I'm totally bragging. How obnoxious!"

"Not at all. I'm enjoying hearing all about it."

"Enough about me. Do you have kids?"

"I do. Anneke is eleven and Lukas is six. Their mother and I divorced three years ago."

"Wow, three years and nobody has snatched you up? Have you been locked in a room since then?"

He laughs. "I've dated. But I hadn't found a strong connection with anyone yet."

Ashley's cheeks burn. She is definitely feeling a strong connection. Is he? Obviously there is strong physical chemistry here. But Andrick also seems to really want to know about her.

"I have to be honest with you. My husband and I just filed for divorce. Just. As in, last month." Ashley blushes, embarrassed and a little ashamed.

"I'm sorry."

"He fell in love with someone else," she says softly.

Andrick frowns. "Well, I think he's crazy, and I'm very sorry you've had to endure that. Would it be insensitive to say that I'm glad he did?"

Ashley's cheeks burn. "No, it wouldn't."

"Ashley." The back of Ashley's neck tingles at the mere sound of Andrick saying her name. Her physical reaction surprises her. "Have you ever been to Sweden?"

Her eyes lock with his. "No, I haven't. But so far I like the people."

***

Dessert is quite an experience. Ashley enthusiastically orders ile flottante, a meringue floating on a sea of creme anglaise. She's never actually had it before, but has seen the Barefoot Contessa make it on the Food Network. The name of the dessert translates to "floating island". This one has a nest of golden spun sugar sitting on top of the meringue like a wispy crown, and it is just as delicious as it is impressive. The meringue is soft and cloudlike, and the chilled vanilla custard has the subtle essence of lemon zest. Finely chopped pistachios add another layer of color and texture. Ashley comments that it's like an edible masterpiece. Andrick orders a decadent chocolate mousse, and they share like they are a couple.

When the dessert dishes and coffee cups have been cleared away, they hold hands over the table and sip cognac out of snifters.

"Ashley, I know we've just met, but I feel very connected to you."

"I feel the same way," she agrees, amazed at this gift that the universe has surprised her with this evening. She would kiss Rishika when she saw her. If not for Rishika, they would be eating room service in their fluffy hotel robes.

"I don't want to say goodbye yet. Will you come with me tonight?"

Ashley doesn't want to say goodbye yet, either. They're just scratching the surface. It's very odd. Clearly there's quite a physical attraction here, but she too, cheesy as it sounds, feels a strong cosmic connection to Andrick, and she knows in her heart that there's potential to go deeper. Plus, her loins are on fire.

"Yes, I will," she whispers. In the background, she sees Lorelei, Katherine and Rishika drunkenly stumble into the restaurant looking for her. *Oh, gosh,* she thinks, both embarrassed and amused. "But only if I can bring my friends."

# Chapter 42

A limo waits at the entrance of the casino. Laughing and sloppy, Lorelei, Rishika, and Katherine take the driver's proffered hand and climb into the limo. He closes the door when they have all piled inside.

Lorelei claps her hands. "I've only been inna limo once before," She slurs. "On ma prom night. I'm gonna tryta remember this."

"Let's take a picture," Rishika suggests.

"Yeah!" Lorelei agrees.

Lorelei sprawls across Rishika's and Katherine's laps. They lean their faces together with wide smiles, and Rishika takes a selfie.

"Excuse me, sir," Katherine says to the chauffeur. He lowers the glass. "Is there a drive-thru we can hit?"

"Of course, madam."

"I'm dying for some curly fries."

\*\*\*

Meanwhile, Andrick and Ashley sit in the front seats of a silver Aston Martin parked in front of the limo.

"Are you sure they'll be okay?" Ashley asks.

"I promise they'll be right behind us. I always use Henri as my driver when I'm here, and he is very trustworthy."

Ashley smiles. "Okay."

Andrick throws the car into drive and they zoom off. The Aston Martin flies through the streets of Monte Carlo. Ashley throws her arms up in the air and cheers.

*\*\*\**

Later, when Lorelei, Rishika and Katherine have arrived at Andrick's accommodations with bellies full of Le McDonald's, Ashley makes sure that they are in their room, safe and sound. It doesn't take them long to plop onto the beds and become dead to the world.

Andrick told her to take her time making sure her friends were comfortable, and he waits by the rail overlooking the glistening water.

There has been a progression of anticipation, beginning with tender touches of hands at dinner while they got to know each other's hearts. During the invigorating joyride through Monte Carlo, Andrick's thumb rubbed the inside of Ashley's hand, sending shockwaves through her entire body.

When she leaves her sleeping friends and finds him, he turns towards her and smiles. He holds out his hand and she takes it. They stand at the railing looking at the giant Mediterranean Sea that sparkles like a dark sapphire while they stand under a black sky dotted with diamonds. When Andrick turns toward her, it's like the universe is telling her, *Your love life is not over. Here you go.*

And then they kiss. It's slow at first, feeling the feather-light touch of each other's lips for the first time and then progressing deeper, their arms sliding around each other. And, oh, to kiss someone new for the first time in so many years. It's so exciting and new.

And now they hold hands as they walk down a hallway to Andrick's room. The anticipation is building through Ashley's pulsing body. With each step, Ashley understands how stifled she has been. During the exquisite dinner, Ashley felt herself unburdening herself and becoming more *her*, layer by layer, with each epiphany that she revealed to both herself and Andrick. She is ready to unleash the pent-up sexuality that has confined her for so many years of not fully being desired, not feeling encouraged to express the bottomless fount of love inside of her. It's about to burst open like a dam breaking, and Andrick has no idea.

He leads her into his room and closes the door.

"This is really nice," she says as she walks into the room, all dark wood and navy blue.

"Thank you," he says.

For a moment Ashley feels a little shy, but she also realizes that her body feels so alive, so full of static and adrenaline. She realizes that she's been sleepwalking through her womanhood, and now she feels awakened. *Oh, my God, the anticipation of this! I get to be with this man all night in this room. Doing whatever we want.*

Andrick walks halfway to her and stops, his eyes an invitation, welcoming and promising to nurture her needs if she walks the few steps to him.

She walks towards him and they interlace their fingers, standing closely, face to face. Somehow without talking, with only hands touching, a conversation takes place.

He moves the hair away from her face and kisses her. It is loving and gentle and urgent. What a kiss.

Andrick kneels down on one knee and puts Ashley's high-heeled foot on his thigh. She gasps.

He smiles at the sight of her dainty foot, her petal pink nail polish, and unbuckles the clasp on her gold strappy heel and removes it.

As each shoe comes off, so do any last fears and inhibitions. Andrick's warm strong hand trails gently up one of her legs as he stands up to face her. It's the most erotic thing that anyone has ever done to her, and she's still fully dressed.

"Ashley?" he questions. She moans softly. *God, his voice is tantalizing.* "Ashley?"

"Yes?" she breathes.

"I'm going to take off your clothes now."

She gasps. He may not even have to make love to her. He is seducing her with a few well-said words.

"Is that okay?"

"Uh, yeah," she says, preoccupied. And then she comes to and smiles devilishly. "But yours are coming off first."

# Chapter 43

Rishika, Lorelei and Ashley begin to stir on a huge bed, still wearing their ball gowns. Their once beautifully styled hair is disheveled and their artfully applied smoky eye makeup is now smudged. It's definitely a morning-after look.

"Oh. My. Gosh," Rishika says.

"Why do we keep doing this? It's like we haven't learned anything," Lorelei says with her arm over her eyes.

"Where are we?" Katherine asks. "The last thing I remember is having burgers and milkshakes in a limo."

Lorelei looks around. "Where's Ashley?"

They all look at each other, trying to remember.

"Where are Anna's ashes?" Katherine asks, worried.

"They're there in the Louis Vuitton," Rishika answers, gesturing to the nightstand. She walks over to the window and opens the shades. "What the fuck?" She looks at Lorelei and Katherine with wide eyes. "We're on a boat!"

"What?" Katherine cries.

"All I see is water!"

"What did we *do* last night?" Katherine asks, worried. "What the hell did we do?"

"Oh, my God," Lorelei cries, panicking. She fans herself with her hands. "It *is* like *Taken*! When the rich king of India buys the virgins at the rich guy's auction and they become his harem!"

"India?" Rishika repeats. "I'm offended by that."

Lorelei looks annoyed. "Okay, fine. When the rich king of an undisclosed country in southeast Asia purchases the virgins as his sex slaves and steals their sacred virginity!"

Rishika throws her a look. "Okay, Grandma."

Katherine chuckles and points at Lorelei. "Back Door Grandma. That's your new nickname."

Rishika snickers and high-fives Katherine.

Lorelei looks thoroughly miffed. "I am never telling you about my sex life again." Lorelei's naturally full and curly hair is currently huge and fluffy, some still pinned up, but most of it has fallen out of its once-lovely updo and it poofs out everywhere.

"You need a brush," Rishika remarks.

Lorelei narrows her eyes. "I hate you right now." There's a knock on the door. Lorelei jumps. "Oh, God. This is it!" She assumes a karate stance, and Katherine shrugs and picks up a vase. Rishika rolls her eyes and opens the door to reveal a man dressed in a butler's uniform.

"Good morning, ladies. I am Gustav, and I am at your service. I would like to inform you that breakfast will be served on deck when you are ready."

Lorelei remains in her karate stance. "Uh, okay. That sounds lovely, thank you."

"Mr. Sjoeberg asked me to purchase some swim attire for you this morning."

"Uhh, Mr. Who?" Rishika asks, suspiciously.

"Mr. Sjoeberg," Gustav answers. "—Andrick."

Katherine snaps her fingers. "Andrick. The Viking!" she says, putting the pieces together.

Gustav appears puzzled, yet lifts a few clothing boxes and gift bags from a silver dolly behind him in the hallway. "May I?"

"Sure," Katherine responds awkwardly. She puts the vase down.

Gustav enters the room, sets several clothing boxes on the bed, and returns to the hallway.

"Thank you, Gustav," Lorelei replies.

Rishika closes the door. "So, we're not stolen virgins anymore?"

"I could use some food," Lorelei replies.

"You're weak."

Katherine puts the boxes on the bed and opens one. She holds up a racy black one-piece bathing suit with so many holes of various sizes in it that it could hardly be characterized as a one-piece. "Whoa."

Rishika opens a box and holds up a white lacy monokini. "Um… this is not really my style."

"Oh, no. Oh, no. Oh, no," Lorelei whines as she pulls out a teeny-tiny bright-pink string bikini. "They're like Barbie clothes!"

"Gustav is a total pervert," Rishika says.

"We can't leave this room wearing these!" Lorelei cries.

"Girls, we have to," Katherine says. "They're gifts. We can't be rude." She looks at the tag. "Besides, this is Gucci and I would never pay this much in real life!" She pumps her shoulders up and down, excitedly.

"You know what? Maybe this is what I would've worn if I was in Europe twenty years ago." Lorelei wears a doubtful and scared expression.

"Good girl." Rishika chuckles and then suddenly gasps. Her hands fly up to her mouth.

"Oh, my God, what is it?" Lorelei cries, as if she can't take anymore surprises.

"Holy shit!" Rishika's arms soar into the air like a champion's. "We won a shitload of money last night!"

There is a moment of silence and eyes wandering, recalling the events of the previous night. Lorelei shrieks. Katherine's jaw drops. They start screaming and jumping up and down together in a group hug.

# Chapter 44

Ashley's eyelids flutter open and her blue eyes peruse her surroundings. She is enveloped in dark gray sheets. Her back is to Andrick and he has her pulled in tight to his body with his strong arm wrapped around her. Her mouth breaks into a wide smile. She thinks back to the incredible hours she has spent in this room with this man. Fantasies can come true. A virile and hunky Viking did have his way with her below deck on his ship. And she had her way with him. She giggles internally. Her friends will love that visual.

She recalls the events of the night. When her dress dropped to the floor, it revealed her body confined by tight spandex. "Oh, shit," she whispered. "I forgot about that. I'll just take it off real quick."

"Don't you dare," he replied with an amused look in his eye. As he peeled off her Spanx, they laughed and kissed. And then all joking stopped.

Ashley smirks and closes her eyes tightly, screaming in her head that this has actually happened.

Sensing her movement, Andrick pulls her in tighter. His embrace feels protective, loving and sincere. It feels *amazing*. Ashley rolls over and studies his sweet face. Suddenly, her heart aches. This is about to end. Today she will get on a train and never see this man again.

"Good morning, darling," he says with his eyes closed.

*Darling.* In a Swedish accent. It's the most beautiful and sexy sentiment she's ever heard. He opens his eyes, kind and crystal-clear blue, and smiles at her. Something deep inside her warms.

She returns a shy smile. "Good morning."

"You're very pretty in the morning," he says.

"So are you. I mean, you're very manly in the morning. Manly and brave. Your name is perfectly accurate. I need to stop talking."

He looks at her, amused. "I'll help you." Andrick tenderly grabs the back of Ashley's head and kisses her deeply. The kiss escalates and she rolls on top of him.

# Chapter 45

Lorelei, Katherine and Rishika have ditched their ball gowns. Finding a delightful assortment of toiletries in the bathroom, they washed the morning-after makeup off their faces, brushed their teeth and hair, and in turn, found the bravery to put on the super-skimpy bathing suits and kitten heels.

Showing a whole lot of skin, they self-consciously slip out of their room. They sneak down the hallway, not knowing who is behind these other doors.

Lorelei attempts to cover herself with a giant sun hat. "Funny that these humongous hats and jeweled sandals were purchased, but cover-ups were not thought of."

"Let's not be ungrateful," Katherine remarks with a wry smile.

"I haven't worn a monokini since junior high," Rishika says, amused. "It's kind of fun." Her toned body looks strong and sexy in the skimpy suit.

"It is not fun," Lorelei snaps. "I've had six children, you skinny bitch. I'm in my own personal hell right now."

They climb the spiral staircase that leads outside. Rishika gets to the top first and sucks in her breath at what she sees.

"You're about to get over it."

They emerge on the deck. The sun-kissed Mediterranean Sea glistens all around them.

\*\*\*

Ashley yells out in pleasure. Andrick rolls off of her.

"Wow," Ashley breathes. "I had no idea. No idea! It's like I understand a whole new foreign language."

"You speak it well," Andrick says as he catches his breath. "I think our bodies were meant to be together." He kisses her forehead. Ashley nods and sighs happily.

"I wonder how my friends are doing. I hope they're not upset with me."

# Chapter 46

Once they emerged from below deck, Lorelei, Katherine, and Rishika realized just how grand this one-hundred-sixty-four-foot yacht actually is. The fixtures and decor are all white, clean and streamlined. There are rows of comfy pine chaise lounges and white cushions on either side of an inviting rectangular swimming pool encased in a mosaic of aquamarine, sky blue and white tiles.

Gustav has brought them frothy cappuccinos and aspirin, and they lounge side by side on chaise lounges in their skimpy bathing suits, huge sun hats and sunglasses as their bodies begin to absorb the caffeine and pain reliever. Lorelei's hat rests on her torso, covering her abdomen.

"You know," Katherine says, "it's just us out here, and damn it, we look spectacular."

"I am getting more comfortable," Lorelei agrees.

"Just own it, girl," Rishika says.

Lorelei removes the hat from her body and places it on her head. She stretches like a cat in the sun. "This Mediterranean sun feels amazing! So much better than ours."

"It is the same sun, you know," Rishika teases.

"It's just packaged better here," Katherine quips.

Gustav appears with a cart containing crystal champagne flutes, a stainless steel ice bucket chilling a bottle of champagne, and a carafe of freshly squeezed orange juice. "Ladies, would you care to move onto mimosas?"

"Only if it's true champagne from the region of Champagne," Lorelei says in a nasally voice.

"Of course, madam."

"I'm joking!" Lorelei laughs. "We'll each have one, please. Sorry."

Rishika casts Lorelei a faux scolding glance. "Can't take you anywhere."

Lorelei giggles and sighs contentedly as she takes in the clear baby blue skies, the sun shining on the calm cobalt water. The yacht bobs ever so gently. "This is so once-in-a-lifetime. I wish Adam was here to enjoy it."

"Maybe we'll take another trip sometime and bring the husbands," Rishika suggests.

"Yes!" Katherine agrees.

Gustav pours their mimosas and hands one to each of them.

"Thank you, Gustav. Thank you, Viking. Thank you, Ashley. Thank you to everyone who is responsible for this moment," Katherine says.

Rishika smiles and thinks of Anna for a moment. "Yes."

A second butler rolls up with a silver cart loaded with ingredients. "Good morning, ladies. I am Emil. May I offer you a crepe?"

Rishika shakes her head. "This just keeps getting better and better."

\*\*\*

The air in the bathroom of Andrick's stateroom is velvety and vaporous, fogged up with sex and steam. Andrick's and Ashley's wet bodies wrap around each other under the powerful spray of hot water. Aromatic citrus body wash and suds make the situation even more slippery and intoxicating. A sensuous dance of lips and limbs moves rhythmically. Andrick has taken over every nerve ending in Ashley's body. Even her ears thrum. Suddenly, an image appears in her mind of her and Pierce having obligatory Friday night sex and then falling asleep, their bodies turned away from each other. It's a very sad image, but in this moment, it amuses her. And then Andrick does something to Ashley that wipes Pierce from her thoughts.

# Chapter 47

Katherine moans in ecstasy as she takes a bite of crepe filled with melty Nutella, sliced bananas, Grand Marnier, and flaked coconut. It leaves a smudge of chocolate on the side of her mouth. "Oh, yeah," she says as she licks whipped cream off her index finger.

She glances over and finds Lorelei and Rishika staring at her. "Would you like to be alone?" Rishika asks.

Lorelei laughs.

"How did Emil know that this was the perfect combination?" Katherine asks, bemused. "It's like he understands my soul." She takes another bite.

Ashley appears, walking like a cowgirl with a filled champagne flute in hand. She wears a tasteful royal blue one-piece bathing suit with a lacy white cover-up. She absolutely glows from the inside out.

"Well, well, well," Katherine says coyly.

"Are you limping?" Lorelei asks.

"I've never had multiple orgasms on a yacht," Ashley says and takes a playfully suggestive sip of her champagne.

Lorelei and Rishika scream. Embarrassed, Ashley shushes them.

"Multiple?" Katherine says, envious.

Andrick appears wearing sky blue swim trunks and an unbuttoned white linen shirt, revealing a peek at his tan, chiseled stomach and chest. Katherine's eyes widen.

"Good morning, ladies. I've been a terrible host. I apologize for my rudeness. I hope Emil and Gustav have been keeping you happy this morning."

"More than you know." Katherine wipes the corner of her mouth with a cloth napkin.

"Thank you so much for your hospitality, Andrick. We've had a lovely morning," Lorelei says.

"We're happy if Ashley is happy," Rishika says protectively.

"That is all I want, too." Andrick grabs Ashley's hand and smiles at her. She smiles back at him, radiant. Rishika looks questioningly at Katherine.

"I hope you don't mind that last night I asked the captain to take us on a short morning cruise," Andrick says. "I thought you would enjoy the view."

"It's been so beautiful," Katherine comments.

"Not that we had a choice," Rishika mutters and takes a sip of her mimosa. Katherine shushes her.

A gorgeous man in his early thirties walks sleepily out on to the deck. He has sandy blonde hair, bright aquamarine eyes and is slim with a washboard stomach. He wears teeny-tiny white Speedos. Rishika chokes on her mimosa. Lorelei and Katherine look confused.

With the ladies speechless, he is unaware of their presence. He approaches the swimming pool and dives gracefully into the water.

"The plot thickens," Rishika says.

He bursts up through the surface of the water like Poseidon.

"Good morning, Sebastian," Andrick says. Sebastian swims to the edge of the pool, lifts himself out with flexing triceps, and grabs a folded towel from a small table. "Ladies, I would like to introduce my brother."

"Of course," Rishika says, dryly.

"Oh," escapes from Katherine's mouth.

"Oh, my," from Lorelei's.

"Good morning," Sebastian says as he walks over, drying himself. "I'm sorry, I'm still waking up. I thought I was alone."

"It's okay," Katherine says. "Hello! I'm Katherine." Katherine offers her hand and Sebastian kisses it.

"Very nice to meet you, Sebastian. My name is Rishika," Rishika says coquettishly, and offers her hand to his mouth for a kiss.

"Lorelei," Lorelei says. Sebastian smiles, takes her hand and kisses it.

"Beautiful names," he remarks.

"And *this* is Ashley," Andrick says.

Ashley smiles and nods at Sebastian.

"They are all visiting from America," Andrick continues. "California, specifically."

"Fantastic. It is very nice to meet you all."

The ladies all smile coyly and gush niceties to Sebastian.

"Would you like some breakfast?" Andrick asks Ashley.

"Love some," she answers. "Let's sit over there." She casts a *sorry, not sorry* look at her friends. Andrick leads her to a lounge chair and Emil rushes to their assistance.

"Do you think our husbands set this up as a test?" Lorelei asks quietly.

"If they did, I may fail," Katherine says under her breath.

"The pool is *not* cold," Rishika says, suggestively. Lorelei elbows her. "Ow."

"You are so crass," Lorelei scolds.

"You say crass, I say observant. Let's call the whole thing off." Rishika takes a sip of her champagne.

"May I join you, ladies?" Sebastian asks after pulling on a t-shirt and shorts.

"Please!"

"Yes!"

"Of course!"

Lorelei, Rishika and Katherine gush, their voices overlapping. Rishika sits up on her chaise and pats the empty spot at the lower end of it. He sits.

"So, what do you do, Sebastian?" Katherine asks.

"I'm an artist," he says as he accepts a Bloody Mary from Gustav and nods in appreciation.

"Really?" Lorelei says. "I'm an art teacher! I actually wanted to be an artist, but life led me to teaching. What a blessing to pursue that."

"Would you like to see some of my work?"

Lorelei puts her hand on her chest. "Oh, my goodness, yes."

Rishika and Katherine smile at Sebastian and sit up tall and poised like poodles, waiting for their invitations. Sebastian stands and offers his hand to Lorelei, who accepts, and he helps her rise from her lounge chair. They walk away, leaving Katherine and Rishika, their smiles slipping from their faces.

"I guess that's what happens when you try too hard," Rishika remarks.

"Well, I'm going to have another crepe," Katherine says. "Emil?"

Emil rushes over from Andrick and Ashley's side of the pool.

"I'll have one, too," Rishika says as Sebastian leads Lorelei away with her arm in the crook of his. "Is this what rejection feels like?"

Katherine casts a look of disbelief at her. "Yes."

"Ugh. I don't like it."

Sebastian and Lorelei disappear below deck. "Do you think we should chaperone them?" Katherine asks.

Rishika shakes her head. "Nah, she's morally stronger than we are."

Emil prepares the crepes. "We shall feed our libidos with Nutella,"

Katherine declares, holding up her mimosa to make it official. "Load me up, Emil."

"Of course, madam. Would you care for something savory this time? Might I suggest ham, gruyere, spinach and bechamel?"

"Please," Rishika says, intrigued. "I need some protein. Maybe I'll swim a few laps after this one." She inhales the fresh salty air. "This is glorious."

"I'll stick with chocolate," Katherine says.

"You're going to make yourself sick," Rishika warns.

"Chocolate, please," Katherine confirms.

"Of course, madam."

"Please. Call us 'mademoiselle,'" Rishika suggests.

"Of course, mademoiselle."

# Chapter 48

Sebastian leads Lorelei into his studio. It's filled with sculptures of people, some completed, some works in progress. Some of them are full-length, some are busts.

"You're a sculptor? Oh, my goodness." Lorelei walks around in awe, taking in all of the art from all sides. "Wow. These really are amazing. Sebastian, you're talented!"

"Thank you," he says humbly.

"So lifelike." She shakes her head.

"Are they?" he asks.

"Yes," she says, surprised. "Don't you think so?"

Sebastian throws his arms up in the air, frustrated. "I'm missing something lately. I'm not inspired." He sits down on a stool. "I'm starting to wonder if I'm wasting my time."

Lorelei rushes to him and takes his hands. "Honey, I can relate. I was so sure that while I was on this trip away from my responsibilities, finally out in the great big world after all these years, I would be inspired and the art would be flooding out of me like a monsoon."

"But, no?"

"Not at all. I've been dying to feel inspired, and I've had the depressing realization that even though inspiration is all around me, it's not inside me."

"Why?"

Lorelei sighs. "Maybe I've missed my window. I no longer possess that zest, that hunger. Maybe I'm just not meant to be an artist, after all. I'm a great teacher"—she nods—"I'll admit that. But my own original art has been nonexistent for years."

Sebastian looks at her, but doesn't know what to say.

Lorelei shrugs. "Well, you know what they say, 'Those who can't do, teach.'"

Sebastian squints his eyes in disagreement. "No."

"No, what?"

"No, I'm not buying that. You know in your heart if you're an artist. I can tell by hearing you talk about it that you live it and breathe it. What is your medium?"

"Sketching, pastels, paint."

"You need to do it whenever you can, even if it sucks. You need to practice. And, eventually something will really move you."

Lorelei smiles. "Well, now look who the teacher is. Okay, I will try." She exhales a breath. "I will try. Alright. My turn. May I give you some feedback about your sculptures?"

"Please."

"They're really quite beautiful." She walks around, studying them more closely. "The features are very realistic. But what makes your subjects special? Like her." She points to a statue of a woman, barefoot, wearing a sundress. "What about her makes me stop and study her? Why should I be captivated by her? It's one thing for someone to be pretty, but something else entirely to be interesting. Her expression is a little blank. I want to know what she's feeling. What are her hopes? What are her flaws? How do you, as an artist, tell her story?"

Immediately a light of recognition appears in Sebastian's eyes. But, while he is excited to apply this lesson, he is also disappointed.

"You are so right." He hangs his head and exhales. "Look at all of these missed opportunities."

"Now, hold on. They are still quite good. Artists learn and evolve. It's interesting to watch an artist's style unfold over time."

"You see? I admire you. Even if you don't feel like you have the zest for it right now, you've *seen* more. You *know* more."

Lorelei narrows her eyes in thought. "I never thought of it that way. But I really haven't seen much."

"Surely you have. As artists, it's our job to observe life, wherever we are."

Lorelei nods, agreeing with this insight. She takes a deep breath, pleased.

"Thank you, Sebastian." She walks up to him and takes his hands. "Boy, did I need that."

"As did I."

"You'll find your inspiration again. I'm positive about that."

"I think I just have." Sebastian looks at her, seriously. "Please. Pose for me."

"What?" Lorelei laughs.

"I want to tell your story."

"Oh, no." She scoffs and waves him away.

"But I must," he says, his aquamarine eyes intense, eyebrows furrowed. "Look at you. You are art waiting to happen."

"Oh, goodness. I never show this much skin. This bathing suit is a little inappropriate," she mutters, somewhat conspiratorial.

"You have a very sensuous body."

"Sensuous! Really?" Lorelei says like he's crazy.

"What do you mean, 'really?' Yes. Absolutely." Sebastian rushes around the studio, preparing. He washes his hands then heaves a large fresh block of clay onto a table.

"Well, thank you." Lorelei blushes.

Suddenly, the room soars with sweeping opera music.

"Oh, my."

"I'm ready to tell a beautiful story. The story of Lorelei..."

"Leibovitch."

He looks taken aback. "It's like a song! 'Lorelei Leibovitch!'" he sings, operatically.

Lorelei giggles. "Don't be silly."

"You have no idea how beautiful you are." He rushes up to her and guides her to sit on a stool. He fluffs her vibrant red hair. "There is something about you. You have a gypsy soul."

"That's ironic. Before this trip, I'd barely left the U.S."

"You have a wanderlust, I can tell. You have this wild and free energy wanting to burst out."

"Oh, Sebastian, you have no idea."

"The lines at the corners of your eyes tell me that you laugh a lot."

Lorelei smiles. "Well, yes. Usually at absolutely moronic things. Like Will Ferrell movies and potty humor."

"Your beautiful stomach..." Lorelei covers her stomach self-consciously. "No. Don't cover it. It tells me that you are a mother."

"That's an understatement," she remarks dryly.

"How many children do you have?" Sebastian begins to form the clay.

"Six." She chuckles.

"Six? Six human beings have grown in the warmth and happiness of your belly? Incredible!"

Lorelei nods, considering the importance of it. "Yeah," she whispers. "I guess that is pretty amazing. I loved being pregnant, actually. I felt special. Everyone holds the door for you when you're pregnant. My husband, Adam, always waited on me hand and foot. Each pregnancy felt different. I felt like I already knew my children when each of them was born."

"That must have been extraordinary." Sebastian's hands work furiously.

"It really was."

"And those breasts. You breastfed your children, no?"

"Oh, yes. Until they were all two." Lorelei begins to feel more comfortable. "Actually, my youngest son, Gideon, totally favored this one." She glances down and touches her left breast. "That's why it's a little bigger than the right one."

"Really?" Sebastian leaves the clay for a moment and approaches her to get a better look. "Extraordinary. I didn't know babies did that." He runs back to the clay and works it quickly and passionately. "It upsets me when women are embarrassed about their bodies. Every body is beautiful. And each one tells a different story. I learned that from the great art teacher, Lorelei Leibovitch."

"Ha." She winks at him. "Sebastian, you're right. My body *is* beautiful," she says, feeling empowered. "Why have I been so shy and self-conscious about it my *entire* life?" She reaches behind her neck and unties her bikini top. "How many mimosas did I drink this morning?" she jokes, aware of her sudden bravery and exhibitionism. She laughs out loud, a beautiful bell-like sound, and the wispy bikini top floats to the floor. "That wasn't so hard," she says. Her red curls cascade onto her bare shoulders, her signature hoop earrings peeking out.

Sebastian uses a tool to make details in the clay. His eyes dart feverishly from Lorelei's body to the clay and back.

Lorelei hops off the stool and begins to peel off her bikini bottoms. She pauses for a moment. "I have a birth mark. My husband is the only one who's seen it. Well, and my parents." She thinks a moment. "A few doctors." She chuckles.

"Add me to the list!" Sebastian says, and they erupt into laughter.

# Chapter 49

Rishika and Katherine have moved to the swimming pool. They lie in the shallow sunning area that is just a few inches deep, cooling their sunbaked bodies in the water. They look like movie stars in their provocative bathing suits, giant sun hats and sunglasses.

"I'm kind of worried about Ashley," Rishika says. "She's so vulnerable right now, and this guy has her eating out of the palm of his hand."

"She's getting back on the horse. I think it's good for her," Katherine counters. "Coming off of Pierce's unfaithfulness, and her feeling unworthy and undesirable, a sexy tryst in Europe is exactly what she needs. And it doesn't get sexier than this."

They look over at Ashley and Andrick, who lie next to each other on chaise lounges. He says something that makes her laugh. Her contagious laughter causes him to join in and he grabs her hand.

"Besides," Katherine continues, "I think *he's* the one who's eating out of *her* hand. He seems to be really taken with her."

"Yeah," Rishika says, skeptical. "Maybe. But he's a one-night stand. I don't want her to be heartbroken. He has so easily swept her away with all of this. He's swept all four of us away with all of this. Come on. How often do you think this guy has his butlers run off to purchase swimwear for spontaneous guests? Or maybe he just keeps a stash in the closet."

Katherine shrugs. "I think he's nice." She smiles as she watches Andrick stand and open an umbrella over Ashley. "I really do."

\*\*\*

Plates of fresh fruit and fluffy omelettes folded into triangles rest on Andrick's and Ashley's laps. Andrick takes a bite of his omelette. "It seems that you are transitioning to a different chapter in your life. What do you want your future to look like?" he asks.

Ashley chuckles. "I feel like you ask me things people have never asked me before. Well, you ask me in a way I've never been asked before."

He waits for her to answer. She thinks about it.

"When I return home, I will start looking for a job. I'm not excited about it, but maybe it could be a good thing. I enjoyed that work once. I'll have to figure out how to juggle things, how to keep things as consistent as I can for the kids. I guess when we figure out the custody, I'll have some time by myself to fill. I think I'll want to fill that time. It will be strange to not have the kids with me. It will be sad, I think." She offers a sad smile. "Are you sorry you asked?"

"Of course not."

"I guess I haven't allowed myself to picture what my new life will bring. I am getting a little more used to the idea. It's beginning to not feel so scary." Andrick nods and squeezes her hand, supportively. "Actually, recent evidence shows that there are still amazing things in store for me."

They smile at each other.

"Of course there are. There's room for new dreams and plans."

"Mmm," she muses, hopeful. "I believe you're right."

"Is there room for me in that future?"

His question surprises her a little. She wants to say yes, but she looks at him tenderly and shrugs. "I don't know."

"Why don't you stay with me?" He sits up on the lounge chair and swings his legs around to face her. "We can get to know each other better and have some time to figure it out."

"I really wish I could," Ashley says. She thinks about it. "I desperately wish I could. But I told you why we need to get to Greece."

"No. I understand. I wouldn't talk you out of doing that. But come back afterwards. Or I'll come and meet you."

Ashley laughs. "I have kids."

"And I have kids. We can introduce them to each other and they can become friends. We'll take them skiing in the Alps and snorkeling in the Great Barrier Reef."

Ashley wants to laugh, but she can see that Andrick is actually serious. Ashley puts her hand on his. "That sounds amazing. Really, it does. But, I have to get back to the real world."

"This is real, isn't it?"

"I have to get back to my real world."

Andrick lets out a heavy-hearted exhale. He folds his hands with his forearms on his thighs and looks down at the floor. It saddens Ashley to see him look so disappointed.

"Andrick," Ashley begins, her tone serious. "Can I ask you what you like about me?"

# Chapter 50

The ladies aren't sure which would be worse, doing the walk of shame back to their hotel in ball gowns or skimpy bathing suits. Gustav goes in their place to retrieve their luggage so they won't have to decide. In the comfort of the yacht, they shower, primp and dress in sundresses and sandals.

Andrick and Sebastian escort the ladies down the ramp to the marina and to the limo where their suitcases wait. Andrick insisted that his driver take the ladies to the train station, and Ashley insisted that this is where they would all say goodbye. She knows that holding Andrick's hand driving to the train station together would have been torture.

"Poor Ashley," Katherine whispers to Rishika. "She looks like she's seen a ghost."

Ashley is very quiet. She has been since Andrick answered her question. *What do you like about me?* A simple question, but the answer was the most beautiful thing she's ever heard. She was an idiot to ask it because she already knew that this relationship has no future. Hearing Andrick's honest words, hearing the image of her through his eyes, broke her heart, and she is certain that if she and Andrick tried, she would fall more and more for him. And when the logistics just didn't work and they failed, it would crush her. And she can't take that. She has already been through enough.

Ashley and Andrick face each other, hand in hand. Ashley looks like she could cry at any moment. "This has been incredible," she says softly. *"You* are incredible."

"Ashley."

She hears the affection that he has for her when he merely says her name.

"I'll miss you," she says. "Thank you for being so sweet. I enjoyed seeing myself through your eyes. I really needed that."

He wraps his arms around her. "You're exquisite," he whispers. "I want so much happiness for you." She kisses him so strongly that tears spring to her eyes.

Rishika feels uncomfortable at witnessing this exchange. She doesn't hear the words, but she sees the passion, and it's like watching a movie. How could something so over the top be real? For God's sake, they just met. Ashley doesn't need another defeat. This is not good at all, and Rishika has had instincts against it from the beginning.

Closer to the limo, Sebastian gives Lorelei a hug. "My muse." She smiles. "You've inspired my most honest piece ever. I feel rejuvenated."

"*I* feel rejuvenated. Thank you."

"Remember how beautiful you are."

"I will. Remember how gifted you are."

Andrick and Ashley join the group at the limo. They hold hands.

As they all stand facing each other, a strange energy hangs between the group. The ladies just had the time of their lives with these perfect strangers, a grand adventure on a yacht in Monaco. Yet it's overshadowed by an air of melancholy. The two gentleman are equally hesitant to let them go.

"Thank you so much for having us, Andrick," Katherine says. "I'll never forget this experience."

"We've had a blissful time," Lorelei says.

"Thank you for your wonderful hospitality," Rishika echoes.

"It has been my great pleasure," he says. Rishika, Katherine and Lorelei look at Ashley when he says this.

He grabs Ashley's face and gives her a simple and sweet kiss on the lips and then one on each of her hands. "Goodbye."

\*\*\*

They ride silently in the limo. They all look out the windows as they drive away from Port Hercule, the sun dancing on the glittering dark blue-green waters.

"Why did you do that?" Katherine asks.

"Do what?" Ashley asks.

Katherine makes a face. "Sabotage that."

"Can it be more than just a vacation fling?" Ashley asks.

The divider of the limo is down and Henri stares straight ahead at the road.

"We all know it was more than that. We all felt it. He's amazing, Ash."

Ashley closes her eyes as a tear escapes. "I know he is. But what am I going to do, FaceTime a man who lives in a different hemisphere? Do you think I want to get my hopes up and get hurt again? I was being realistic. You have no idea how much I want Andrick." Her voice drops to a whisper. "I was being realistic."

"What about that thing we said at the Hofbrauhaus?" Lorelei asks. "Europe is magical. Anything is possible."

"Europe *is* magical," Ashley agrees. "But we don't live in Europe."

# Chapter 51

The silence continues, and it fills up the room of their private train cabin. Eventually, their very late night gets the best of them and they each succumb to sleep.

The cabin is hot from the sun baking through the window and Lorelei begins to stir. She sits up sluggishly to find Ashley staring out the window. Rishika and Katherine enter their cabin carrying cardboard cups of coffee and sandwiches wrapped in plastic wrap.

"Thanks," Ashley says.

"Oh, thank you," Lorelei says as she stretches. "Goodness, I needed that nap."

Katherine sips from a can of ginger ale. She didn't purchase a sandwich for herself. "Why on earth did you let me eat all of those chocolate crepes? You were not looking out for me."

Rishika laughs. "I tried. But you were not hearing me." She takes a bite of her sandwich and turns to Lorelei with a devilish smile. "Hey. How have we still not talked about Sebastian? Were you a bad girl?"

"Whatever do you mean?" Lorelei asks innocently.

"Spill it."

"Of course not. I'm Adam's girl to the bitter end. We talked about art and exchanged our own insights about how the other can improve. That's all. It was inspiring."

"Okay, okay," Rishika concedes. "Inspiring, indeed."

They eat and sip their coffees in silence.

Finally, Katherine asks, "You okay, Ash?"

Ashley shrugs and smiles, a smile that indicates she is not happy, but appreciative of her friend's concern. "I'm okay. I think I did the grown-up thing by recognizing that a relationship with a man who lives halfway around the world would not likely work." And then she adds under her breath, "But gosh, I wish it could."

"I think you're right," Rishika remarks. "Besides, you just got out of an eighteen-year relationship. I think you need to take a beat and become independent again."

"She's independent," Lorelei remarks, defending her.

"I don't mean that in a condescending way. I just mean that you've been a part of a unit for so long, perhaps you need to just be you for a while. Don't you think you need a little time before you're ready to move on?"

"My marriage has been over for a while now. I think I'd like to move on."

"Pierce moved on," Katherine points out. "Why shouldn't she?"

"Besides," Lorelei says, "Andrick is wonderful. How are we to control the timing of when we meet the right people? Ashley, I don't think you should miss this opportunity. He's *wonderful.*"

"I'm with Lorelei," Katherine agrees. "Andrick is God's gift to women. And he's crazy about you, Ashley! You should call him right away."

"I didn't get his number. Or give him mine."

There is a moment of silence. Katherine and Lorelei look at each other.

"Are you crazy?" Lorelei screeches.

"Oh, do not worry about that." Katherine whips her phone out.

"I'm on it." After a moment, Katherine has located Andrick's Facebook and Instagram pages. "Here you go. You can message him right now if you want to." She hands Ashley the phone. "Do it, do it, do it," she chants.

"I'm sorry," Rishika jumps in. "I hate to be a downer about this whole thing. Andrick *is* a catch. He seems to be the whole package and more. But, come on. He's too good to be true. Didn't anyone else think it was strange how head over heels he seemed about Ashley so quickly? If it *was* sincere, is it possible that he's one of those men that falls in love really easily and then falls out of love just as easily? When the next incredible woman turns his head, will he ditch Ashley and fall in love with her?"

The feeling in the train cabin dramatically changes. Any pep in Ashley's attitude visibly deflates.

Katherine shoots daggers at Rishika with her eyes. "Stop shitting on her love story," Katherine attempts quietly.

"I'm just trying to protect her," Rishika loud whispers back.

Ashley closes her eyes, annoyed. "I can hear you both. It's fine."

"Ignore her," Lorelei says.

"It's fine."

***

After hours of the ladies sliding in and out of sleep, nibbling on snacks, staring out the windows in silence as they listen to music on their phones, the terrain outside begins to change. Rolling hills are now dotted with olive trees and vineyards.

Lorelei sketches the countryside. Sebastian gave her a lot to think about. He's right, she knows more than she did as a young woman in her early twenties. She is so much wiser. And maybe before this she hasn't seen much of the world, but beauty is everywhere, not just in Europe. However, recognizing beauty isn't her problem. It's creating it. She told Sebastian to dig deeper. How can *she* do that? It's so much easier said than done. It's okay, though. If she's not meant to be a renowned artist, that's okay. She's not going to put pressure on herself. She's going to sketch and paint because she loves to. Even if it sucks.

For the first time on their trip, Katherine is not working during their train ride. She simply stares out the window. They pass a beautiful ivory villa with a long gravel driveway lined with cypress trees. "We're in Italy," she says, expressionless.

The others look out at the Italian countryside. In the distance, what looks like an old castle sits atop a hill.

"Italy. Oh, my goodness, I can't wait," Lorelei says.

"It's so lovely," Rishika remarks.

"If I knew it would've taken me this long to return, I might not have left." Katherine doesn't say this wistfully. She says it regretfully.

Rishika turns to her. "Oh, my gosh. You're thinking about Italian Guy."

"Who's Italian Guy?" Lorelei asks.

"Don't you remember?" Rishika asks. Lorelei shakes her head, looking so in the dark. "Katherine fell in love with an Italian guy when we were here. Like, head over heels in love. At the end of our trip, when Ashley, Anna and I flew home from Greece, Katherine came back to Rome and spent the rest of the summer with him."

"Really?" Lorelei asks, flabbergasted.

"You didn't know that?" Rishika asks.

Lorelei shakes her head and shrugs.

"I forgot about that!" Ashley exclaims, momentarily coming out of her Andrick slump.

Katherine sighs. She continues to look out the window. "His name was Francesco…"

"Yes, that's it! Francesco!" Ashley interrupts.

"…and, he was one of my true loves. But I was starting law school that fall. I was going to return to Rome the following summer and each summer until law school was over. That was our plan."

Lorelei is dumbstruck. "How do I not know about this? This is huge."

"You were probably busy taking Lamaze classes," Rishika says flippantly. What sounds like a dig to Lorelei, is only intended as the honest truth. Lorelei fell off the face of the earth when she had Phoebe. And the rest of her friends were nowhere near having kids, so at the time, they didn't get it.

"You had a lot on your mind," Ashley says gently.

"Right." Gosh. Lorelei really did miss a lot that happened during that trip, Lorelei thinks. Until this moment, she thought she had just missed having experiences of her own. She didn't realize that she also missed important moments in her friends' lives. How did she not even know about one of Katherine's true loves? She thinks back to that summer when she was seven months pregnant preparing to have a baby right out of college. She *was* in her own little world. And when Phoebe came it was even worse. The first month was all about trying to successfully breastfeed and squeeze in a little nap for herself when she could. And Phoebe had horrible reflux and colic. Lorelei was submerged in a fog of minimal sleep and the scary reality of just trying to keep a little human alive. There was no time to think about anyone else. She turns her attention to Katherine. "What happened?"

"He told me he would wait for me. We wrote letters. We called occasionally. Communication wasn't as easy as it is now. There was no Skype or FaceTime. I didn't even have a cell phone yet. But you can't just kind of commit to law school. I fully immersed myself in it. It was my priority. And then I met James. And, you know, law school and James became a package deal. I was immersed in him, too." She shakes her head. "I just abruptly stopped contact with

Francesco. He had no idea what happened."

"Why?" Lorelei asks.

"What could I do? Write him a letter that I met someone else?"

Ashley and Rishika look at each other. "That might have been fair," Rishika offers.

"I couldn't," Katherine says. "He kept writing for a while. And eventually he stopped."

"Is he still in Rome?" Lorelei asks, dying for more information.

"I have no idea."

"Are you going to look for him?"

Katherine scoffs. "No." The intonation goes up at the end. What Katherine intends to sound like a preposterous notion sounds more like a question.

"Have you been thinking about him this whole trip?" Rishika asks.

Katherine blows out a heavy breath of air.

"Shit, Katherine."

"Off and on," Katherine says a little defensively. "I've been trying to avoid the thought of him. When I was planning our route, I wondered if it would be best not to go to Rome at all. But I couldn't do that to you guys. And in a way, I've been waiting to return for twenty years."

# Chapter 52

The ladies disembark the train at the Roma Termini Train Station and take the metro to Campo de' Fiori where they take a short walk to the famous square of the same name. The sky is dark, but the square is lit up and busy as the night life gets underway.

"I did some research on the train," Lorelei begins. "This square is historic. Back in the Middle Ages, this area was a meadow of flowers, which is what Campo de' Fiori translates to. The first church here was built in the late fourteenth century. Later it was used for commercial use, like horse sales. There were actually public executions! Uh, somewhere around here… Okay, there it is." She points to the far side of the square. "That's the Statue of Giordano Bruno, a philosopher who was burned *alive* for heresy," she says with amazement.

"That's horrible," Ashley comments.

"Now there are tents set up daily for a market. Just buy your groceries where someone was burned alive at the stake! Isn't that crazy?"

Rishika smiles at Lorelei's enthusiasm. "It *is* absolutely amazing the extent of history that we're in the presence of. There need to be more movies set here. I need to think on that."

They check into their suite at a boutique hotel. The living room is gift-wrapped like a fancy present with green wallpaper with gold-leaf jacquard. A gold and crystal chandelier dangles from the ceiling over a mustard velvet settee and two velvet wingback chairs. The two bedrooms have tufted velvet headboards, elegant coffered ceilings and wall sconces. Small chestnut writing desks in each bedroom invite you to sit down and write on postcards containing photos of the Sistine Chapel and St. Peter's Basilica to send home to loved ones. Outside, an awning shades a small balcony, where a pot of red geraniums sits on the wall with vines hanging down. The attractive space welcomes you to sit on two dark brown rattan chairs and enjoy the view of Campo de' Fiori. The ladies run around clapping their hands together in their anticipation of enjoying this beautiful suite and drinking coffee on the balcony in the morning.

It's late, though. They had a leisurely morning basking in the sun on Andrick's yacht. It's crazy that they were there only this morning. The eight-hour train ride filled up the rest of the day. They opt for dinner at a ristorante just across the square where they dine on fantastic chicken cacciatore and spaghetti. They retire to bed, Ashley and Rishika in one room and Lorelei and Katherine in the other, to rest up for all they will attempt to pack in during their stay in this glorious city.

***

At eight o'clock the next morning, Rishika, the early riser, returns from a jog, which included several sets up the legendary Spanish Steps, to find the ladies still sleeping. She bursts into the room that Lorelei and Katherine are sleeping in. "Buongiorno! Rome is awake and you're missing it!"

Ashley shuffles into their bedroom sleepily to see what the commotion is. "What's going on?"

Katherine and Lorelei sit up in bed and rub their eyes.

Rishika holds a box.

"Up and at 'em, ladies. I got us cream buns for breakfast. To the balcony!"

The sleepyheads drag two more chairs out to the balcony as Rishika distributes the goods.

"What, pray tell, is this?" Katherine asks, intrigued, when Rishika passes her a thick piece of bread with an equally thick layer of what looks like white frosting.

"I came across a *pasticceria*," Rishika says with an exaggerated accent, "and this is, apparently, the thing to eat for breakfast around here. It's sweet bread with whipped cream on it, and it's definitely not paleo."

"Wow." Lorelei opens her mouth wide to bite into it. "It's lovely," she says after a few chews.

"Thanks, Rishika," Ashley says.

"Sorry I didn't deliver caffeine. The lady in the pasticceria instructed me to drink espresso with the cream buns to cut the richness, but I forgot that you can't get espresso to-go in Rome. So, sorry, I had my espresso already. I had generous intentions."

"Ugh, and there's no coffee maker in the room," Katherine pouts. She likes her coffee immediately upon waking.

"I guess that's what's wrong with Italy," Ashley comments sleepily.

"Well, culturally, Italians take their espresso together in the bars. Bars are what we would call cafes," Katherine explains to Lorelei. "Italians like their espresso super hot so they would never walk around with it and drink it leisurely like we do. They either stand and drink it quickly at the counter or sit. I think it's a lovely custom. It encourages socializing." To Katherine, Italy is perfect. There is absolutely nothing wrong with it, except, of course, that it led her to a broken heart.

# Chapter 53

It's a warm and humid day, and the ladies move from the Forum to Circus Maximus to the Colosseum. They use their imaginations to fill in the blanks of the ruins and attempt to visualize what it all looked like during it's prime.

Despite the fact that three of these four ladies have seen the Colosseum before, they are still beyond impressed. As they walk around the various levels, Katherine reads facts off of her phone. "Dating back to 70 AD, the Colosseum used to house up to eighty thousand people. The things that used to occur here! Executions, competitions, religious events, and re-enactments of wars. The floor was sometimes flooded for mock sea battles. The Colosseum still stands with about one third of its travertine rock in place, with the exception of what has been lost over the years to stone robbers, rock taken for building materials and damage from earthquakes. "

"Absolutely incredible," Lorelei remarks as she takes countless photos. "Can you imagine being here for some of those events?"

As they stand looking out across the lower level of the Colosseum, Ashley feels so moved by the immensity of it. She experiences such a strong pang of missing Andrick. She wishes that he could be here, that they could see this together, that they could share many more moments, big and small.

\*\*\*

They walk down the street towards the Spanish Steps, their last destination before they will head back to the hotel for a little siesta and then out again for a late dinner, or rather what is customary in Italy. Katherine stops and stares across the street at a restaurant.

"What is it?" Lorelei asks.

Katherine is frozen. "That's it. Where Francesco worked."

"I *knew* it was around here somewhere," Rishika says.

"Rishika," Ashley chastises.

"As if I could ever forget," Katherine utters darkly.

"You have to see if he's there," Rishika says.

"I don't think I can." Katherine starts blowing out panicky breaths.

Lorelei watches Katherine, perplexed. It's so strange to see her like this. Katherine is and has always been the even-keeled one. The one who has everything under control. This guy, who Katherine hasn't seen since she was a young woman, has her completely losing her cool.

"Come on," Lorelei says. "What are the chances that he still works here after all this time?"

"It was his family's restaurant," Katherine answers.

"Oh. Then you have to go in there! You've waited two decades for this opportunity!"

"And what? I'm married, and I'm sure he's married, too. We've both moved on."

"That's good. It's no big deal, then," Lorelei concludes.

"It doesn't sound like you *have* totally moved on," Rishika says. Katherine looks sharply at Rishika. "I'm not trying to rock the boat here. Just..." Rishika sighs and softens. "Katherine, if you don't go in there, you're going to wonder about Francesco for another twenty

239

years. That sounds like torture to me. You've got to finish it."

"I don't know," Ashley says. "What good can come from this?"

"Closure," Rishika retaliates. "For both of them. Doesn't sound like he ever got it, either."

"Closure would probably be a good thing," Ashley agrees, cautiously.

"Which would be worse, Katherine?" Rishika asks. "Seeing Francesco or missing the opportunity to see Francesco?"

Katherine looks pained. "I'm honestly not sure."

# Chapter 54

"Come on, come on," Lorelei encourages and grabs her hand, inching her across the cobblestone street. "You'll just be an old friend saying hello."

"Be the bigger person," Rishika says. "You kind of owe him this."

Katherine looks at Rishika and nods.

She tentatively walks into the restaurant and the ladies follow her. They stop just inside the entrance. The restaurant is a classic trattoria. Each table is dressed with a simple white tablecloth, a small vase holding a few daisies, and a bottle each of olive oil and balsamic vinegar.

A waiter comes out of the kitchen. He's young and gorgeous. Katherine breathes in sharply and freezes.

"That *can't* be him," Lorelei announces to no one in particular.

Katherine walks up to the young man. "Scuse."

"Si?" the handsome young man says.

"Um, conosce Francesco Moretti?"

"Si. He is my father," he answers with a beautiful Italian accent.

"That makes more sense," Lorelei states.

"Wow. That explains the crazy resemblance," Katherine says and laughs nervously. Rishika, Ashley and Lorelei smile in the background. "Okay. Is he here?"

"No," he says. Katherine nods, both disappointed and relieved. "But he should be back very soon. Would you like to wait?"

"Yes!" Lorelei, Rishika and Ashley chime in simultaneously.

Katherine manages an embarrassed smile. "He was a good friend of mine a long time ago. My name is Katherine."

The young man extends his hand warmly and she shakes it. "I am Matteo. It is wonderful to meet a friend of my father's. Please sit down."

Moments later, Matteo has them sitting at a large round table drinking Chianti and dipping bread in olive oil.

"I think I could just drink this olive oil," Lorelei says, astounded.

"It's better than our olive oil," Rishika says. "And so is this bread."

"What else can I get you while you wait, some pasta?" Matteo asks.

"This is perfect, thank you," Katherine says.

He nods and leaves to tend to other tables.

As he walks away, Katherine exhales. "This is a mistake. We've been sightseeing all day. I'm gross. We're leaving." She stands up.

"No!" Lorelei says.

"Sit back down," Rishika says.

"You know," Katherine says, pointing at Rishika, "I'm getting tired of your bossiness." Rishika raises her hands in surrender, and Katherine sits back down.

Rishika fishes through her purse and pulls out a little makeup bag. Without warning, she spritzes Katherine with a small bottle of honeysuckle body spray. "Here's a mint," she says as she drops one into Katherine's hand. She hands her a compact and lip gloss. "This and this, and you're good."

"Thank you."

They all dip bread in olive oil in silence while Katherine primps.

"It's so strange that we're here," Rishika comments as she looks around.

"Uh, yeah. Obviously," Katherine says shortly as she closes the compact.

"I know it's weird for you. But, we all spent a lot of time in this restaurant that week. Francesco's family was so nice to us."

Ashley nods. "They really were."

"His parents don't seem to be here," Rishika remarks. "That's sad."

"A lot changes in twenty years," Katherine concludes.

Lorelei pats Katherine's hand. "Tell me how you and Francesco met."

Katherine takes a breath and relaxes. "Well, the four of us came here for dinner on our very first night in Rome. We stumbled across this place as we were headed to see the Spanish Steps. We sat—" Katherine points at a table in the middle of the restaurant—"there, and Francesco was our waiter."

"God, he was hot," Rishika interrupts.

"We all liked him," Ashley admits, "but we could tell almost immediately that he had eyes for Katherine."

Katherine smiles.

"When we were done eating, he left his shift early and took us to the Spanish Steps himself." Katherine sighs, deeply, and turns to Ashley and Rishika. "Do you remember what it felt like to see the Spanish Steps for the first time?"

They both smile at her and nod.

"Overwhelming," Rishika says.

"Magical," Ashley agrees.

"When I looked up at the steps, I felt Francesco's hand slip into mine and..." Her shoulders rise suddenly, and she breaks from her story. "I just got chills thinking about it. I knew he was going to be someone special to me."

"Katerina?" a beautiful, deep voice says. Katherine's eyes widen.

243

All four of the ladies look up and there is Francesco, handsome and distinguished with thick black hair and eyebrows and kind eyes the color of the boldest espresso. He has strong shoulders and wears a classy sports coat and jeans. He seeps Italian sexiness.

"Holy shit," escapes Lorelei's lips. Ashley elbows her. "He's even hotter than the young one." Ashley elbows her again. "Ouch! Stop it!"

Katherine and Francesco stare at each other.

"Francesco," Katherine says with a hint of pain, but also wonder at seeing him again. She rises from her chair.

"Katerina," he shakes his head like he can't believe it.

Katherine and Francesco rush to each other and embrace. He lifts her off her feet and spins her around. The ladies look at each other, wide-eyed.

"Holy shit," Lorelei repeats.

"You already said that," Ashley whispers.

"It still applies," she whispers back.

"What are you doing here?" Francesco asks.

"I'm traveling through Europe with my friends," Katherine says. "You remember Rishika and Ashley." The three ladies stand up and smile.

"Of course! Ciao!" He steps towards Rishika and Ashley, one at a time, and kisses them on both cheeks.

"It's really good to see you," Rishika says. She's surprised how happy she is to see him. It's funny how you can go decades without even thinking about someone, and then being in their presence feels really good. Francesco was always a really nice guy, dynamic and fun.

"And this is Lorelei," Katherine says.

"Piacere." He follows suit with Lorelei.

"It's very nice to meet you," Lorelei effuses.

"Where is the other one? The teddy bear?" Francesco asks. They look at each other.

"Anna," Katherine responds. "Um." She looks at her friends. "She died about a month and a half ago. Of brain cancer."

Francesco's smile falls. "Oh, no. I am so sorry. That is a tragedy." He shakes his head. "She was a beautiful woman. It's funny, I remember her perfectly. She was so funny, so full of life." The ladies look at each other and smile.

"You remember her as the teddy bear?" Lorelei asks, touched.

"Si. She was so little, and whenever she saw me, she would throw open her arms and offer me this huge soft hug. She was like a little cuddly teddy bear. So friendly. So welcoming."

"That was totally her," Lorelei muses.

"How are you?" Katherine asks.

"Perfetto." Francesco grabs her again and pulls her into another embrace. "It's so good to see you. I can't believe you're here. You're like a vision." He holds her at arm's length and smiles at her.

Katherine smiles, her cheeks rosy.

"Please. Let's sit. Matteo!" Francesco calls.

Matteo appears. "Si, Papa?"

"Bring us some food. Lots of food. My American friends have returned."

# Chapter 55

The table is covered with a carafe of Chianti and plates of various starters, which they feast upon as they catch up. There is prosciutto and figs, deep-fried zucchini flowers stuffed with mozzarella, a frittata with peppers and potato, and piselli con prosciutto. The latter is green peas, onions and prosciutto sauteed in butter and sprinkled with mint.

"I've died and gone to heaven," Lorelei says.

"Pass me those figs, please," Rishika says and Ashley does so.

Ashley, Rishika, and Lorelei eat with gusto while Katherine and Francesco gaze at each other.

"You are married," Francesco says, eyeing Katherine's wedding ring.

"Yes," Katherine answers.

"Of course," Francesco says, as if it is a given that she would be.

"I have eleven-year-old twin boys," Katherine continues. "Brice and Beckham." Francesco nods. "And Matteo, how old is he?"

"Eighteen."

"Wow. So, not long after we lost touch."

"Lost touch." Francesco puts his glass of wine down. "Yes. I had to move on with my life."

Katherine's shoulders visibly slump. Rishika, Ashley and Lorelei look at each other, uncomfortable with the tension in the conversation, uncomfortable for Katherine, uncomfortable for poor Francesco who was dumped without any explanation.

"Matteo is so handsome," Ashley says.

"Grazie," Francesco says.

"Are we going to meet your lovely wife?" she continues and takes a bite of crusty bread.

"Sadly, my wife died four years ago."

Ashley coughs on the bread. She holds her hand up, signaling that she'll be okay.

Katherine slaps her on the back. "My condolences. I'm so very sorry to hear that."

***

Francesco walks the ladies outside.

"That food was incredible," Lorelei gushes. "The fried zucchini flowers were beyond!"

"Grazie, grazie," Francesco says proudly. "Please come back anytime. You will always be family here."

"It was such a pleasure meeting you, Francesco." Lorelei offers both hands and Francesco takes them both warmly.

"It was wonderful to see you again." Rishika gives Francesco a huge hug.

Ashley follows suit. "You were always so good to us."

"Oh, ladies, it is always good to see old friends. I am so very happy to see you again. And I am truly sad to hear about Anna. Please come back while you are here."

"Ciao," Katherine says. Her energy is difficult to read. "Thank you." She exhales. "Francesco."

"Katerina, would it be alright if we had a little time together? I would like to speak to you alone."

She looks at her friends. Rishika and Lorelei nod at her, like, *Of course, what are you waiting for?* Ashley looks apprehensive.

"Of course. When?"

"How about now?"

"Okay. Um."

Rishika jumps in. "We need to show Lorelei the Trevi Fountain. We'll see you back at the hotel. Ciao, Francesco."

"Ciao, bella."

# Chapter 56

Katherine and Francesco walk down a Roman street. He keeps looking over at her, smiling. "I keep thinking you're a mirage."

"I know what you mean."

"It took you a lot longer to return than I had anticipated."

Katherine looks ashamed. "I know. I'm sorry."

"More than twenty years have passed since I received a letter or a phone call from you." He stops walking and grabs her hands. There is a sadness in his eyes. "What took you so long?"

"My life took a turn and I…"

"Katerina," Francesco interrupts. "Let's not beat around the bush. Haven't we done that long enough?"

She nods. "Yes. The truth is, I met James… and I was a coward. There's no excuse for it. I couldn't bear to tell you that I met someone and that I wasn't coming back."

"Why couldn't you tell me? Not knowing what happened was hard for me. It was hard for me to move on. When I met Angelina, she had to work hard to break down those walls."

"I'm so sorry. I don't know. Maybe because I knew that if I talked to you, you would try to talk me out of it. Maybe I knew I would *let* you talk me out of it. And I realized which direction I wanted my life to go."

Francesco nods.

"I was determined to get my law degree in America…"

"And marry James," Francesco finishes for her.

"Yes," she says quietly.

"It's okay. It looks like life turned out how it was supposed to. I loved my wife very much. Angelina was beautiful and kind. She was my angel on earth, now she's my angel up above. She gave me four children and we have one grandson."

This makes Katherine smile. "What? You're a grandfather? I can't believe it!"

"Well, Matteo is somewhat of a Casanova."

"Hmmm. I can picture it."

He elbows her, playfully. Katherine slips her arm companionably through Francesco's. They walk along in contented silence and approach the Spanish Steps.

She smiles. "I knew you would bring me here." She takes in the view for a moment. "Wow," she breathes in awe. "This is one of my favorite places in the whole entire world. I can't believe I'm here again. After what feels like a lifetime." A tear runs down her face. "It brings so much back."

"Katerina." He wipes her tear away. "Don't cry."

"I didn't know I was going to."

"Let's sit." Francesco leads her up several steps and they sit, surrounded by other couples and tourists.

"It was hard for me, too," Katherine says. "You were really special to me. I knew that James was right for me, but it didn't take away the love that I had for you." She looks at him with sad, wistful eyes.

His own dark brown eyes are intense and serious. They hold hurt and love. He takes her hand with both of his and holds it in his lap as if it is something so precious. "Time has been good to you. You look just the same."

"Oh." She smooths her hair. "I look a mess! I've been all over this city today." She smiles at him. "You look the same, too."

Francesco looks at Katherine's face thoughtfully.

"I think I should walk you back to your hotel. But if your friends will allow, I would like to see you one more time before you go."

Katherine nods. "How about we meet for an espresso in the morning?"

"Caffe, a trip around the world… Whatever you suggest, I would not refuse you."

# Chapter 57

Katherine pushes a tomato around her plate from her caprese salad tower.

Rishika has found a hot new restaurant known for its new spin on Roman classics and its inventive desserts. With their usual planner preoccupied with thoughts of her old flame, Rishika has taken over.

"The Trevi Fountain was something out of a dream. Now, when I hear 'Three Coins in the Fountain,' I'll know what Frank Sinatra was singing about. Katherine, we'll have to go back so you can go."

"I've been there before," Katherine says, shortly.

"Right." Lorelei casts a glance at Rishika, who raises her eyebrows.

"So, Lorelei, how is Phoebe feeling?" Ashley asks.

"Horrible morning sickness. Well, all-day sickness, really. We all know it's not just in the morning."

"Poor thing," Ashley replies. "But, it's all worth it. With the sacrifices come a lifetime of love."

"It's true," Lorelei agrees. "I haven't even thought about how a sweet new little life will be coming our way. It's just the timing and the drastic life changes and sacrifices for Phoebe I can't wrap my head around."

They are interrupted by the noisy breaking of a crusty roll. Katherine focuses on it as she swirls a hunk around in her dish of olive oil.

"Katherine," Rishika says.

"Hmm?" She looks up.

"Where's your head at with this whole Francesco thing?"

She shakes her head and exhales. "I don't know. I'm troubled. We're meeting for coffee in the morning."

"Why?" Ashley asks. "I thought you were going to get your closure today. I thought you were going to give him closure."

"Come on. We all know closure doesn't occur within one conversation. You of all people understand that, I'm sure."

"Are you comparing closure of my eleven-year marriage to closure of a relationship that ended twenty years ago?"

Katherine looks at her sharply. "I may not have been married to Francesco, but, with a few different turns in my life, I might have been. That's what's so hard. I'm seeing the other option. Francesco and all of this." She waves her hands around to indicate Rome itself. "It hurts my heart. It's like I can see my twenty-two-year-old self over there, and part of me wants to tell her, 'Don't leave.'"

Ashley's eyes widen. "Do you really mean that? Not leaving would mean that you wouldn't have met James, wouldn't have married him, wouldn't have had Beckham and Brice. Do you really wish your life had turned out differently?" When Katherine hesitates, Ashley throws her hands up in the air. "I'm flabbergasted, Katherine. You have a wonderful life—a successful and fulfilling career, great kids, and a husband who would do anything for you. How can you imply that you would have chosen Francesco over all of that?"

"I don't know. I mean, I don't mean *that*. I'm just thrown. It's like I'm looking back on that moment that I got on that plane that took me away from here, and I can see so clearly that it was the crossroads of my life. Obviously, I didn't know that at the time, but, in retrospect, it was the single moment that changed my life forever."

For a moment they all ponder this.

"Of course I love my life and my family, but I also suddenly long for the life that I might have had here. With Francesco."

"You loved him that much?" Lorelei asks.

"Oh, God, yes."

"He's very different from you," Lorelei comments. "What attracted you to him?"

"Well, initially, it was physical chemistry and sparks that wouldn't quit. I'm serious." She shrugs. "I was twenty-two. But he was also really kind. I could tell by observing him at the restaurant that he was devoted to his family. We always had so much to talk about. We wanted to know everything about each other. Our personalities were really complementary, and we just clicked. He was a hard worker, and he looked forward to the day he would take over his family's restaurant. That was expected of him, and he was perfectly happy with that.

"On the flip side, James has always had the desire to keep climbing. James and I had the same career goals and we began to strive for them together. I admired him from the start and always wanted to know what he was thinking."

Ashley shakes her head and stabs two gnocchi with her fork. *Now we're comparing Francesco and James?*

"It's like James has always inspired me to push and climb, and with Francesco, I was able to stand still. In a beautiful way."

"What do you think a life with Francesco would've looked like?" Rishika asks.

"I suppose we would have worked side by side in the restaurant."

Ashley interrupts her. "Sweetie, you are a dynamo in the courtroom. You would have preferred to be a waitress?" Lorelei narrows her eyebrows at Ashley. "I'm not trying to be condescending. I just mean that you're a successful lawyer. You've been working every free moment that you've had here since we got on the plane. You love your work. The other life would have been so different." She raises her hands in surrender. "I don't think it would have been enough for you."

"I know, but isn't it possible that I could've been divinely happy living a simpler life here in this magical city with a man I loved and our children? Maybe I wouldn't be stressed out all the time. Maybe *I* would be the one attending the boys' school functions and not Shu or my mother-in-law."

"I think that's a matter of you achieving work-life balance at home, not contemplating the parallel life that you didn't choose," Ashley argues.

Katherine waves away the notion with her hands. "Of course, of course. I'm fine. This has just been very traumatic and strange."

"Yeah," Rishika agrees with weight.

Lorelei nods supportively.

Ashley chews her gnocchi without making eye contact. *I have a really bad feeling about this.*

# Chapter 58

Katherine and Francesco meet at a bar across the street from his trattoria.

As soon as her eyes meet his, she feels that the energy is different than yesterday. There is something wrong. He's sitting at a table and stands to greet her.

"Buongiorno," he says, but his tone is detached.

"Buongiorno," Katherine returns. "How are you?"

"I am fine. Let's get some caffe and a pastry."

They do so and sit outside with their espresso and rolls as the morning business of Rome breathes around them. They sit in silence, in a painful awkwardness. Francesco lacks his usual warmth and charm, and to Katherine, it feels horrible.

"Francesco, what is going on?"

"Katherine, this is very insensitive of you."

*Katherine?*

"You broke my heart when we were kids. We spoke of a future together. We were in love. And then you disappeared from my life for what I thought was forever. I always wondered. It's not like I could just buy a plane ticket and track you down. I didn't have the money for that. And in my heart, I could feel it. I didn't feel like you'd been in an accident or you were sick and unable to write to me.

I sensed that you had cut yourself out of my life. How could you do that to someone that you supposedly loved?"

Katherine leans back in her seat, astonished by this outpouring. Just as she's about to respond, he continues.

"And now you waltz back into Roma after twenty years, come to my trattoria and assume that I'm going to forgive you. Just like that. Like time has healed everything. It is cruel for you to be here because you are going to break my heart again."

Katherine is floored. But, really, what did she expect? That time alone has healed his wounds? That the fact that they both married other people and moved on with their lives would rectify how she handled things? She isn't quite sure what to say. "I'm sorry. I didn't know you felt angry about it."

"Of course I feel angry about it. Do you know how long I've felt angry about it? Of course my impulse yesterday was happiness at seeing you again. But I was caught off guard. Again, you have the control. You knew you were coming. You were able to prepare yourself, but I just suddenly see you and I'm supposed to have my emotions ready? You broke my heart. I loved you."

"Francesco," Katherine says, overwhelmed.

"I would like to walk." He finishes his espresso in one decisive sip, stands and walks away from the table.

Stunned, Katherine sits at the table for a moment alone before realizing that she is being left. She knocks back her espresso, stuffs the bag of rolls into her purse, and stumbles after him.

"Francesco, wait."

"Now that I've had time to think about it, I'm angry," he says, a few steps ahead of her. "Do you think I slept last night?"

"I… I couldn't get you out of my mind either, and I'm sorry, I've been pretty self-centered about this. I haven't been thinking about your feelings. Then or now."

Francesco walks briskly ahead. "Please!" she shouts.

Francesco turns around and waits for her.

"I'm sorry. Francesco, I'm so sorry for all of it. For then and for yesterday. It didn't occur to me that I was catching you off guard because I was so consumed by how I was feeling. Every time I've gotten on a train in the last few weeks, I panicked because I knew I was getting closer to you."

"And why was that so bad?"

"Because I didn't just break your heart, I broke mine!" Katherine's composure cracks and shows the vulnerability that she's been hiding.

Francesco's face twitches, unreadable.

"I'm sorry, Francesco," she persists, almost begging. "All those years ago, I was a coward, and I wasn't thinking of you. I was only thinking that the path that I wanted couldn't include you, and I couldn't bear to tell you that. I was selfish and weak, and I don't expect you to forgive me, but my heart *wants* you to." She doesn't realize until now that tears are streaming down her face.

There in the middle of the cobblestone street with people meandering by, they just stand, hands at their sides, facing each other.

Francesco lets out a pained exhale.

"I didn't know if I should see you or not," Katherine continues. "I didn't know if I *wanted* to see you or not. Both would be torture, but which decision would I regret less? And now I realize that again I was only grappling with how my decision would affect me. I didn't take into consideration that interrupting your life would be a bad choice for you."

Francesco takes a few steps towards Katherine and takes both of her hands. "As difficult as it is, I never thought I would look into your eyes again. I never thought I would hold these hands. So I am glad for this moment." He brushes his thumb across Katherine's cheek to wipe away her tears. He smiles gently. "Let's find a place to eat our breakfast."

And so they walk to a bridge over the Tiber River where Katherine pulls the bag of rolls out of her purse and they begin to nibble on them and talk of other things.

Francesco speaks of his children—Matteo, Valentina, Giovanni, and Sofia. And Katherine tells him all about Beckham and Brice.

They fill each other in on twenty years of life—their marriages, Francesco's restaurant, Katherine's law career, and Francesco's first grandchild. As they share the things in their lives that they love, Francesco stops feeling resentful, Katherine stops feeling guilty, and the conversation flows out in the easy energy that they shared so long ago.

# Chapter 59

Hot and sweaty from a day in Vatican City seeing Saint Peter's Square, Saint Peter's Basilica, and the Sistine Chapel, the ladies, including Katherine, all reconvene back at the hotel to lounge and freshen up for dinner. Rishika, Lorelei and Ashley are happy that Katherine is at peace about her time with Francesco. She briefs them about how angry he was, how she apologized profusely, and that they now understand each other.

Lorelei has arranged for a cooking class by a well-known Roman chef. Once a week he leaves his restaurant and hosts the class in his very own home.

Ashley stands at the door holding her purse, wearing a flowy skirt, a white wrap top and wedge heels. "We should go, girls."

Lorelei and Rishika emerge, Lorelei in dressy jeans, a flowy floral kimono and platform sandals, and Rishika wearing black cigarette pants, a silky tank top and gold sandals that lace up her ankles.

Katherine appears with her makeup done and her hair pulled into a low casual chignon, but still wearing a silky robe.

"You're still not dressed?" Lorelei asks.

"Girls, I'm not going to go to the cooking class."

"Why not? Don't you feel well?" Lorelei asks.

Katherine hesitates. "I'm having dinner with Francesco."

Ashley gives her a sideways glance. "You just spent the whole day with him. I don't understand. First you didn't want to see the guy. Now you're spending all of your time with him. What's the goal here?"

"We… we still have a lot to talk about. We just need to talk about a lot of things."

"So, are you saying that the two of you need to talk some more?" Rishika quips. She pats Katherine on her shoulder as she walks out the door.

"Have fun and do what you need to do to get closure," Lorelei says, reassuringly.

Ashley hangs back for a moment. "Katherine," she says, her eyes intense. "Be careful."

\*\*\*

Lorelei looks at her phone as she, Ashley and Rishika approach an apartment. "This must be it."

Ashley knocks on the door. They hear chatter inside, footsteps, and then the door opens to reveal a gorgeous man in his early thirties dressed in a black chef coat and pants. His chestnut brown hair is short with bangs that swoop across his forehead. He has eyes that are almond-shaped and the color of dark chocolate, an arched nose, full lips, and a slight dark stubble covers his face.

"Buonasera," he greets with a wide smile. "I am Enzo, and I will be your chef tonight."

"Ciao," all three of them say with silly smiles. After they introduce themselves, they join the other students in the living room where they sip Aperol spritzes. Chef Enzo brings Ashley, Lorelei and Rishika their own glasses containing a combination of tangerine-colored Aperol, Prosecco and club soda.

After a few introductions, the ladies learn that the couples consist of a mother and eighteen-year-old daughter from Sydney, second-marriage honeymooners in their sixties from Phoenix, and a husband and wife from a suburb of Dublin celebrating the wife's fiftieth birthday.

As they socialize and continue to sip their aperitifs, Chef Enzo brings out trays of bruschetta and carciofi alla Romana, which is simply entire artichokes filled with parsley and garlic and cooked in olive oil. He then toasts to a lovely evening together and they head into the kitchen to begin.

Chef Enzo explains that he grew up in Rome and attended culinary school in Florence, but it was his dream to return to his hometown and run his own restaurant. He explains that as the bruschetta and artichokes illustrate, Roman cuisine is made with fresh and seasonal ingredients that are prepared simply. This evening they will learn how to make a Roman favorite, cacio e pepe, from scratch.

They all stand around a butcher-block island, each with a small pile of flour in front of them in which they form a well. They add an egg and use their fingers to mix and transform it into dough.

Being the domestic goddess that Ashley is, she completes her task quickly and perfectly. She, of course, has made her children and foolish soon-to-be ex-husband homemade pasta many times.

Chef Enzo walks around observing his guests and comes up behind Ashley.

"Excellente," he praises her.

They share a smile, which causes Rishika to raise her eyebrows at Lorelei.

"Alora, you can roll your dough and form long rolls like this." He covers Ashley's sticky, doughy hands with his own to show her the motion of pushing and pulling the dough.

She casts a smirk to Rishika that translates to *I already know how to do this, but okay, show me.* Rishika tries not to laugh. The rest of the couples stop what they're doing and watch in awe of this almost erotic moment that resembles the messy and sensuous pottery wheel love scene from the movie *Ghost.* Pushing and pulling. Pushing and pulling. Pushing and pulling.

"Grazie," Ashley says and removes her hands.

"Si, I think you've got it," Chef Enzo says, flustered. "Uh, you can form it into rolls now." He assists a few more of his guests and then addresses the group. "Alora, we will all start to form our spaghetti."

After they have put their pasta through a press and received its long thin ropes, they drop it in boiling water. Enzo instructs the birthday girl to remove the al dente pasta with tongs and transfer it to a large bowl, where her husband adds grated pecorino romano cheese. Rishika ladles in hot starchy pasta water, and the daughter grinds coarse fresh black pepper over the mixture.

"Work quickly," Enzo instructs as the mother tosses it all together. The ingredients form a decadent sauce that coats the pasta and wafts a savory aroma to their noses. "Okay. The dish is finito. We can eat."

Everyone claps with anticipation.

They move into the dining room where they sip Enzo's thoughtfully paired white wine, bright with flavors of citrus and orchard fruit. They pass around the large bowl of cacio e pepe, family style, and serve it onto their plates. As they taste their creation, they rave in awe of how spaghetti with cheese and pepper can be so divine. The sheep's milk cheese is sharp and salty, the pepper adds a simple yet powerful spice, the sauce is creamy, and the homemade pasta is fresh and pure. It's incredible. Chef Enzo has proven his point. The simple dishes of Rome that have been prepared for hundreds of years are unparalleled. The dish is savored along with happy conversation.

"Excuse me, friends," Enzo says. The chatter quiets, and all eyes turn to their host. "Thank you all for being guests in my home tonight. It has been such a pleasure to know you. This is where the class ends." There are moans of disappointment. "My intention is that you will now go out into the Roman nightlife to a beautiful ristorante and resume your meal with the main course, salad course, and of course, something dolce. I hope we can all call each other friends and that our paths will cross again in the future." He lifts his glass one more time. "Chin chin!"

"Chin chin!" Everyone cheers and clinks wine glasses.

As the guests of the cooking class rise from the table and give each other their best wishes for a wonderful trip, Chef Enzo pulls Ashley off to the side.

"Ashley, may I have the pleasure of taking you to dinner?" he asks as his gaze burns into her eyes. He's so boyishly cute and *Italian.*

"Oh. Thank you so much, Chef Enzo…"

"Per favore, call me Enzo."

"Enzo. Thank you for the kind invitation, but I really should stay with my friends."

"Of course. How about tomorrow?"

She smiles graciously. "I'm so flattered. But things are complicated for me right now. I'm sorry, but I have to say no. It was such a pleasure to meet you, and I loved taking your class."

"Piacere," he says, disappointed, and kisses her on both cheeks.

# Chapter 60

Francesco pulls out Katherine's chair, and she sits down at a small table on the rooftop of a hotel. They can see the tops of churches and buildings, the nearby Pantheon, Piazza Navona, Piazza della Rotunda, the black sky above them, and the warm glow of illuminated night life below.

"This is incredible."

"I wanted to bring you somewhere special. But I'm not trying to sweep you off your feet," he adds as an afterthought.

She laughs.

Katherine wears a sleeveless long black cotton dress that hugs her body and strappy black heels. Her skin glows from the humid air and from within.

Their wine glasses are filled with a dark, rich Montepulciano, and they dip bread into sumptuous olive oil. They talk of places they've vacationed over the years, the sad experience of their parents' deaths, and what will come next with this phase of life. There is so much to say.

"Katerina?"

She looks up at him and is surprised to find eyes that are very serious.

"I've been upset with you for a very long time. How I feel about you is complicated. My memories of us held so much happiness and promise. When I stopped hearing from you, I would go to the Spanish Steps, to the gelateria in Piazza Navona where you loved the peach gelato, to the Trevi Fountain where we made so many wishes. It was so painful. Those places were missing you. After a while, I would go to those places and I would feel so bitter."

Katherine's heart sinks. *I ruined the Spanish Steps, Piazza Navona and the Trevi Fountain for a Roman. That's evil.*

"I... I was so naive," she begins, flustered. "Not naive. Self-absorbed. I didn't realize that I had affected how you would feel in those places. But, duh. I was petrified to even come to Rome, to have to relive being here. And you live here. It was so cruel."

"Yes. That is how I felt. But what I'm trying to tell you is... first I was heartbroken, and then I was angry, and then I met Angelina. We started out as friends, and she knew that I was hurt. She told me that those places existed before my memories with you. She told me that I needed new memories of those places. And so I made new memories with her and our children. I moved on."

"Angelina knew about me?" Katherine asks, both surprised and embarrassed.

"Of course. Did you tell James about me?"

"No. Not because you weren't important. We never talked about our previous relationships."

He nods.

"The reason I tell you all of this is because my feelings for you have had to evolve over the years, and now I find another opportunity. I am ready to forgive you."

"Oh, Francesco. I don't even feel like I've done enough to apologize. I..."

He cuts her off. "I forgive you."

Katherine reaches across the table and takes Francesco's hands. "Thank you."

# Chapter 61

Despite Chef Enzo's intention for his students to go on to finish their dinner elsewhere, Ashley, Lorelei and Rishika are stuffed, but determined to find just a little more room in their bellies for gelato. In a gelateria located in the Piazza della Rotunda, they peruse the glass case that displays a variety of gelato—a deep red raspberry, a light orange cantaloupe, a creamy white base dotted with chocolate called stracciatella, which is the classic chocolate chip, and lovely subtley-green pistachio, to name a few. Most of them have a topping to indicate what the flavor is—scalloped lime halves, whole strawberries, half of a fresh pineapple, pieces of a chocolate bar. Rishika chooses nocciola, which is sweet, nutty hazelnut. Ashley chooses a tart green apple that is fresh and light like a sorbet, and Lorelei chooses cioccolato all'arancia, an intense dark chocolate with the orangy flavor of Grand Marnier liqueur.

Moments later, they are sitting on a bench looking directly at the Fontana del Pantheon illuminated with white lights at its base, with the glowing Pantheon looming behind it. They savor their decadent gelato with tiny plastic squared spoons as they marvel at the extraordinary view.

"You should have gone to dinner with Enzo," Rishika says, shaking her head. "Hot, young, robust, Italian Enzo."

Lorelei nods in agreement. "He was a doll! He could seduce you not only with his svelte body, beautiful face, and dreamy accent, but also with his fresh pasta." Rishika nods, amused.

"Yeah, for a day or two before we leave. Why are you guys encouraging me to have trysts with men I'm never going to see again?" Ashley asks.

Rishika laughs. "Because we can't."

"It's true," Lorelei agrees. "We're totally living vicariously through you." She thinks for a moment. "But, also, because you can. Your love life is open now. You can do whatever you want. And we want you to be happy," she adds seriously.

Ashley smiles. "Thank you. Yeah, this trip has opened my eyes quite a bit. That the end of my marriage doesn't mean *the end*."

"If I'm honest, though," Lorelei interjects, "I really want to see you with Andrick. I can actually see a long-term relationship with him."

Rishika makes a doubtful expression, though, looking down and poking at her gelato, Ashley doesn't see it. "I think you need a rebound to get over your rebound."

Ashley nods and takes a bite of her gelato. "I'm completely confused by all of this. I'm still processing the combustion of my marriage, and all of this sudden attention from men is so strange."

"You have a different energy, Ash," Rishika says. "You don't give off the sad, stifled, married-to-Pierce vibe that you used to. You just resonate authentic, happy Ashley. 'I am Ashley, hear me roar!'"

"Well, that sounds obnoxious."

"Um, no. I love it."

"I love it, too," Lorelei agrees and smiles.

"Thanks. And I suppose it's easy to be those things on vacation, but I'm feeling the premonition that when we get home, it's time to be responsible Mama Bear again. With the divorce coming, the kids have short- and long-term challenging times ahead. I need to put them first. Besides, I need to get a job, and I probably need to sell the house and find a new place to live. Things are about to get crazy. I can't see myself being distracted by an international relationship attempt or even dating in San Francisco."

"You're an incredible mom, Ashley," Lorelei says. "I know you will protect your kids and be sensitive to their needs. But don't you deserve to be happy, too? And don't Elizabeth, Teddy and Ryan deserve to have a happy mom?"

"Mmm." Ashley nods, hearing it, but not quite responding, and then smiles slightly. "Thank you for all of your support on this."

"Of course," Rishika and Lorelei both return.

"So, what do you think Katherine is doing right now?" Rishika asks.

"I hope she's eating dinner in a crowded restaurant," Ashley says.

"It's so wildly romantic," Lorelei says wistfully. "Seeing your first love after twenty years. In Rome."

"I'm very uncomfortable with all of it, and I really don't think you two should encourage her," Ashley says. "Especially you, Rishika. You're acting like this is a joke."

"I'm not. *I* enjoyed seeing Francesco yesterday after all these years. It was nice. Wasn't it?"

"Of course."

"I wouldn't mind spending more time with him myself. All I'm saying is of course they have a lot of catching up to do."

"This is serious," Ashley persists. "I think we're witnessing Katherine on the verge of making bad choices."

Lorelei and Rishika ponder this.

"Surely not," Rishika remarks.

"I feel for Katherine. I can see that she's really struggling here," Lorelei says reasonably. "It's sad having regrets. She's looking back on an important scene in her life that meant a lot to her, and it's in the past."

"I get that. But what is she planning on doing?" Ashley questions. "Bringing it out of the past and ruining her marriage? Breaking up her family?"

"Do you really think Katherine would do something drastic?" Rishika asks. "Katherine is the most logical and level-headed person I know."

"I trust her," Lorelei agrees.

Ashley shakes her head. "I think she is so shaken by seeing Francesco again and being back in Rome, that she's lost all reason. We're talking about her cheating on James. *James.* They've always been a rock-solid couple, and he is a *good* man. I'm not going to just stand by and watch her break his heart."

# Chapter 62

Katherine and Francesco feast on a simple, yet perfect margherita pizza, with a crust so thin and a tomato sauce so pure, it is completely unlike American pizza.

They laugh as they eat. They look into each other's eyes. When one of them says something funny, the other grabs the other's hand. They are back in sync, like kindred spirits.

They move on to espresso and share tiramisu. Eating al fresco on this rooftop in Roma feels magical.

*I don't want this to end,* Katherine thinks. A bold thought occurs to her. *Maybe it doesn't have to.*

***

As Lorelei, Ashley and Rishika finish their gelato, a man walks over to his parked moped.

Lorelei looks at them with a smirk. "Hold on a second." She walks toward the man.

Ashley and Rishika look at each other.

After Lorelei talks to the man for a minute, he mounts his moped and Lorelei climbs on behind him.

Rishika and Ashley stand up.

"What are you doing?" Rishika calls.

"I've always wanted to do this!"

Ashley frowns doubtfully.

"I'll be right back!" Lorelei calls as they speed off.

Ashley and Rishika raise their eyebrows and sit back down on the bench.

"Why is everyone stressing me out?" Ashley asks.

"Not me," Rishika says. "I'm now the dependable, drama-free one. How times have changed."

\*\*\*

When Francesco and Katherine are done with their meal, they walk arm in arm looking in the high-end shop windows. Katherine moves to interlace her fingers with his. The energy running from one to the other is electric and deep. It just feels *right*.

"This has been an incredible evening," Katherine croons.

"I can't tell you how much I have enjoyed spending this time with you."

"Francesco, is this what life would be like here with you?"

Francesco turns to Katherine. "What are you asking me?"

"What if I took the wrong path? What if this is where I'm supposed to be, with you? What if this is our second chance?"

Francesco looks astonished.

She continues. "I've thought about you through the years. And when I have, my heart has hurt."

"I know what you mean."

"I still love you, Francesco."

"I love you deeply." He pulls her to him and kisses her intensely. When they pull apart, Katherine has genuine love in her eyes, but Francesco's eyes are mixed with love and conflict. "I'm going to walk you back to your inn."

"Take me to your home."

He looks at her, pained. "Oh, Katerina. I want to do that. You have no idea. But that is something that we will not be able to return from. You need to know what you really want."

"I want you."

He takes both of her hands, lifts them to his lips and kisses them. "Then, tell me that tomorrow."

# Chapter 63

After waiting for an hour on the bench, Rishika and Ashley decide to go back to the hotel. They've called Lorelei's phone six times, and she's not answering. They're very worried, but mostly they're pissed.

They sit on the balcony wearing their pajamas, but it's hard to enjoy the beautiful view.

"When do we call the police?" Ashley asks.

Rishika glances at her phone. "It's only been an hour and forty-five minutes. They won't do anything."

Ashley nods. "I can't believe she did this. God, I hope something bad hasn't happened to her."

They hear the click of the door and rush into the living room where Lorelei stands with a guilty look.

"I'm so sorry," she says.

"Are you alright?" Rishika asks.

"Yes. I'm sorry."

"Okay, good. What the hell happened?"

"We grabbed a drink and then the guy wouldn't bring me back."

"You grabbed a drink?" Ashley repeats, flabbergasted.

"He said it was the best bar in Rome."

"Oh, I'm sure," Ashley mumbles.

"We were worried," Rishika says. "We called you repeatedly."

"My phone died. I'm so sorry I worried you."

Ashley sighs and looks at Rishika. "I'm going to bed."

"I think I will, too," Lorelei says, humbly. "I really am sorry."

"I'm just glad you're safe. I'm going to sit out here for a while," Rishika says, thoroughly annoyed.

*** 

When Katherine returns and steps out onto the balcony, Rishika is still sitting out there.

Rishika eyes Katherine's form fitting dress and heels. "Wow. You look great."

"Thanks."

"How was your night?" Rishika attempts neutrally.

"It was lovely," Katherine says, trying not to give away too much. "How was yours?"

"It was fine. The cooking class was awesome. Just... let's leave it at that."

"Okay," Katherine says, suspiciously.

"Katherine..." Rishika hesitates, unsure how to navigate this conversation. "Would you like to talk this out with me? I'm sure you have a lot of confusing emotions happening."

Katherine smiles, resigned. On the one hand, she wants to. She wants to just gush about her huge crazy emotions about Francesco, but for now, she feels like she should keep all of that to herself. She wants to enjoy it before her friends judge her for it. "Maybe tomorrow. I'm exhausted. But thank you."

"Okay. Good night."

Katherine retreats to the bathroom to take a shower and get ready for bed. In the privacy of the little shower, she is free to revel in replaying her time with Francesco, her kiss with Francesco. For now, she allows herself to soar in the clouds.

# Chapter 64

Katherine didn't sleep much. Every nerve in her body was on fire and her mind was consumed with Francesco. She had so much to think about. She loves the man. She misses him. Part of her wishes she could turn back time and have never left Rome at all. What should she do? She has to see him again this morning.

She rises early. As the other ladies sleep, Katherine dresses in a long yellow sundress and canvas espadrilles and applies her makeup quietly. She steps outside onto the balcony and appreciates the morning ambiance of Rome—the bustle of the day starting, the vendors setting up the market in Campo de' Fiori, people walking to the bar to get their espresso. It's so crazy how she *feels* the air here on her skin. She feels *being* here. It feels right. This is where she appreciates life. This is where she feels alive.

Francesco was so thoughtful to send her home last night. She was acting impulsively. He knows that the decision is hers. Clearly, they both want to be together. But she's the one who has so much to lose, who has sacrifices to make.

Ashley steps out on to the balcony, dressed. "Good morning," she says, guarded.

*Shoot,* Katherine thinks. *I missed my opportunity to sneak out of here without getting the third degree.* "Good morning," she returns, attempting to sound normal.

"What did you end up doing last night?"

"We had a very nice dinner."

"In a restaurant?"

"Yes, this beautiful rooftop ristorante had the most perfect margherita pizza."

"That sounds nice." After an awkward moment, Ashley says, "Katherine, what are you doing?"

"What do you mean?"

"I feel like you're pretending you don't have a husband and family back home. I'm worried about you."

Katherine attempts to remain casual. "Francesco and I are just spending time together. He's a dear old friend."

"That's a lie and you know it," Ashley barks.

Katherine is taken aback by Ashley's tone. "Goodness. Why are you overreacting?" She opens the sliding glass door and goes into the living room. *This is just too much before coffee. Why is there no coffee maker in here?*

Rishika and Lorelei have just settled onto the settee in their pajamas. Their energy is also a bit strained from the events from the night before.

"Buongiorno," Lorelei says cheerfully, trying to lighten the mood.

Ashley follows Katherine into the room. "I'm reacting this way," Ashley continues, "because I want to know what's going through your head. I'm trying to save you from yourself."

Katherine turns and faces her. "If you must know, I'm considering staying."

"What?" Rishika sits up.

Lorelei straightens, attentive.

"*Staying?*" Ashley repeats.

"As in not going home?" Rishika confirms.

"Yes," Katherine says, unnerved.

"You are talking crazy," Ashley persists. "You have a wonderful husband! And he loves you very much. You have two sons, Brice and Beckham. Remember them? Your life is practically perfect and you're about to throw it away. Not only that, but you love your job. You're obsessed with it. Are you willing to just toss that aside, too?"

"I don't know!" Katherine cracks. "I haven't thought about all of the details yet." At Rishika's dubious look, she says, "Look, I'm not taking this lightly. It's not like I just met an attractive man on this trip and I want to have a fling with him. This is someone I loved! Someone I thought I was going to spend my life with. I've waited twenty years to see him again. And now that I have, it's like, how did I live so long without him? Don't you guys get it? Life is short! If there's anything we want to do or say to someone or anything we want to change, we've got to do it before it's too late!" She takes a deep breath and tries to calm herself. "This is my second chance."

Ashley fumes, shaking her head.

Lorelei jumps in, trying to remain level-headed. "But, sweetie, you're not going to get a second chance with your actual family in your real life after you mess that up. Do you really think they'll forgive you if you choose Francesco over them? Do you think your children will not be devastated? That they won't judge you for this forever and need therapy when they're adults?"

Katherine doesn't answer.

Ashley takes a deep breath. "I called James."

Katherine's head whips towards Ashley. "What?"

"I called him last night when you were out doing God knows what. He has a right to know what's going on over here."

"What did you tell him?"

"That you've been spending all of your time in Rome with an ex-boyfriend and you're on the verge of making some terrible choices."

Wide-eyed, Katherine covers her mouth with her hands. "You had no right to do that," Katherine says, appalled. "Where's your loyalty?"

Ashley is equally flabbergasted. "My loyalty is to you. I've spent my time in Rome feeling deeply disturbed about this *for you*. I'm helping you save your marriage because you're not capable of seeing the right path right now. Where's *your* loyalty?"

Katherine avoids the question. "You crossed the line," she seethes.

Ashley doesn't waver. "You're welcome."

Katherine throws her arms in the air. "Wow. I can't. I have nothing more to say to you. I am so furious!"

"And I'm disgusted by your behavior. You're no better than Pierce."

Katherine sucks in her breath. Rishika and Lorelei watch from the settee with horrified expressions. "How can you say that to me?"

"Because you're dangerously close to it being true."

"You guys," Lorelei interjects. "Come on."

"I need some fucking espresso." Katherine grabs her purse from the table by the door and flees the hotel room.

Ashley stomps into the bedroom and slams the door.

"This is not right," Rishika says, shaking her head. "This trip is about friendship. It's about remembering and honoring Anna."

Lorelei makes a face. "Well, that was a nice segue."

"What are you talking about?"

"Oh, my gosh, we get it! Anna loved you the most! We all miss her, okay?"

"Of course we do," Rishika says, perplexed. "Relax."

"Who elected you to be Anna's spokesperson?"

Rishika casts her a dirty look. "What's your problem?"

"Just that this entire trip, you've made it very clear that you were Anna's best friend. Not just this whole trip, actually—for as long as I've known you. And you've been rubbing it in our faces!"

"So sue me for grieving for my best friend. I've known her my entire life. At moments, it seems like I'm the only one who *is* grieving. That's what this trip is about, remember? Not for trying to redo your twenties and having a full-blown midlife crisis. I'm sorry you missed your twenties, but that's so far in the past, so grow up."

"Grow up? I've been a mom since I was twenty-two! I've raised six children. I had to grow up. You, on the other hand, would have no idea what I'm talking about. You disappeared when I had Phoebe. You're the one who lives a life of leisure."

"Because I don't have kids I live a life of leisure? I run an entire department at a major studio. I have an extremely demanding job!"

"It absolutely blows my mind," Lorelei says with venom, "that Anna chose you to be her contingency plan."

Rishika's eyes widen. "How do you know about that?"

"Oh, we all know about it, and we all think it's utterly insane! Like you are qualified to raise Camila and Alexa if something ever happened to Kevin. If anything, it should've been you who…" Lorelei stops herself, and the color drains from her face.

"Who died." Rishika nods. "It should've been me who died."

"No. Of course not."

"Because nobody needs me." Rishika shakes her head, taken aback. "Wow. You really mean that, don't you?"

Lorelei's eyes fill with tears. "I…"

"You know," Rishika interrupts her, "we used to have a lot in common, but that's just not the case these days. Maybe it doesn't make sense for us to be friends anymore."

"We haven't been friends for a long time, and you know it," Lorelei whispers. She rushes into her bedroom and closes the door before sobbing can be heard on the other side.

Rishika walks out onto the balcony.

"Rishika," Ashley says behind her, gently.

Rishika stares out over the piazza. "Do you feel the same way about Camila and Alexa?" she asks without turning around.

Ashley hesitates. "I feel like…"

Rishika turns toward her and her eyes narrow. "Forget it. This trip down memory lane is over. I'll go to Mykonos myself."

# Chapter 65

Ashley leaves the hotel suite. With Lorelei and Rishika staying in separate bedroom's, they are able to stay out of each other's way. They dress quickly, and Rishika gets out of there first.

She leaves the hotel and strides down the cobblestone street, enraged by feelings of deceit. She suddenly knows that Ashley, Lorelei and Katherine have been talking behind her back about her and her part in the will for the entire trip. She knows that they think it's preposterous that she should be trusted with the responsibility of raising someone's most prized treasures, their children. She knows her friends believe that she would fail miserably. And she knows that Anna put a lot of thought into it, which makes it all the more baffling. A tiny piece of her is angry at Anna for putting her in this situation. What makes Anna think she would want this? But mostly, Rishika is embarrassed because she knows that her friends are absolutely right.

# Chapter 66

This early in the morning, the Spanish Steps are not yet crowded. Ashley sits there in the morning light of Rome, a softness resonating off of the old beautiful buildings. She is so livid at Katherine who is acting selfishly out of emotion and lust, presumably as Pierce did when he met Maggie.

She doesn't want James to go through that. She doesn't want Brice and Beckham to go through what her kids have gone through. She doesn't want her friend, who she respects so much, to stoop so low.

James is on an airplane to Rome, and it's her doing. It was a brazen move, but she did it because she loves Katherine and she doesn't want Katherine and her family to go through the same turmoil that has torn her own family apart. She knows it was the right thing to do, but that it was quite possibly at the expense of their friendship.

What will happen when James arrives? Will he get here before Katherine has done something she regrets, something that James will be unable to forgive? Or will Katherine choose Francesco and leave James and her children? The best-case scenario, however unlikely, Ashley suspects, will leave Francesco brokenhearted by Katherine a second time. Nobody wins here.

Her thoughts shift to her own family situation. She pulls her cell phone out of her purse and begins to look at photos of her kids. Somehow she has to share Elizabeth, Teddy and Ryan with a stranger who has helped break her family apart. That just really sucks. It makes her feel sick.

She swipes through her favorites in her photos and comes across their family photo from Christmas. She studies Pierce's face and realizes that she doesn't actually want to be with him. She's sad that it didn't work out and that they weren't better together than they were. He really didn't love her the way she wants to be loved and adored. Their kids are the ones who will suffer the most from this. It's sad that the five of them won't sleep under the same roof again, won't wake up on Christmas morning together. She will move on, she is sure of that. Her discomfort is that they will all have to adjust to new schedules, her children going back and forth between Mom and Dad.

But, oddly enough, she is okay that she won't be with Pierce, and that is a new realization. She's not grieving over the loss of him anymore, she's grieving over the loss of family life as they know it. She will just have to be strong for the kids, and make it as positive an experience as she can. And that means being upbeat when it's time for the kids to spend time with Pierce... and Maggie. She inwardly groans.

Ashley looks at a selfie that she and Andrick took on the deck of the yacht as they ate their breakfast in the sun. The hurt of Pierce leaving her, of him deceiving her and betraying her is still so fresh. Is she ready to move on with someone new?

Can she trust Andrick? What about Rishika's instincts about him? That he falls in and out of love easily. That he will hurt Ashley.

What Ashley feels for Andrick is strong even though she just met him. The feelings of missing him are overwhelming. Is it love? *Can* it be love? Or is she just in a place of desperation? Of needing someone to love her? Maybe Rishika is right. Perhaps she does need a period of aloneness and independence. But, if she gives herself that time, Andrick will be gone with the wind. She'll find someone else eventually… but it won't be him. Surely, he will meet another wonderful woman, and soon.

On the flipside, she was so dependent on Pierce, when he pulled the rug out from under her, she was completely lost. She can't let that ever happen again. And even if she took the plunge with Andrick, how can it possibly work? How could they sustain a relationship on two different continents? It's a fairy tale.

*But come on! Listen to yourself! Trust yourself! You know how you feel about him!*

She thinks about her conversation with Andrick by the pool. When she asked him what he liked about her, he looked into her eyes. There was such honesty and sadness in them.

"It's how you make me feel," he replied, and then he took a moment to think about it. "From the first moment I saw you fishing an olive out of the top of your dress, you had me smiling. I thought, 'This is a woman who is so adorable when she thinks no one is watching, she has my heart paying attention before we've even exchanged one word.' To wake up with you for one morning and to see those eyes and that smile made me feel love before my day had even started. I would do anything to hear that laugh every day. And the conversations we shared seemed like just a glimpse into a companionship that could last for a lifetime. When you speak about Elizabeth, Teddy and Ryan and how you love them so much, you make me wish that you were a mother figure for my own children. When you speak about your sadness in your marriage ending, you make me want to ensure that you'll never be sad again. And the times that you are sad and I can't prevent it, I want to be there to hold you and make you feel better. I know that we haven't known each other very long, but I want the opportunity to know you completely."

When he finished, Ashley looked like she'd seen a ghost. She was so moved, but so saddened that she had to give up something so beautiful before it barely started.

She suddenly realizes that when she told Chef Enzo that things were complicated for her, it wasn't because her husband left her and she's going through a divorce. It's because she's in love with someone else. The complicated part is that she doesn't know how to let it unfold.

What the hell was she thinking? Telling Andrick no, leaving him behind? This man wants to love her. She didn't even know that men like Andrick existed in real life. And he sees her for who she really is. Maybe she just needs to have faith, give him a chance. What more does she need than that heartfelt poetic admission of love? A lightning bolt? A kick in the ass?

She whips her cell phone out of her purse and finds Andrick on Facebook. She selects the button to send him a message, and she begins to type.

# Chapter 67

Lorelei heads north towards Piazza Navona. She feels so lost, so horrified by her behavior. Her fight with Rishika got so ugly. How could she say those horrible things to her friend? It's unforgiveable.

And then there was last night. She feels remorse and embarrassment about those events. It was intended to be an innocent ride on a moped in Rome, something fun and crazy that she could pack away in her arsenal of European backpacking memories that she's trying so desperately to hoard. But it went too far. Of course her friends were pissed off at her. Of course they were worried about her. The truth is, she was afraid. When the man, whose name she didn't even know, tried to kiss her and refused to take her back to Piazza del Rotunda, she realized that she had put herself in a dangerous situation, the type of situation that she cautions her daughters about, the type of sketchy situation she has been trying to avoid this entire trip. Her cell phone was dead. She got on the metro by herself in a city she was not familiar with late at night.

What is she doing, really? All of it. The brazen gambling at the roulette table. Thank God she did not lose her money. What would Adam think of her had he seen her pulling out a thousand dollars like it was nothing? Surely, he would be disappointed by her other behavior as well. While he's home dealing with the Phoebe situation, she's been trying to be as irresponsible as she could possibly be. She's been trying to turn back time and be a girl in her twenties with no responsibilities and an entire unwritten future ahead of her.

Lorelei enters the Piazza Navona. Like Campo de' Fiori, the square is surrounded by cafes, ristorantes and bars, and vertically, there are hotels and apartments. But, here, the awe factor is amped way up. For this is the home of three very impressive fountains, the first one dating back to 1574. Lorelei did her homework about these works, reading about them on the train from the French Riviera, and she has been anxious to see them and study them in person.

Lorelei first comes to la Fontana de Moro, the Fountain of the Moor. In the middle of the fountain is a Moor, or an African, but it is possible that he was originally intended to be Neptune. He is standing in a shell and taming a dolphin. He's surrounded by four kneeling tritons blowing into shells.

By the time she saunters over to the middle of the piazza, Lorelei is feeling a little better. Immersing herself in this legendary art history is helping her to get her mind off all of the crises she and her girlfriends are experiencing. Being in her element of art is helping her to feel more like herself.

She spends a lengthy amount of time studying la Fontana dei Quattro Fiumi, the Fountain of the Four Rivers which was commissioned from the great Gian Lorenzo Bernini in 1651 by Pope Innocent X. In the middle of the square, this fountain cannot be ignored with a base of rocks holding sculptures of four gods and an Egyptian-style obelisk reaching high into the sky at almost one hundred and fifteen feet. The four gods personify the four ancient rivers—the Nile, the Ganges, the Danube, and the Rio de Plato. The river gods are surrounded by various animals: a serpent, a sea monster, a dolphin, a crocodile, a dragon, and a lion. Most impressive to Lorelei is the horse bursting through the center of the rocks with such intensity. There is so much going on in this monument, so many details, so much theatricality, and so much backstory that tells what was going on in Rome at the time when this fountain was created.

Lorelei is astonished at the movement and symbolism that Bernini portrayed out of marble and stone. She wonders if Sebastian has been here before and seen these works. He could certainly learn from the incredible storytelling techniques of Bernini.

She moves on to the last fountain in Piazza Navona, la Fontana del Nettuno, or the Fountain of Neptune.

She sits down on a bench facing the fountain. This fountain is actually the first one that was created. Like the Fountain of the Moor, it is much simpler than the Fountain of the Four Rivers, adding balance to both sides of the piazza. But what is so unbelievable to Lorelei is that although the basin of this fountain was created in 1574 by Giacamo della Porta, the rest of it came much, much later. The statue of Neptune wrestling an octopus in the center of the fountain, and the mermaids, sea monsters and dolphins that flock the perimeter were designed by Antonio della Bitta and Gregorio Zappala, respectively, in 1878. The basin waited three hundred years to have statues in it, to be completed. Three hundred years.

*Better late than never.* Lorelei smiles inwardly. *Oh, the irony and symbolism.*

Lorelei looks around and takes it all in, the ambiance of this piazza, the immensity of being in the presence of all of this. People sip espresso and enjoy breakfast at the sunny outdoor tables. Sightseers take selfies and photos of the fountains. An old man in his eighties at the bench adjacent to her gazes up at Neptune.

Lorelei finds her gaze lingering on the old man. He holds such wonder in his eyes for the statue of Neptune. She wonders what his story is. Where is he from? For what reason is he so enamored with this fountain? Did he come here long ago and finally make it back after fifty years? Or did he always long to come to Rome, but work, finances, his family, or a sick wife delayed his visit until now? He is clearly so grateful to be sitting on a bench in the presence of this legendary fountain in the middle of Piazza Navona in the Eternal City. Lorelei realizes that regardless of what his path was to get here, he is here now. He gets to experience it now. *Better late than never.*

And so does she. Suddenly, Lorelei has such a moment of clarity. The story of this man resonates with her. *The story, the story, the story.* She pulls the sketchbook out of her tote bag and opens it. She puts a pencil to the paper and it begins to move. The focus of her drawing isn't the powerful Neptune or the flailing, fighting octopus or this legendary piazza that dates back to the first century AD. The story is the old man himself. His emotion at finally being here at this fountain. Each line on his face is a story from his past. He gazes up at the fountain, marveling at its beauty and history, marveling at the strength of Neptune, like his own determination that got him here after everything, like his own physical strength when he was a young man.

Lorelei sketches furiously and a tear runs down her face. The dormant artist and the newly discovered storyteller within her have been unleashed. She wouldn't change the path her life has taken for anything. She loves each of her children—Phoebe, Aislinn, Hadley, Atticus, Celeste, and Gideon, all so different, each one a gift. Her family is big and loud and messy. She is married to a supportive friend and dependable companion who she still loves dearly. Her days feel so unorganized and busy as she rushes from home to the students that she loves, the opportunity to inspire them, as her own high school and college art teachers inspired her. And now she is here, experiencing adventures during the trip of a lifetime, in this magical place where art exists at every turn. She is so blessed.

# Chapter 68

Rishika sits down on the edge of the Trevi Fountain. Everything has come to a head, and Rishika is doubting all of it. What an absolute mess. She thinks about what she said to Lorelei, about them not having anything in common anymore. In college, they just clicked. But, actually, they didn't have a ton *in common.* They were completely different then, and that was what they loved about each other. They were as thick as thieves. Actually, Lorelei was the first *best* friend Rishika ever really had other than Anna. Afterwards, life kind of took them in different directions. "Kind of," nothing. Once Lorelei had her first child, she was gone with the wind. She was all about her family, and Rishika went years without seeing her until Anna started hosting the Christmas brunches.

Is it true that they shouldn't be friends anymore? For years, Anna has been their only connection, and now she is gone.

*Anna is gone.*

A tear escapes down Rishika's cheek, and then another. She puts her face in her hands and sobs. She has herself a really good cry, something she has rarely indulged herself in in her life, but lately the release of it feels so necessary.

For her, this trip is solely about honoring Anna, about putting Anna to rest. About Anna's death. To Ashley, Katherine and Lorelei, this trip is about reminiscing, experiencing, living. The truth is, she couldn't have survived this trip without them. They made it bearable. They made it fun. They made it *amazing*.

She looks over, and a few feet away from her sits Anna on the edge of the fountain. Anna closes her eyes, and, one at a time, she throws three coins over her shoulder into the water. The image of it breaks Rishika's heart. What could a dead girl be wishing for anyway?

Anna notices Rishika watching her. "When in Rome, you know?"

Rishika sighs. "Oh, Anna. I'm so confused. I have a million questions."

"Like…"

"Like, why the hell did you pick me to raise your daughters if something ever happens to Kevin? Why have I been seeing you on this trip? And how am I supposed to continue life without you when I don't know how to *do* life without you?"

Anna's eyes are compassionate, yet strong. "Okay, first of all, I pray and I feel in my heart that Kevin will be with our girls for a long time. He needs to raise them. He needs to be there when they have babies. He needs to be a grandpa. But I needed a back-up plan, and I would always choose you to be my back-up plan for anything."

"But, you know I've never been a kid person. I would do a horrible job. I don't have a nurturing bone in my body."

"Yes, you do," Anna says. Rishika looks doubtful. "And I worry that if you didn't have that responsibility to my daughters you wouldn't keep in touch with them. I need the three of you to know each other. I need the three of you to be important to each other. You have to promise me that."

Rishika exhales. "Of course, that makes sense. And it's my fault that you felt like you had to worry about that. I'm so sorry that I've been so selfish, that I haven't put in much effort. Of course I promise you."

"Alright, good." Anna smiles. "Next. You've been seeing me because I knew you that you needed to. I knew that you needed to see me being happy. And I am. I'm not in pain anymore. I knew that you needed me to tell you that it's okay to have fun without me, that it's okay to move on with your life. So listen to me already. I want you to move on. You *need* to move on.

"Which brings me to your last question. Your life will go on without me no matter what. It already has. You're married to your soul mate. You have a career that fulfills you, that you are supertalented at. You have three amazing women who love you very much. And they are struggling, too, in their own ways. And they need your strength. You all need each other's strength."

"We're a mess right now."

"Then fix it."

Rishika makes a face.

"Oh, you're going to tell me that friends can't have fights? That's a laugh if I ever heard one."

This makes Rishika smirk. "We fought like sisters."

Anna smiles. "Of course we did."

"Anna, I'm so sorry I didn't let you say the things you wanted to say to me. So please, tell me what they are."

"I just did, Rish. This is the conversation I wanted to have with you. It's okay. You weren't ready then. I know it was hard for you to prepare to let me go. That's my Rish, stubborn to a T."

"Oh." Rishika exhales a huge breath, unburdening herself. "Okay."

"Also, I wanted you to make sure I get to Mykonos. And here we are, on our way, and it's been incredible." Anna beams. "You have a life of extraordinary moments ahead of you. Savor them."

"Wait. Why do I feel like you're leaving me?"

"Because you have a life to go live. Be happy, my sister. I love you.

And, by the way, one of my wishes was for you."

"Anna!"

But Anna is gone. The vision of her is gone. And, Rishika *feels* that she is gone."

# Chapter 69

At the bar across the street from Francesco's trattoria, Katherine sits at a table by the window. Occasionally, she can observe Francesco as he serves customers at tables near the window and outside. She is painfully conflicted.

Until Ashley compared her to Pierce, she did not really comprehend the magnitude at which she would be hurting her family. Seeing Francesco swept her away, swept her away from reality. Her real life seemed so distant, as did any consequences to her actions.

In the wee hours of this morning, lying in bed wide awake on adrenaline, she fantasized of a new life with Francesco. In some of the visions, she and Francesco hadn't married other people or had any children, and as a result, she wasn't betraying or abandoning anyone. They were still in their twenties with a clean slate waiting for them to make choices together. In some fantasies, Brice and Beckham were their biological children together, and the twins lived a simple life here in Rome where Katherine was a very hands-on mother. But these visions are complete fiction. They aren't real. They are fantasy.

She watches Francesco, the same man, yet with reminders that twenty years have passed—a handful of gray hairs have joined his thick black hair and frame his face, and there is a wisdom in those dark brown eyes, a sadness. In the years without Katherine he has loved a wife deeply and grieved deeply when she died. He is a father and a grandfather; he has a family that does not include her at all. Their lives have taken them in different directions, and she cannot pretend that this is a second chance. It is not.

The moment that Ashley said she called James was like someone snapped their fingers and brought Katherine back. She is not a single woman. She does not have a clean slate in front of her with free choices that don't impact anyone else. She got swept up in the idea of doing it differently the first time, the concept of her choosing a different life way back then. But she made her choice then and she has three men back home whom she loves with all of her heart as a result.

These are conclusions she could only come to while watching Francesco from afar. Here, she is not clouded by their intense chemistry, the look in his eyes, the need to kiss him, the pull to hold his hand and be his companion.

She wishes she could have had it both ways, that somehow she could go back in time and have a second parallel life in which both paths exist and succeed. But that is not how life works.

# Chapter 70

Lorelei adds detail to her sketch.

Rishika suddenly appears behind the bench and peers down, studying Lorelei's sketch, the look of wonder in the old man's eyes as he gazes upon the Fountain of Neptune.

"Wow. You're a storyteller," Rishika comments. Lorelei looks behind her, surprised. "That never occurred to me before. Interesting that we both look for great stories."

"I never did before," Lorelei says, resigned, trying to read Rishika's energy. "I always thought inspiration had to come from me internally. It's something new I'm trying out."

"It's working," Rishika says and smiles tentatively. "Maybe we're more alike than we think." Rishika walks around to the front of the bench and sits down next to her. "Hey."

Lorelei sits up straight. "Hey. What are you doing here? And how did you find me?"

"Well, I knew this was on your list of things to see, and I got lucky. We need to talk," Rishika says. Lorelei looks down at her hands. "Are you okay?"

Lorelei closes her sketchbook and looks at Rishika.

"I am now." Lorelei shakes her head and her eyes tear up. "I didn't mean what I said. My life is no more important than yours because I have kids. That's a preposterous notion and a horribly mean thing to say. I promise I don't believe that. I'm so sorry. So, so sorry."

"Thank you." Rishika looks Lorelei in the eye. "I feel like you're really mad at me."

Lorelei nods, but for a moment, she doesn't respond. She's been pondering the source of her anger at Rishika for a while now. She's felt a negative energy towards her for years. At first it was just annoyance, but has recently bloomed into full-blown anger. But it's difficult to articulate. She knows that she has silently judged Rishika for her choices, and she has finally put her finger on it.

"Okay. This is a lot of layered stuff that has been building up for years," Lorelei says. Rishika nods. "First of all, once I had Phoebe, you and I started having less in common. I felt like you kind of dropped me, and the disconnect just kept getting wider over time, and I kept getting more and more resentful."

Rishika nods. "It's true. You didn't imagine that." Rishika blows out a breath. "I didn't know how to relate to you. When you had Phoebe, I was so far from the mind space of getting married and settling down. So I wasn't ready for my friends to. And certainly not ready for you guys to have kids."

Lorelei nods. "I wasn't ready either. I was terrified, actually. I could have used your support."

"Mmm," Rishika says, regretful. "I wish I had realized that. I'm sorry. You know, when you had Phoebe, I felt like *you* dropped *me*." Lorelei looks at her as though this never occurred to her before. Rishika continues. "Saying that out loud, I hear that it's ridiculous. Obviously, you were crazy busy at the time, but I still felt that way. And it still hurt."

Lorelei nods. "I was in survival mode during that entire first year. I had no idea what was going on with anyone else besides Phoebe, Adam and myself. However, friendship is a two-way street. I should've reached out to you once the dust settled."

"I'm sorry, Lorelei. I know I haven't been there for you. I haven't been a friend to you for a long time."

"It's okay. I'm seeing now that I haven't either. And it's total news to me, which validates how self-absorbed I really was. I apologize for that." After a beat, she says, "There's more. The truth is, I've often found myself feeling jealous of you."

"Why?"

"You're everything I'm not," Lorelei says a little sheepishly. "You're always meticulously put together, you're in amazing shape, you never seem stressed out, and I always think, 'Well, if I didn't have any kids, I'd have time to take care of myself, too.' And it just seems like you're exactly where you want to be in your life. You're so very accomplished. I remember your dreams and aspirations of working in the film industry back when you were eighteen years old. I remember you shooting student films on campus and then interning at the studio and then working as a production assistant on low-budget independent movies around town. You knew that you wanted to be a creative executive and you've meticulously worked your way to the top. You've done it! And gracious, until this moment, I didn't realize how damn proud I actually am of you. But, my path hasn't worked out as planned at all. Not one bit. So instead of being proud and celebrating with you, I've let it manifest into jealousy."

Rishika nods, digesting all of this. Lorelei takes advantage of the pause and continues.

"But it goes beyond that."

"Shit, there's more?"

"I told you it was layered."

Rishika nods, encouraging her to finish.

"Of course, after graduation I was bummed that I didn't get to come with you girls to Europe. And then I got so busy, I never really dwelled on it again. Until this trip. When we arrived in Germany, I started realizing just how much I missed. I missed a chapter of my youth. I missed extraordinary bonding time with you ladies, including Anna, and life-changing experiences. Obviously, I love each of my children and I wouldn't change any of that, but I wish I could have had that time to do all of the crazy things you girls did in your early twenties. Maybe then I wouldn't be throwing down a thousand dollars on a roulette table, riding on the back of a stranger's moped, and taking my clothes off for a hot young artist I've just met." At Rishika's shocked expression, Lorelei throws her arms up into the air. "Totally more innocent than it sounds. I promise." She smiles and lays her hands in her lap. "But now I realize that I was also doing all of that for Phoebe, because I'm terrified that she's going to miss that soul-searching chapter of her youth."

Rishika's huge brown eyes are wide. "Wow. That's a lot of stuff."

"I know."

"We're going to need to delve deeper into that 'naked with Sebastian' conversation later."

Lorelei laughs. "Okay. I figured."

"I mean, you can't just expect to drop a bomb like that into the conversation without total elaboration."

"I'm aware." Lorelei puts her face in her hands for a moment in embarrassment.

"Was he naked?"

A bellow bursts out of Lorelei's mouth. "No!"

"Okay, good." Rishika's expression turns thoughtful. "You know, perhaps you shouldn't assume that Phoebe is going to miss out on everything. Who knows what life will throw her way or what she will go after. She is, after all, a different person who will likely have her own path."

Lorelei's face brightens and she looks surprised by the new

perspective. "That is… incredibly good advice. I think I'm going to need to put that on a coffee mug and read it often." They sit quietly as Lorelei digests this. "Everything might be okay, after all."

"Of course it will be." After a few beats, Rishika says, "Hey. There's something you should know."

Lorelei looks at her, unsure.

"Sometimes I'm jealous of *you*."

"Come on," Lorelei scoffs.

"No, really. This entire trip you've been getting texts and phone calls from your kids and DM's from your students. You have so many people who love you and vie for your attention."

"Sometimes that's a curse," Lorelei jokes.

"I'm not kidding. You're loved and you're blessed. When it really comes down to it, I've got Craig and Penelope. I really enjoy my colleagues, but they're not family. Who's going to take care of Craig and me when we're old? You guys are so fulfilled by your children. I mean, I truly feel fulfilled by Craig and my work, but…"

"Well, there you go," Lorelei says supportively.

Rishika nods but continues. "I love my life, but there's a teeny part of me that worries, in ten years, am I going to decide that I'm missing something? Am I going to decide that we need family? If I do, it will be too late."

"You've always been so adamant that you don't want children. Do you really think you'll regret it?"

Rishika looks thoughtful. "No, I don't think so. But it's possible."

"Well, goodness. Every person alive could say 'what if' about something. I think each one of us has proven that recently."

"That's true."

"When we are old, my kids will take care of you and Craig."

Rishika looks truly touched. "Really?"

"Of course. Families come in many forms. We've known each

other for half of our lives. In my book, that makes us family."

"Thank you. That really means a lot." Rishika's face still holds concern. "I have to be honest. I have struggled a lot with Anna choosing me to take the girls should anything happen to Kevin. It's such a humongous responsibility."

Lorelei looks thoughtful. "This is not something Anna would have taken lightly. She knows all of your many qualities, and she hand-picked you for the job."

Rishika scoffs. "That's really generous of you to say. We both know you're more suited for that responsibility."

Lorelei shakes her head. "Anna is Camila and Alexa's mother. She knew what is best for them, and she had her reasons. And it's not anyone's place to question that."

Rishika looks sheepish. "I haven't even spent that much time with them. I feel so ashamed. I always just wanted Anna to myself. Even though she went through so much to get them, I avoided putting in the work to get to know that part of her."

"It's not too late," Lorelei says.

"It's not?"

"No. And there is only one way to make it up to Anna."

Rishika exhales, nervously. "What if they don't like me?"

"Just be yourself."

Rishika makes a doubtful expression. "Will you help me?"

Lorelei smiles. "Of course."

"Okay." Rishika smiles. "Remember how close we were in college?"

"How could I forget? We were like *The Odd Couple*. We were such an unexpected pairing. I think that was our superpower."

"I think the tide is turning for us. I think the Odd Couple is back in business." In an uncharacteristically affectionate moment, Rishika opens her arms wide. Lorelei scoops into the bear hug and wraps her arms around Rishika's lower back with her head under Rishika's chin. Ironically, it looks like a mother nurturing her young. "I almost forgot." Rishika pulls away. "I bought you something."

"You did?"

Rishika hands her a small brown paper bag with cord handles and white tissue paper inside. Lorelei pulls out a tiny baby onesie that says 'Ciao' on it. Her eyes soften.

"Oh! It's adorable! Thank you."

"It's so *tiny*," Rishika says with wonder. "You're going to make a wonderful grandma."

Lorelei wipes a tear from her face. "I'm going to be a grandma."

"Yes, you are! Congratulations."

"And you are going to make a wonderful great-auntie."

"I'm starting to realize that I'm fated to be an auntie. Maybe that's kind of brilliant. I can spoil them, but I don't have to keep them."

"It's totally brilliant. Why didn't I think of that?" Lorelei jokes.

# Chapter 71

James sits on a velvet chair in the lobby and rubs his eyes. He has sat here for the last two hours. He is tired from the long flight, a flight that he could not relax on, could definitely not sleep on, could not even focus on a movie. He could only worry about the fate of his marriage. Has Katherine had an affair? He feels like that is what must've happened, otherwise Ashley would not have called him. He is on edge, alternating between furious and terrified.

Katherine walks into the small lobby of the hotel. She looks emotional and exhausted.

"Katherine." James stands up.

"Oh, my God." Katherine runs to him. "James." They embrace, and tears pour from her eyes.

He pulls away and looks at her.

"Are you okay?" he asks.

"Yes."

"Good. What the hell is going on?"

\*\*\*

They manage to make their way up to James' recently booked room before really getting into it.

"Tell me everything," James instructs.

"Well," Katherine begins hesitantly, "I reconnected with someone I used to date here. His name is Francesco, and..."

"I can see your face. You obviously did more than date."

Her face falls. She sits on the bed. She is so upset, she is at a momentary loss for words. How does she explain it to her husband?

"Katherine. For God's sake, just tell me."

She looks at him with sad eyes. "I loved him very much. I thought I would move here and marry him after law school."

James' face registers the timing. He met Katherine at the end of their first year of law school.

"Our relationship ended abruptly. We didn't have any closure."

"That must've been hard. You should've told me about him."

"I'm so sorry, honey." She grabs his strong hands, but he takes them away.

"What exactly are you sorry about?"

Her face falls. "I've been spending time with him. We... kissed."

James' face tightens. "What else?"

"That's all."

"Did you sleep with him?"

"No."

"Katherine."

"No," Katherine says, adamantly.

The relief on James' face is obvious. "Okay, that's good. That's good," he whispers again to himself. "But Ashley called me and told me I should come to Italy. What else happened?"

"I... was having a hard time with it. I was considering... staying." Katherine looks down. She can't believe she is actually saying these words out loud to her husband.

"*Staying?*" This is worse than the fact that his wife kissed another man. James looks truly shocked. "Staying. What does that mean?"

"Staying with him," she whispers.

"What about us? What about our sons?"

Katherine shakes her head, not knowing how to explain it. Saying it out loud to James makes her realize how extreme a concept it was. Before this moment, she didn't see the wrongness to it when it was something she was only considering. Seriously considering. She hadn't sinned *yet*. She hadn't really taken action. But, admitting this and seeing the reaction on his face is another story.

"Why would you stay in Italy with a man I've never even heard of?" At her silence, he says, "Is life so bad back home? Is our marriage so bad?"

"No," she says.

"Do you not love me anymore?"

"Yes, I love you."

"Well, that was really convincing." James paces around the room.

"Yes, I love you! I'm so sorry, honey." She goes to him and tries to hug him.

He puts his hands up in front of him to stop her. "I think you should go back to your room."

Katherine looks taken aback. James' hands stay up, emphasizing the wall that is up in front of him.

Katherine nods. She exits his room and goes down the hall. She enters her suite and rushes out onto the balcony.

What has she done? There is a trust, an innocence to their marriage that is now gone. She feels its absence.

She leans against the wall of the balcony and looks out at the city of Rome. The air feels different now. It feels sad. This isn't her city. As much as she loves it, there's a sad nostalgia to it. For her, this city will now represent heartbreak, complicated emotions, loss of trust, and remorse.

She paces back and forth in a state of panic. Seeing her husband's face knocked clarity into her. A decision that she was earlier wrestling with now seems inconceivable. She suddenly feels desperate for James and the family and home that they built together.

She leaves her room and runs down the hall to James' room. She knocks on the door, and when he answers, she begs for forgiveness. His dark eyes hold so much hurt. *She* has hurt him. The man she has been with for almost two decades. He has been a loving and reliable husband. Loyal and kind. And he feels betrayed.

"Katherine. I need to process all of this. Alone."

# Chapter 72

When Ashley lets herself into the hotel suite, she hears sobbing. She rushes into the bedroom to find Katherine lying on the bed, an absolute mess.

"Oh, sweetie. What happened?"

"James is here. I told him everything. He's furious. Actually, it's not even that he's furious. It's his disappointment. I've really... damaged what he thinks of me."

"I'm sorry." Ashley *is* sorry that this is happening, that Katherine and James are having to deal with this, that they are both in pain, but she's certainly not sorry that she called James. She's steadfast that that was the right thing to do.

"You were right. What was I thinking?"

Ashley wants to say, *You weren't*, but instead, she sits down on the bed and rubs Katherine's back.

***

When Rishika and Lorelei return to the suite, they find Katherine on the settee with her head in Ashley's lap, Ashley caressing her hair.

Katherine sits up and tearfully fills them in on the current events and how James is in a room down the hall, adamant that he has some time to himself.

"Well," Lorelei says, "the good news is that you didn't yet reach the point of no return with Francesco. Hopefully James can get past the other stuff that isn't *totally*"—she makes a hopeful face— "unforgiveable."

"Francesco wouldn't let us get to that point last night."

Ashley purses her lips. "Francesco is a good man. It's just not to be."

Katherine nods. "I know you're right. I should've listened to you sooner. I didn't want to listen. I know you were just trying to help me. I'm sorry."

"It's okay. I'm here for you."

Katherine leans against Ashley like a child leaning against her mother.

"I shouldn't have encouraged you," Rishika says. "I just felt like you needed to talk about all of it."

"None of this is anyone's fault but my own. What a mess I've made."

There is a knock on the door. Katherine jumps up and runs to it, revealing James. He enters the room.

"Hello, ladies." He nods, but doesn't smile.

"Hi, James," Lorelei says.

"Well," Rishika says, "I'm ready for an aperitif."

"I'm dying to try a negroni," Ashley says. "Rachel Ray made one on her show and I've been meaning to get the ingredients for months."

"Thanks," James says.

As they pass by them, they pat and squeeze both Katherine's and James' arms and then grab their purses from the table by the door.

When they've gone, Katherine clears her throat. "Um, let's sit on the balcony."

"Okay," James answers sternly.

Katherine pours them each a glass of Chianti from the uncorked bottle in the kitchenette.

"Thank you," he says when she joins him outside. They both drink silently for a moment.

"I know I've messed up big time. I can't make excuses for my behavior or for what I've been thinking, but I do want to explain myself. I think... I'm going through some sort of midlife crisis. Oh, my gosh, did that just come out of my mouth? It sounds so cliche and like the stupidest justification ever."

James' expression doesn't change. "I can't believe you were ready to leave me. What have I done wrong?"

Katherine grabs his hands. "Nothing. This is going to sound so bad. I wasn't thinking about you. I'm sorry. I was thinking about me. About me at age twenty-two when life was open-ended and I was in love for the first time. On this trip, I've been thinking, 'How did I get here?' I'm forty-two and I'm in a job that consumes me. I think about it all the time. I was checking my email when we were at the Louvre." She blows out a breath and shakes her head. "I hardly see Brice and Beckham. You and I never spend quality time together. My current life is a rat race."

"How does that explain how you were going to leave me for another man?"

"Well, part of it is that I saw the alternative. Living a simple life here with Francesco."

James' cheek twitches at hearing his name. "And the other part?"

"The other part is that I had this serious relationship with someone, and when it ended I never dealt with those feelings."

"Katherine, that's life. We all have past relationships that we think about. But you don't go back to them and give them another try when you're married."

"You're absolutely right."

"So, when you and I met, you were in love with this Francesco guy? Great."

"Honey," Katherine begs with her eyes. She sniffs as tears run down her cheeks. "I was the one who ended it. Because of *you*. I married *you*. I loved you more."

The words flow over James, who's unconvinced.

"Look. I'm starving," he says. "I'm going to go back to my room and take a shower. I want you to find us a place to eat that you've never been to before. And we'll go there and we'll talk some more."

# Chapter 73

They sit at the table and the waitress takes their drink orders.

"Two negronis, please," James says. The waitress smiles and walks away. "I figured something stronger than wine was in order. Thought I'd take Ashley's recommendation a second time. She seems to be full of good advice lately."

"That she is." Katherine purses her lips, awkwardly.

"I'm devastated by this. It breaks my heart that you wanted to be with someone else."

"I know. I wasn't thinking straight. I wish I could turn back time."

"You can't." He exhales. "Just let me talk for a while." She nods. "Our lives have gotten away from us at home. It's not just you. We both need balance. You think I haven't thought about Kevin? How suddenly his wife is gone and he'll never see her again? How his kids will never see their mom?" His voice cracks.

Katherine furrows her eyebrows, surprised. It didn't occur to her that Anna's death might have James pondering life.

"We need to spend more time together," he continues. "You and me. Us and the boys. We need to figure out how to decrease our workload. Not just you. Me, too. You're the one who's been working to make partner. Maybe I should slow things down a little at work."

"But work is important to you, too."

James shrugs. "Maybe I could work from home more often. We are going to devise a plan to put some balance in our lives," he says firmly. "And when we get home, we will start marriage counseling. I insist on that."

"Okay. Yes. Does that mean you'll take me back?"

"You're my wife. You chose me and I chose you. Don't forget it again."

"I won't."

He softens. "I chose *you*. And I love you. I probably don't tell you enough." He puts both of his hands palm up on the table. She puts her hands on his.

The waitress delivers their negronis and leaves.

He raises his glass. "Now, let's enjoy the rest of this evening because I think I'm done with Rome."

Katherine smiles and raises her glass. She knows she will have to tell James that she's sorry a million more times. She looks at his face, his loyal, dependable and handsome face. The face she fell in love with. He's worth it.

"To us."

# Chapter 74

The next morning Francesco waits at a table outside his trattoria. When Katherine walks up to him, he nods with sad eyes.

"Buongiorno, bella."

"Buongiorno," she returns. He pulls out a chair for her and she sits. She attempts to smile at him. "It's time for us to say goodbye."

Francesco nods. "I know."

They sit in silence for a moment.

"There was a part of me," Francesco begins, "that thought maybe God was giving me a second chance with you. But I understand that can't happen. Loving you was and has been a blessing."

"Francesco…"

"But you are not mine to keep. This is not how I would have you. This is not how Angelina would want me to move on with my life."

"I'm so sorry that I'm hurting you again." Katherine bursts into tears.

"No, tesora. I've been lucky to love two amazing women in my life. And I realize now that I do want to love again. Also, it was time to finish this."

"I wish it could be different."

"But do you?"

"You know what I mean. I wish I could live two different lives. I wish I could have both."

"I do know what you mean. You were my first love, Katerina."

A few tears stream down Katherine's face. "And you were mine."

Katherine puts her hands on his face and looks into his eyes. They wrap their arms around each other.

***

Across the street, James, Rishika, Ashley and Lorelei sit at a table by the window and watch Katherine and Francesco engage in a loving embrace. James insisted that Katherine had him as a chaperone looking on, and the ladies insisted that James had support.

Ashley glances at James.

James blows out a breath. "It's okay," he says with a stern face. "That's goodbye."

# Chapter 75

The trip from Rome to Athens is a short two-hour flight, and they arrive in time for a late lunch. Europe is incredible in that after a short period of travel you can arrive in a completely different culture with its own cuisine and it's own rich history. They have a quick meal of Greek gyros with savory lamb and cucumber dill yogurt tzatziki on pillowy pita bread with strong coffee before heading to the Forum and the Acropolis for a little sightseeing.

Their group has a completely new dynamic—James. With Lorelei, Rishika and Ashley's blessing, he has chosen to stay on to their final destination. He, too, has expressed a desire to lay their dear friend to rest.

The energy between Katherine and James is… interesting. There are moments that they seem like the usual Katherine-and-James unit. Other times there is a strain of awkwardness when James looks off into space, silently contemplating what went down in Rome. Katherine constantly reaches for his hand and searches his eyes, her way of silently apologizing. The other ladies are fine with it. They love James and are grateful that he and Katherine are working things out.

This European adventure is losing steam. Their true purpose for all of this travel is a mere two days away, and they can all feel it.

# Chapter 76

The next day the ladies and James board a ferry that will carry them across the Aegean Sea to the small island of Mykonos.

Four and a half hours later, they sit on the deck eating sandwiches purchased from the snack bar. Lorelei looks up from her lunch and her breath catches. "Is that it?"

A vivid seaside city is small but visible.

Ashley looks up and her face brightens. "Yes! There it is!" The ladies and James stand up from the tables and rush to the bow of the ship.

"It's unreal," Lorelei says, full of awe. *There it is,* she thinks. *The place that Anna loved so much, we've come halfway across the world to deliver her here to her final resting place. It's so beautiful and so sad.*

"It's just as I remembered it," Katherine says wistfully, and she turns to James. "Isn't that incredible? I haven't been here in twenty years and it's just as I remembered it." James smiles and puts his hand on her shoulder. "It *feels* how I remember it."

Katherine becomes suddenly aware of a little knot inside her heart. It clenches and aches, and as the blurry image of Mykonos grows and becomes more clear, so does the knot. She realizes she's looking at a real-life image of Anna's painting. She remembers the excitement in Anna's voice when she saw the painting at the swap meet. "Oh, Anna," she whispers. "How can you not be here for this? How can you be gone?" Katherine turns to Rishika. "She's gone." She says it as if it's a totally new realization. "She's really gone."

Rishika nods. "Yes."

"We're here, but this is where *Anna* wanted to be. *She* wanted to come back. This is not what she meant!"

Lorelei's eyebrows furrow. *Katherine's the one who planned this trip. The reason we are here is because it was Anna's favorite place. What doesn't Katherine understand?*

"Honey," James says gently. He touches her arm. He's never seen anything like this from her before. "Are you okay?"

"No! I'm not!" Tears spring from her eyes. "I'm not ready to say goodbye. I don't want to be here already."

Katherine's friends look at her in horror. It's like, where has Katherine been all this time? It's been a month and a half since Anna's death, and it's taken her this long to realize that Anna isn't coming back? Putting Anna to rest has been the entire point of the trip and it's as if Katherine, one of the most intelligent and logical people they know, has just realized the ramifications of death. Anna is dead and she isn't coming back.

Katherine runs along the rail a ways toward the stern of the boat, away from Mykonos, where the view is all open ocean. "Oh, Anna," she sobs. "No."

"What is happening?" James asks, thoroughly confused and concerned.

Rishika, Ashley, and Lorelei look at each other, wide-eyed, brows furrowed.

"She's finally mourning," Rishika says to both herself and the rest of them. It's in this moment that Rishika understands Katherine. She has judged Katherine for not showing true sadness towards Anna's death. She felt angry toward Katherine, even. Rishika suddenly realizes that they have all processed Anna's death differently, have all mourned differently. They all care deeply for Anna. They've all been affected by losing her. She sees the devastation that Katherine's subconscious has been holding inside in denial, and now it has cracked, releasing it all.

"Anna!" Katherine shouts.

Rishika bursts into tears. Ashley and Lorelei start to sniffle. Rishika runs to Katherine. Just as Katherine yells again, Rishika leans over the rail and yells with her out to the sea.

"Anna!"

Rishika grabs Katherine and pulls her to her body, and they shudder with sobs. Lorelei and Ashley look at each other, and without spoken words, they run to the rail and take over while the other two just hold each other up.

"Anna!"

Katherine and Rishika peel apart from each other on one side, still with one arm around the other, red faces streaked with tears, and face the ocean and resume their cries to their friend. They call to Anna in a chorus through the wind as if she is out there lost at sea, waiting to be rescued, as if their voices will lead her back to them. When their voices are tired and rough, they turn and melt into one another, with hands grasping heads and arms wrapped around each other's bodies like an octopus. They hold each other and they cry.

James stands, watching this strange yet moving ceremony, his face covered with tears. Rishika's eye catches his, and the only change in her position is the wave of her hand from Katherine's back as she motions for James to join them. And he does.

# Chapter 77

As each of them steps off the boat and onto the pier, it feels very melancholy. They are in Mykonos. Twenty years ago, Anna, Rishika, Katherine and Ashley spent four glorious days here basking in the sun talking about guys, talking about what they were going to do after they graduated, eating great food and getting a tan. At night they partied and danced in whitewashed bars. Now they are here without Anna. Tomorrow they will distribute her ashes on the shore of a beautiful beach.

They walk quietly down the pier, pulling their luggage, the wheels of their suitcases clattering over the bumps of the wooden planks. Ashley stops walking for a moment and just looks around, causing the others to do the same. Deep turquoise water glitters around them, a sandy beach at the end of the left side of the pier. The countless whitewashed buildings provide a shocking color contrast in the background. The beauty is wasted on them. It's almost too sunny, too sparkly, too brilliant. It's obnoxious.

Rishika catches Ashley's eye and they share a sympathetic look.

"Are we supposed to be excited that we're here?" Ashley asks. It's kind of intended to be rhetorical, but they all ponder it nonetheless.

"It's the end," Lorelei says. "On so many levels. I'm not ready to say goodbye to Anna or Europe or any of you. I don't want to go home and do life without you ladies right by my side. Without your constant support."

Rishika grabs Lorelei's hand and purses her lips, sympathetic. "Well, we are here to fulfill Anna's last wish, so I guess we should try to be. Excited, that is." Though she doesn't sound excited at all.

"It will be an honor and a privilege to do so," Katherine says. "I just can't fathom how we're going to get through it." James slips his hand into Katherine's. She exhales and pushes forward down the pier.

A yacht toots its horn. "Ashley!" a faint voice calls.

Ashley's ears perk up as she registers that her name has just been called. She looks around. The ladies and James turn around. A yacht is pulling into the harbor.

"Ashley!" the voice calls again, a little louder.

"Is that…" Rishika squints her eyes to focus her vision. "Andrick?"

"Andrick?" Ashley says, both surprised and guarded. They can see the figure of a man standing on the bow of the yacht. Her tone changes to excitement. "Andrick?" Her hands fly to cover her mouth.

"Ashley!" his voice calls out over the water. The far-off image of him is of him standing with one leg bent, presumably his boot propped up on a wooden box. One hand holds onto a weathered rope dangling above him. He looks like a virile Erik the Red.

Ashley inhales, now positive that it is her love who has sailed the seas to find her. She drops her luggage and takes off into a sprint down the pier. "Andrick!"

"Holy shit," Rishika says with awe.

"Who the hell is that?" James asks. "Should I go after her?"

Katherine puts her hand on her husband's arm. "Don't you dare," she says with a smile. Off his bewildered expression, she explains. "Pierce cheated, he left her, they're done. This is the new guy, and we *love* him." She claps her hands.

Ashley gets to the end of the dock and pulls off her espadrilles.

"No!" Andrick shouts across the water. "Don't, Ashley!"

Without hesitation, Ashley leaps feet first into the water, her long willowy sundress ballooning like a parachute.

Lorelei sucks in her breath, as she watches the spontaneous and possibly dangerous move.

From the bow of the yacht, Andrick reacts immediately, diving, his sculpted arms piercing the water. He sails under the water dolphin-kicking towards his love.

"Is this really happening?" Lorelei asks wistfully, with her hands clasped under her chin.

"This might be the best thing I've ever witnessed in my life!" Katherine says as she squeezes her husband's hand.

"I might have to agree," James says and kisses her hand.

Rishika's mouth hangs open.

Andrick bursts through the water only meters away from Ashley, who scoops at the water, one arm at a time, in a less graceful freestyle-type move.

"Andrick... You came... You found me," she says between strokes as she swims towards him.

"Nothing could have stopped me," Andrick says.

They have just about made it to each other and he reaches out and pulls her the rest of the way to him. She grabs his face and they kiss. A kiss so urgent because they thought they had had their last, but this one will be the first of so many more. They laugh and tread water and kiss each other.

From the dock, Lorelei, Rishika, Katherine and James jump up and down and cheer for them. Caught up in the emotion, and having just witnessed a master-class on romantic gestures, James scoops Katherine off her feet, as a prince would do to his princess, and kisses her deeply.

***

After Andrick and Ashley swim back to the pier and find a ladder to climb up, James, Katherine, Rishika and Lorelei excitedly greet Andrick and express their happiness to Ashley. They all walk together and resume pulling their luggage toward the village. Ashley and Andrick walk behind the group, holding hands, Andrick pulling Ashley's suitcase.

Ashley is positively giddy. "I can't believe you came. I *missed* you. I was so sad in Italy. Who is sad when they're in Italy? But I thought I'd never see you again!"

"I missed you so much. I'm sorry. Forgive my intrusion. I know this is your private time for saying goodbye to Anna and laying her to rest. I will give you and your friends privacy and space."

"Oh, I've had enough space from you, mister." She stops walking and pulls him to her and kisses him.

James, Katherine, Lorelei and Rishika walk ahead. Lorelei glances back at the kissing couple and smiles.

Katherine glances at Rishika. "You're uncharacteristically quiet."

Rishika shakes her head. "Remember all that one-night-stand shit I was spouting off when we left Monaco? I was wrong."

"Wrong? I have an announcement to make, world. Rishika Badami Cooper was wrong."

"Oh, shut up," Rishika responds.

"Ha ha, the cynic turns romantic," Lorelei says.

"Never say never," Katherine boasts.

"I know," Lorelei says. "All I can say is, Pierce who?"

James raises his eyebrows. "What the heck have you ladies been up to the last few weeks?"

The three ladies look at each other and laugh.

"So much," Lorelei says. "So much."

As they draw close to where the pier meets the sand, Rishika notices a man with two little girls playing in the water in matching bathing suits. Rishika squints her eyes. "That man looks like Kevin."

"Oh, my God!" Lorelei squeals. "It's Kevin!"

The ladies leave their suitcases on the edge of the sand and run towards them. Lorelei and Katherine run to Camila and Alexa and scoop them up. Rishika runs to Kevin and hugs him.

"What are you doing here?"

"A few days ago, I had this really vivid dream. But actually I don't think it was a dream at all. I felt a finger poke me firmly on my forehead, and I heard Anna say, 'Get there.'" He shrugs. "We couldn't miss this."

Rishika's eyes fill with tears. "I'm so glad you're here." She turns to Camila and Alexa, in the arms of Lorelei and Katherine. "Hello, cuties," she says. "You have no idea how happy I am to see you." She smiles at them, appreciating like never before how very much they look like their mom.

# Chapter 78

They all, every one of them, sit at a long table inside a second-story restaurant. The large doors to the balcony are open, letting in the golden afternoon light as a warm, salty breeze ruffles the branches of fuchsia bougainvillea around the doorway. A feast is laid before them on the table. There are plates of grape leaves stuffed with ground lamb and rice; spanakopita, layers of crispy filo, spinach and feta cheese; fresh salad of chunks of tomatoes, cucumber, olives and feta; moussaka, ground beef cooked in tomato sauce layered with eggplant and a creamy bechamel sauce; souvlaki, skewers of seasoned chicken served with tzatziki, and glasses of retsina wine.

Camila crunches into her triangle of spanakopita and nods approvingly. Little conversations bubble across the table until Kevin taps his glass.

"As we all know, Anna adored this island. She was a lifelong beach girl. She told me that when she was a little girl, she and her family would wake up early on a summer day in preparation of a day trip to Santa Monica Beach, her anticipation was akin to going to Disneyland. The beach chairs, cooler, umbrella, boogie boards, shovels and sand toys would be sitting in the driveway, ready to be loaded into the van. They would drive the forty-five minutes to the beach and stay all day. She and her brothers would sit on their boogie boards and her mom would pass out tuna sandwiches and Pringles, and they would each get their own can of soda. Inevitably, she would crunch on a few grains of sand no matter how hard she tried to not get sand in anything. Anna would boogie-board and get tossed by the waves, her hair tangled with salt water and sand. She loved every moment of it, as she used to tell me."

Rishika smiles and swallows hard as she relives the memory of the little dark-haired girl wearing a pink bathing suit with Strawberry Shortcake on it. Many times Rishika had been on those beach trips with her.

"Anna told me that when she saw Mykonos for the first time, it took her breath away," Kevin continues. "She'd never seen a more beautiful seaside town. She tried to describe to me how clear and blue the water was and about the lazy days she spent lounging on the beach with her very best friends."

Katherine, Ashley, Lorelei and Rishika look at each other and smile.

"She said it was paradise. So, even though what we're about to do tomorrow will be really emotional"—his voice catches—"really hard for us, I would like it to feel like a celebration. I know that I, for one, was not ready to celebrate at Anna's funeral, even though that's what she wanted us to do. With that said, the day after our ceremony, I've rented a catamaran with a full crew." Smiles spread across everyone's faces. "The captain will take us to grottos around Mykonos where we will swim and snorkel." Ashley claps her hands in excitement and Camila and Alexa follow suit. "We will have a nice picnic onboard, drink wine, toast to Anna repeatedly, and create more wonderful memories together on this magnificent island."

"That will be beautiful," Lorelei says.

Rishika nods. "A true celebration of Anna."

"Sounds like a wonderful occasion, Kev," James says.

"Yes," Kevin says, "I believe it will be. So. Let's please raise our glasses to Anna, my beautiful and anything but forgettable wife, Camila and Alexa's loving mother, and a dear friend to all of us."

"Hear, hear!" Katherine cheers.

They clink glasses and drink their wine.

Kevin leans towards Andrick and James and says something to them. They push away from the table and stand.

"Well," Kevin starts again, "as if we have any more room in our bellies, us guys and my little princesses are going to get ice cream."

"Yay," Alexa cries and jumps out of her chair. James takes her little hand in his.

"Do they have mint chip here?" Camila asks.

"I don't know," Andrick replies and pulls out her chair. "Let's find out." He winks at Ashley. She smiles back as a warm happiness fills her.

Rishika, Lorelei and Katherine glance at each other, wondering what is going on as James, Alexa, Camila and Andrick leave the restaurant. Kevin stays seated at the table.

"I have something for you ladies," he says. Lorelei, Rishika, Katherine and Ashley look at each other. "Anna wrote you all a letter. I had to write it down for her, she was too weak to write it herself. But I wrote it down word for word." He smiles. "Even the things I didn't want to write. I'm sorry. I was so overwhelmed that I forgot to give it to you before you left. But I felt that you needed to read it before you distributed her ashes. I feel like it was Anna's way of getting the girls and me here. I don't know how each of you have been feeling in accepting all of this, but I feel like after tomorrow, we all need to come to a new place where we can mostly think of our happy memories with her." He looks off for a moment and nods solemnly. "I'm including myself in that goal. With that, there are some things Anna needed to tell you." The girls look at each other, mystified. Kevin hands Rishika the letter and stands up. "She sure loved you guys." He walks out of the restaurant.

# Chapter 79

The ladies look at each other silently for a moment.

"I'm nervous," Ashley says.

Katherine grabs Ashley's hand.

Rishika's heart pounds inside her chest. She holds out the letter to Lorelei. "Will you read it?" Rishika asks, her eyes pleading.

"Of course." Lorelei smiles comfortingly at Rishika. Lorelei unfolds the stack of pages and takes a deep breath. "'Rishika, Lorelei, Ashley and Katherine. My girls. I'm so sorry. I know that you probably think that it's dumb that I'm apologizing, but I know that I've caused you all pain. I'm sorry that I left you. Please know that I wanted to live another lifetime with you as my very best friends.'" Lorelei's voice cracks. She looks up with tears in her eyes. "I don't think I can read this."

The ladies all sniffle. Ashley pats Lorelei's hand. "You can do it. None of us can do any better."

"Okay." She takes a deep breath, steadies herself and reads from the letter. "'I have a few things to get off my chest and set straight.'" The ladies all exchange glances. "'Yes, I know it's kind of passive-aggressive of me to say this while I'm dead and you can't argue with me.'"

"Gosh." Rishika scoffs and chuckles at Anna trivializing the fact that she's dead. Ashley looks at Rishika and her mouth curves into a faint smile.

Lorelei continues. "'I guess that's the perk of writing a letter from beyond; what I say goes.' There's a little happy face after that." They smile.

"'Ashley,'" Lorelei looks at Ashley, whose smile turns serious. "'I'm so sorry about the whole Pierce fiasco. When I talked to you about it before your wedding, I meant it out of love because I was really concerned for you, but I know it drove a wedge between us. One sure-fire way to alienate someone is to talk shit about someone they love. Remember that when your kids are in love with someone you're not fond of. They may have to come to that conclusion on their own. You'll have to use your judgment about whether to tell them how you really feel. It hurt me that your marriage to Pierce didn't work out. I really wanted it to. I really hope that the next man is deserving of your heart because, Ashley, you are a treasure. There is true love out there for you, I absolutely promise. I want you to be happy. I want you to be cherished. As for Pierce, I will haunt him from the grave. Just kidding… Not.'"

They laugh.

Ashley nods as she accepts these words from Anna. "I forgive you, Anna. Please forgive me for how I acted." She sniffles and blows her nose on a restaurant napkin.

"We know she does," Rishika says sympathetically.

"Thanks."

"Your turn," Lorelei says as she passes the letter to Katherine.

Katherine reads, "'If you've heard the news, I know you're probably all caught off guard and confused about my choice to leave Camila and Alexa to Rishika, should something happen to Kevin.'" Katherine glances up and they all regard each other a little awkwardly. "'Rishika, you're probably the most shocked, ha ha. Obviously, Kevin is still here, but he's going to need your help. All of you. My girls will need strong women in their lives, not just now, but always. And while I've been lying here thinking about the things I need to say and plan out, I've been thinking mostly about Alexa and Camila. If one day, God forbid, they become orphans, I have to have a plan. That is the idea that terrifies me the most. I have to make sure they're going to be okay. When I had my string of miscarriages before we did IVF, you all took care of me in your own way. That last one was a doozy since we were so far along. Lorelei, you sat with me and stroked my forehead, telling me that it would be alright. Katherine, you did the laundry and cleaned the house so I wouldn't have to worry about all of that. Ashley, you flew down for a weekend and cooked our meals and arranged for friends to drop off food when you left. Rishika, you binge-watched *Sex & the City* episodes with me for a week. But when you decided that I'd done enough self-loathing, you told me to get my ass out of bed and bullied me into taking a shower and getting dressed. You drove me to work. I was so pissed at you. Remember we fought about it?" Rishika nods. "'I told you that you didn't get it because you didn't want kids. A pretty mean thing to say, but true, I felt. You may not have understood my pain, but you understood me. You gave me the tough love that I needed to push forward, the relentless tough love that only a family member would give. And that's what you are, my true sister. You are strong, and my girls need that strength. Rishika, you're so many things that I'm not, and I want you to share those things with Camila and Alexa. And guess what? You need them, too. I'm worried about you, worried about leaving you.'"

Rishika grabs a napkin and holds it over her eyes.

Katherine stops reading for a moment. "Are you okay?"

Rishika removes the napkin. "Yep. Keep going."

Katherine nods and continues. "'Camila and Alexa are my minimes. When you miss me, hang out with them. Camila has my caring, nurturing side and Alexa has my sense of humor and my smart mouth, which I didn't always appreciate. They will crack you up. They're special and phenomenal, and you're going to be blown away by what they will teach you. They're going to need support in the qualities that are unique to each of you. I'm counting on you all to love them and take care of them for me.'"

"I promise. I absolutely swear to," Rishika says solemnly.

The girls nod at each other. "We all will, Anna," Lorelei adds.

Katherine hands the letter to Ashley.

Ashley reads, "'Lorelei, I know after I got married I kind of distanced myself from you.'" Lorelei looks up. "'I don't even know if you realized it. I struggled to get pregnant for so long, and it seemed like Adam barely had to look at you to get you pregnant. It was really hard for me. I was jealous.'" The ladies look at Lorelei.

"I noticed," Lorelei says quietly. "But I didn't know the reason."

Ashley continues. "'I was too ashamed to ever share this with you. And you were so sweet and comforting to me when I had my miscarriages. I want you to know that even when I was feeling jealous and resentful of you, I was admiring you as a mother. You were our trailblazer into motherhood! While we were out partying, you were doting on your sweet baby Phoebe. And when your kiddos kept coming, you were an endless supply of love and wisdom. You were always the mother I hoped I could one day be. Please forgive me for all of that.'"

Lorelei shakes her head. "Of course I do," she whispers.

Ashley continues. "'Katherine. You and I shared the same major and we chose the same career. We were always very competitive with each other. There were times in college when we really pissed each other off, as a result, but girl, you sure pushed me to be better. No one else in the world inspired me to work harder than you did. Thank you for that.'" Katherine nods, smiling. Ashley passes the letter to Rishika.

"Girl, you inspired me, too," Katherine says.

Rishika holds the letter, hands shaking. "'Lastly, I'm counting on all of you to take care of Kevin. After a respectable period of time, he's going to need a woman. Like in fifteen years.'" Rishika's voice breaks off into a boisterous laugh. Lorelei, Ashley and Katherine join in. Rishika looks at the letter, lets out a happy sigh and continues to read. "'I'm joking. Much sooner. Help him find a good one, someone the girls will really like, who they can look up to and love. Someone you will all be great friends with. Just make sure she's not quite as beautiful as I am. Beautiful, no doubt, just a notch or two below me. And with smaller boobs.'" The ladies laugh. Rishika looks at the next sentence and stops. She steels herself before looking at Lorelei, Katherine and Ashley. "'I love each of you.'" Rishika dabs at her eyes and they each sniffle and wipe tears away. Rishika shakes it off a little and continues. "'It's okay that we've all had our less-than-perfect moments with each other. Trust me, I've had plenty of time to lie here and reflect about this kind of stuff. I've realized that the reason we've all fought like sisters over the years is because we *are* sisters.'" The girls reach across to each other and hold hands. "'You know all of my flaws, and I know yours. With many friendships, you just give that person the best of yourself, but with us, we love and accept each other despite our shortcomings, and maybe even because of them. God put us at LMU at the same time so we would find each other. We were meant to be. You've enhanced my life more than you'll ever know. Don't be too sad for me. I've lived a beautiful and fulfilling life, and I have each of you partly to thank for that. Keep having adventures so that I have fun stuff to watch from above. Occasionally toast some champagne to me. Kiss each other for me and kiss my babies and Kevin. I love you with all of my heart. Anna.'"

Rishika puts down the stack of papers and looks up. Katherine, Lorelei, Rishika and Ashley look at each other with tearful eyes and nod. Only sniffling can be heard. They rise from the table and meet each other in a group hug. For a few moments, they just hold each other and weep.

"God, she was awesome," Lorelei says as she cries.

"The best," Katherine confirms.

"Anna, we promise to do everything you asked of us," Ashley says.

"We love you so much, and we always will," Rishika says. After a few minutes of sniffling, Rishika pulls away and nods at Ashley, Katherine and Lorelei. "We're going to be okay." She takes a deep breath. "We can do it. We can say goodbye to our girl."

\*\*\*

Alexa and Camila happily lick chocolate ice cream cones. Kevin, James and Andrick sit with them on a bench below the restaurant.

"Opa! Opa!" come the sounds of the ladies' familiar voices and dishes splintering into large ceramic shards.

"Okay, they finished reading the letter," Kevin says.

James' eyebrows furrow. "It sounds like they're throwing dishes. Is that a good thing?"

Andrick smiles. "In Greece, it is."

Kevin exhales. "They're going to be okay."

James puts his arm around Kevin. "We all are, brother."

Sail boats line the horizon and the waves therapeutically lap against the rocky shore.

"Haha, you have some on your nose," Alexa teases her sister.

Kevin smiles at his daughters. "Yeah," he agrees softly.

"We have to pay for those dishes, don't we?" James asks.

Kevin laughs. "Yep."

# Chapter 80

It has been a lovely day of relaxing on none other than Agia Anna Beach. This beach has rows of comfortable sunbeds shaded by grass-covered umbrellas. The group has vowed to enjoy their time here, for throughout the European journey, this has been the destination all along.

And so, they have spent their day nibbling on sandwiches and sipping frappes, the frothy iced coffee drinks that are so well-known in Greece. They have enjoyed oceanside massages while Camila and Alexa have splashed around in the cool blue-green waters in their frilly white one-piece bathing suits and red heart-shaped sunglasses.

Now it is dusk. The group has taken private transportation to the secluded shore of Fokos Beach. There are no sunbeds or umbrellas, no bustling beach bars or restaurants, no flocks of people. It is quiet and calm here. As the sun lowers, it casts a beautiful glow onto the beach. Pink blurs into orange that blurs into yellow above the horizon. Rishika, Lorelei, Ashley and Katherine wear long flowing sundresses. Alexa and Camila wear pretty little matching yellow sundresses. The ladies have French-braided sections of each other's varying manes of hair, as well as Camila's and Alexa's. Some of them have a complete braid, some just a small braid in their flowing sea-salted waves. Anna's ashes have been transferred from the trusty plastic Tupperware container that journeyed around Europe to a lovely blue and white Greek vase, which Kevin hugs with care. Kevin, James and Andrick wear untucked collared shirts and shorts. They all walk with bare feet in pairs and trios down to the beach.

Kevin sits down, nestles the vase at his feet, burrows his feet into the damp sand and closes his eyes. James and Andrick squat down and dig in the sand with Camila and Alexa.

Rishika squeezes Kevin's leg gently and takes a handful of ashes from the vase. She stoops down in front of Camila and Alexa, smiles into their eyes and lays ashes onto the sand in front of them. They dig with colorful plastic shovels. Kevin, James and Andrick begin to fill little buckets with sand and assist the girls in building what will be a grand sandcastle on this paradise beach.

Lorelei, Katherine, Ashley and Rishika exchange meaningful glances and scoop out ashes into cupped hands. They walk to the water's edge and wade in a few inches of the cool water, taking a moment to gaze out at the vast ocean. A gentle tide brings waves in and waves out, waves in and waves out, in a comforting cycle. They look at each other and nod.

Katherine looks down at the white ashes in her hand, all that is physically left of her friend. Her eyebrows furrow and her eyes fill with tears. Next to her, Lorelei turns and they lock eyes.

"It's okay," Lorelei whispers. Lorelei inhales and her expression turns decisive. She throws her handful of ashes up into the air with both arms, with ballet-like movements, and a gentle breeze whisps it away into the Aegean Sea.

Seeing this gives Katherine courage, and she begins frolicking in the shallow surf, slowly opening her hands and letting the breeze take the ashes with it.

Rishika and Ashley dance around sprinkling ashes in the low water. Occasionally they go back to Kevin to get more ashes from the vase. Tears run down all of their faces. Of course, they are tears of sadness, as well as so many layers of emotions. They are tears of acceptance, tears of love, tears of goodbye. All of them, who are so loved by Anna, are sending her to a peaceful rest.

At this, the golden hour, everything and everyone seems to glow. As Anna's most beloved friends skip and frolic around on the wet sand, throwing Anna's ashes into the breeze, they begin to see images of her life in their minds.

They see Anna singing with a mug of weissbier at the Hofbrauhaus. Throwing her arms into the air at the top of the Eiffel Tower. Writing in her journal as she sits on the Spanish Steps. Dancing in Mykonos and breaking dishes on the floor.

They see Anna in a wedding dress at the front of a church as she says her vows to Kevin. With a full belly, pregnant and glowing. Cheek to cheek with Kevin in a hospital room as they hold their newborn daughter. They see themselves rushing in to meet the newborn baby.

They see Anna running around her backyard with Camila and Alexa. Greeting her parents and her brothers at her front door with open-armed hugs.

Rishika, Lorelei, Katherine, and Ashley dance around, letting out joyful whoops, as Anna's ashes take flight on the breeze. It's like an ancient ceremonial dance.

The sun continues to lower, turning sparse clouds pink and purple. It reflects off the water, off the dark wet sand. The water darkens with the absence of light, but the sun casts a glowing yellow trail across the water to them, like a portal away from them but to something else. The breeze feels tranquil, transporting, magical.

Suddenly, Anna is dancing with them. And this time, they all see her. There is surprise and shock and joy in Lorelei's, Ashley's and Katherine's eyes at seeing their beloved Anna. Like girls in their twenties, they dance around joyfully, without a care in the world.

Anna throws her arms into the air and dances with beautiful abandon. She looks around Mykonos and nods with satisfaction.

With happy tears in her eyes, Rishika lays both of her hands on her heart and mouths *I love you* to Anna.

Anna mouths, *I love you, too.*

"Rest in peace, my dear friend," Rishika says, out loud. And with that, she releases Anna to go to a place of peace where she can watch over them.

Anna kisses her hands and sends the kiss to all of them with a smile. She walks over to Camila and Alexa, who add scoops of sand to their sandcastle. Anna stoops down, looks at their faces and kisses both of them on their noses, though they don't know it.

"I love you, Mommy," Camila says.

"Love you, Mommy," Alexa mimics.

Anna stands back up and steps over to Kevin, who is now standing and watching with wonder and appreciation as the ladies dance around. Anna stands in front of him, rises to her tiptoes and places a loving kiss on Kevin's lips. His expression changes as though he feels her presence.

"I love you, my sweetheart," Anna says.

"Goodbye, my love," Kevin whispers.

The last sliver of sun disappears into the horizon. But, tomorrow, it will rise again.

# Epilogue

# The Next Generation

Three American girls in their early twenties hang out in the common room of a hostel. Stephanie and Tess sit on the floor on either side of a coffee table and play checkers. Raven peruses the used books on a bookshelf just behind the couch. She pulls out the <u>Let's Go To Europe 1996</u> book.

"How strange. This guidebook is from like twenty years ago." She chuckles. "Why would they still have it here?" She sits down on the couch and as she opens the book, a photo of Anna, Rishika, Katherine and Ashley falls out and onto the floor right where Stephanie is sitting.

Stephanie picks up the photo and looks at it. "Aww, they look so fun." She passes it across the table to Tess, who looks at the photo and smiles.

Raven reads aloud from the first page. "'Dear traveler, this book is tried and true. It led us to many adventures that will stay with us forever. I challenge you to take this with you and go to some of the places we highlighted. Highlight a few of your own and then pass it on. Europe is magical. Anything is possible.'"

"I love that," Tess says. "Let's do it."

# Lorelei

From the moment that Sebastian sculpted Lorelei in his art studio afloat in the Mediterranean, she has been completely energized. The muse within her has awoken, and so the artist within her has awoken. It was the old man at Piazza Navona, though, who helped her to realize that she is not just meant to teach, which she loves, she is also meant to create.

When Lorelei returned home from her trip, she cleaned out the guest room that had turned into a catchall for a rarely used treadmill, plastic tubs of wrapping paper, and bags of the kids' outgrown clothes that needed to be donated. For about a week, she stayed up late and rearranged and organized.

One side of the room is now her art studio. She brought in an old easel that had been forgotten in a corner of the garage. A table now holds a can of clean paint brushes, sponges, and a new set of oil paints. A stack of empty canvases leans against a wall in the corner of the room.

On the wall hangs the framed sketch of the old man gazing up at the Fountain of Neptune. It will always be special to her. It was her epiphany moment—the moment, really, when she became an artist at age forty-two. It also represents the moment she became at peace with herself and her life. That sketch kicked off what Lorelei will always view as "the summer of painting", for since then she has been an overflowing fount of creative expression.

Next to that hangs a painting of the backs of five ladies staring out over Paris from the top of the Eiffel Tower. Herself, Ashley, Rishika, Katherine… and Anna. Because when they had their special moment at the top, admiring the panoramic view of the City of Lights, Lorelei knew in her heart that Anna was there, too. This was the type of powerful art that she wanted to create down by the Seine. Her inner voice just hadn't mustered it up yet. On the flight home from Europe, the image began to take form. Her mind's eye was speaking to her, loud and clear.

Lorelei's sketchbook from the Louvre sits open on the art table. It contains a depiction of Rishika sitting in a chair with an espresso on the table next to her. Even though the view that she was looking at was spectacular—whitewashed buildings with bright blue trim and the Aegean Sea in the background, it is a medium shot of Rishika from the bust up. Lorelei saw this image the morning after they distributed Anna's ashes. The expression on Rishika's face is subtle, but if you know the story, it's profound. There's sadness, relief, growing peace, and the promise to live the rest of her life to its fullest. To those who don't know the story, the subject's face holds an expression of mystery and nuances, not unlike the Mona Lisa.

Now, Lorelei sits in front of her easel, a smudge of dandelion-yellow paint on her left cheek, her paintbrush dancing across the canvas, lost in her own world as an angsty Florence + The Machine song wails inspiration.

She paints a picture that will be a gift for Kevin. It is of Camila and Alexa on a beach making a sandcastle. Camila scoops sand up with a blue plastic shovel and Alexa packs down sand into a red plastic castle-shaped cylinder with her little hands. Lorelei is currently putting the finishing touches on Anna's angelic eyes that can be seen in the swirling yellows and pinks of the sunset over the ocean behind the girls. The girls are wearing yellow sundresses, and the sun glints highlights onto their dark brown locks, blowing lightly in the breeze. Their expressions are… happy. Obviously, there is a sad subtext to what they are doing, but they were blessed to have a mother as amazing and kind as Anna, and they are blessed as she watches over them still. Their lives will go on. To Lorelei, the image is a juxtaposition of heaven and earth, life and afterlife. She nods, satisfied because it stirs such strong emotion in her, both longing and contentment, and to her, those are the best kinds of paintings.

Downstairs, Adam opens the front door to reveal two delivery men.

"Delivery for Lorelei Leibovitch."

"Yeah, that's my wife. Come on in."

They carry a box in and set it on the round table in the entry way.

"We are instructed to unpack it for you, sir."

Adam shrugs. "Sure."

As one delivery man hands Adam a clipboard to sign, the other unpacks the box. Adam thanks them, they leave, and he is left perturbed, looking at a sculpture of a naked woman.

"Lorelei, did you order a sculpture?" he calls up the stairs.

He leans at the waist, checking out the sculpture. Long, curly hair cascades over bare shoulders. The woman's left breast is slightly larger than the right.

"Interesting," he murmurs. He reads aloud the brass tag on the marble base. "*Gypsy Soul* by Sebastian."

In awe, Adam studies the woman's face. Her eyes crinkle as a laughs bursts from her mouth.

"It's uncanny." His expression changes as he chuckles. "Nah."

He walks around the circular table and peeks around at the sculpture's buttocks. He notices the distinct birthmark, and his face contorts into recognition.

His voice echoes through the house.

"Lorelei!"

# Ashley

Andrick drives a Jeep and Ashley is in the passenger's seat. He puts his hand on her knee and they smile at each other.

Ashley texts Lorelei, Rishika and Katherine. *On our next adventure and I'm thinking of you girls. I'll send pics soon. By the way, I know it's way ahead of time, but I would love to host Christmas brunch this year! How about we rotate houses every year? I know it's farther for you girls, but I'll be settled in a new place by then and we can make it a girls' weekend. I promise to make crepes with Nutella! Love you.*

The ladies immediately respond. *Sounds great! I'm in! Love you! I'll be there. Perfect! Have fun!*

"Mommy, I'm hungry." Ryan's little three-year-old voice breaks Ashley from her thoughts.

Ashley turns towards the backseat rows where Elizabeth, ten years old; Teddy, six; Ryan, three; Lukas, six; and Anneke, eleven, sit. "I told you to eat more of your lunch, sweetie."

"I'm hungry, too, actually," Anneke says in an adorable Swedish accent. "Do you have any snacks?"

Teddy groans. "I'm hot. It's hot here."

Ashley sighs at Andrick and he laughs. "He's not wrong. It's quite hot. And I'm kind of hungry, too."

A laugh emerges from Ashley's lips and she nudges Andrick's arm.

"How many kids are in this car?" she asks.

"Mom, you have a new comment on your blog," Elizabeth says. Rishika was right. Ashley is really good at being fashionably domestic. Her new lifestyle blog has a handful of subscribers and she really enjoys photographing food and writing about entertaining. What she doesn't know is that in six years, HGTV will offer her her own show on throwing stylish children's birthday parties.

"Sweetie, please get your head out of your phone and look out the window." Ashley extends her hand back to the middle row.

Elizabeth tsks. "You were just on your phone." She begrudgingly passes her phone up to Ashley.

"Holy shit!" Lukas shouts.

"Lukas, watch your mouth," Andrick says sternly.

Ashley looks past him out the driver's window and her eyes widen. "Holy shit!" she exclaims.

Andrick looks out his window. Majestic giraffes walk with long gaping strides just outside their Jeep in the African landscape.

He slows the Jeep to a stop and they all stick their heads out the window and sunroof. The kids go crazy. Ashley and Andrick smile at each other and lean together for a kiss.

"Mom, can I have my phone back to send a picture to Daddy?"

Ashley returns the phone to Elizabeth and grins. "By all means."

# Katherine

Katherine and James dine in an elegant restaurant. They hold hands across the table.

Katherine and James started going to marriage counseling when they returned home from Greece. They have learned the not-so-uncommon issue that Katherine works a lot and so does James. Dr. Phifer is helping them make plans for how to balance their work and kids and how to make connecting with each other more of a priority. They have been instructed to go on a date every other week and to not talk about work while they are on their date. So here they are.

Back in her natural habitat, it's hard for Katherine to believe her behavior in Rome. She loves James, Brice and Beckham so much. What the hell was she thinking? She knows she was caught up in the moment with Francesco, not thinking clearly at all. Well, they definitely have closure now. Now, she can move on. And sweet and kind Francesco can too. Hopefully he will find an incredible and single woman to spend the rest of his life with.

With some reflection, she has realized that she had some kind of midlife crisis, brought on both by Anna's death and being back in Rome with her first love. Nothing excuses it, of course, but she definitely sees it all more clearly now. Now she just has to prove to James that he was and is the love of her life, to redeem herself, and to rebuild the trust. *Just.*

He says he forgives her. Most days she believes him. Some days he regresses, and some days she is bitter that she still has to prove herself. But James knows that Katherine is trying, and Katherine knows that James is trying, and they are committed to putting in the work together.

"I was thinking about something Dr. Phifer said to us today," James says. "About how when you were in Rome you were exploring the path you had not taken in your life."

Katherine nods. "Yes?"

"I like her idea that we should explore something new and adventurous together."

"I was thinking about that, too," Katherine says. "That's a fun idea."

"Maybe we should try living somewhere else for a period of time. It would be us exploring an unknown path together. I'm talking big, like another state or another country."

Katherine looks surprised. "That's pretty drastic."

"Yes. But I'd be willing to talk about it, if it's something you want to do."

She smiles at him, touched. "That's really generous, honey." She spreads butter on a roll and purses her lips as she considers some factors. "Would the firm let us do that? Would we rent out our house? Would we enroll the boys in school there or would they do online school?"

"I haven't thought about all of the details, but I think we need to shake things up." He tips back some champagne.

"Maybe. That *would* be an adventure." She shrugs, considering it. "Or maybe we could just try anal sex."

A spray of champagne shoots out of James' mouth all over their table.

# Rishika

Alexa and Camila stand on the front doorstep of a huge turmeric-colored Mediterranean house in the Hollywood Hills. A small pink suitcase covered in butterflies sits on the ground in front of each of them, and Kevin stands behind them.

"Go ahead, sweetie. Knock," he encourages.

Alexa knocks softly on the front door and then a little harder.

The door opens to reveal Rishika, nervous but determined. "Hello!"

"Hi, Auntie Rish," Camila says, a little shyly.

"Hi, Auntie Rish," Alexa follows.

Rishika hugs the girls in a tight embrace. She sighs. "Hi, sweet girls. Hi, Kev."

Kevin and Rishika hug each other tightly, extra-long, and give each other a kiss on the cheek. "Love you," she says before they pull away. "Come on in. We thought we should camp in the backyard tonight. Does that sound okay?"

"Yes," Camila says looking up briefly, a slow smile emerging.

"Yes," Alexa mimics and begins to jump up and down.

Kevin puts the girls' suitcases at the foot of the stairs and they follow Rishika through the lavish living room.

"Uncle Craig has it all set up. He set up a tent, but if we're uncomfortable, we'll just come in and sleep in beds," she says conspiratorially. "We're going to roast marshmallows and make s'mores, and, God help us, Uncle Craig even has his guitar out." She lowers her voice. "And he cannot sing. But he doesn't know that I think that so we'll humor him."

The girls giggle.

"Penelope is in the backyard, too, and she's going to go crazy when she sees you. I've got lots of outfits we can put on her later."

The girls' eyes widen with excitement.

"Okay!" Alexa shouts.

"Kevin, will you join us for dinner before you go?"

"I'd love to."

"Good. Grab a beer. Grab one for me, too, please."

"You got it," he says and disappears into the kitchen.

"Girls, beer?" Rishika asks.

Camila and Alexa furrow their eyebrows at each other. "No, thank you…" Camila says with a weird expression.

"You sure?" Rishika asks.

"We're literally children!" Camila says through a giggle.

"Oh, I forgot. You're very tall for your age," Rishika says, feigning seriousness. Camila and Alexa look at each other and cover their mouths, giggling. Kevin's laugh can be heard from the kitchen.

Rishika opens a French door and they walk into the backyard.

"I'm reading this script about a little girl who befriends an ugly lizard. It's kind of a 'don't judge a book by its cover' thing. I'm going to tell you all about it and I want you to tell me if it sounds dumb."

"Okay," Alexa says.

"*I* have an idea for a movie," Camila says bravely.

"Really?" Rishika says, playing along.

"A little girl becomes friends with fairies and she eats this poisonous mushroom and becomes small and they go to this magical fairyland."

"Huh," Rishika says, intrigued. "The mushroom thing has been done in *Alice in Wonderland*, of course, but we'll figure that out. Tell me more."

After dinner, when Kevin has left to hang out with some buddies, Camila and Alexa ask Rishika if they can bake cookies. Rishika turns to Craig, the cook of the household.

"Do we have stuff for that?" she asks him. When he assures her that they have all the ingredients, she pushes him out of the kitchen. She wants to do this alone with Camila and Alexa, so she looks up a recipe on her phone, and they get to work.

In addition to the standard chocolate chip cookie recipe, the girls have decided to also break up the leftover graham crackers, chocolate bars and cut-up marshmallows and add them to the cookies.

After an hour and a half of chaos in the kitchen, the cookies are in the oven. Rishika let the girls do all the measuring and the egg breaking, so it looks like a bomb of flour, eggs, and s'mores has exploded all over the kitchen counters and floor.

"I'm tired," Alexa says, "Can we watch a movie?"

"Well, first we have to clean up this horrendous mess," Rishika says firmly. Camila and Alexa look discouraged. Rishika smiles when an idea comes into her mind.

"You know, when your mom and I were little, we used to do this thing to make cleaning up more fun. We used to pretend we were on a game show and the announcer would say"—she puts on a deep and theatrical male voice— "You have five minutes to clean up this mess, and if you succeed... you will win... one million dollars!'"

The little girls' eyes widen.

"And would you win it?" Alexa asks.

"Well, kind of. We would set a timer, start picking up toys as fast as we could, and the timer would always go off before we were ready, and the announcer would say, 'You have one more minute.' And after a few more adjustments of the time, the room would be clean. And we would jump up and down and scream, 'We won a million dollars!'"

"Did you *literally* win one million dollars?" Camila asks, amazed.

"Well, we would pretend to win it. It was still pretty exciting, though."

"That's crazy," Alexa says and laughs. "Do you know other stories about my mom when she was a little girl?"

Rishika makes a face and scoffs. "Are you kidding? I know *hundreds*. After we clean up, and win *a million dollars*, I'll tell you some."

With big, brown eyes that look just like Anna's, Alexa looks up at Rishika with admiration. It hits Rishika in the depths of her heart. And just like that, she's in love.

# The Next Generation

The three backpackers from the hostel, Stephanie, Raven and Tess, trek along a weathered trail. Tess has the trusty <u>Let's Go To Europe 1996</u> guidebook tucked into her backpack. A gray sky looms around them. It's not a gloomy gray, it's romantic and beautiful, like a sky from another century. A medieval sky. They are surrounded by blankets of thick, verdant coastal grass on one side, and on the other ragged sea cliffs that nose-dive into the Atlantic Ocean. They've been hiking for three hours from Doolin, with the soundtrack of crashing waves on a continual loop, the invigorating sea-spray filling their nose and lungs. Charlie, their spry guide with white hair and ruddy cheeks, has recounted hours of Irish history and folklore in a cheerful melodic tongue.

"Well, lassies, we've arrived." Charlie swoops his arm in a half-circle to illustrate the finish line of their journey.

"Thank you, Charlie." Stephanie launches herself at the old man with a huge bear hug. Tess and Raven follow.

Charlie laughs boisterously. "The pleasure was mine."

The ladies run to the concrete wall that looks out over the Cliffs of Moher. The seemingly never-ending expanse of the Atlantic lies in front of them in a panoramic array. On either side of them, they view the coastline of the dramatic cliffs, the most shocking of green on top, and layer upon layer of striated dark brown rock and bright moss, descending to frothy, churning sea foam as the frigid waters crash onto the rocks below.

"Why do I want to cry?" Tess asks, her voice thick.

"Because it's the most powerful, most beautiful sight you've ever seen in your life," Stephanie answers. "At least, that's how I feel. It's so vast and full of possibility."

"I've got this crazy feeling in my chest," Tess says. "I feel so inspired, so motivated."

Raven shakes her head. "Girls, there's such a giant world out there beyond that ocean. Don't you just want to see it all?"

"Absolutely," Stephanie replies.

"You know, we're never going to forget this moment, for as long as we live," Tess says.

They put their arms around each other.

"Those girls that left the guidebook were right. Being up here makes me feel like anything is possible," Stephanie says, wistful. Tess nods.

Raven looks at them with a sure smile. "It is."

# Acknowledgements

Nobody knows more than my family how much I put into this book, and I thank John, Izzy, and Brady Womack for cheering me on. John, thank you for going along with me when I started calling the office in our house, "my office." To me, there is no better place to work on these books. It's my little haven. I appreciate you for being my favorite IT guy, even though it's your least favorite thing in the world to do next to hanging pictures. Izzy, I thank you for offering me your artistic opinions while I made various decisions about the cover of *Taking Her to Mykonos* and for remaining patient with me when I panicked and wavered back and forth repeatedly. Brady, your way of telling me that I'm doing a great job is to say, "Mom, you're famous!" I always appreciate your support and optimism! Izzy and Brady, the world is your oyster. I thought about you both while I was writing about all of the fabulous settings in this book which I was blessed to visit. There are so many remarkable places to explore and people to meet in this world. I hope you'll be curious about them, and I hope we can embark on some of those adventures together.

To my parents, Esther and Terry Sneed, it's because of you both that I studied abroad in Rome and backpacked through Europe during my college years. I know it was scary for you to send me into the unknown when I would call once a week from a payphone to tell you that I was alive and having fun. Dad, you were afraid that I was going to fall in love with an Italian and never come home. Look! I married a Texan instead and followed him to Oklahoma! Much, much closer! Regardless of your fears, you both gave me your blessing (and credit card) and made it possible for me to have those experiences that changed my worldview forever. I'm so very grateful.

To Christina Kasendorf, Helena Danni, Rachel Mashhoud, Dimple Bhasin, and Kate Murray, thank you for being my beta readers and reading *Taking Her to Mykonos* before anybody else. I truly appreciate the time that you devoted to it, your honest and constructive feedback, and your excitement about the book! Becky Blackwood, thank you for proofreading my back cover blurb for me, right on the spot! Katherine Cook, thank you for answering my very last-minute texts about grammar.

To my girlfriends, *The Ladies*. I thought of you all often while I wrote this book. I thought about how we are a crazy diverse bunch, all so different in strengths and personalities, and that's what makes us so much fun. In this way, you inspired the ensemble of characters in *Taking Her to Mykonos*. Can you imagine us on the loose in Europe together? You're my village through life and motherhood, and you enrich my life so much. We love a good cheese platter, a good potluck, a good cocktail, a good girls' weekend, and an hours-long dance marathon to some good 90's rap. Who else is blessed with a text string of twenty-four ladies weighing in on any and every topic that pops up 24/7? I love how we laugh and talk about everything. *Everything.* You know what I'm talking about.

To Ashley Farasopoulos Brooks, Magaly Gomez, Allison Fox, Sebastian Parker, and Frank Weitzel, it's been twenty years since we backpacked through Europe together, but I will never forget you guys and the once-in-a-lifetime moments we shared, such as river-rafting in Interlaken, drinking weissbier at the Hofbrauhaus, picnicking below the Eiffel Tower before climbing its many stairs to the top, cheering at a World Cup soccer game in Paris, and sleeping in a park in France when the train station was closed. Certainly, there are some crazy moments that I won't mention here! Two decades later, I still proclaim that that trip was one of my best life experiences. Ashley, you were there for all of it, starting from getting on a plane together at LAX. We were roommates in Rome, and then we backpacked every city together, up until the moment we left Greece. After the others flew home one by one, you and I were the last two standing after four weeks! You learn a lot about someone when you travel that long together. You were amazing, and we made a great team. And for that, I had to give you a namesake character. I hope this book inspires some reminiscing of our amazing international moments together. And Kathleen Lungren Jobe, you were my BFF in Rome, my favorite place of all! It was so nostalgic to write about my characters going to the Spanish Steps, Trevi Fountain, and Colosseum, where we had so much fun with our other study abroad classmates. I'll never forget our jogs through our neighborhood of Monte Mario, as well as our Italian language lessons with the locals!

To the Delta Zeta Sorority, it was so special to be given permission to use the Delta Zeta name as the sorority that bonded Anna, Rishika, Ashley, Katherine, and Lorelei in a lifelong friendship. Even though I don't often see my DZ sisters, I love you all, and I cling to our wonderful memories of sisterhood and fun!

Thank you to my editor, RJ Locksley. Your notes are always insightful and right on. You so easily provide clever suggestions for my stubborn story roadblocks, and I appreciate that you find my many, many mistakes. You are so good at what you do.

Thank you to Marina and Jason Anderson at Polgarus Studio for formatting *Taking Her to Mykonos*. Thank you for working so patiently with me with the countless changes that I made! You did a fabulous job.

To the team at Deranged Doctor Design, this is the second time that you've created a gorgeous book cover for me. Thank you so much!

And to my readers, one of the absolute best things about being an author is when you reach out to me and tell me how my book affected you and how you related to the characters. For so many years, my writing lived inside my laptop for my eyes only. I can't tell you how fulfilling and riveting it is to share my heart, soul, and humor with you and then for you to connect with me and share with me how you felt about it. Your encouragement inspires me to write more! So, thank you from the bottom of my heart.

# Book Club Discussion Questions
## *Taking Her to Mykonos*

Hi, friends! Please get together with your favorite book people and discuss *Taking Her to Mykonos* while you sip some wine and demolish a beautiful charcuterie board. Feel free to reach out to me. I would love to Facetime you and answer some of your questions or attend your event if I'm close by! I love a good charcuterie board. Here are some questions to get the party started. Have fun!    -Julie

1.  Of the four main characters, Anna is the one we spent the least amount of time with, yet she is the driving force of this book. Did you feel connected to her? Did you feel the loss of her?

2.  How did you feel about Katherine's reaction to Anna's death? What first impression did she give you when she was handling the organization of the funeral?

3.  If you were asked to distribute a friend's/loved one's ashes, would you be willing to do it?

4.  When the ladies climbed into the cargo truck, Katherine remarked, "There are a few things we will not be duplicating." Rishika said, "Well, obviously." Did you wonder what those things might have been? Could you speculate some crazy things they might have done while backpacking in their twenties that they wouldn't be willing to do this time?

5. Some of the ladies were envious of the younger patrons at the Hobrauhaus recalling their own rose-colored optimism and go-getter attitudes from their younger years. Could you relate to that conversation? If so, how?

6. Which character did you most relate to?

7. Which European destination or adventure was the most fun for you to experience through the characters?

8. If you could go on a girls' trip anywhere in the world, where would you go? Who would you go with?

9. Anyone up for a quick game of "I've Never"? (Also known as "Never Have I Ever", but I recall it as "I've Never" from my college days.)

10. If you and a group of girlfriends were going to do a dance-off that represented a time from your "youth", what song would you choose?

11. How did you feel about Rishika seeing Anna? How did you rationalize what was happening? Did you view it as escapism or did you believe that Anna was really appearing to her? Or did you have another explanation?

12. Did you relate to any of the midlife crises in the book?

13. Like Lorelei, is there a dream that you still want to realize?

14. Leading up to Rome, could you guess why Katherine had hesitation about returning to Italy?

15. How did you feel about Katherine's interaction with Francesco in Rome? If you had been in Ashley's shoes, would you have called James? Did you agree with how James handled the situation?

16. Do you have a love from long ago that you still think about?

17. How did you feel about Lorelei's regret about missing out on her self-discovery phase in her youth? Was her wild behavior in Europe justifiable?

18. How did you feel about Lorelei's sculpture posing session with Sebastian?

19. Let's talk about Ashley's romance with Andrick...because we want to!

20. Rishika didn't know how to go on living her life without Anna. Was there a time that you lost someone and you didn't know how you were going to move on?

21. How did you react to Katherine's breakdown while approaching Mykonos on the ferry?

22. There were a lot of varying personalities and quirks in the characters. Were there any that bugged you or that would be difficult for you to travel with for two weeks?

23. Through her final letter, Anna came to peace with some of her struggles with her friends. Are there any struggles or disagreements with friends that you would want to resolve if you had to say goodbye?

24. If you could recommend that I write one more scene in a different city or country in Europe, where would it take place?

25. If you could have joined the ladies for any of their European meals, which one would it be?

26. Did the ladies have any adventures that you would be uncomfortable doing now?

27. Have you ever distributed the ashes of a loved one? What was the experience like?

28. If you could choose anywhere in the world for a loved one to distribute your own ashes, where would it be? Why?

29. How did you feel about the ladies retiring the <u>Let's Go To Europe 1996</u> guidebook? How did you feel about ladies from a younger generation finding it?

30. Were you happy with where the epilogue scenes left Ashley, Katherine, Lorelei, and Rishika? What would you like to imagine happening to their characters after the book ends?

31. Can you come up with an alternate title for this book?

32. (And my very favorite question...) Who would you cast to play the characters in the movie of *Taking Her to Mykonos*?

Photo by Kimberly Cordova Photography

Julie Sneed Womack is a Los Angeles native who lives in Oklahoma with her husband, two children, and a cat or two. She studied screenwriting at Loyola Marymount University, and her debut novel was *Tea with Isabel*. She has had the pleasure of teaching preschool and elementary school children, and mostly of calling herself a stay-at-home mom. When she is not writing or hanging out with her favorite people, she is taking photos of cows, bales of hay, and sunsets.

Julie would love to connect with you!
Instagram @juliesneedwomack
Facebook/juliesneedwomack
Goodreads/juliesneedwomack

Did you enjoy *Taking Her to Mykonos*? Please take a moment to rate it and write a review on Goodreads and Amazon. Thank you!

Printed in Great Britain
by Amazon